L. D. Smithson was born in Staffordshire and now lives in Ilkley with her husband and their three children. She is an occupational psychologist and a crime writer.

CW01335698

www.penguin.co.uk

Also by L. D. Smithson

THE ESCAPE ROOM

The Shame Game

L. D. SMITHSON

PENGUIN BOOKS

TRANSWORLD PUBLISHERS

UK | USA | Canada | Ireland | Australia
India | New Zealand | South Africa

Transworld is part of the Penguin Random House group of companies
whose addresses can be found at global.penguinrandomhouse.com.

Penguin Random House UK,
One Embassy Gardens, 8 Viaduct Gardens, London sw11 7bw

penguin.co.uk

Penguin
Random House
UK

First published in Great Britain in 2025 by Penguin Books
an imprint of Transworld Publishers
001

Typeset in 10.8/13.95 pt Minion Pro by Jouve (UK), Milton Keynes
Printed and bound in Great Britain by Clays Ltd, Elcograf S.p.A.

The authorized representative in the EEA is Penguin Random House Ireland,
Morrison Chambers, 32 Nassau Street, Dublin D02 yh68.

A CIP catalogue record for this book is available from the British Library

isbn: 9781804991695

Penguin Random House is committed to a sustainable future
for our business, our readers and our planet. This book is made
from Forest Stewardship Council® certified paper.

For Kathryn, Nicola and Tom.
I promise this isn't inspired by us.

Prologue

Since that day, when the thing happened, I've become something of an expert in shame. I've observed it like any good researcher, looking for its origins and its antidotes, and the closest thing I can compare it to is a self-replicating fungus. You see, emotions like anger or fear, when starved of fuel, lessen over time. But shame is an entirely different beast. It starts with the smallest of ideas: that sense of being found wanting. But what happens next is the really clever bit, because shame starts to feed itself. Moments of joy become things of which you are not worthy. Moments of sadness become exactly what you deserve. Setbacks, obstacles, challenges, difficulties all feed the shame: they are evidence of your inadequacy and insignificance. And so the shame grows; feeding, fuelling, and infecting every positive aspect of who you are, what you've achieved, and what you hope to be. I honestly believe it is one of life's most destructive forces.

All I had to do was release the first few spores, then sit back and let shame do its thing.

1

RYAN

Friday, 3.30 p.m.

Ryan raced from the air-conditioned coolness of his office into the heavy heat of the midsummer heatwave. He was late, as he knew he would be.

Camille would not be pleased. For the past month, she had spent every waking hour on this party.

'Thirty is a big deal for a woman, Ryan,' she insisted. He had wanted to take her away for the weekend, maybe to visit her parents in Monaco, but she was determined to recreate the late-afternoon garden parties her parents used to host during her childhood. Designer-clad members of Monaco's elite all sipping champagne in the Mediterranean sun. A tall ask in the middle of the Yorkshire Dales, where the threat of a traditionally soggy British summer looms large. But Camille had fortuitously picked a corker of a day.

Ryan had not celebrated his thirtieth at all. Back then, he'd been facing the end of his cycling career and not knowing what he was going to do with the rest of his life. Plus, he was single and his daughter Rosie had just turned ten, making him feel old before his time. He wished he could go back and tell his younger self not to worry. *You'll be offered TV work, start your own charitable foundation, meet your soulmate and have Ethan, your little man.* It turned out that the twists and turns of life were more unexpected and delightful than any mountain pass he'd ever had the pleasure of riding.

The estimated arrival time on the taxi's sat nav said Ryan would be twenty minutes later than he'd promised, but he was pretty sure the gift in his bag would redeem him. She had pointed it out as they'd walked past Lister Horsefall, the fancy jewellers on the corner of The Grove in their hometown of Ilkley.

'It must be a wonderful store to have something as gorgeous as that in their window.'

He'd played his part well, paying little attention to the sparkling item then quickly changing the subject to leave her wondering: *Has he seen it? Will he remember it?*

It was a game they both enjoyed.

'Any chance you can shave a few minutes off that ETA?' he said to the driver.

'I'll do me best. Not often we get trips like this these days. This cost-of-living crisis is a nightmare for us cabbies.'

'You have my wife to thank for that. I usually cycle to and from work but I'm under strict instructions to not turn up sweaty to her birthday party.'

'Clever man. Do what the missus asks.'

'Yes, well, I don't look as good in tight Lycra these days. I'll give her that.'

'Must be tough growing older when you're married to a model.'

Ryan met the man's gaze in the rear-view mirror.

'My wife is a big fan of the cycling,' said the cabbie.

'She's clearly a woman of taste.'

As the driver went on to complain about some of the more ignorant characters he'd had in his taxi recently, Ryan watched the giant golf balls of RAF Menwith Hill pass them by. It meant

4

they were nearing Harrogate and Ryan was pleased to see the driver had already shaved four minutes off their ETA.

He listened to his daughter Rosie's voicemail message for a second time.

'Hi, Dad. I really wanted to be there for Camille tonight but I'm not sure I can take the drama. Mum is kicking off again and I just want to keep the peace until my exams are done. Sorry. You know I love you. See you on Monday.'

Ryan considered calling her back and trying to convince her to come, but he knew that wasn't fair. She was the one who would face the flak from her mother if she did. Steph had done her best to try and drive a wedge between them over the years, constantly harping on about how he'd broken up the family. And no matter how many times he stressed, 'I left *you*, Steph, not Rosie,' it fell on deaf ears.

'If your Dad really wanted you there he wouldn't have put the party in the middle of your exams,' she'd said to Rosie, who'd passed the message on to Camille. As though Camille could change the date of her birthday, and forgetting that Rosie only had one more of her GCSEs to sit. She'd decided she was going to work for Ryan instead of studying for her A Levels. For the first time since she was a baby, he'd get to see her every day.

Ryan imagined what might have happened if he'd turned up late to Steph's birthday party when they were together. It would have resulted in a public showdown where she told him, and anyone in hearing distance, that he was a waste of space. A fuck-up who couldn't be trusted. At least he was now free of the woman. Well, as free as you could be when you shared a sixteen-year-old daughter.

A notification pinged on his phone. He lifted up the screen, expecting another excited message from friends who were heading to the party, but what he saw expelled all the air from his lungs in one swift rush.

The text contained a link to an article on the BBC News page.

5

The image was of Ryan crossing the line with his hands aloft as he won his Tour de France stage.

'EX-BRITISH CYCLIST RYAN FALLON EXPOSED', read the headline.

Ryan's hand began to shake as he pressed the link and watched it expand. Now it filled his phone from top to bottom.

'All right, mate?' said the driver, his eyes on the rear-view mirror and Ryan's reaction.

Ryan scrolled quickly down the article, scanning the text before pausing on the picture of his wife. Her hand was raised to shield her face but the grief was still clear to see. She hadn't called. Why hadn't she called? Feeling a cold weight settle in his stomach, he carried on scrolling, past a few pictures of himself to a final one showing the logo of the Fallon Foundation, the charity he had founded to encourage children of all abilities to take up cycling.

The car stopped at some lights as Ryan began to re-read the article from the beginning.

'Everything OK, mate?' said the driver again.

Ryan's shirt felt hot and tight around his neck and his hands were sweaty making his finger slip on the screen as he scrolled. 'Yeah, I'm fine.'

This would finish him.

His life was imploding in the precise way he had managed to convince himself would never happen. He had gotten away with it for so long. And the further away from the deed he had moved the easier it was to tell himself no one ever knew.

And now they'd all know. His wife, his kids, his friends. Oh God, his parents.

The shame crawled through his body like a living thing.

2

ISOBEL

Friday, 3.30 p.m.

The council's office provided a quiet, cool escape from the bustling city centre that was baking in the summer sun. The weather really had changed dramatically over recent years. It was quite frightening if she gave herself time to think about it. Was this really a world she wanted to raise a child in? How would she cope with the judgement in the next generation's eyes when they realized what their predecessors had done to damage the planet?

Isobel suppressed the flutter of nerves that skittered across her stomach whenever she thought about the life-long responsibility she and Annie were hopefully going to be taking on. They had been fostering Joshua for a year, and today they would find out if they were approved for adoption. She couldn't imagine life without the toddler bouncing around them; she wanted nothing more than to be told she would be his mummy for ever.

The clock above the reception said 3.32. Annie was late.

Chill out, I'm coming, I'll never let you down, she heard Annie's voice say in her head. As a freelance journalist, Annie was used to asking for extra time as she realized she wasn't going to hit a deadline. Isobel was the opposite. She valued timekeeping, seeing it as the essence of self-management and politeness. It was how she had been raised. Which parent would Joshua take after, she wondered, or would there be some other innate approach inherited from his biological parents?

Isobel rolled her shoulders and moved her head from side to side. Last night's shift had been long and complicated, she could feel it in the muscles of her back and neck. If she had time she would book a massage, but they were the kind of life luxuries other people enjoyed. She had thought when she made it to consultant, her life would have more balance. As a junior doctor she had watched the consultants above her head home for a weekend of golf and thought how wonderful it must be. But somehow, now she was here, there was always some extra responsibility that demanded her attention and stole her free time. Annie used phrases like *pushover* and *people pleaser* to explain it, but Isobel thought the truth was closer to feeling like an imposter. She was a woman in a man's world. She'd worked hard to become a doctor, a leader, a scientist, and she wanted to hold on to it.

Truth be told, for much of her life, she had been so keen to hide the truth about herself that she'd invested every waking hour in proving to her dad that she was as good as any man.

You say I can't, I'll show you I can. You say I'm not good enough, I'll prove you wrong. But at what cost? Years of repressed emotions, of hiding who she really was and what she really wanted. Not until Annie turned up in her life did she even realize the terrible toll it was all taking on her sanity.

'Just tell them you fancy girls,' Annie had said, making it sound far easier than it felt. Fortunately, it hadn't been as difficult as she thought. When Isobel did finally pluck up the guts to tell her parents a few months later, the moment passed without drama.

3.34.

The receptionist was losing patience with the person on the

8

other end of the phone. She repeated her instruction to turn left after Waterstones with barely disguised irritation.

Isobel looked hopefully towards the door before checking the text that pinged on her phone. It was a link to a news story: CONSULTANT NEONATOLOGIST AT LEEDS CHILDREN'S HOSPITAL DISGRACED . . .

Her heart began to beat just a touch faster as she read the headline. There were a total of twelve neonatal consultants within Leeds Children's Hospital. In the time it took for the link to open out into a *Daily Mail* news page, she thought about her colleagues, hoping it would be one of them and not her.

Mrs Isobel Walters.

Isobel stared at her own name, unable to read any of the words around it because she knew what they would say, and she knew what they would mean.

She would be suspended, investigated and most likely struck off. It wasn't so much the error she had made – that awful, regrettable lapse of judgement. It was the lie. The General Medical Council did not take kindly to probity failings; honesty and integrity was foundational to the medical profession. Her father would be proven right. She would be found wanting. And what about Annie? How would she view the wife she had always been so keen to show off about now this was out?

Isobel forced her thumb to scroll down the article even though her brain refused to assimilate what her eyes were seeing.

When she'd received the voicemail asking for Annie and her to come in to see the agency decision-maker, Mrs Howell, today, she had assumed this was to inform them of the adoption panel's decision. 'Who wouldn't think a paediatrician was a perfect parent for a child?' their social worker had said. The irony of it brought a wave of sickness so strong, Isobel had to swallow back the bile for fear of throwing up on the polished floor.

In the article, Mrs Howell had given a quote. Isobel's thumb froze a fraction above the screen. *No, no, no.*

'We can't comment on pending adoption applications, but I assure you safeguarding the children is our priority.'

That said it all.

Joshua wasn't going to be theirs.

3

PAUL

Friday, 3.30 p.m.

It was a straightforward case in many ways. Paul's client was accused of arriving drunk at his father's house and beating him to death with a beer bottle after an argument. His defence that 'It wasn't me' was somewhat discredited by the forensic evidence, which included his fingerprints and DNA on the murder weapon. But there was always a story to these things. People don't simply beat their father to death out of the blue with no instigating factors. The origins of such crimes begin many years earlier and build over time until a final straw breaks the camel's back. Paul's job was to uncover that story and set it out to the jury in a manner that built a degree of empathy: under different circumstances this man could be any one of us.

Paul had managed it pretty well in this case. The victim was one of those small-town gangster types who bullied his way through life. The defendant's sister had given a particularly powerful description of a childhood spent cowering behind furniture hoping that the wrath would not come her way. The prosecution were arguing that no one deserves to die like that, beaten and broken in the safety of their own home. But sometimes, some people do deserve it.

He read through his closing argument one more time. This was where he could bring it all to life, draw out the emotion and show his client as a man who was driven to the act by a terrible father. The guy was unlikely to get off completely, but a manslaughter conviction would be a significant achievement. It was entirely in Paul's reach if he played it right.

The room where he sat was cold, cramped and dark, but Paul liked the claustrophobia of it. There were other rooms in the Leeds Crown Court building he could have used, ones with windows and easier access to drinks and snacks, but they didn't force his brain to fight its way out of a corner quite like this one.

He nearly ignored the alert on his phone. He was on a roll, his neurons firing at pace as he practised and perfected his closing. The problem was that any breaking news story was a possible future job.

A few moments won't hurt, he told himself. He could stretch his legs, visit the gents' then return to the job in hand refreshed, or so said the voice of justification in his head.

Criminal Barrister Paul Reece-Johnson Accused of . . .

Paul stood up, his chair scraping loudly across the floor. His hands were balled tightly into fists; he could feel the sweat forming down his back and around his neck.

Paul had never heard of the article's author, Carl Baker. He wasn't one of the regular court reporters Paul had a good degree of rapport with. So why had he come for him? Had someone tipped him off? Was there another, more culpable person behind all of this?

Was this Kyle Renton's doing? If Renton had evidence of Paul's past there was a good chance he could use it to get out of jail, and what then? Paul's career and reputation would be left in tatters, but he suspected that might not be revenge enough for the likes of Renton.

A soft knock on the door broke Paul out of his trance.

'Five minutes, Mr Reece-Johnson.'

'Thanks,' he managed to say.

He needed to park this and focus on the job at hand. There were only the closing arguments to be done and then the jury would be sent to deliberate. If the prosecution didn't mess about, he'd be done in a matter of hours. He just had to hope no other news outlets picked this up before then. If he could stop it in its tracks early, he might just be able to escape this unscathed.

Paul collected his documents and made his way back to the court room. His fists were still tightly balled as he tried to ignore the voice in his head.

It's all too late.

4

MANDY

Friday, 3.30 p.m.

Waiting at the lights on the central reservation of Leeds inner-city ring road, Mandy watched her bus depart from the station opposite. Tears welled in her eyes and she took a deep breath to rein in the emotion.

I am not going to cry in the street.

Mandy was only yards away from the new fine-dining restaurant where she had just interviewed for a job as the head chef. She had known within moments of the interview starting that she was out of the running. The owner-manager had opened with a brazen statement about wanting to create the premium dining spot in the city, hence requiring a 'name chef': someone to compete with Michael O'Hare at the Man Behind the Curtain or *MasterChef*'s Chef Jono at V&V. This was not her.

She had no doubt passed the paper sift simply because of her brief stint as a TV chef over fifteen years earlier. Back then, she thought she'd made it. All her friends were still starting out in their first post-university jobs, and she was already on national television once a week. She was the famous friend whom everyone wanted to accompany to the National TV Awards.

Mandy pressed the pedestrian crossing button again even though it was already lit up. Cars passed in a constant stream with no sign of slowing and the air was thick with exhaust fumes. What was the rush anyway? Her bus was gone, and the next wouldn't be for at least an hour. In years gone by she'd have seen such a setback as a nice opportunity to wander around the shops, but she couldn't afford the temptation any more. The job wasn't hers and there were no more interviews on the horizon.

She wiped a stray tear from her cheek and looked over at the new John Lewis building to her right, its silver and black exterior shimmering in the summer sun. The site had once housed Milgarth Police Station, where Greg had worked when they first met. She wondered how he was. She hadn't spoken to him for nearly a month now, which would have been unthinkable when they were together. Their daily calls would number three or four, never less than two. So entwined were their lives that neither of them could go more than a few hours without checking in and saying hi. When had it all gone so wrong? How?

Recording the TV show had been exciting at first, but she had begun to tire of the strict schedule, not to mention the misogynistic culture that prevailed. Why did she need hours in make-up so she could bake a soufflé? And why did the director think it was OK to move her into position manually, his hands lingering on her waist longer than they should?

Greg had been her greatest joy and her biggest failure. She had left the TV job to move back up to Yorkshire from London after meeting him on one of her train journeys home to visit her parents. He had proposed within a year.

Greg was already a sergeant and on the accelerated promotion track so he could provide a good life for them. He was a breath of fresh air, a man of principle who wanted to make the world a better place. She had fallen hard for his good heart, intelligent eyes and mop of blonde curls. They were supposed to have lived their whole lives together. They wanted a family who they could spend their summer weekends camping and cooking outdoors with, who would fill the cold winter nights with the sound of sibling rivalry and laughter. Their house should have been busy, loud and full of love. But that was not to be.

Years of IVF had taken their toll. Greg was a detective chief superintendent now, passionately focused on his job and, it would transpire, his detective inspector.

Mandy felt the all too familiar weight of hopelessness settling upon her once more. She needed to do something constructive. The counsellor she had been referred to by the GP had told her to concentrate on taking control in such moments: 'Do something productive to stave off the darkness.' But what?

She stared at the little red man and willed him to turn green so she could at least move from her trapped position between two carriageways. He seemed to stare back with an air of obstinance. *Whatcha gonna do, make me?*

Paul. She could go to see Paul. He had said he was running a big trial this month so couldn't make it to Camille's fancy party. Mandy had blamed the interview even though she knew it would be over in plenty of time for her to still make it. But she couldn't cope with all that joy right now. The Crown Court was on the other side of town, but she had nowhere else to be so why not walk up and see if he's there? Paul would make her feel better. He always made her feel better.

The buzz of her phone in her hand made her jump a little. She had forgotten she was still holding it after checking the bus time-table. Needing something to distract her from the indignant stare of the little red man, she looked at the screen.

Former TV Chef Mandy Coulters Suspected . . .

She knew what was coming even before her shaking finger touched the link and she watched the *Yorkshire Post* page open up, revealing a photograph she had managed to make herself forget over the years.

Only two things of note had occurred in her past: the brief stint on TV and the other thing.

Underneath the photograph, the paper had printed a quote from Mandy's seventy-one-year-old dad: 'I will stand by my Mandy no matter what.' Her dad was old. She knew he would defend her until his dying day, but she couldn't put him through this.

Mandy looked up and saw her life disintegrating. She had told herself that being broke and alone was the worst thing life could throw at her, but somewhere deep in her psyche she had known it was not the worst. This was. This thing that the world now knew.

She looked to her right. There was a break in the traffic after the little white Mazda and before the Amazon Prime van. The van must be doing at least forty. It would have decent brakes but not such a great stopping distance. She knew the stories and the statistics from Greg's time working on traffic. Mandy looked at the little red man for the last time, but now she willed him to remain stubborn.

'Help me out, you little bastard,' she said under her breath as she waited a few more seconds and then took two determined steps into the road.

5

THE SHAME GAME:
A TRUE CRIME DOCUMENTARY

Episode 1 of 3 - The Players

EXT - WHITE WELLS, ILKLEY - DAYTIME

A large white cottage fills the screen. The
lush green moorland surrounding it is bathed
in sunlight, but the front of the building
is cast in shadow. A teenage girl walks
across the cobbled courtyard. She wears
cream shorts with a black hoody, and black-
and-white checked Vans. Her fair hair is
tied in a ponytail, and it swings a little
as she moves across the screen.

TEXT on the screen: ROSIE FALLON, DAUGHTER
OF RYAN FALLON.

Rosie passes a small stone porch that
extends from the front of the building. The
wooden door on the front of the stone porch

is white and windowless. Next to the porch,
attached to the building, is a triangle of
stone steps, four high on each side, that
go nowhere. Next to this is another white,
windowless door. The camera zooms out to
show the breadth of the cottage. It is made
up of four conjoined blocks of whitewashed
stone, each rising to a different height.
The whole thing stretches out wide, and as
the camera pulls back further to reveal its
position high up on a hill, it is possible
to see that these man-made cubes of white
are overshadowed by an impressive stone crag
that rises up at its rear.

TEXT on the screen: WHITE WELLS BATH HOUSE,
ILKLEY, WEST YORKSHIRE.

                    ROSIE FALLON

    This is where it happened.

Rosie sits on the weathered picnic table in
front of the Bath House. She pushes a stray
hair that has escaped from her ponytail
behind her ear as she speaks.

                        ROSIE

    It's funny now, to look back and
    think of all those plans I had. I
    thought my life was predictable.
    I thought I knew what was coming
    next. I'd decided to leave school
    and work with my dad so I could
    focus on cycling. I had this dream

of getting to the Mountain Bike
World Championships. But in the
space of one week, everything
changed.

Rosie looks over at the building and the
camera zooms in on a sign above the second
white door. It has an arrow pointing to the
porch that reads, 'BATHS'.

Without looking back at the camera, Rosie
continues to speak.

                    ROSIE

    This is the first time I've been
    back since. It used to have so
    many great memories. Dad and
    I would come up here every New
    Year's Day and take the plunge.
    Loads of people do it. My friends
    say I should come again and jump
    in, as if all the freezing water
    will change what happened.

Rosie looks back at the camera.

                    ROSIE

    But if I've learned anything from
    all of this, it's that you can't
    erase the past, especially the bad
    stuff.

6

RYAN

Friday, 4.10 p.m.

The taxi drove slowly along the sweeping driveway of Rudding Park. Ryan looked up from his phone. The luxury hotel's car park was about half full and he wondered how many of Camille's guests would have seen the article by now.

Where was Camille and why hadn't she called? He checked his phone to be sure, but there were no missed calls or messages.

'Thanks, mate,' Ryan said to the driver, wishing he could go somewhere and hide.

The hotel reception was out of sight, around the perimeter of the building. He had visited here with Camille the previous weekend and they'd walked through how the whole party would be laid out on the terrace area outside the Clocktower, the hotel's restaurant. People would be greeted with glasses of champagne and French-style canapés as they circulated and soaked up the sun while a young guitar player serenaded them with an acoustic set of Camille's favourite songs. She had been so animated as they talked it all through with the events manager. Ryan wondered if he would ever see her smile at him again the way she had that day.

Laughter floated in his direction and his heart sank. Most of those here awaiting the celebration wouldn't have seen the news yet. He really was going to have to say it all out loud. He paused for a moment to steel himself.

Focus. Don't think about the past. Don't worry about the future. Concentrate and take control.

It was a mantra he'd been coached to repeat as a cyclist to manage his nerves.

'Baby, you made it!'

The sight of Camille stopped him in his tracks. She looked stunning. Her blonde hair shone in the sun and her model's body was draped in a blue silk dress.

'Hi,' he managed to say as he braced himself for what was to come.

'Ryan, you look like you've seen a ghost. Aren't you going to wish your wife a happy birthday?' His mother's words sounded light and humorous on the surface but there was a steely undertone that he recognized well. It was the same tone she had used since he was a child whenever she thought he was showing her up.

'Sorry, yes, wow . . . erm, happy birthday . . . honey.' He added the last word a little nervously, expecting an admonishing look from his wife as he leaned in to kiss her. But she simply kissed him back and giggled.

'I don't think I've seen you look at me like that since the first night we met. When you were too scared to say hello.' Camille grinned at Ryan's mum. 'You were right. This dress was a great choice.'

The women chinked their champagne flutes as they shared a conspiratorial look.

Ryan felt a cold dread settle in his stomach. Camille and his mother didn't know. He was going to have to tell them himself. He looked at the handful of guests milling around the entrance. How long before one of them saw the article and said something? How much time did he have to find the right words?

Camille took his hand. 'Come see, it all looks wonderful.' She pulled him into the hotel and towards the terrace at the rear.

'Camille, honey,' he said, forcing her to stop and look at him.

'What is it?' She looked down and saw the small bag he was carrying and her hands flew to her mouth. 'Oh! Baby. You didn't?' Her wide eyes looked joyful but not at all surprised. The reaction caused him to smile on instinct. She had known he would do as he was instructed.

'Yes, of course. I love you.' He took hold of her wrists. 'You know I love you, don't you?'

Her eyes questioned him for a second and then she shook the expression away. 'Of course I do. Especially now.' She made a grab for the bag and he let her take it, watching her place it on a side table and remove the wrapped box as he decided how to handle this.

Behind his wife, Ryan saw the vice president of the American bicycle brand he had ridden when he won his Tour de France stage. The company had recently agreed to lend their support to the Fallon Foundation. When Camille had invited the VP to attend today, he'd said he'd be delighted to experience a traditional European drinks party.

But in the article, the VP had been quoted saying the brand had no desire to be associated with someone like Ryan, no matter how well-meaning his charity might be. The man continued to walk purposefully towards them and, to add salt to the wound, he was accompanied by Ryan's father.

Steven Fallon was Ryan's hero. He had been a professional footballer in his youth, playing for Sheffield Wednesday and Blackburn Rovers before being forced to retire due to a knee injury. Ryan had grown up watching men greet his dad with genuine awe, shaking his hand vigorously and asking for an autograph, even if they were in the supermarket doing a weekly shop. His dad's success had inspired Ryan to achieve his own in cycling, and he had wanted to inspire his kids in the same way.

Camille threw her arms around his neck and kissed him full on the lips.

'It is magnifique,' she said, holding up her hand to show him how the bracelet sparkled on her elegant wrist.

'Well, I would say that gift was something of a success. I may need to know your secret, Ryan.' The VP's booming Texan accent filled the hotel lobby.

Ryan nodded as he braced himself for the criticism that was to follow. This was going to be his life now – bracing himself for people's low opinions of him. He may as well start practising how to take it.

'Oh my gosh, I forgot to ask if you'd heard from Isobel?' said Camille. 'Ryan did you hear? Isobel and Annie are getting to keep Josh.'

Ryan was staring at the VP, who was smiling widely at him. It struck Ryan as particularly cruel to take pleasure in someone else's downfall.

'That's brilliant,' Ryan said.

'Lift it off the page, son. Your best friend just became a mummy.' His dad slapped him on the back and it was enough to jar Ryan back to reality.

He looked at his dad, Camille and the VP. None of these people were angry with him, which was especially weird for the VP. There was no disappointment or disgust in anyone's eyes.

'Sorry, can you give me a minute. I'll be back in a sec.'

Ryan hurried to the toilet where he entered the first cubicle and locked the door. He took his phone from his pocket and opened the BBC News app, scrolling through all the day's stories. There was no mention of him. Closing the app, he opened Google and typed his name into the search bar. The results included his Wikipedia page, a few old cycling stories and his company website. Finally, he viewed the open pages on his phone, knowing he hadn't closed the article when the taxi pulled in.

The sight of it miniaturized on his screen brought back the dread. It was real. He pressed to enlarge it, and the image flickered a couple of times before the page refreshed and defaulted to a white screen. Website Unavailable.

Ryan looked back at the text which had sent the link. It came from an email address rather than a number: Shame@pm.me.

Ryan leaned back against the cistern. Was it a prank or a threat? He should feel relieved, but he didn't. The article was out there. Someone somewhere had it. He would have to tell everyone it was coming.

He had thought that being exposed out of the blue in the press was as bad as it could get, but this would be so much worse.

7

ISOBEL

Friday, 3.35 p.m.

Isobel watched as Annie carried Joshua into the building. His arms were outstretched towards Isobel as he called out, 'Bye, Mama!'

He muddled hi and bye all the time, but this occasion struck Isobel as particularly poignant. Tears welled in her eyes as she tried in vain to think of what she could say to explain or apologize. Joshua would eventually forget them both, she knew. He was too young to form any real lasting memories, but Annie would have the next few moments seared into her mind for the rest of her life.

'I'm so sorry,' Isobel said as the two most important people in her universe reached her.

'I'm the one who's late,' said Annie, wiping some crumbs off Joshua's chin with the side of her index finger. 'It's "Hi, Mama," Joshy. Say "Hi, Mama".'

'Hi, Mama,' Joshua repeated, rubbing one eye with his podgy fist.

'Is he tired?'

'Oh, I expect so, he flat out refused to nap. I nearly lost my sh—' Annie stopped then said, 'rag. It's like the little monkey knew something big was going on today.'

You can say that again, thought Isobel.

'Good afternoon, ladies.' Mrs Howell approached them from the end of the corridor. Her sensible low-heeled black court shoes made a click-clack sound against the tiled floor.

'Annie—'

'Here's the lady who's going to make our dreams come true, Joshy,' Annie said, her attention focused entirely on the agency decision-maker.

'Annie?' Isobel touched her wife's arm.

Annie looked at her properly for the first time. 'You look awful. Are you sick? Did something happen at work?'

Isobel caught sight of her own reflection in the mirror behind reception. She had inherited dark caramel-coloured skin from her Syrian mother, but right now her complexion looked waxen and grey.

'I'm fine.'

'Now then, young man, can I have a quick cuddle?' Mrs Howell held both hands out.

You can't take him, Isobel shouted in her head, but no words came out as she helplessly watched her wife hand Joshua over for the final time. There would be no elongated goodbyes. That would only upset Joshua. It would be professional and quick, just like in the hospital when a child needed to be taken away from its panicking parents for surgery.

'OK then, shall we go through to my office?' Mrs Howell said.

'Are you OK?' Annie mouthed, taking Isobel's hand and giving it a squeeze as they followed.

'No. I'm sorry. I'll make it all right. I promise.'

'What do you mean? What's going on?'

Isobel didn't respond as, ahead of them, she heard Mrs Howell say to Joshua, 'Today you all get to become a for ever family. You are going to have a wonderful life with your mummies, little man.'

The next twenty minutes passed in a blur. Isobel was aware of hands being shaken, forms being signed and many kind words being shared from Mrs Howell. The voice in her head told her to stop the whole thing and come clean about the article, but her gut said no. Once these papers were signed it would be so much harder for them to take Joshua back. They would have to wait out the inquiry and that would give Isobel time. She tried to smile and look normal but she could feel Annie's eyes on her.

On the way out of the building, Isobel excused herself and went to the ladies' room to throw up.

'Spill,' said Annie after she had fastened Joshua into his car seat and climbed into the driver's side of their Volvo.

'I don't know what you mean.'

'Why were you so quiet? You barely cracked a smile when she told us Joshua was going to be ours. Are you feeling OK?'

'I was nervous.'

'Why?'

Isobel returned Annie's inquisitive stare. Most people would accept 'I was nervous' as an explanation for looking and acting out of sorts, but not her journalist wife. Oh no, she smelled a story and like a bloodhound she would chase it down.

'There are rumours of an inquiry at Harrogate paediatric unit, suggestions that some misconduct might have occurred back when I worked there.' Isobel had to give Annie something and this was as close to the truth as she could bring herself to get because the article had disappeared. She couldn't make sense of it. When she had visited the ladies' room, Isobel had looked for it again on her phone. She had been certain that they'd quoted Mrs Howell but she must have been mistaken and she wanted to see for sure. But it was gone. And when she searched the *Daily Mail* website, it was not listed.

'On any of your patients?'

'It's yet to be confirmed.'

Isobel could feel the weight of Annie's silence. The article must have been sent to her as an advance warning. She knew Annie would be able to tell her how these things worked and what rights she had to stop such a story, but no matter how hard she willed herself to ask, she simply couldn't make the words come out.

Annie began to talk about all her plans for their life with Josh as she drove them to Camille's party at Rudding Park. Meanwhile, Joshua sang 'Hickory Dickory Dock' over and over from his car seat. Isobel reached through the gap in between the front seats so she could hold her son's hand. *Her son.* He was really theirs, and Isobel would do everything in her power to keep it that way.

8

PAUL

Friday, 5.45 p.m.

He half expected a handful of reporters to be waiting for him as he left court and he was relieved to find there were none. For the past few hours, he had pushed his own concerns aside and done his best for his client, but now he had handed the baton to the jury it was time to focus. He reached his car, a Porsche Panamera, and carefully hung his jacket on the hanger in the rear. He had looked up the number on his walk to the car, so he could call as soon as he set off for his drive through the city.

'Mira Hussain,' said the plummy editor of the *Guardian*'s law desk.

'Mira, it's Paul Reece-Johnson KC here. I'm calling to request the immediate retraction of Carl Baker's article.'

'Sorry, Paul. I'm not sure I understand. Who is Carl Baker?'

Paul pulled up at the lights next to two young men in a red Golf GTI. The driver pumped his accelerator a few times when he saw Paul's car, the growl of the engine accompanying an inane grin from the young lad in the passenger seat. Paul ignored them.

'Is Carl Baker not one of your journalists?'

'No. What was the article?'

Paul realized he needed to get off this call quickly. 'Does he work on a different desk?'

'Never heard of him. Let me check here.'

Paul could hear Mira tapping on her keyboard.

'So, not a freelancer either?' He wanted to be sure of what she was saying. The article he had been sent had opened on to the *Guardian* website and been fully branded.

'No. We have no one of that name. What is this about Paul? You sound annoyed.'

Paul apologized, saying he must have been misinformed, and hung up before Mira could quiz him any further.

The last thing he needed was a journalist of Mira Hussain's calibre digging around in his past.

Vanessa was upstairs on a Teams call with her managing partner when Paul arrived home. He was used to hearing their conversations about billing hours and staffing issues. As a partner in a corporate law firm, his wife earned almost double his salary, such was the difference between commercial law and criminal law. He flicked on the kettle and placed his laptop on the kitchen island. He had checked his phone in the car and found no trace of the *Guardian* report so now he needed to dig deeper. Who was Carl Baker, why was he pretending to work for the *Guardian*, and why was he threatening to expose Paul?

He had concluded that the article he'd been sent was a threat of some kind. The email address attached to the text message said it all: Shame@pm.me. This was someone's attempt to scare him. And it had worked. He'd been so thrown by the thing he hadn't paid any attention to the sender of the article. He had since sent a text back asking 'Who is this?' and 'What do you want?', but thus far he'd had no reply.

Though the article may be fake, one thing was true: someone had uncovered the truth about Paul's past. He could only think of one person with a reason to go digging on him: Kyle Renton.

If that was what was going on here, the baiting nature of the article made more sense. Renton hated Paul for putting him away and would revel in the idea that he was guilty of something.

Vanessa came into the kitchen. 'Seb says hello. He asked if you were doing that charity golf tournament next month.' Vanessa wore a silk blouse and pencil skirt even though she had been working from home today. She poured away his untouched mug of now-cold tea and reached for two wine glasses.

'Yeah, maybe. I'll have to see what's happening.'

She poured them each a generous glass of Viognier and took a sip. 'You're back earlier than you said. We could have made Camille's big do after all.'

Paul reached for the glass and took a long slug of the crisp wine. 'You said you didn't want to go.'

'No. I said I didn't fancy spending hours discussing the merits of shirt dresses versus wrap dresses with a room full of fashionista darlings.'

'Or in other words, you don't want to go.'

'You are twisting my words, darling. I would never stop you from playing out with your friends.'

'They are your friends too, Ness. Or at least they're supposed to be.'

'Who poked your cage?' Vanessa leaned back against the range cooker. 'Did Larry the Lamb get the better of you?' She referred to Larry Lonegan, the prosecuting KC in his current case.

'What do you know about imposter news sites?' Paul said, changing the subject.

'Those fake news vehicles? I know one of our clients got stung by incorrect market information that had been posted about a competitor by a fake newspaper. I think it was called the *Financial Tribune* or something along those lines.'

'No, more like mimicking a legit news source like *The Times* or the *Independent*.'

'Anything's possible, I expect. Think of those financial phishing emails that take you to a site that looks like Barclays then pump you for your account details. Is this about a case?'

'Mmmm, not sure yet. It's disturbing what people can do and how real they can make it look.'

'You need to check the hyperlinks and the adverts. If they don't go anywhere, then reader beware.'

Paul studied his wife as he downed the rest of his wine. Would she stick by him if this came out? He knew she loved their large house in the small hamlet beyond Ilkley Moor, and their biannual holidays – one luxurious, one adventurous – not to mention their expensive clothes, fast cars and well stocked wine cellar. Even with a salary like hers, that lifestyle would take a hit without his income . . . But did she love *him*? He was pretty certain she was still attracted to him, given the healthiness of their sex life, and that she still enjoyed his company. But did she love him and, if so, did she love him enough to stick by him? Of that, he wasn't entirely certain.

9

RYAN

Friday, 5.45 p.m.

The sight of Isobel carrying little Josh provided Ryan with a touch of light relief. He was struggling to tune in to the party vibe despite finding no trace of the story about him each time he checked – which was regularly. Fortunately, people were either too engrossed in what they were saying or too tipsy to pay attention to him. Camille would probably spot something was off if she wasn't so busy being the centre of attention.

'You three are a sight for sore eyes.'

'Struggling to hold your own with the great and good, hey, Ry?' Annie kissed his cheek. She was never one to miss the chance of a friendly slap-down.

'I expect he's been charming everyone he meets and throwing around his dad jokes,' said Izzy.

'Er, you're supposed to be my bestie.'

'Hi, hon.' Isobel passed Josh to Annie so she could give Ryan a hug. It felt a little tighter than normal. Maybe he wasn't masking his mood as well as he thought.

'So, did it all go OK today?' Ryan asked before Isobel could quiz him.

An odd look crossed Isobel's face before Annie replied.

'We are officially Josh's mummies. Our fab family of three.'

'It's a huge relief,' Isobel said, and Ryan sensed that she really meant it.

'Surely there wasn't any doubt? You guys are meant to be,' Ryan said, reaching out his arms. 'Can I have a cuddle?'

The little boy curled into Annie's neck and pushed his thumb into his mouth.

'Sorry, he's knackered. No nap today.'

'I hear you. Ethan's still a nightmare without a nap.' Ryan ruffled Joshua's hair. He loved kids at this age; all podgy and cuddly. He remembered when Rosie was that small and every time he picked her up or put her down he would plant a big kiss on her head. At sixteen, she would only entertain a kiss from her dad under strict pre-agreed circumstances, such was the threat of social suicide.

'This is quite the do,' said Annie. 'I'll freshen up our little monster here, then we can go and find Aunt Camille.'

'The perfect wife,' said Ryan to Isobel as Annie walked away. 'Thanks for coming. Camille was upset when Mandy and Paul said they couldn't make it.'

Ryan, Isobel, Mandy and Paul had been close since high school. Back then, there had been a lot of laughter and some good parties before they had all headed off in different directions for university. The fact they had all ended up back in Yorkshire and in each other's lives again was a source of great joy for Ryan. These were his people, and they kept him young.

'I'm not surprised it was a stretch for Paul if he's got a trial on,' Isobel replied. 'I hoped Mandy might change her mind. It must be hard going to things without Greg, but it's us, you know? *She's* our friend. Anyway, at least the real A-listers are here.'

She smiled and nodded over Ryan's shoulder, and when he turned around, he had to blink a couple of times to confirm to himself that it really was Rosie walking towards him.

'Surprise!' she said with the largest grin on her face.

'You look beautiful,' said Isobel, admiring Rosie's figure-hugging black dress that, in Ryan's opinion, made her look a few years too old.

'Nanna bought it for me,' she said, giving a twirl and then smiling at Felicity, the woman in question, who was hanging back as Rosie greeted them. 'She said as Mum was working tonight, she'd bring me down and come back to collect me later.'

'What Stephanie doesn't know won't hurt her,' said Felicity. The mother of Ryan's ex looked a little out of place in her casual clothes. 'We'll need to have you back before midnight, mind,' she said to Rosie. 'So I'll ring you when I'm on my way.'

'Like Cinderella,' said Isobel to Rosie, and the two of them giggled.

'You're welcome to stay and have a drink,' Ryan said, but knew this would not go down well with Camille. There was no love lost between his new wife and his ex's family. But he felt it was only polite to offer.

'No, no. I'm a simple taxi service tonight.'

'Thanks, Nanna, love you,' Rosie said, giving her a kiss. 'I'm going to find Camille. I have a gift for her.'

Ryan felt a burst of pride for his girl as he watched her rush away to find her stepmum. He knew every parent probably thought their child was the best, but his really was.

'Stephanie tells me you're adopting your little one, Isobel,' Felicity said.

'They signed on the dotted line today,' Ryan said and watched Isobel fill with pride.

'The hard work starts here, then.'

'Best work there is. He's a little star.'

'Long may that continue.' Felicity smiled but it looked a little forced and Ryan wasn't sure what to say next. He had no doubt

36

Steph had been hard work as a child. He caught Isobel's eye and she raised her eyebrows a touch.

'Well, that was awkward,' said Isobel once Felicity had headed off.

'Kind of her to bring Rosie, though.'

Isobel rubbed his arm. She knew better than most how hard he'd had to work to keep the peace for Rosie's sake.

'So is it all confirmed with Greg?' he said to change the subject. 'Has he really moved in with the woman from work?'

'Oh, yeah. I feel so sorry for Mandy. They were the one couple I always thought would be together for ever.'

'Isn't that what they always say? I figured it would be Paul and Vanessa who'd split. You know, when she finally realized she was too good for him.'

'Don't be mean.' Isobel gently slapped his arm. There was a long-standing joke in their group of friends that Ness would someday see the light and find a real man to marry. Paul went along with the joke but it was obvious he hated it, which only made it funnier.

'I'm gonna miss Greg.' It struck Ryan that if the truth about his past had come out while Mandy and Greg were still together, the police officer might have insisted they cut contact. Greg could be quite judgemental about those who didn't toe the line. Then again, he was an adulterer, so his stance might've surprised them.

'I know. It makes you wonder if we can ever have one of our dinner parties again. How Mandy will feel alone at the table. It's really sad.'

'She'll be OK. If we take care of her as well as you guys took care of me after Steph, she'll soon be back on her feet.'

Isobel stared past him and didn't respond.

'Earth to Izzy.'

'Huh?'

'I lost you for a minute there.'

'Sorry, I just had a feeling . . .' She scanned the gardens and tree-lined borders around them. 'Ignore me. I'm sleep-deprived. Josh has been teething.'

Ryan watched her walk inside and then scanned the gardens himself before following her. He'd been having a weird feeling too. Was someone out there, hiding in the trees and watching him? He dismissed the idea. The article was making him paranoid. Whoever was coming for him didn't need to spy on him; they had everything they needed already.

10

RYAN

Friday, midnight

The dance floor was in full flow to the sound of the Black Eyed Peas. Camille and her friends bounced around in bare feet singing at the top of their lungs. Ryan had moved outside on to the terrace where it was quieter. His head ached from the stress of the day, and the need to keep up a facade and pretend that everything was normal. A few other party stragglers were already sat outside, each with half-drunk glasses of wine or whisky. The night was still warm and Ryan closed his eyes.

Rosie had been collected not long after Isobel and Annie left to get Joshua to bed. He was so happy for Isobel and Annie, and so sad for Mandy. Seeing Isobel and Annie become parents would be an extra blow on top of Greg's betrayal. She had been so desperate for a family and experienced truly dark times as the IVF failed time and again. He knew she had floated the idea of adoption past Greg, but he was against it for some unknown reason. Whatever hassle might be coming Ryan's way he needed to keep it in perspective. He had two healthy children.

The vibration in his pocket made him stiffen in his seat. He opened his eyes and took out his phone.

From: Shame@pm.me

Do you want to know a secret?

Ryan looked around at the party guests, all busily chatting. When he was sure no one was watching him, he opened the full message.

Yours is not the only secret. Someone is hiding something that you really need to know.

WHO HURT AUDREY RAYE?

If you can find out by 3.30 p.m. on Friday, I will keep your secret.

If you cannot or will not, your secret will be shared with the world.

If you involve the police, I will go to the press.

Clues can be provided, but at a cost.

Start the clock.

Happy hunting . . .

Audrey Raye. Ryan recognized the name but for the life of him could not place it. He opened Google and typed it in. A few social media links came up first: various Audrey Rayes on Instagram and Facebook. Back on Google, there was a podcast episode entitled, 'What Happened to Audrey Raye?' Ryan read the brief description.

Of course, that's why the name was so familiar. Audrey had been a pupil at his school. She was a few years older than him and had been found seriously injured at the side of the road near the golf club. He remembered how Ilkley had been full of speculation about what had happened to her for years. The police couldn't even be sure if she'd been hit by a car, thrown from one or even jumped from one. Audrey had survived but with serious brain damage that meant she could not recall what had happened to her.

He hadn't known her. He'd been away at university when it happened, Audrey in her early twenties. But had somebody in his life been involved? Is that why someone was challenging him to uncover the culprit? He immediately thought of his mum's erratic driving; his dad would often tell her to slow down or indicate before taking a turn. The idea brought a wave of nausea. He walked back to the doors to the party and looked for his parents. His dad was holding court with Camille's football-mad cousins and his mum was on the dance floor, twirling and laughing without a care in the world. Would he expose them, or anyone else he loved, to keep his secret?

11

ISOBEL

Friday, midnight

Isobel received her message while sitting on the floor of Joshua's nursery, holding his hand through the bars of his cot. It was the only way to get him back to sleep if he awoke in the night, and often involved her or Annie sitting here for a good thirty minutes until he was in a deep enough slumber to be able to extract your fingers without waking him.

Isobel had been scrolling through various news outlets on her phone. She told herself she was simply staving off the boredom but in reality it was driven by paranoia. And now she'd been given a reprieve and a chance to make it all go away again.

Yours is not the only secret. Someone is hiding something that you really need to know.

WHO BETRAYED YOU IN ENGLAND FIRST AT THE ROYAL OAK?

If you can find out by 3.30 p.m. on Friday, I will keep your secret.

If you cannot or will not, your secret will be shared with the world.

If you involve the police, I will go to the press.

Clues can be provided, but at a cost.

Start the clock.

Happy hunting . . .

Isobel stared at the question. *Who betrayed you?* Only the people closest to you could be guilty of a betrayal, like Greg with Mandy. So that meant someone she loved had done something to hurt her. Her mind immediately went to Annie. She was the person who could inflict most pain, but Isobel could never imagine that she would. Annie had been her salvation; her best friend and ally through so much. But that was her heart talking. Her head knew that anyone was capable of anything given the right conditions. She had discussed this with Greg and Paul many times over the years. The people who passed through the justice system were less often bad, and more often either broken or faced with a catastrophic set of circumstances.

The other word that jumped out at Isobel was 'FIRST'. 'Who betrayed you in England first?'

How many times had she been betrayed by someone close to her?

12

PAUL

Saturday, 8.30 a.m.
6 days, 7 hours left

Paul didn't read his message until the next morning. He and Vanessa had finished the bottle of Viognier and moved on to a Rioja with the steaks he cooked, after which they'd made love and he'd fallen into a comatose sleep. When he awoke at 6 a.m. with a kick drum pounding in his head, he crept out of the bedroom and headed to the kitchen for paracetamol and water.

Sitting at the breakfast bar, he stared at the message, unsure whether this was good news or bad. He had wanted to know what game someone was playing with that article and now he knew. It was blackmail. Someone was using his past to make him do their bidding.

Yours is not the only secret. Someone is hiding something that you really need to know.

WHO CHEATED JUSTICE ON 22/07/2012?

If you can find out by 3.30 p.m. on Friday, I will keep your secret.

If you cannot or will not, your secret will be shared with the world.

If you involve the police, I will go to the press.

Clues can be provided, but at a cost.

Start the clock.

Happy hunting . . .

Paul swore under his breath.

'Someone is hiding something.'

Someone who knew too much, Paul feared: 2012 had been a critical year for him. Not that anyone else knew that. Plus, his dastardly deed hadn't been done until October of that year, and this related to something which had occurred in July. He thought of the friends he'd had back then, people he'd considered kindred spirits. Had one of them cheated justice? And why was that relevant to him? He could think of a number of possibilities but none that settled the writhing nerves in his gut. Paul had long cut off contact with those people. They weren't good for him. They had infected his mind and blurred the line between supporting a cause and committing a crime. And once he had hooked up with Vanessa, she was adamant that these people could be harmful to both their careers. Was this one of them coming after him? Had they heard of his success since he'd left them behind? Were they coming to balance the scales? And if so, why taunt him with someone else's secret?

What if this somebody knew everything?

What then?

Paul knew there was only one answer. He would have to find a way to keep them quiet.

13

Mandy, Mandy, Mandy, why did you go and do that? Did you think it might save you from me? That I would forgive what you did because you died? Silly, silly girl.

If you knew how patient I've been, you would understand that forgiveness is not an option. You have to pay for what you did whether you are here or not. There's no get out of jail free card in this game.

I'm looking at your brother's Facebook page right now. He's been a great source of intel over the years. Quite the prolific poster, isn't he? Unlike you. You rarely posted anything apart from the odd happy birthday on friends' walls. But your brother, he likes to document his life by posting endless selfies and photos of family gatherings. This morning he's posted a message saying: 'My wonderful sister. May you rest in peace, Mandy.' I doubt very much that you will. Peace is the last thing you should be feeling.

If only you'd hung around long enough to see this thing out. You'd have realized you were in good company with those awful friends of yours. Maybe that's why you all stuck together like glue. What is it they say about flies and shit?

The point is that it was inevitable. Your goody two-shoes friend Isobel might have delayed things, but this was your destiny. I was always coming for you.

14

RYAN

Saturday, 8.30 a.m.
6 days, 7 hours left

Ryan needed more coffee. He'd been up since 5 a.m. listening to the podcast he had found on Audrey Raye, narrated by a true crime fan with a penchant for drama. Everything was expressed with an almost breathless, 'no one saw' or 'no one would ever know'. Ryan had a feeling that the guy was trying to place more mystery around the event than was warranted. To confirm the fact, he read all the articles he could find about her accident from that time.

Audrey had been seen leaving work in her boyfriend's car. She had been found badly injured and unconscious hours later at the side of the road. The boyfriend said they'd argued and she'd insisted on walking home, and there was no evidence that he was lying. So that was that. As the podcaster said, no one else had seen a thing.

He did discover that Audrey still lived in Ilkley, according to Facebook, and could often be found feeding the ducks at the tarn near White Wells on the moor. Ryan knew the area well – it had been at the end of a mountain biking trail he'd enjoyed as a teenager. Maybe he would take a walk up there later and see if he could find her.

Ryan's phone rang and he frowned. Why was Greg calling him? Mandy's husband hadn't been in contact much since the separation. He was a DCS in the police, though. The cold dread Ryan had felt yesterday returned. Had his blackmailer already gone to the police? For a second, he considered letting the call go to voicemail.

'All right, Greg. Everything OK?'

The line remained quiet long enough for Ryan to think Greg had lost connection or hung up. He was about to end the call when he heard what sounded like a strangled cough.

'Greg?'

'Sorry to call so early, Ryan.' Greg's voice had its usual commanding tone but was accompanied by a rasping quality, as if the man had a truly awful sore throat. 'I thought you'd want to know as soon as possible. Mandy died yesterday. A road traffic collision.'

Ryan sat back in his chair. 'How? Where?'

'On the inner ring road. She had been for a job interview and was heading back to the bus station. It doesn't look like the driver was speeding and he hadn't been drinking, we're checking his phone to make sure he's not guilty of driving without due care and attention.'

Greg was in work mode and Ryan let him talk. It was a practised speech, he guessed, one Greg was tripping out to everyone he was having to break the horrible news to this morning. Ryan wondered how Mandy would feel about that. They were still married, so Greg was legally her next of kin, but would she want him breaking the news to her nearest and dearest given how things had ended?

'I can tell our group if you haven't already spoken to Paul or Isobel.'

'Thanks. No, I haven't. You were my first call.'

Ryan wondered if he had been the easiest option for Greg. Perhaps the adulterous husband would worry about receiving a stern reception from Isobel, Mandy's oldest female friend, and Paul, her ex-boyfriend.

Ryan offered to lend any further help that Greg needed, and Greg promised to let him know the funeral details as and when they were sorted. Then they hung up, and Ryan wandered around the ground floor for several minutes, feeling numb.

He found himself staring out of his dining room window into the garden. Two birds swooped down to the fish pond, took a drink and flew away. When had he last seen Mandy? What had they talked about? It was hard to remember. He did recall the first time he'd ever seen her, though. That had been at school. She'd been moved to his form group halfway through their first term at high school after pulling a prank on her previous form tutor which involved a balloon and some flour. She had arrived that first morning in a whirlwind of energy, loudly announcing herself to the group then plonking down in the seat next to Paul and blowing him a kiss. That was Mandy. Full of life and always up for a bit of mischief. God, he couldn't imagine a world without her in it.

'Daddy, Daddy, come play with me.'

Ethan ran into the dining room carrying a half-eaten piece of toast covered in chocolate spread. Camille must be feeling rough this morning if she was giving in to their son's demands for sugary treats and then allowing him to run around the house with a chocolate grenade gripped tightly in his sticky hands.

'Let's take your breakfast back to the kitchen, buddy,' said Ryan.

Camille was sitting at the large wooden table with a mug of untouched black coffee cradled in her hands. She was wrapped in a baby-pink dressing gown with unbrushed hair.

Ryan took Ethan's toast and placed it on the plastic *Paw Patrol* plate before wiping his son's fingers with a baby wipe from the packet Camille permanently kept on the table.

'How's your head?' he said gently to his wife.

She met his gaze. Her face was pale and the bags under her tired eyes were darkened with the remnants of last night's mascara. She looked rough.

Ethan began racing around the table making engine noises. Normally, Ryan would tell his son to calm down or to keep the noise down, but today it provided a good distraction as he whispered the words he needed to.

'Greg just called. Mandy was hit by a car yesterday.' Ryan's voice broke a little and he swallowed hard. Camille's eyes became alert and focused as she squeezed Ryan's hand. He knew what her next question would be. 'She didn't make it.'

Camille's hands flew to her mouth and she made a high-pitched wailing noise that had Ethan screeching to a halt. She reached out for Ryan and pulled him into a tight hug and he could feel her sobbing into his neck.

Ethan came over and placed his hands around his mum's waist.

'It's OK. Everything's OK,' Ryan said as he rubbed Ethan's back. 'Mummy's OK. She's just tired after the party. Do you want to watch some TV?'

TV in the morning was another no-no in their home, so Ethan was understandably excited. He made a dash for the playroom and the TV before his dad could change his mind.

'What happened? Do you know?' Camille's French accent was strong, which was often the case when she was upset or tired.

'All I know is she was crossing a road in the city centre after her interview.'

'It's too awful to imagine. And we were all dancing and celebrating. Poor Mandy. Poor Mandy,' Camille closed her eyes tightly, stemming the tears that flowed down her face. 'How is Greg?'

'He sounded pretty cut-up, as you'd imagine. Making these calls must be horrific. I said I'd call Izzy and Paul for him.'

'OK. I will have some painkillers and take a shower. Your mum said she'd have Ethan today if we felt poorly, so . . .'

'Good idea. I'll run him over in a bit. I'll explain what's happened.'

Ryan wondered if he could mention Audrey Raye to his parents when he was there, then felt immediately guilty. This was not the time.

15

ISOBEL

Saturday, 9 a.m.
6 days, 6½ hours left

'From a journalist's point of view, if you were tipped off that something untoward had happened at a pub somewhere, but you didn't know which exact pub, and you only had a name like the Royal Oak, how would you go about it?' Isobel asked Annie, watching carefully for her wife's reaction. The question was genuine, but she also needed to find out whether the name of the pub meant anything to Annie.

Annie was feeding Joshua porridge and pretending it was a train. 'I'd ask my police contacts if they knew anything. Why do you ask?'

There was no panic on Annie's face.

'It's in this book I'm reading. The journalist seems to find information a bit too easily and I wondered how realistic it was.' She was pleased with herself for coming up with such a convincing lie so quickly. 'What if it isn't a police matter? What if it's like the scene of a betrayal or something?'

'Like someone having an affair?'

Annie hadn't reacted to the word 'betrayal' either. 'Yeah, let's say you knew someone in the public eye had been betrayed at a pub called the Royal Oak. How would you investigate that?'

'Is the rough location of the pub known?'

Isobel realized she had assumed the pub was local if someone she knew had betrayed her there, but then she remembered the reference to England in the message. How many hundreds of Royal Oak pubs might there be across the whole country?

'Because I suppose I'd start with a list of all the Royal Oak pubs in the area, then systematically visit them. In my experience, you can dig up dirt on anyone if you're focused and friendly enough.' Annie flashed a smile but Isobel didn't return it.

The lack of any reaction from Annie to the pub name or the idea of someone being betrayed should be making her feel better, so why wasn't it? The nauseous anxiety churned away at her insides and Isobel tried to stem her line of thinking, not liking the conclusions it was trying to lay out.

Annie's internal lie detector was finely honed. Ordinarily, she would be all over Isobel about why she was really asking about this. It was unlike Annie to buy the 'I'm reading a book' story. So why had she done so today? Why wasn't she at all curious about these questions? Even yesterday in the car, when Isobel had said there was a potential inquiry into misconduct at Harrogate Hospital, Annie had not really reacted. As if it wasn't a surprise to her.

In my experience, you can dig up dirt on anyone if you're focused and friendly enough.

Did Annie know? Had someone told her in a pub called the Royal Oak?

Isobel wanted to run from the room, from the house, from the possibility that her wife had found out what she'd done. But she was unable to move.

'Are you going to answer that?'

Isobel looked at her ringing phone. It was Ryan.

*

Two hours later, Isobel sat outside Ryan and Camille's trying to compose herself before going in. Annie had insisted she go to Ryan's alone. Her wife had said the angst wouldn't be good for their son, but surely she knew that Isobel needed her now more than ever?

Today should have been so happy. Time for Annie and her to be with Josh and enjoy the start of their proper family. Instead, she was drowning in grief. Mandy was the first person Isobel came out to. She had raised her eyebrows before laughing loudly and saying, 'Good grief, Izzy, how daft do you think I am?' It turned out her friend had long suspected the truth. Mandy had known Isobel better than anyone for as long as Isobel could remember. They had held hands in the playground at primary school, hugged each other better over every unrequited crush as teens, and stood in the front row of each other's wedding holding each other's bridal bouquet. Their lives were deeply entwined. It was impossible to look back on her life without finding Mandy close by in every memory.

Isobel choked back the sobs that threatened to engulf her. Why had Annie refused to come? How could she abandon her in this?

Paul's Porsche pulled into the drive and parked behind her. Vanessa was wiping her eyes with a tissue and checking her reflection in the wing mirror. Isobel had never seen Vanessa emotional.

Once inside, Isobel sat at the end of the kitchen table with Vanessa on one side of her and Ryan on the other. Camille served them tea as Isobel tried not to focus too much on Paul. He looked devastated and Isobel wondered how Vanessa felt about that. Vanessa knew Paul and Mandy had been a couple at school but, as far as Isobel was aware, she didn't know how badly the breakup had affected Paul. That he'd gone off the rails for quite a while afterwards, once turning up in the pub when Mandy had first started dating Greg, acting like the whole group was cheating on him for daring to be nice to Mandy's new boyfriend. After that, they'd all lost touch for a while and it wasn't until Vanessa was on the scene that Paul reappeared in their lives.

Looking at him now, his face ashen and his eyes heavy with sadness, she was reminded of how he'd once confessed in a drunken state that Mandy was the love of his life. Isobel sensed Paul was haunted by the idea that he wasn't good enough for Mandy. She wondered if Vanessa sensed the same.

'What was she like when you met her?' asked Camille. She had been the last to join their group of friends, so had known Mandy for a fraction of the time the rest of them had.

'Crazy,' said Ryan with a small laugh. 'Like a whirlwind of energy.'

'Remember that time she stuck one of those individual portions of brie cheese under Mr Strickland's desk then told us all to deny we could smell anything whiffy?' said Paul.

'But then Sharon Vardy blurted out the truth because the open windows were making her cold,' said Isobel. 'Mardy Vardy was such a wimpy suck-up.'

Isobel, Ryan and Paul started to laugh, and the story led into another and then another.

'Then there was that time she brought her dad's prize goat into school and it ate Mrs Wheeler's vegetable patch. Remember? Wheeler had been growing them with her special needs group,' Ryan said.

'Oh God, I'd forgotten about that. She had to go and explain herself to the headmistress.' Isobel wiped tears of both grief and laughter from her face. 'And she had to go and buy a load of cabbages and carrots from the greengrocer,' she said, barely able to finish the sentence.

'How did she get a goat into school?'

Vanessa's question had Paul, Ryan and Isobel looking at each other with blank expressions.

'I have no idea,' said Isobel, who had walked the half mile to school most days with Mandy.

'I bet Jimmy brought it in his car,' said Paul.

The group agreed that Mandy's older brother was the most likely explanation. He tended to do whatever Mandy asked him to.

It felt good to laugh and remember.

'I can't believe she's gone,' said Isobel, and the mood shifted. Paul excused himself to visit the bathroom and Camille got up to make more tea.

'She would have liked you all remembering her like this,' said Vanessa.

A loud knock on the door disturbed their quiet moment of reflection. Ryan went to answer, leaving Isobel with Vanessa.

'Congratulations, by the way. We heard the adoption went through at last,' said Vanessa.

Raised voices in the hallway caught Isobel's attention a moment before Ryan's daughter Rosie came in. Isobel saw a look of surprise cross Camille's face before she smiled broadly.

'Hi Rosie, we weren't expecting you today.'

Rosie smiled then looked back towards the hall and her mum's raised voice.

'She'll have to revise here, Ryan, because I'm very upset.'

'I'm not saying Rosie can't stay. You know I'd never turn her away. I'm simply saying we're all upset, Stephanie.'

Isobel braced herself for what was to come. Ryan's ex was a woman of two distinct characters. On a good day, she would greet you with the kind of saccharine niceness that made her appear sweet-natured and innocent. Then on another day she would be venomously cruel, lashing out with grand generalizations about how Ryan *always* let her down, or throwing around brutal insults. Once, she called Camille a trashy dog because she had dared to post a picture of herself with Rosie on Instagram.

'You don't understand, Ryan. I'm a single parent. I don't have someone helping me like you do.'

'Stephanie, you are not a single parent. We co-parent. Rosie is with me almost half the time.'

'Yes, but you have Camille to help when she's with you. I have no one.'

'I was under the impression your mum and dad help out a fair bit.'

Isobel wanted to tell Ryan not to bite. When Steph was in this kind of mood there was no reasoning with her. It was best to simply let her vent and avoid getting dragged in. Isobel had witnessed it time and again over the years.

Camille busied herself in the kitchen, wiping surfaces that were already clean and straightening the dishes on the drainer while Rosie concentrated on her phone. Isobel wondered at the stress it caused them both when things kicked off.

'I can't believe you're all here together without me. I was her friend too,' Steph said, her voice becoming shriller and less controlled.

Isobel saw Camille glance at Rosie.

'Wish me luck,' Isobel said quietly so only Vanessa could hear. Paul's wife smiled a little. She was not one to get involved in these things.

'Hey, Steph. It's awful, isn't it?' said Isobel, walking to the other woman and giving her the briefest of hugs. Just enough to deflate the anger, she hoped.

For a moment, Steph's scowl remained in place, but then her face softened and she turned her attention away from Ryan.

'I don't think any of you understood what she was going through. I wouldn't be surprised if she did this to herself.'

'Stephanie!' Ryan glanced back towards the kitchen to where Rosie was.

'What? How would you know what was going on with her,

Ryan? You were all too busy, but I've been there for her every day. She was my best friend and now I've lost her.'

Isobel had to hold her breath to stop herself from reacting. This was not the day to play tit for tat on who was Mandy's closest friend.

'I need to be alone,' Stephanie said as she walked out of the house without saying goodbye to her daughter.

'She'll be going straight to her mum's for sympathy. She can't spend a minute on her own, that woman,' Ryan said, then returned to the kitchen.

Isobel stood alone in the hallway, thinking about what Steph had said. *I don't think any of you understood what she was going through. You were all too busy.* Was that right? Had they let Mandy down? Had *she* let Mandy down? Mandy knew she was there for her if ever she needed anything, but then work had been hectic and life with Joshua could be chaotic.

Isobel felt fresh tears roll from her eyes.

16

PAUL

Saturday, 11.30 a.m.
6 days, 4 hours left

Having excused himself from the chat around Ryan's kitchen table when things became a bit too raw, Paul was now standing in his friend's lounge.

In the hours before he heard about Mandy, when he thought his midnight message was the worst thing that could possibly happen to him this week, Paul had started a list. His assumption, looking at the question he had been given – who cheated justice on 22 July 2012? – was that it related to either a crime or a case. It could be the date a crime occurred, or the date a case commenced, reached a verdict, was sentenced, or appealed.

He had begun by looking up people he had been involved in convicting or representing around that time. Had one of those cases gone wrong? Was someone holding a grudge? It seemed unlikely. He'd been a junior on most cases at that point. From his records he could see that he hadn't been in court at all over that week of July 2012. The cases he had been working on included an aggravated assault and a theft, but they had gone on to win both, so it was unlikely either defendant held a grudge. What

59

about the victims, could they be behind this? It seemed unlikely. The cases were hardly the stuff of high drama. Was there anyone who had shown any negativity towards him? Had any of their clients sacked them? It was so long ago he couldn't recall. Paul had noted down the names of the key players in the two cases he had been working on back then. He would look to see if anything significant had happened to any of them after the fact. Had one of the defendants gone on to commit another more serious crime?

Truth be told, he knew he could dismiss a good 90 per cent of the people he had defended and convicted over the years, because they simply weren't smart enough for this. It felt sophisticated. There was something very purposeful about sending that article followed by the challenge. Someone had put thought into it. So that meant he needed to ask a different question. Who in his professional world might want to bring him down? That list was much longer. Life at the bar was competitive and he was a front runner, already standing in for judges as a Recorder on a regular basis. Only last month, a retiring judge had included Paul in a list of barristers tipped for a job on the bench in the High Court someday. The jealousy this stirred up would not have been insignificant, especially given the fact Paul was such a young KC. He thought about his chambers and the colleagues he passed on a weekly basis. Their interactions were polite, sometimes friendly, but rarely warm. He added names of the people who might benefit from his downfall to his list.

There were nine names, including that of Kyle Renton's latest solicitor.

Now he needed to consider what the person behind this wanted. It wasn't as simple as punishing him, or destroying him, or even winning an appeal. If that had been the case the article would have been published straight away. Which suggested Renton's people might not be behind it after all. Whoever was doing it wanted something different. Did they want him scared? Paranoid?

Paul thought for a moment, letting the answer crystallize in his mind.

Motivated. That's what they wanted him to be. They wanted him desperate enough to do their bidding.

For a second time, he searched for Carl Baker. But he couldn't find a journalist with that name associated with any of the main press outlets. Why not? Was that a clue? Someone's little joke?

Paul read his list again. At least it got his mind off Mandy – his grief could easily get the better of him.

They had been talking a fair bit recently. When Greg had finally manned up and told her it was over, she had called Paul. He had been working late in chambers and she had sounded drunk and emotional. She apologized for hurting him so badly all those years ago. She had not realized the pain she had caused until the same had been done to her, she said. He had laughed it off and told her she was being silly, they were kids, it was not at all the same. But he wasn't being entirely honest, and her apology had meant more than he'd let on. After that they had spoken pretty much weekly, and he had concentrated on making her laugh. She always had the most wicked laugh. He knew he couldn't make things right and put her life back together, but he could at least offer some light relief. They had taken to referring to Greg as Plod, a moniker Paul had adopted for years when talking about Mandy's husband but never shared with her. Now she embraced it with all its dismissive and demeaning intent. He had hated seeing her hurt and lost but he had never doubted she would come out the other side and be his bold, beautiful Mandy once more.

But now she was gone, and he would never hear her laugh again.

Paul became aware of a brewing argument between Ryan and his ex, Steph, who sounded annoyed that they had gathered together without her. Steph was a woman who had never left her hometown, spent most of her life avoiding work, and expected her parents and Ryan to pander to her every whim. The woman's inability to see how she impacted on others never failed to startle Paul. Mandy had complained to him only a few weeks before that Steph was fussing around and revelling in the drama of her breakup. Paul figured Steph was looking for an ally in her man-hating.

Paul focused on his list again; it would be better to focus his anger on something more productive, like answering this damn question. He had no doubt he would do it in the given seven days.

The lounge door opened and his goddaughter greeted him with a smile.

'Hey, Rosie-bear,' he said, putting his phone away and wrapping her in a big hug.

'Sorry about Mandy,' she said into his shoulder. She was getting so tall now. 'I loved her lots.'

Paul looked at the wall behind her and swallowed. 'And she loved you, Ro-bear. Like you were her own.'

Rosie pulled back and looked at him. There were tears welling in her eyes. This was probably Rosie's first experience of death. Not like Paul, whose own mother had passed away when he was seven. It was a pain he could still feel now if he ever allowed it to resurface, and a loss made all the worse by having a shitty bully of a dad. Vanessa once suggested his dad's anger was related to losing his wife and being a single parent, but Paul saw that as no excuse for the brutality he'd been subjected to. If it hadn't been for Ryan and his family, Paul wasn't sure where he'd have ended up. They'd given him a safe place to come home to. He'd spent many a night in their spare room, escaping Dad's latest temper tantrum. But more than that they'd celebrated him for who he was. Ryan's mum had given her wonderfully hearty laugh at every joke Paul had told, and Ryan's dad had told him he was a bright lad whenever they'd been discussing sports or whatever was going on in the news. They redefined him, told him he was worth something and taught him that he didn't need to be from the right family or the right social class to live his dreams, he just had to work hard. That's what Ryan's footballer dad had done. And later, Ryan would go on to prove the same when he cycled into the history books – his mate, at that time the youngest Brit to win a stage of the Tour de France. It was true to say the Fallon family had played a massive part in all Paul had achieved.

'You OK, Ro?' he asked.

'I don't know. I don't know if I'm supposed to be crying more.'

'Hey, there are no rights or wrongs with grief. You just do you, OK?' he nudged her chin with his fist.

'What's with the white-soled pumps, by the way?'

Paul looked down at his feet. The shoes were a new and rather expensive purchase from Harvey Nichols. 'What? You can't recognize a bit of class when you see it?'

'Er, yeah. I'm just not seeing it anywhere near your feet.'

'All right, Paul Smith. What are you wearing anyway, did they forget to attach the rest of the material to your T-shirt?'

'It's a crop top and it is actually cool.'

'Cool meaning cold? I hope you're not wearing that out with Gary or Glen or whatever his name is.'

Rosie's cheeks flushed. 'Gus, actually.'

'Gus, actually,' Paul parroted back as he placed an arm around Rosie's shoulder and walked with her back to the kitchen. 'I bet your dad's chuffed to bits that you're dating Toby Phillips's son. We went to school with Toby, you know?' Paul knew there was no love lost between Ryan and Toby.

Rosie shrugged.

'So long as you know he's not acceptable as a boyfriend until he's been vetted by Uncle Paul.'

Rosie's sigh sounded exasperated, but she leaned her body close to his as they walked and he was grateful for the unspoken expression of affection.

What would she think if she ever found out what he'd done? It was a question he could not bear to face the answer to.

17

THE SHAME GAME:
A TRUE CRIME DOCUMENTARY

Episode 1 of 3 – The Players

INT – BOB ADAMS'S LOUNGE – DAYTIME

The elderly man sitting on a floral sofa has grey hair and a bushy beard. He's wearing a blue and green checked shirt with jeans.

> VOICE (O.S.)
>
> Hi, Bob. Could you look directly into the camera and introduce yourself.

> BOB ADAMS
>
> Aye, all right. I'm Bob Adams. Will that do?

                    VOICE (O.S.)

Great, thanks. So how long have
you lived in Ilkley?

                         BOB

All me life.

                    VOICE (O.S.)

So you know the community well.

                         BOB

Most of 'em. It's not a big town.
Not when it comes to gossip, if
you know what I mean.

                    VOICE (O.S.)

And was there any particular
gossip about any of the four
friends?

                         BOB

Well, there was a lot of interest
around the cyclist, Ryan. We
were very proud of the lad in
the town. People would tell you
if they'd seen him, you know.
'I saw Ryan Fallon cycling,' or 'I
saw Fallon in Booths.' That's
the local fancy supermarket. I go

to Tesco but if you're in Ryan's
crowd you shop at Booths and
pay twice as much for the same
thing so it feels like you're
getting sommat better. I didn't
know him as such, meself, but I
knew Paul's dad, John, as he was
often in the pub on a weekend,
and Mandy's family were friends
of ours, so those two I watched
grow up.

                VOICE (O.S.)

And Isobel?

                BOB

Can't say I had the pleasure. Her
parents lived up on the hill in
Middleton. A bit too fancy for the
likes of me.

                VOICE (O.S.)

So, you said there was gossip?

                BOB

Ha, well, most of it was nonsense,
but there was this one rumour
about Paul. Not sure if it was
true, but some said he'd fathered
Ryan's daughter, Rose, is it?

Rosie.

BOB

That's right, aye. Well, I 'ave
no evidence of the fact but that
was the talk back in the day. They
reckoned Steph had claimed it was
Ryan's because he was a better bet
at the time. Not sure that turned
out to be true, though. Last I
heard, Paul was raking it in with
his fancy barrister job. So if the
rumour's true, the lass backed the
wrong horse.

Bob Adams laughs the deep, rasping laugh of a
lifelong smoker.

18

STEPHANIE

Saturday, 11.45 a.m.

Stephanie sat in the car and tried to still her shaking hands. Why did she always get like that with Ryan? She hadn't wanted to have a go at him but it was so unfair of them to all get together without her. It had been the same ever since she and Ryan had split up; their friends had made it clear that they were his friends really. What had she ever done to make them treat her like she was nothing? She wasn't so bothered about Paul, but Isobel and Mandy backing off had hurt.

Steph hadn't been exaggerating when she'd said she and Mandy had become close recently, but she could see that Ryan and Isobel didn't believe her. The truth of the matter was that Mandy had reached out to Steph after Greg left because no one really knew the empty, hollow ache of rejection unless they'd lived through it. Steph had enjoyed their new bond. It felt good to finally have someone in her life who understood. Tears stung her eyes and she blinked them away. She was going to miss Mandy so much. No one had even bothered to call her. She had heard the news on the local radio. Imagine that. On impulse, she dialled Greg's number and left a message asking him to call her back. When he didn't, she continued to call every few minutes until he finally picked up. She expected he didn't want to speak to Mandy's friends for fear of what home truths they might tell him, but she wasn't going to let him avoid her.

'Did you not think to call me about Mandy?'

'Sorry, who am I speaking to?'

'It's Stephanie. Can you imagine how hurtful it was for me to hear it on the news?'

'Sorry, Stephanie, there have been a lot of calls. I didn't realize you and Mandy had become close.'

'Well, no, you wouldn't have.'

'OK, sorry about that. I'll let you know about the funeral as soon as I have details. I need to go now.' Greg hung up before Steph had time to say anything more.

The cheek of the man. Not that she was surprised. Ryan had adopted the same cold, distant manner with her after they separated. It was something she and Mandy had compared notes on. Mandy had thought it was down to embarrassment and not wanting to cause any more hurt, but Steph had told her, 'They're just cowards, Mandy. They don't want to look at you and see the harm they've caused.'

Stephanie pulled up outside her parents' house and buzzed the electronic gates open. She knew her mum was annoyed with her at the moment. They had rowed yesterday morning about Steph needing to pay more rent on the house her parents had bought for her and Rosie. Her parents were both retired and living off their pensions now, and with the cost of living rising, her mum had said Steph needed to contribute more. Goodness knows where she expected Steph to get the extra cash from. She already worked three days a week at the local hotel and they were long days. She had Rosie to take care of and bills to pay. It wasn't like her parents couldn't afford to help her out. They had plenty of savings and this house must be worth a fortune. The row had ended with Steph storming out.

Stephanie walked to the front door and let herself in, hoping that the news about Mandy would stop all of that in its tracks. They wouldn't pressurize her while she was grieving.

She paused in the hallway to read a text that had arrived from her friend Fleur.

Holy crap, Stephy! I just heard about Mandy Coulters.

She died!!!!!

I'm at work but will call later. Hope you're ok.

F xxxxx

Stephanie smiled. It was nice to know someone was thinking of her. Classical music was playing loudly from the kitchen, which meant her dad was cooking one of his *MasterChef* creations. Maybe she could get an invite for dinner, given how upset she was.

'Hi, Dad.'

'Hello, Stephy. How are you?'

'Not great. Did you hear about Mandy?'

Her dad scraped the remains of the peppers he'd been chopping into a large pan on the stove. 'I did, yes. Very sad. I liked Mandy. She was one of the good ones.'

'And there aren't many of those,' she said, finishing one of her father's favourite phrases.

The two of them smiled at each other and Steph flicked on the kettle. 'I'll make us a cup of tea.'

Her dad patted her arm as he passed her to fetch a punnet of mushrooms from the fridge. 'Are you staying for food?'

'Well, Rosie's at her dad's so I'm all alone.'

'That sounds like a yes from my favourite daughter.'

'I'm your only daughter, Dad.'

'Still my favourite.'

Steph loved these moments, when it was just the two of them together. Why couldn't she find a man like her dad? Someone to take care of her like he did for her mum. It wasn't fair.

When her mum arrived back from the shops half an hour later, yesterday's argument wasn't mentioned. Ordinarily, Steph might have pushed for an apology but she was taken aback when her mum squeezed her hand as she passed. She was not a touchy-feely person.

'Have you heard the news about Mandy, love? Graham at the butchers just told me.'

Stephanie swallowed back the tears and nodded. 'I spoke to Greg.'

'Did he say what happened? It's like history repeating itself – Mandy's mum passed when she was not much older than Mandy. Karma really is a bitch, isn't it?'

'I don't think you mean karma, darling,' said Stephanie's dad.

'I'm just saying. Her mum died young after a stroke and now Mandy.'

'That's what's called a coincidence, Felicity, albeit a very sad one.'

Stephanie's mum tutted but didn't bite. Dad was well-read with a talent for crosswords and he couldn't help pulling Mum up on her misuse of words. Her mum came to sit next to Steph and, as Dad cooked, they reminisced about Mandy, discussing what an arse Greg had been and how awful he must feel now.

'*That's* karma,' said her dad, in the only contribution he made to the conversation.

19

Sunday is a day of rest, but I bet you're not resting, are you, folks? Oh no, I expect you are tearing your hair out trying to solve my puzzles. I can almost see the sweat on your brows and the steam coming from your ears. I bet you're locked in your home offices and snapping impatiently at any family members who dare to disturb you. Such is the importance of your task.

Or has Mandy's sad demise distracted you? I certainly hope not, because the questions you have been set are not easy to solve. You will need every second of the week I have given you. Because even when you find the answer, you will discover a new dilemma in front of you. You will need time to think.

What should I do? What am I prepared to do? How important is avoiding the shame of it? Who will I sacrifice?

It's all very exciting. I wish I could see inside your homes and watch you ferreting about in panic. I would enjoy that. But that kind of intrusion of privacy goes too far even for me.

20

RYAN

Sunday, 10 a.m.
5 days, 5½ hours left

It was an overcast morning with a faint drizzle, like the sky was mourning Mandy. For a few seconds after he'd awoken, his mind was clear of all the pain and panic. But then it came back in a tsunami of grief and the gut-wrenching knowledge that life would never be the same again.

Today, he needed time alone. Not least because he wanted to get to the tarn in the hope of seeing Audrey.

He had found the reference to her daily visits on the Ilkley community group. Someone had asked, 'Who is the lady I see at the tarn every day while walking my dogs? She feeds the ducks and is always alone. She looks a little vulnerable and rushes away if I ever try to say hello.' The response had come back to say it was Audrey with a link to the newspaper article about her accident.

Ryan leaned his bike up against the small shelter with a wooden bench where an old man sat with his pet dachshund.

'Morning,' said the old man.

'How are you?' said Ryan as he removed his helmet and hung it on the handlebars of his Pinarello bike.

'I used to watch you ride. You didn't have an Italian bike then – it was American. The white one.'

Ryan smiled. He was always surprised how varied in age cycling enthusiasts were. 'Are you a cyclist too, sir?'

'How can you not be when you live in Yorkshire? Nothing like you lot, though. We had big heavy bikes that needed real muscles to get you up the hills.'

Ryan didn't feel like laughing but he knew it was the polite and normal thing to do. No need to spread his angst to unsuspecting strangers, especially those who took the time to talk cycling with him.

He and the old man chatted for fifteen minutes or so about the merits of carbon bike frames and the wonderful routes that snaked around their shared hometown. By the time Ryan saw a woman in a crumpled raincoat appear on the other side of the water with a carrier bag at her side, the sun had broken through the clouds and begun to warm the day.

Mindful of the comment on the community group that said Audrey rushed away from the lady trying to say hello, he didn't directly approach her. He had come prepared with some bread for the ducks, and took up position a little way along the waterside and watched for a moment. The small island in the middle of the tarn was home to half a dozen trees that hung low over the water, their reflection creating a glistening display of leaves below where the mallards swirled in front of Audrey. She was whistling and clicking as she threw handfuls of what looked like rolled oats into the water, sending the ducks into a frenzy.

He felt bad attracting their attention away from her, but he needed to strike up a conversation somehow. He reached into the bread bag, took out a slice of malted white and began breaking it into pieces before tossing it into the water. He half expected that Audrey wouldn't pay any attention to him at all but as soon as his first handful of bread hit the water, she screamed at him.

'I feed the ducks! I feed the ducks! Only I feed the ducks.'

Despite the shouting, her face wasn't curled up in rage, she looked frightened and there were tears in her eyes. Ryan closed the bread bag and held his hands up towards her.

'Sorry. I didn't realize. I'm sorry.'

Audrey turned abruptly away to look at the ducks. 'There used to be thousands of ducks here. I've been coming for hundreds of years and there were thousands and thousands of ducks back then but people started feeding them and they left.'

Ryan stayed quiet and watched her throw in another handful of food.

'Only I'm allowed to feed them. They told me only I can feed them. No one else, no one else.' In a moment of lucidity, she turned his way and pointed at the bag in his hand. 'You can't feed ducks bread. It's bad for them.'

Ryan tried to catch her eye. 'Sorry. It's Audrey, isn't it? I didn't mean to upset you.' Her eyes looked to his left, to his right and above his head, but never at his face. 'I'm Ryan. We went to the same school. Ilkley Grammar. I was a few years below you.'

'I've been feeding them for hundreds of years. There used to be thousands and thousands of them.'

Ryan realized this was hopeless. Poor Audrey. Had this been her life all these years? While he was winning races, gaining fans, falling in love, having kids, was she coming here and doing this?

'I was sorry to hear about your accident. Have you been OK?'

'Thousands of ducks. All gone now. All gone.' She walked a little further away from him and resumed her whistles and clicks.

Should he ask her if she recalled what had happened? He knew it was both inappropriate and pointless. In the last eighteen years, how many times had she been asked by the police, amateur sleuths and well-meaning locals? If she knew anything, someone would have found out by now.

'Bye, Audrey. Sorry again,' he said as he walked past her to fetch his bike.

He had been pinning his hopes on this conversation giving him something to work on. He had less than a week to solve a mystery that had eluded the professionals for nearly two decades. It was hopeless.

21

ISOBEL

Sunday, 3 p.m.
5 days, ½ hour left

In the early hours, as she lay next to her sleeping wife, Isobel had been unable to ignore the dread. Despite the suffocating sadness that had landed on her life with the loss of Mandy, her fear shouted louder. What if someone had betrayed her in a Royal Oak pub by telling Annie what she had done all those years ago? How would Annie have reacted? Might she have been so incensed that she decided to make Isobel squirm? It certainly wasn't beyond Annie's skills to write that article and lay out in black and white the devastation Isobel's past would bring to bear on their future. She may even have been able to post it on a news site then have it taken down. Isobel was ashamed to realize she did not know enough about her wife's profession, or level of influence, to know if that was a possibility. Had she been giving Isobel a chance to come clean before they took on Josh? Or had she been hoping that Isobel would deny it, say it was all lies and ask Annie for help rebutting it. And of course, Isobel had done none of that, which must have screamed her guilt at Annie. There was no way back from that. She would have to try to explain it in her own words and hope that her wife might, in time, find a way to forgive her.

She nearly did it too. As dawn broke, she had reached for her wife's warm hand under the covers and entwined their fingers, hoping to hold on to her through the coming storm, but then Annie had turned and kissed her full on the mouth before pulling her close so that their whole bodies were entwined.

Isobel had offered to take Joshua out for the day while Annie was working on a story. It had not been your traditional kid's trip out – she had done the rounds of the Royal Oak pubs in driving distance. The nearest one was in Keighley. It was a Timothy Taylor's pub with stone floors and leather Chesterfield-style sofas. It smelled of beer and chips and a beam above the bar quoted Frank Sinatra saying, 'Alcohol may be man's worst enemy, but the bible says . . . love thy enemy.'

She knew there was only really one person who could have betrayed her, as only they knew the truth of things, and surely that person would only be incriminating themselves by telling on her. What made more sense was that her fellow wrongdoer had told a third party who was now bent on exposing them both.

Just make the call and ask.

Next, she had driven to the Royal Oak in Bradford to find it closed and abandoned, with blocked up doors and windows. After that, she had driven over to Harrogate, where she had worked as a junior doctor at the hospital, to visit the four Royal Oaks in the surrounding area. It was a fruitless search. She wasn't even sure what she was expecting to find.

After a long day of driving, Joshua was getting weary of the car. Her last attempt to put him in his seat had been met with an arched back and bolt-straight limbs. She had succeeded in the end, but not before a lot of squealing on his part and a lot of pleading on hers.

Isobel had just one more stop before she returned home, and

it was going to be the toughest of the day. She pulled up outside the semi-detached house in Horsforth. There was a large hanging basket by the door filled with a rainbow of flowers, and in the centre of the front window sat a heart-shaped ornament. Isobel's chest felt tight. She hoped to God that Mandy had never seen this, though she expected that she had. If she were Mandy, she wouldn't have been able to stop herself driving past her ex's new love nest.

A memory of helping Mandy and Greg move into their for ever home filled her head. She recalled scrubbing the oven and cleaning the two en suites as Mandy and Greg helped lug boxes and direct the removal men. Afterwards, the three of them had sat cross-legged on the lounge carpet eating fish and chips out of the paper, swigging champagne and laughing. They were always laughing. Isobel looked at that heart ornament in the window again. What had gone so wrong for Greg to walk away from all he and Mandy had?

'Sorry to disturb you,' she said when Greg opened the door. 'I won't stay long. Josh is sleeping in the car.'

'Thank you. You really didn't need to,' he said, taking the tin of cake from her. She had baked her lemon drizzle that morning knowing it was Greg's favourite and wanting an excuse to ask the question that had been bugging her since Stephanie's visit to Ryan's yesterday.

'It's only a lemon drizzle. I thought it might keep you all going while you're doing the tough stuff. I mean, you and Mandy's family,' she corrected, not wanting him to think she had intended the cake for him and his new girlfriend.

Greg's half smile told her he knew what she was saying.

'Also, I wanted to ask something and it's a bit delicate.'

'I suspected there was more to the visit, Isobel.'

'Sorry. I don't want to be . . . you know . . . causing any extra pain and I didn't want to ask her dad or brother. It's just that

Mandy had been pretty down lately and I wanted to check there wasn't any suggestion ...' Isobel stopped short of saying the words. If Mandy had done this on purpose no one would feel more responsibility for that than Greg. She shouldn't have come, this was cruel.

'That she took her own life?'

Of course the police officer would be matter-of-fact about such things.

'I don't think she would, I just, I don't know . . . sorry, Greg. I don't know what I was thinking.'

'You were thinking you wanted to know the truth of what happened to your friend. That's perfectly natural, Isobel. But rest assured, Mandy didn't do this on purpose. It was a tragic, stupid accident that could have been avoided. We have the driver and two other eyewitnesses saying Mandy was looking at her phone instead of the road. She made a mistake.'

Isobel was not aware she was going to ask the next question until she heard herself saying it. 'What time did it happen?'

A few moments later, Isobel was back in her car listening to Joshua's heavy breaths. At approximately 3.35 p.m. on Friday afternoon, Mandy was looking at her phone instead of the road. That was the same time Isobel had been waiting in the council building and had received that article.

What were the chances that was a coincidence?

22

THE SHAME GAME:
A TRUE CRIME DOCUMENTARY

Episode 1 of 3 - The Players

INT - FALLON FAMILY HOME - DAYTIME

An attractive woman sits on a blue velvet
sofa. She has a soft French accent and is
dressed head to foot in black. When she
crosses her long legs, it is possible to see
that the heels of her shoes are high.

TEXT on the screen reads: CAMILLE FALLON.
EX-MODEL. WIFE OF RYAN FALLON.

> CAMILLE FALLON
>
> Of course I didn't suspect that
> anything odd was going on. We
> had just heard about Mandy
> and everyone was freaked out.

No one was behaving normally,
you know?

Everyone had come to ours on
Saturday. Well, except for Annie,
who stayed home with the little
boy, and we tried to make sense
of it. Mandy was loud and funny
and warm. You could hear her laugh
from the other side of a house,
you know.

                VOICE (O.S.)

Had Ryan told you about the
messages he'd received at that
point?

                CAMILLE

Non. He had said nothing. He kept
it all locked inside.

                VOICE (O.S.)

Did that hurt your feelings, when
you found out?

                CAMILLE

But of course, I am his wife. I
wanted him to share everything
but I understand he was scared
and then so, so devastated about
Mandy. He spent most of Sunday out

on his bike, escaping. It was a
sad, sad time.

VOICE (O.S.)

How close were all the friends?

CAMILLE

Well, I came into the group last
and Ryan told me, we are all big
friends and you will love them and
they will love you. But were they
all close? I don't know. Sometimes
yes, sometimes no. Because I was
new to an established group, I
think that I saw some of the
friction more clearly.

VOICE (O.S.)

Between who?

CAMILLE

Well, Ryan and Paul. They always
had such a lot of competition. It
was friendly on the surface but I
always would think it comes from
something deeper. Paul and Mandy
had history, and I don't think
Greg or Vanessa were always so
comfortable with that. Isobel was
the only one I never saw anything
with. She was the peacemaker. I do

wonder if without her they might
have drifted apart over the years.

                    VOICE (O.S.)
So when did you realize something
was going on?

                    CAMILLE

I would like to say that in
hindsight I saw the signs, but,
it would be incorrect. I was busy
with my son, trying to run the
home and do whatever I could to
make life easy for Ryan. Sure,
he was distracted and irritable
at times, but I figured he loved
Mandy and was going through a lot.
I never saw any of it coming.

23

RYAN

Monday, 7 a.m.
4 days, 8½ hours left

@BeAshamed

A glimpse of what might be . . .

#4daystogo

'Timeline: Lance Armstrong's journey from deity to disgrace'
Guardian news

The *Guardian* report was from 2015 and summarized the seven times Tour de France winner's fall from grace following a doping scandal. The retweeted article had over 500 comments attached, which Ryan began to scroll through.

Armstrong displays all the symptoms of someone sociopathic.
Biggest cheat in sporting history.

Smug and deluded.

Lance Armstrong cheating at riding the bicycle doesn't surprise me.
Cyclists think the rules don't apply to them.

Armstrong was stripped of his medals and forced to quit his cancer charity. Turns out he was the cancer.

He put himself on a pedestal as some kind of hero then destroyed anyone who tried to expose him. Maybe his cancer was the universe trying to tell him something.

Yeah, like fuck off and die already.

Ryan closed the app. It was nothing he hadn't read before. When Armstrong was exposed, the whole cycling community, along with the world, pored over the details. But reading it again now had the desired effect. What had it felt like for Armstrong to fall from such heights? How did it feel to become the poster boy for cheats in sport, taking Ben Johnson's crown? Ryan had not done anything as extreme as the likes of Lance Armstrong, but everyone in cycling knew the man cast a dark shadow over the sport. People had been suspicious of cyclists ever since Armstrong and his era of riders was exposed. If records were broken, questions were asked. If rumours began, they were impossible to shake. The court of public opinion had little time for mitigating factors or extenuating circumstances. It was the same for any person in the public eye – if you mess up your name is forever linked to the scandal. Because the internet never forgets.

Ryan opened the app again and clicked on the sender of the message: @BeAshamed. He scanned down their list of posts. It was a stream of hypercritical rhetoric about everyone from MPs and media personalities to bad drivers and rude coffee shop workers. He'd heard about these corners of social media, where people hand down judgements and stir up negativity, but reading it first-hand made him feel unclean. This was where his name was waiting to appear, in a community of bitter people who take pleasure in running others down. He could just imagine how they would revel in sharing his scandal. Could he track down the sender of his blackmail through this account? The idea was appealing until he realized it would be beyond his technical ability, especially in under a week.

After breakfast, Ryan drove Rosie to school, having to tolerate a typically irritating call from her mother on the way. He was endlessly impressed with how his daughter managed Steph. Even when Rosie was under fire with a barrage of criticism, she remained calm and almost detached, extracting herself from the conversation as soon as she could. But what would be the long-term effect? He didn't like to think too hard about that.

'I'm very proud of you,' he said before she climbed out of the car. 'Good luck today.' She had her final GCSE exam. Her mum appeared to have forgotten.

'I'm proud of you too.'

She often parroted back any compliment he gave her. It was her way of deflecting the attention, but today her words landed heavily on his heart.

24

PAUL

Monday, 7 a.m.
4 days, 8½ hours left

@BeAshamed

A glimpse of what might be . . .

#4daystogo

'Third time unlucky for "named and shamed" barrister as he is finally
Disbarred' – Legal Futures: legalfutures.co.uk/latest-news

The forwarded tweet was from November 2017, when Henry
Taylor, an immigration barrister in Sheffield, had been found
guilty of repeated misconduct. Paul remembered the incident and the feathers it had ruffled within the profession. It
was one of the first disbarments he had followed on Twitter
rather than in the traditional print media. He had enjoyed con-
versing with colleagues across the country about how such
reckless behaviour had brought their profession into disrepute.
Now he read the stream of rage in the replies with a renewed
perspective.

Who do these Barristers think they are? They're not above the law.
They should be setting an example.

I think it's disgusting how elitist nobs like Henry Taylor act.

Corrupt bastards, the lot of them. They shouldn't be struck off they
should be strung up.

Henry Taylor QC, stands for Quite a C@#t

He should be stripped, whipped and paraded around the streets like
the criminal he is.

Henry Taylor QC wanted power so he could do as he pleased.
And I know where he lives.

Paul read the last tweet a couple of times. Shit, this stuff got scary
quick. In a matter of six tweets, a barrister struck off for fraud was
being threatened with physical attacks. Paul looked back at the tweet
which brought him into all of this. *A glimpse of what might be.* How
would such trolls react to his past? It didn't bear thinking about. He
googled Henry Taylor and discovered the man now lived in New
Zealand with his family. Paul was dismayed that a man who had
already lost his career had been further punished by public opinion
to the extent he felt he needed to leave his country of birth. How was
that justice? The punishment should fit the crime. It was the essence
of a civilized society and the court of social media was perverting
that. Paul would not be driven to such extremes. He wasn't being
bullied by anyone. He would fight to the bitter end.

He looked into the source of the tweet but found no useful personal details attached to the @BeAshamed handle. All he found
was an account which had been running since pretty much the
birth of Twitter that appeared to be dedicated to spouting vit-
riol about the shameful acts of supposedly shameful people. And
depressingly, the account had over 10,000 followers.

25

RYAN

Monday, 9 a.m.
4 days, 6½ hours left

Sitting in the car outside Rosie's school, Ryan made a decision. He had to prioritize. He couldn't afford for this situation to be placed on the back burner, so he called the charity office and told his PA he was taking a few days off due to a bereavement.

He knew he'd made absolutely no progress finding out who had hurt Audrey Raye and he was fast losing time. And so, when a text arrived from Shame@pm.me during his drive home, asking if he wanted a clue, he didn't really think it through. Whoever was doing this knew the damage exposing his secret would do to Ryan's world. It would not only trash his reputation, it would ruin his career and leave his relationships in tatters. Especially those with his parents, which he could not countenance.

And so he said yes.

The reply came within minutes.

Location, location, location.

26

ISOBEL

Monday, 9 a.m.
4 days, 6½ hours left

@BeAshamed

A glimpse of what might be . . .

#4daystogo

Isobel clicked on the retweeted message and read the string of comments that followed it.

@BeAshamed

Just found out a doctor at our local hospital has endangered the lives of children WTF??

Tell us who they are. We will name and shame and the lowlife will never work again.

Remember Nassar, the sports doctor. They stabbed him.

The nausea Isobel had been feeling since Friday bubbled up her throat. She took a deep breath and swallowed back the saliva swilling her mouth. She was in the consultants' lounge at work, about to do her rounds, and she wanted her mum.

She'd not slept much at all. She kept thinking of Mandy stepping in front of that van. Had she known what was happening? Had she felt any pain? Was it all Isobel's fault?

'Isobel, the chief exec's PA is looking for you,' one of her colleagues called from the doorway. 'You and the CMO are needed ASAP. Hey, are you OK?'

Isobel gave some platitude in response and barely noticed the various people smiling and saying good morning as she walked to the CEO's office. Three months ago, she had been appointed as the clinical director for children's services at Leeds Children's Hospital. It was a whole new level of responsibility, and she had yet to come to terms with leaving the clinical environment and walking down the carpeted corridors of power.

The chief medical officer was already sitting in one of the two large cushioned chairs in front of the chief executive's desk. The CEO herself sat behind the desk, which was piled with paperwork. They were supposed to be a paperless trust, but the CEO liked to hold reports in her hand. She said they felt more real that way.

'Isobel, take a seat.' The CEO continued typing on her keyboard; her fingers hitting the keys hard and fast.

Isobel nodded hello to the CMO and then looked at the papers pinned to the noticeboard. They included the trust values, a leaflet on speaking up and speaking out, and an anti-bullying poster. It came to something when you had to instruct grown adults how to behave.

'Right. We have a bit of an issue,' said the CEO. 'Our local MP has been in touch requesting a review of the paediatric cardiac unit's outcomes. He's noted a dip, which I know you will both tell me is the normal ebb and flow of these things, but unfortunately we can't ignore this. It's the downside of this data being out in the public domain. I'm going to need you to put your heads together and come up with a plan, ideally by close of play. This MP is not a man to back down.'

Isobel had never met the local MP, but she had heard him speak on a number of occasions and from what she could tell he was a typical Tory. It was all about profit margins and value for money, and the constant need to monitor metrics that don't necessarily drive patient care. She wasn't a fan. Plus, the paediatric cardiac unit was something of an easy target. There had been a threat of closure back in the 1990s after the Bristol heart scandal, where staff shortages and leadership failings had led to a high number of babies dying after cardiac surgery. A whole raft of such units were subsequently closed, but Leeds Children's Hospital had fought hard to keep theirs as, despite being small, its outcomes were strong.

'And to add insult to injury,' the CEO continued, 'he's claiming to have been tipped off that one of our senior neonatal consultants has a compromising incident in their past which should have been disclosed.'

Isobel felt like all the air had been sucked out of the room.

'What kind of incident? I think we'd be aware of anything like that, don't you, Isobel?'

Isobel didn't hear much of what the CMO went on to say, such was the volume of her heartbeat pounding in her ears. What were the chances this would happen now? It had to be another warning shot across the bow.

Isobel walked back to the ward in a daze. Her mistake was in the past, she had been working at a different hospital, so why come for her now? And why contact Mandy too? It didn't make any sense.

Then, suddenly, she knew who she needed to speak to.

27

RYAN

Monday, 9.30 a.m.
4 days, 6 hours left

Ryan had been studying the news reports from the time of Audrey's accident. They said she had been found a few hundred yards along from the golf clubhouse on the same side of the road – on the stretch he was walking now, away from Ilkley and towards Bolton Abbey.

Location, location, location. Why had that been his clue? The accident happened nearly two decades ago, there could be no evidence here now for what had occurred, if there had ever been anything. He stopped to let a silver 4x4 pass and tried to imagine Audrey walking here. She had been in her early twenties, it had been dark and she was possibly upset after a row with her boyfriend. Ryan thought of Rosie and how easily she could find herself in a similar situation. She was fairly independent already at sixteen, and Ryan knew it was getting harder and harder to protect her. One of the main downsides of being separated from her mum was that at least half the time he had no idea where his daughter was. It was a horrifying train of thought to imagine her here, discarded and dying at the side of the road. Audrey had been discovered by a farm worker on his way to work. Reports said if she'd been left much longer, she was unlikely to have survived.

He looked over the hedge and across the field beyond. A few sheep grazed the grass. What was he supposed to be looking for?

His ringing phone disturbed the peace and quiet. It was the office.

'Sorry to call you. I know you said to hold the fort but Sophie really needs to speak to you. It's urgent.' His PA sounded stressed, which was unusual.

'Everything OK?'

'I'll let Sophie explain.'

Sophie was their PR manager at the charity. A no-nonsense mother of four who had worked for the large agency in London that had represented him after his Tour de France stage win. Ryan had convinced her to relocate north with her family when he'd set up the Fallon Foundation.

'I had a call from a journalist this morning – they wanted a comment from you about an up-and-coming story. A scandal surrounding a British cyclist.'

Ryan closed his eyes.

'Ryan?'

'I'm here. What's the story?'

'They're not saying. I said we could hardly comment without more information. They claimed a couple of your old teammates are planning to put out statements denying any involvement, though. Suggest anything to you? I advise we draft a statement too, so we're ready to go once things develop.'

Should they? Was that a good idea? If he could stop the story, a denial would be the right move. But if he couldn't, and let's face it he was making little progress, it could be fatal. Sophie had once told him, deny what you can, admit what you have to, but never lie. She couldn't save him from an out and out falsehood.

'Can I call you back?'

Sophie was quiet for a second before she agreed. No one listening would ever detect it, but it told Ryan she understood. Another piece of advice she'd given him was if there was something he needed her to manage, to buy them time. *If we're in a meeting, ask for a break; if we're on a call, ask to call me back.* It was a way of tipping her off. Her job was not only to make him and the charity look good, but to avoid them looking bad at all costs.

Ryan walked back to his bike, putting his helmet on over his earphones. He needed to think it through. How much to tell Sophie. What to hold back. He had to get this right if he had any chance of reducing the fallout.

As he began heading back, he realized that part of him was becoming resigned to the inevitable. He might not be able to stop this.

28

PAUL

Monday, 3 p.m.
4 days, ½ hour left

At 10.15, the jury in the case against his client (the man who had beaten his father to death with a beer bottle) had delivered their verdict: manslaughter, by reason of diminished responsibility. It was the best outcome Paul could have hoped for, and it also left him free to work from home all afternoon.

Paul was realizing that he might need to get creative in tackling this blackmail situation. He'd had to set 'Carl Baker' aside, on account of there being no leads to suggest it wasn't a fake name, but he figured he still had two significant lines of enquiry.

The first involved contacting his old associates and seeing if they could cast any light on who might be brazen enough to attack him like this. But he knew that opening that channel of communication had risks. It had taken him years to shut down the many and varied requests for legal assistance he used to receive to get people out of dubious spots.

His second option was to seek help from Mitchel Bleacher, a local crime boss who might be able to find out whether Kyle Renton's people were behind this. He knew Bleacher would help him because Paul had put Renton away for killing Bleacher's grandson. But again, Paul knew such a call for help would have consequences. With men like that, a favour begets a favour which begets a favour.

The knock on the door was a relief. He could decide later.

'How are you doing?'

Isobel looked awful, like she hadn't slept for days. Her olive skin had taken on a yellowish tinge and there were dark rings under her eyes.

'Oh, you know. Shitty. How about you?'

Paul shrugged. It would serve no useful purpose to air his despair over Mandy or his worries about saving his own skin. He focused on making coffee instead.

'I need some advice, Paul.'

'Legal?'

'I don't know, maybe . . . hopefully not.'

'Sounds intriguing.'

'I went to see Greg yesterday. Something Steph said freaked me out a bit—'

'I wouldn't worry too much about that harpy's ramblings. She's got a very slack hold on reality, that one.'

Isobel smiled a little. 'She said Mandy had been really down lately and that we'd all missed it. Then she said she wouldn't be surprised if she'd done it on purpose.'

'Don't be stupid. God, she is full of shit. She was getting on Mandy's nerves, I'll tell you that much for free.'

'Was she? So they weren't getting close?'

'Steph might have hoped so, but you know Mand, she had little time for an emotional drain on her best days.' He sat with her at the breakfast bar.

'Had you seen much of Mandy after the split? I was so busy and I feel awful that I wasn't checking in more.'

'We spoke a few times a week.'

Isobel's eyebrows rose. Paul knew what they all thought of his continuing affection for Mandy. If Isobel had known they were talking so frequently she would no doubt have advised caution. *Be careful with your heart, Paul*, she would have said.

'You don't need to feel guilty. She didn't expect everyone to rally around. She was coping.'

'Did you speak to her last week?'

Paul had to think. The case had been heavy-going, he'd been working day and night. 'Er, no, not last week.'

'Right.' Isobel frowned into her untouched coffee.

'Sorry, can I just check, did you say you went to ask Greg if Mandy had done herself in?' Paul laughed. Way to stick the knife in and twist it. He only wished he'd thought to do the same himself.

'He was adamant she didn't. I felt terrible. I shouldn't have gone.'

'Oh, I'm sure his new girl will rub it better.'

Isobel shuffled in her seat and pulled at the cuffs of her blouse.

Paul waited. He knew when a client had something on their mind and wanted to confess.

'I received something on Friday and I'm worried Mandy did too.'

Paul sat a little straighter. 'What kind of something?'

'A warning. Someone threatened to go to the press about something that happened at work years ago. But they made it look . . . as if it was already out in the world.' Isobel met his gaze and Paul hoped he was keeping his expression as unreadable as possible. It sounded the same, but caution was the order of the day here. He couldn't risk anyone finding out about his past, especially not Isobel.

'OK. I'm sorry to hear that, but what makes you think Mandy was involved?'

'The timings. I received it at around three thirty, and that's the time Greg said Mandy had been distracted by her phone and stepped into the road. What are the chances?' Isobel looked hopeful. Did she want him to confirm her suspicions or dispute them? 'You think I'm crazy, don't you?'

'I'm thinking it sounds like you've had a tough weekend.'

Tears welled in her eyes and she nodded.

What are you guilty of, Isobel? he thought as his well-honed instincts for self-preservation kicked in.

'This threat you received. What did they want?' he said.

'Erm, they sent a text saying someone had betrayed me and I needed to find out who. If I can't find out by Friday, then they'll expose my . . . thing.'

'Betrayed you as in told someone what you'd done?'

'Yeah, I assume so. They sent me a mocked-up newspaper article revealing what I'd done.' Isobel let the point hang and Paul nodded. 'I think Mandy might have received something too, and then, today, whoever is behind this started dropping hints at work.'

'Dropping hints how?'

'The local MP contacted my CEO and said he'd been told one of the neonatal consultants had a dubious incident in their past.'

Shit. Was this arsehole planning to contact his chambers? Paul was not as protected as NHS employees. If you're not earning enough, you're out. If you're not good enough, you're out. His was a do or die environment.

'Have you tried calling the number that texted you?' Paul asked this in part because that's what he would ask if he had no personal insight into this situation, and in part to confirm they were being targeted by the same person.

'It's not a number. It's an email address.'

Shame@pm.me, Paul figured.

'Do you have any hunches as to who is doing this?' he asked.

'I've been trying to work that out. If it's just me, then possibly an ex-colleague or even a disgruntled parent? Parents with poorly kids can be pretty intense, and if they've lost a child . . .'

'They're looking for someone to blame?'

'Not all of them. But extreme situations can cause extreme reactions. You taught me that.'

'Hmmm.'

'But if it's me *and* Mandy, that changes things, which is why I came. You knew Mandy best. Was there anything in her past she might have wanted to hide?'

'Gone are the days when she would confide that in me.'

Isobel looked crestfallen. She'd wanted him to confirm her hypothesis. She didn't want this to be only about her. He could understand that.

He was feeling a weird kind of relief from knowing this wasn't only happening to him. But it did beg the question: why was someone targeting them? He'd assumed this was someone from his personal history but if Mandy and Isobel were being threatened too, that changed things. He knew he should tell his friend she wasn't alone in this, but something instinctive was telling him, *Not yet.*

'Would you feel comfortable telling me exactly what you've been asked to find out and I'll see if I can help? If you're nervous about that, you could always pass me a tenner and secure my services as your legal advisor.'

'You've got enough money. And I trust you. I'm desperate this doesn't blow up in my face. The adoption authorization is barely dry on the paper.'

Paul waited. Maybe this could help him answer his puzzle.

Isobel took out her phone and read the words exactly. Paul recognized the preamble. It was exactly the same as his own message, and then she said, 'Who betrayed you in England first at the Royal Oak?'

Paul had been taking a sip of coffee and almost spat it across the polished wood.

Fuck.

Thankfully Isobel was still reading the words that followed so missed Paul's reaction. By the time she looked up, he'd recovered.

'Cryptic,' he said as he listened to Isobel's account of visiting Royal Oaks in the area. He couldn't tell her she was wasting her time. That she was barking up the wrong tree. That she'd misread the words. Because the person who had betrayed Isobel was currently serving her coffee in his kitchen and he knew he had to do everything he possibly could to make sure she never, ever worked that out.

29

ISOBEL

Monday, 4.30 p.m.
3 days, 23 hours left

'Hey, babe. Good day?' Annie called out from the kitchen as Isobel entered the house.

'Mama?' said Joshua with what sounded like a mouth full of food.

'We're having shepherd's pie.'

'Sounds good,' Isobel managed to say as she removed her shoes. 'Just going for a shower.'

'Oh dear. Mama's had one of those days, Joshy. Let's finish our din-dins then we can cheer her up.'

Isobel managed to make it to the en suite before sinking to the floor and letting the sobs engulf her. She had hoped Paul would help her to make some sense of it all. Instead, he'd asked her what she'd done and, when she said she'd prefer not to say, he'd looked irritated. She had expected support. He was one of her oldest friends, someone she thought would have her back no matter what. But clearly she'd misjudged things.

And if that's how Paul reacted, how would everyone else respond? Would they have that same judgemental look in their eyes?

I've let them all down.

She thought of Josh and fresh tears ran down her face. She had wanted to be the best of mums, someone he could rely on to guide him and give him every opportunity to live his best life. But how could she do that if she had no job? If she lost her profession and her ability to earn a living. Where would she go next? What would she do? She couldn't expect Annie to support her.

Isobel tried to conjure up the words to tell her wife. *'I'm so sorry, Annie. I never meant to let you down. I feel utterly broken. Every space in my head is filled with despair and desperation. I wake in the night and look at you sleeping and I'm panic-stricken . . .'* None of it sounded like enough to excuse the admission which would have to follow.

She had never felt more alone.

30

PAUL

Monday, 4.30 p.m.
3 days, 23 hours left

'Did I hear that right?'

The arrival of Vanessa in the kitchen made Paul jump. She had been ensconced in their garden office all day while he worked indoors and he'd almost forgotten she was around. He looked at his wife, who stood at the island with her hands flat on the surface. Eyes wide. Tone irritated.

'What did you hear?'

Isobel had left not long before.

'Who betrayed you in England first, yada yada. You do realize if she works out what that means, it's not only you who's buggered. If this comes out, a good deal of those lowlifes you put away will think they've got just cause to appellate their convictions and then the whole justice system will be buggered, not to mention the victims.'

'I am aware.' He was also aware that there was more to it than even she and his blackmailer knew. If this thing came out, everything else might too and that would be a game-changer.

His mind flicked back to the small room at the back of the

Royal Oak with its stone floor and open fire. The tables had been small, wooden circles around which they had perched on low, cushion-topped stools. It was his first taste of being admired and that had become a drug in which he willingly indulged. He'd wanted them to look up to him, to see him as a man of influence even though he was barely more than a boy. So he'd gone out to impress them. Out in the deep. Far too far.

'You'd better tell me what's going on.'

Paul briefly summarized the situation for his wife. She had already heard most of it, so it was pointless playing it down.

'So what are you going to do about it?'

Paul knew exactly. As soon as Isobel had revealed that she had been tasked with investigating him, he'd connected the dots pretty swiftly. He had thought 22 July 2012 related to something he had been involved with at the time, but when he realized it might be associated with one of his friends, he knew exactly who that might be. When Vanessa had walked in, he'd been googling the date along with Ryan's name, and, as he suspected, it was the day Ryan had won the twenty-first stage of the Tour de France.

Paul thought about the wording of his question. *Who cheated justice?* He had understandably zoned in on the word 'justice', but now he could see that was a red herring. The important word was 'cheated'.

Ryan's win had been out of the blue. A massive achievement. Ryan was a junior member of his team, only there to support the lead riders, who'd be challenging the likes of Bradley Wiggins and Chris Froome of Team Sky. He wasn't there to win something; which only made his talent all the more impressive. But what if talent wasn't behind the win? The Lance Armstrong scandal had been reaching its zenith, and it was just a few months later that he finally confessed. He had said he only did it because everyone else was doing it. If you didn't dope, you didn't win.

Paul looked at the picture of Ryan crossing the finish line with one triumphant hand up in the air.

'I've got it under control,' he said.

'You better have, because I'm not getting wrapped up in this, do you hear me? This will not torpedo my career.'

Paul knew what she was saying: *If this comes out, I walk out.* He wasn't going to let that happen.

Back in his office he texted his blackmailer.

You asked me to tell you who cheated justice on 22 July 2012.

I suspect it was Ryan Fallon.

Am I correct?

He pressed send and waited. *Take that Carl Baker, or whatever your name is.* Three days, it had taken. This dickhead had severely underestimated him. It had crossed his mind it could be Annie. She certainly had the skills to both research people's secrets and write journalistic copy. He, Ryan and Mandy could be collateral damage in some domestic drama. But he wasn't sure he bought the idea that this was Izzy's wife having a strop. One thing he was sure of, if he found out that it had anything to do with Mandy's death, he would hunt down whatever evil prick was doing this and burn their world to the ground.

A message came back.

You are correct.

But do you know how?

Paul sat back in his chair. *Shit.* Despite the relief at having nipped this nonsense in the bud, he was gutted. Paul looked up at the signed cycling shirt framed on the wall. He had bragged about Ryan, told people his story whenever he had the chance and basked in the reflected glory. Finding out his best friend had cheated was a kick in the nuts. Paul thought about all the stories Ryan had told over the years. Stories of brutal training regimes, beating impossible odds and joking around with the superstars of cycling as if he was a part of a special gang. All told to enraptured audiences who hung on his every word. Paul wasn't sure if he admired Ryan's audacity or judged him for it. He'd have made a good barrister.

But did it really change anything? Ryan was still Ryan. It wasn't the friendship- and career-destroying bombshell Isobel had been tasked to uncover.

He took a few moments to think about his next message.

I suspect doping but I don't care.

I did your stupid task so I'm going to need some assurance that this is the end of it.

Paul paced as he awaited the response. He was going to need to draft up something legal. A non-disclosure agreement of sorts. And once he had a guarantee that his past would stay where it belonged, his next task was to go on a hunt to find out who it was that thought they could do this to him and get away with it.

But then the next message arrived and the reality of things became clear. This prick was only just getting started.

If you want your secret to stay hidden, Paul, you need to tell the world what Ryan did.

You need to ruin him or I will ruin you.

Welcome to the Shame Game.

31

Ah, Paul. You always thought you were smarter than everyone else, didn't you? I can almost hear you congratulating yourself on working out that Ryan was the one who had cheated just before I told you what comes next: him or you.

It was a toss-up, deciding whether to give you Ryan or Mandy's secret to uncover. Obviously, Isobel had to have yours. She'll be appalled by who you really are. But with you, I could have gone either way. Mandy was your first love, but your bromance with Ryan includes an extra bit of hero-worshipping on your part. Safe to say both of their secrets were likely to change your opinion of them. I could have picked either, but in the end I chose Ryan because I knew it would hurt you the most.

32

THE SHAME GAME:
A TRUE CRIME DOCUMENTARY

Episode 1 of 3 - The Players

INT - CAFÉ - DAYTIME

The woman sitting at the café table is thin and wiry. Her face is a mass of deep wrinkles and her blonde, wispy hair falls unstyled to her shoulders.

TEXT on the screen reads: LESLEY CARTER, RETIRED BUS DRIVER.

> LESLEY CARTER
>
> What you have to understand is I had an odd route at that time, the number sixty-two, which ran from Keighley to Ilkley.

Keighley is a working-class town,
you see, it's had a lot of social
issues over the years, there was
a heroin problem for a while and
they even had a bomb scare back
in the nineties. It's the kind of
place you'll often see a bit of a
scrap in the street from the late
bus, and that's just the girls, if
you know what I mean.

The woman laughs and it sounds as if her
throat is lined with sandpaper.

EXT - BUS ROUTE - DAYTIME

As LESLEY continues to talk, the screen
shows an aerial view of the route running
from an urban town along a dual carriageway
and through a few rural villages before
rising over lush green moorland and dropping
into the valley towards the spa town of
Ilkley.

                    LESLEY

And then Ilkley is the other
extreme. There's a lot of money
over that side of the hill. You'd
still get a bus full of rowdy kids
at school closing, but they were
better dressed and there was less
swearing.

INT - CAFÉ - DAYTIME

                    LESLEY

        I say this so you understand why
        I didn't react. I don't even think
        I got out of my seat. I think the
        things I'd seen in Keighley had
        desensitized me. I figured, they're
        just blowing off steam, it'll pass,
        because ninety-nine per cent of the
        time these things do.

                    VOICE (O.S.)

        Is that a regret?

                    LESLEY

        Oh, aye. Especially considering
        what happened after. They were
        young and when you're young you
        can be really bloody stupid, can't
        you? You think you're so funny
        and clever and that there's no
        consequences to what you do and
        say. I should have got out of my
        seat and given 'em what for. If I
        had my time again . . .

33

RYAN

Monday, 5.30 p.m.
3 days, 22 hours left

Ryan had spent the afternoon in a corner of the office with his PR manager after telling her he had also been contacted by someone who was threatening to expose a story on him. They concluded this was most likely the same anonymous journalist who had contacted her. Though Sophie was irritated that he had not come to her immediately on Friday, she didn't chastize him. Her focus was on what to do now.

He told her the truth of the matter. It was the first time he'd ever said it out loud and it took a lot to get the words out. Sophie was patient and quiet; a woman skilled at not looking shocked by whatever her charge might say.

They agreed that by facing up to this and taking a bit of control, he'd feel less vulnerable. And that had given him an idea. One of his closest friends, Annie, was a regional journalist. Surely she would know the details of Audrey's accident. And then there was Greg. Ryan hadn't seen much of the police officer since his separation from Mandy, but Ryan had known better than to express an opinion or take sides, and so they were still on good terms. If he wanted to find out more about Audrey Raye's accident, he should be speaking to them.

As Ryan opened the front door to his house, he could hear quiet sobbing coming from the kitchen. He took a moment to steel himself before walking into the room.

Ryan expected to find Camille upset at having heard her husband was not the man she thought, but Camille was not the one crying. Rosie was. Camille sat by her side with an arm over her shoulder. His wife looked up at Ryan when he entered and mouthed the phrase, 'Bad exam.'

'Hey, Ro. What's up, darling?'

Rosie crumpled on to the tabletop and buried her head in her arms.

'I'll check on Ethan,' said Camille, and Ryan realized the TV was on in the other room.

He took Camille's position next to Rosie and ruffled her hair. 'Nothing is that bad, Ro. I promise. Everyone has tough exams. It might not have been as bad as you think, and if it was, you can retake. No problem.'

Rosie shook her head and spoke in an angry tone through her sobs.

Ryan managed to pick up that Rosie had misread the instructions, something about answering the wrong number of questions from part one of the paper. 'It's an instant fail!' she said.

'I'm sure they will estimate what mark you would have got from the questions you did answer.'

'No, Dad. I did it wrong. They can't pass me now.' Her sobs became louder.

Ryan wanted to say, *It's only history, it doesn't matter so long as you have English and maths*, but he didn't. This was not the time. She was feeling ashamed and Lord knows he knew what that was like. Being told you were overreacting was not the answer.

'Well, I still love you even though you can't read simple instructions.'

She elbowed him in the ribs and he made a loud 'oww' sound and nudged her back. She nudged him again and the tit for tat continued until he heard a small laugh through her tears.

Not long after, Ryan's parents arrived armed with Rosie's favourite sausage casserole and a large French stick. His mum had always been one to show her love through food. They both hugged Rosie and told her not to worry before Ryan's dad went off to play trains with Ethan.

'How is Paul coping? He was always sweet on Mandy,' Ryan's mum said.

Ryan knew his mum and dad saw Paul as something of a second son. He had spent so much time at their house as a boy and when they spoke about his achievements they did so with an air of pride.

'He's a mess, like the rest of us.'

When they had all finished eating, and Rosie was helping Camille to stack the dishwasher, Ryan took his opportunity.

'I rode up to the tarn yesterday and met Audrey Raye, do you remember her?' He needed to ask his parents about Audrey. He didn't want to believe they might have had anything to do with her accident, but he had to be sure.

'Oh yes. I knew her mum, Sylvia. Lovely woman. She worked in WHSmith for years,' said his mum.

'What happened to her, do you remember? She was really confused today, talking about how the ducks had told her she was the only one allowed to feed them.'

'It was the boyfriend, wasn't it?' said Ryan's dad. 'I heard he'd had his way with her and either pushed her out of the car or she'd jumped out to get away from him.'

'We don't know that, Steve. They never arrested him. Sylvia always said he was a nice boy and very upset by the whole thing.'

'I'd pretend to be upset too, if I'd brain-damaged my girlfriend.'

Ryan's mum shook her head as if her husband was saying something utterly ridiculous, but Ryan thought his dad had a point.

'What do you think happened, then?' he asked his mum, watching her reaction closely. She had always been an absent-minded driver. He recalled that when he was a teenager, she would get irritated with him for pointing out that she needed to indicate before a turn or switch her wipers on when it started to rain.

'I can only go by what Sylvia said. The doctors told her Audrey's injuries were consistent with being hit by a car. She thought the boyfriend's story was probably true. Him and Audrey were always breaking up and getting back together, and apparently Audrey was inclined to storm off if someone had upset her.'

Ryan was relieved by his mother's calm tone and relaxed body language. Without a doubt he would have seen some sign of guilt if she had been involved. She had no poker face whatsoever.

'So she stormed off from the boyfriend and was hit by a car while walking home?'

'It used to be much darker along that back road to Beamsley, plus there was a lot more drink driving going on back then. Folks wouldn't think twice about having a few pints while out in the car. Whoever did it failed to stop so there must be a reason for that,' his dad said.

Ryan's mum nodded. 'Imagine having to live with that. Destroying a poor girl's life. I know she survived but Sylvia became a full-time carer and I've no doubt it contributed to her death. Sylvia wasn't much older than your dad and me when she passed.'

'Imagine how that driver who hit Mandy feels,' said Ryan's dad, which had them all falling silent and contemplating that.

'So we hear Rosie has a boyfriend,' said his mum to break the silence.

Ryan saw Rosie blush across the room. 'Apparently so. Gus Phillips, he's Toby Phillips's son. Do you remember Toby?'

'Oh, I do indeed. Your dad and him were big friends back in the day, Rosie.'

'Really?' Rosie became more interested in the conversation, moving back to the table to join them. 'You never said.'

'I wouldn't call us big friends. We rode together a bit.'

'Toby runs the mountain biking club now, he's really nice,' said Rosie. She had taken up mountain biking when she was around ten years old. It had scared Camille to death when they went to watch her bouncing down the side of Ilkley Moor one Sunday last year, but Ryan was proud of her. 'I know he knew Aunt Mandy well, but Gus never mentioned you.'

'I don't think he did know Mand well. We were just at school together,' said Ryan.

'Yeah, Mandy's brother dated Gus's aunt for years, that's Toby's sister, but apparently they broke up when he cheated on her with one of Mandy's friends.'

'Ooo you are full of the gossip, Rosie,' Ryan's mum said.

It was the first Ryan had ever heard of this. It must have all happened when he was away cycling. He wasn't surprised though. He knew how small towns worked: if families are not connected by relationships or scandals, they most certainly know each other's business.

'Your dad was always trying to beat him, weren't you, Ryan? But that Toby was too good. I think most of your father's competitive edge came from trying to get past Toby Phillips.'

'I'm not sure that's the truth of things, Mum. We used to race together as teenagers, Rosie, when I was mountain biking, but then I switched to road racing.'

'Because he couldn't beat Toby,' said his mum with a smile. She enjoyed a good wind-up. Truth of the matter was, Toby was a better rider off road and Ryan had looked up to him. He was also a couple of years older and very cool. But once Ryan switched to the road, any friendship that had been there was done. Toby had resented Ryan's success and no doubt grown more and more bitter as the years went by and he failed to win anything significant for himself.

Bitter enough to expose you?

Ryan felt the hairs rise on his arms. He had guessed that whoever was coming after him was either a journalist with a career to make or a disgruntled fellow cyclist. But he'd only considered road cyclists, not mountain bikers. What were the chances of Toby's son dating Rosie at this very point in time? They had been dating for a few months, long enough for Gus to have been snooping around in their lives, walking through their home, pumping Rosie for information.

'Are you all right, love? You're as white as a sheet,' his mum said, patting the back of his hand.

34

STEPHANIE

Monday, 7 p.m.

She tried Rosie's phone one more time as she paced around the house picking up abandoned hair bobbles, socks and half-drunk cups of tea. Her daughter could be so ungrateful. When Stephanie had texted the evening before to say goodnight, Rosie had replied with, 'Oh, you remembered you had a daughter then?' Stephanie had immediately called Rosie and when she didn't pick up, she rang Ryan. He was the reason Rosie was so mean and argumentative. Stephanie would never have dared speak to her mother the way Rosie spoke to her. Ryan hadn't answered either, leaving Stephanie to have a restless night seething over what an ungrateful child and unreasonable ex she had.

'Mother,' said Rosie in a flat tone.

'Don't be mean.'

'How is saying your name being mean?'

'Because you said, *mother*, like that. You know what you're doing.'

'Was there something you needed? Because Dad and I are just arriving at Isobel's.'

'Oh, you can go and comfort Isobel but you can't spare me a second thought?'

Stephanie heard quiet words being exchanged.

'What's that? What are you saying?'

'Nothing.'

'Rosie, don't lie to me. I could hear you and your father talking about me.'

'I've got to go, Mum. I'll call you later.'

'Ryan, tell her,' Stephanie had time to say before her daughter hung up. Stephanie screamed out loud in frustration.

'What is going on?' Stephanie's mother asked as she stepped through the front door carrying two bags – a laundry bag full of Stephanie and Rosie's freshly ironed clothes, and a large Waitrose bag that smelled of homemade food.

'Oh, it's Rosie and Ryan ganging up on me again.'

'I'm sure you're exaggerating, Steph.'

'Am I? Am I? I don't think so. He manipulates her, Mum. He always has and you always defend him.'

'I don't think I do. Shall I put the kettle on?'

'I don't want tea. I want my bloody daughter to show me some respect and to understand I'm suffering right now. She has no idea what it feels like to be upset like this. You'd think she'd want to comfort me.'

'Well, maybe you shouldn't have shipped her off to his house.'

'That's not fair. He needs to do his share. This is what I mean about you taking his side.'

'Stephanie, this is not how to be a good parent, you know that, don't you? You need to take some responsibility. Not that I'm surprised. You can barely look after yourself let alone your child.' Felicity placed the laundry bag at the bottom of the stairs and walked to the kitchen.

'Don't be mean.'

'Your dad made you a shepherd's pie without the carrots – I know Rosie's not a fan – and a cheese and bacon quiche. Do you want them in the fridge or the freezer?' Her mum's tone was flat and cold.

'The fridge. They've got me working a double shift again tomorrow. I won't be home until midnight and I never get a chance to eat, so I can have some quiche when I get back.'

'That might be a bit heavy before bed. Maybe have some for lunch before you go.'

'What do you mean? I'm due in at ten. They're so short-staffed at the moment, I'm doing every hour God sends.'

'OK, well, you do what you think is best, then. I'm only trying to help.'

Her mum's tone had gone from flat to frustrated and Stephanie distracted herself by checking her phone. She didn't want another row. She half expected to see a text from Rosie apologizing for cutting her off, but there was none.

'I saw Mandy's dad yesterday at the supermarket, poor man,' Felicity said. 'He was wandering up and down the aisles not selecting anything. You can't imagine, can you, losing a child? I said to him, do you need a hand, Alan? but I'm not sure he knew who I was or even where he was.'

Stephanie couldn't let her mind go there. For all the teenage drama she was facing with Rosie at the moment, the idea of not having her around was too much to bear. 'How old was Mandy's mum when she died?' Steph had not really known Mandy that well until she began dating Ryan, by which point Mandy's mum was not around.

'Oh, gosh, I don't know exactly, but she can't have been much past forty. She lived for a few years after the stroke but she was in a home. I don't think she could speak or walk or anything. If that ever happens to me just put a pillow over my face or something.'

'Mum!'

'I mean it, Stephanie. I wouldn't want to live like that.' Her mum neatly folded the Waitrose bag and placed it in her coat pocket. 'Right then, I'll leave you to it. Your dad wants to drive over to Harrogate early in the morning to visit the rare book shop, so I'm going to do a little retail therapy.'

Stephanie told her mum to have a nice time despite feeling jealous. What she'd give to have a nice daytrip out shopping instead of having to deal with grumpy hotel customers and incompetent colleagues.

35

ISOBEL

Monday, 7 p.m.
3 days, 20½ hours left

Isobel heard Ryan's voice from the bedroom where she had been hiding since returning home, waiting for her red, puffy eyes to calm down. Annie hadn't been up to see what was going on. Josh must be keeping her busy.

The sound of Rosie's voice brought Isobel out of the room. The last of Rosie's exams had been today. She had mentioned it on Saturday when they were all at Ryan's. Isobel should ask her how she'd got on, plus it would be good to think about something else for a while.

On hearing about Rosie's exam disaster, Isobel pulled her into a hug as Annie shared a horror story from her own exams, telling Rosie it really didn't make a difference to anything in the long run. Rosie didn't look convinced, and Isobel remembered what it had felt like to be so worried about your GCSEs. They seemed like the most important and difficult things you'd ever had to do at that age. She released Rosie from the hug and told her to try and forget about it for now. The kind of advice it was easy to give out but hard to follow yourself.

'Can you show me your toys, Joshy?' Rosie said, moving away from the adults and the attention that was making her pull the sleeves of her jumper over her hands.

'Annie, what do you know about Audrey Raye?' Ryan asked once Rosie and Josh were ensconced in the conservatory, playing with building blocks.

'That name's a blast from the past,' said Annie.

'I met her yesterday up at the tarn. I tried to talk to her but she started shouting at me about the ducks and how she'd been feeding them for hundreds of years.'

'Some think she fell or was pushed from a car, but she was more likely hit by one, if I recall correctly. That's what doctors told the police. She sustained head injuries, which explains the duck ranting.' Annie squeezed Isobel's hand and her eyes asked, 'All OK?'

Isobel squeezed her wife's hand back.

'People suspected the boyfriend, is that right? Who was he?' Ryan was saying.

'Er, yeah, that's right. He was from the family who had the Chinese takeaway on Brook Street. Their youngest son, I think? They took a lot of flak and lost a lot of business after Audrey.' Annie was clearly enjoying the trip down some journalistic memory lane. She described the people she had interviewed back then as a rookie reporter, including a few police officers.

'Greg wouldn't have been one of those, would he?'

Isobel felt irritated. Their friend had just been hit by a car and died – why was Ryan bringing up some accident that happened decades ago to a woman none of them knew? And why mention Greg? He had never been an officer around their neck of the woods. It was insensitive and irrelevant. She turned her attention to her phone to escape the conversation, but her mind was inexorably drawn back to the blackmailer's messages.

What she hadn't admitted to Paul when she'd told him about

the anonymous call to work was that she had most likely triggered it herself. She scrolled down to the messages received and
sent late last night.

The clock is ticking.

Are you any closer to finding out who betrayed you?

Can I give you a clue?

OK

Red Cross

Isobel was tired and emotionally drained. Someone out
there knew what she'd done. Had they known all these years
and watched her behaving as if nothing had ever happened?
She thought back to that misjudged moment. She had been
so young and foolish. If only she could go back and do things
differently. Her mind felt sluggish and slow and the constant
sickness in her stomach was getting her down. She kept trying
to tell herself it would be OK. But she knew it wouldn't. Whoever was tormenting her had already started dropping hints at
work. It was only a matter of time before everyone knew the
truth: that she was a weak, pathetic person who had broken
her vow to do no harm in the most awful way. She wanted Ryan
and Rosie to go so she could get Josh to bed and then bury her
head in her pillow.

She had to make the most of that clue. The British Red Cross
provided crisis support around the world and some of her colleagues would no doubt have been involved over the years, if
only in the form of charitable donations, especially in the face
of a humanitarian disaster. But as far as she knew no one in her
immediate circle had ever worked directly for the Red Cross. So
maybe the medical nature of the organization was the clue. Her
mind automatically brought up images from that day; the tears,

the panic, the platitudes. She had been in shock, the enormity of how her selfish actions had backfired screaming in her head: *Do I tell someone? What will happen to me? Will people lose faith in me? Will everyone treat me differently? Will I lose my job?*

Isobel knew she had made mistakes that day. Not only at the point at which it happened, but in the decision to cover up the truth with a lie. She hadn't had a chance to think about what she was going to say. She had walked into a panicked situation and simply said the first thing that came to mind. It was a split-second decision that had snowballed. If she had owned up back then she could see now that the consequences would have been minimal, maybe she would have been sanctioned, but she was only a senior house officer, and by now she would have recovered. But if it came out today, everything would be ruined and she might never be able to make it right. Isobel felt nausea rise up her throat again and she reached for the bottle of wine on the side and poured herself a large glass.

Josh became teary, so Annie took him off to bed. Rosie came to sit with Ryan and Isobel but immediately put her headphones in and delved back into her phone. Isobel turned her attention to Ryan. She knew she needed to make an effort.

'Tough week,' she said.

'Yeah,' Ryan looked away with a frown. 'I need to let you know about something that might be coming. I feel bad mentioning it with Mandy . . . but . . . I didn't want to not say anything.'

Isobel wasn't sure how much more she could take this week, but she smiled to let him know he was fine to talk. Ryan had always used her as a shoulder to cry on. She knew he appreciated her willingness to listen and talk things through, but it was a favour rarely returned over the years, which was becoming an irritation. She loved Ryan to bits, but he could be incredibly self-absorbed when something was going on in his life. She expected it was something to do with his overly devoted parents.

'A story might be coming out in the next few days about a British cyclist.'

Isobel met his gaze. 'What kind of story? About you?'

'Probably.'

She moved closer and dropped her volume. 'Have you seen the article?'

He frowned for a second. 'Isobel?'

'Did someone send you an article about something you've done?' She placed a hand on Ryan's arm.

'How do you know that?'

'Oh God, Ry. I think Mandy had one too. I think that's why . . .' She looked across at Rosie, whose head bobbed gently to some tune Isobel had no doubt never heard of.

'What are you saying?'

'I'm saying, I was sent what looked like a *Daily Mail* article about something I did years ago. It named me and said the adoption committee were reconsidering putting Josh with us.'

Ryan leaned in towards her, his hands clasped over his knees. 'Mine was a breaking news story on the BBC. They had a picture of Camille crying, but I found out later it was a photograph someone papped of her years ago when she was modelling.'

'Did it arrive on Friday before the party, about three thirty?'

'Yeah, probably. Is that when yours . . . ?'

'And Mandy's, I think. She stepped into the road just after three thirty p.m., and witnesses said she had been looking at her phone. Whatever she was sent either distracted her or . . .'

'No way.'

'Someone is targeting all of us. Why?' Isobel looked over at Rosie, who was still engrossed. 'Is this why you're asking about Audrey Raye?'

Ryan told her about his question and how he'd been trying to find out as much as he could. 'I figured Annie would be able to help flesh the story out a bit for me. I did wonder if I should speak to Greg, but then I thought that was insensitive. But if you think Mandy was threatened too, then maybe I should.'

'I don't know. We don't know what Mandy was threatened about. What if it's something Greg doesn't know? I asked Paul if Mandy had anything in her past she might be ashamed of, but he said he had no idea.'

'How's he doing?'

'He looked rough. I feel for Vanessa.'

'Oh, I don't think Ness has anything to worry about.'

'No? He told me that him and Mandy had been speaking a couple of times a week.'

'That doesn't mean anything. You and I talk a lot.'

'Only when you're having a drama.'

'Well, Mandy was having a drama.'

'I'm telling you, it's not the same. I like girls and I never dated you and broke your heart.'

'She didn't break his heart. They were what? Nineteen, twenty? That's like saying I broke Steph's heart. We were all just playing at boyfriend and girlfriend back then.'

Isobel patted his leg. 'There's a reason Steph hates you, you know.'

Ryan looked at Rosie and then changed the subject. 'Greg could give us access to Mandy's phone and messages. What if we offer to put some photos together for the funeral and ask for access to the ones on her phone?'

'But he's a police officer. Can't we just ask her dad or brother?'

'I think it might be a good idea to get a police perspective on the whole thing.'

'My threat says if I go to the police this person will go straight to the press. I can't risk that.'

'Yeah, but Greg isn't really the police, he's just Greg.'

'He holds the fourth most powerful rank in our police force. I think saying "it's just Greg" won't cut it.'

Ryan thought for a moment. 'How would anyone know I've spoken to him?'

'When Greg acts on it?'

'And does what, Izzy? I don't know what they're threatening to reveal about you, but my thing is not a million miles from the truth. Is it illegal to tell the truth about people?'

'This must constitute some kind of harassment or stalking, and if it led to Mandy's death . . .'

'OK, maybe. I'll not mention the threats specifically. But I really do think we should talk to Greg. He's still legally Mandy's next of kin and I really don't want to hassle her dad or Jim about this. At least Greg has some emotional detachment, given he and Mandy were separated. It won't feel so inappropriate.'

Isobel went to top up her wine. She wasn't sure about this. 'What if this someone's watching us? If we go to see Greg together, won't it look suspicious?'

'Fine. I'll go with Rosie. She's finished school now and it will make it look like a normal visit from friends.'

Isobel thought about it. She had taken Greg a cake. It was perfectly reasonable that Ryan and his family might call in too. And Ryan was smart enough to be careful, or at least she hoped he was.

36

THE SHAME GAME:
A TRUE CRIME DOCUMENTARY

Episode 2 of 3 - The Play

INT - BOB ADAMS'S LOUNGE - DAYTIME

VOICE (O.S.)

Can you tell us about that day
then, please, Bob?

BOB ADAMS closes his eyes and adjusts his
position on the floral sofa.

TEXT on the screen: BOB ADAMS. FARM WORKER
WHO DISCOVERED AUDREY RAYE AT THE ROADSIDE.

BOB

I don't like to think about it. It
wasn't a nice thing to come across.
I remember it was dark. There'd

been an emergency at work, so the
boss had called me out and I was
driving along Common Holme Lane and
me car lights caught something in
the road. I thought it was a carpet
at first, sommat fly-tippers had
dumped there, but . . .

                VOICE (O.S.)

You saved her life.

                BOB

What there was of it. Sylvia –
that's her mum – had a terrible
time. Audrey was her world
and she had to have operation
after operation then all that
physiotherapy. It took both their
lives away.

            –   VOICE (O.S.)

Did you see anything at the time
that made you suspect who was
responsible?

                BOB

Nope. Not a thing. And I should
'ave. I should 'ave seen it clear
as day. But I didn't. They were
clever, see. Very clever. Makes
you wonder about folks.

37

RYAN

Tuesday, 9.30 a.m.
3 days, 6 hours left

Ryan had expected his daughter to say she didn't want to come along to see Greg, so he was surprised to find her up, dressed and eating cereal at 8 a.m.

'I just need to bring Ethan's car seat in for Camille – she's taking one of his friends out to the park with them today.'

Rosie nodded, her mouth full of Shreddies.

Ryan exited the house and nearly jumped out of his skin.

Toby Phillips was standing on the pavement opposite the end of Ryan's drive. He had his bike with him but had dismounted.

'All right?' he said, continuing to stare at Ryan.

Ryan walked towards him. 'What are you doing here?'

'Just passing by. Checking out where our lad keeps disappearing off to.'

'He's not here now.'

'Aye. I know. He'll be in his pit 'til lunchtime.' Toby made no move to leave.

Ryan tried to gauge what was really going on. He searched

Toby's face for clues: a look of smugness or satisfaction at having dropped a bomb on Ryan's world.

'Funny, them being a couple.'

Ryan shrugged. 'Why are you here again?'

Toby placed his left foot onto his pedal and pushed his bike into motion, swinging his other leg over and bouncing into his seat as he went. 'Nice to see you, Ry.'

Ryan watched him ride away, fighting the urge to chase after him and drag him to the ground.

Rosie insisted they stop at the Co-op on their way to Greg's new house. She wanted to buy him a box of liquorice allsorts. 'Uncle Greg's favourites,' she said by way of explanation.

Ryan thought about Toby's little visit as he waited. Ryan hadn't seen the guy in years, despite the fact they lived in the same town, and now his son was dating Rosie and Toby was watching their house early in the morning. Maybe he should mention it to Greg, but then he remembered Isobel's warning. They couldn't risk Greg knowing about the blackmail. It wasn't only his reputation on the line now, it was Izzy's too, and maybe even Mandy's.

He'd nearly asked Isobel last night about Mandy's brother Jim and Toby Phillips's sister breaking up because of an affair with one of Mandy's friends, but it felt like petty gossip in light of everything else they were facing.

Greg was outside pulling weeds out of the garden path when they arrived at the neat, semi-detached new build. He raised a hand as they parked. Ryan noted the man had aged since they'd last seen each other a few months earlier. Was that down to the separation or Mandy's death, he wondered.

'Well, that's just lovely, thank you,' Greg said when Rosie handed him the box of sweets, and if Ryan wasn't mistaken, the policeman's eyes became a little glassy.

'You're welcome. I wanted you to know I was thinking of you.'

Greg placed a hand on Rosie's upper arm. He wasn't a hugger, so this was a big gesture.

In the kitchen, Ryan leaned against the counter opposite where Greg stood as Rosie looked at a few pictures and cards stuck to the fridge without making it obvious that she was snooping. Ryan could see one photo of Greg with a woman, presumably the new girlfriend.

'Looks like the funeral will be a week on Thursday at the crematorium, two o'clock. Mandy didn't want anything religious.' Greg spoke quickly, as if he needed to get the information out and dealt with.

'Izzy and I thought we'd make a slideshow of pictures, or print a load out and stick them to some boards, if that's OK with you?' said Ryan.

'Sure. Jim's organizing the wake, so speak to him about it.'

'Izzy was saying Mandy had some lovely photos on her phone of her with the wider family. Would it be possible to get hold of them, do you think?'

'Well, her phone was destroyed, but I expect they'll be backed up on her laptop or in the cloud. Ask Jim about that, too. He has a key to her place.'

Ryan said he would do so. As Shame@pm.me was contacting them via text message, there was a good chance anything they'd sent Mandy would have uploaded on to her laptop or iPad.

'Actually, Rosie, I was going to ask you how you'd feel about reading a poem at the funeral? It's one Mandy has loved since she was a girl and as you were so special to her . . . No pressure, though. Have a think about it,' said Greg.

Rosie looked at her dad before she said, 'Maybe. Can you send it to me?'

Ryan smiled and nodded at his daughter. Mandy had been Rosie's godmother and she'd taken the role seriously from the start. She'd never missed a birthday and had always been on hand to babysit or take Rosie out for the day. Even when she and Greg were struggling with not having their own family, she had never wavered in the attention she gave to Rosie. Once, when Ryan had been grumpy about the fact Mandy remained friendly with Steph, she had told him, 'I know you guys don't get on, but it's important for Rosie to see that someone else likes both of her parents. That way she's not caught in that tug of love all alone.' That's the kind of godmother Mandy was. Rosie was her priority.

The back door to the kitchen opened and a woman wearing running clothes stepped in. She looked a little startled to see them.

'I thought you were doing a long one?' Greg said.

The woman removed her earphones as Greg filled a glass of water.

'That was the plan, but I've been called into work.' She took the water and drank half of it in one go.

'This is Ryan and his daughter, Rosie. Ryan is an old friend of Mandy's, and Rosie is her goddaughter.'

'Oh, that'll explain my burning ears.' She looked at Ryan and her gaze was steady. 'Sorry about your friend. She wasn't making life easy for us, but it's a horrible thing to happen . . . Anyway, I'm off for a shower.' She placed the glass in the sink.

'Ro, can I talk to Greg alone for a sec?' Ryan said. Rosie raised her eyebrows but made her way into the hall, taking her phone from her pocket as she went. 'What's all that about?' asked Ryan, when both women were out of earshot.

'Mandy was finding it hard to come to terms with Lucy and me. She'd been stirring up trouble for a while.' Greg lowered his voice a little, glancing towards the hall. 'Turning up at work to confront Lucy, sending silly messages, you know the kind of thing. Before we moved in here, she even climbed into the boot of my car so she could find out where Lucy lived. I kept hoping she would find a way to move on with her own life, but for whatever reason she couldn't, and it was starting to get out of hand.'

Ryan tried not to show any judgement on his face. He had no right, given that he had ended his relationship with Steph when Rosie was so young, but it still stung to hear Greg's indifference to Mandy's suffering. She was clearly finding it hard to move on because she was consumed with jealousy. He'd had no idea Mandy had been struggling to this extent, and he wondered if Isobel or Steph had. One thing he did feel sure of was that despite the new girlfriend's words, the woman was probably secretly happy that Mandy was now out of the picture.

Ultimately, though, that was Greg's personal business, and Mandy's death left him another step removed from that. He saw the chance to change the subject.

'Tell you what, I wanted to ask you about something from a professional point of view. Did you ever have any dealings with the Audrey Raye investigation? She was found injured years ago in Ilkley, and it's something of a mystery what might have happened to her. I was listening to a podcast about it.'

'I didn't know you were a true crime fan.'

'Oh, no, I'm not. I just bumped into the woman herself recently and was intrigued about what had happened to her. Have you ever heard of the case?'

'Sure. Mandy mentioned it a few times. I don't think there was any mystery, though. It was a straightforward hit and run from what I heard. It happened near her family farm.'

Ryan tightened his hold on the edge of the kitchen counter.

Location, location, location.

'Mandy talked about it?'

Greg widened his stance and folded his arms. 'You guys went to school with Audrey, didn't you? Mandy used to take her a birthday cake every year, up to the residential home.'

Suddenly, Ryan could feel the sun's rays burning the back of his head through the window behind him. Audrey Raye had been four years above them in school. She wasn't Mandy's friend. So why would Mandy be taking her cake every year? Was it out of sympathy, or something else?

Someone is hiding something that you really need to know.

'Dad, are you OK?' Rosie had stepped back in from the hall. *How much had she heard?*

'I was wondering the same,' said Greg.

Please be wrong, please be wrong, please be wrong.

'Can I get a glass of water, please? I think I need to move away from this window.' Should he tell Greg that Mandy and Audrey had not been friends at school, that as far as he was aware they didn't even know each other? Ryan wasn't sure what that would achieve, other than providing more reason for Greg and his girlfriend to look down on Mandy. He could imagine their conversation later. *How odd that Mandy pretended to be that poor woman's friend. That's weird, right?*

'That's really thoughtful of Aunt Mandy, to bake a cake every year,' said Rosie.

'She was often kinder to others than herself,' Greg replied, handing Ryan some water.

'I didn't know she used to do that,' said Ryan.

Greg's steely gaze landed on Ryan for a long moment and then he said, 'Everyone has their secrets.'

'Never a truer word said,' chimed in the new girlfriend as she came back in, dressed in dark trousers and a white blouse with her wet hair neatly wrapped in a bun. 'Everyone is guilty of something. Or maybe that's just the cynical coppers in us, aye babe?' She planted a kiss on Greg's lips.

Ryan felt like the room was closing in. Had Greg known something about Mandy and decided to use it against her when she wouldn't stop hassling his new lover? Is that what the 'everyone has their secrets' comment was about? Greg had gone from being the reliable family man to the adulterer. Perhaps he wanted Mandy to share some of his shame. Ryan knew how angry and irrational a relationship breakup can make you, but would the career policeman do such a thing? Surely not. It was a crazy idea. And why would he dig up dirt on her friends? Ryan and Isobel had never done anything to Greg. Unless Greg was simply using them as cover, so he could attack Mandy in a way that didn't place any suspicion on him as the ex-husband.

Ryan became aware of Greg and the new girlfriend watching him closely. He must look like shit – sweating, mind racing, eyes wide.

He thanked Greg for having them and said they'd see him at the funeral, then he got out of there as quick as he could.

38

ROSIE

Tuesday, 10.30 a.m.

'Well done, Dad, that was really sensitive – bringing up a car accident when that's how Aunt Mandy died.' *And great job sending me out the room first – that kitchen door? Totally soundproof.*

'I shouldn't have come. She said I shouldn't have come. I shouldn't have come,' her dad said under his breath.

Rosie looked out of the passenger window at the fields of sheep. What was going on with him? Why was he so obsessed with this Audrey Raye accident? He'd been asking Aunt Annie about it, and now Uncle Greg.

And then there was the weird conversation she'd heard between him and Isobel last night. She'd pretended to be listening to music as she could tell they were talking about something important, because they were sitting so close and speaking so quietly. She'd heard them mention a BBC article her dad had been sent about something bad he'd done, and the fact Isobel and Mandy had received one too. When Aunt Isobel had suggested this might have made Aunt Mandy step into the road on purpose, she had looked over at Rosie, who made a point of nodding her head along to an imaginary beat. Rosie had then heard Isobel say,

'Someone is targeting us all,' and 'Is that why you're asking about Audrey Raye?'

Who would target her dad, Isobel and Mandy? They weren't people with enemies. She knew her mum was no fan of her dad, but she didn't *hate* him. In fact, Rosie suspected she might still be in love with him. On the morning before her dad had married Camille, Rosie had heard her mum sobbing through the bathroom door. She'd never do anything to deliberately hurt him.

Rosie wiped away her own tears as she thought about Aunt Mandy stepping into the road on purpose. Why would she do that? Rosie thought of that Lucy woman kissing Uncle Greg just now. She had needed to look away. As a child, she used to fantasize about what life would be like if her mum and dad loved each other as much as Aunt Mandy and Uncle Greg did.

Adults can be such idiots.

When they got back, her dad headed out on his bike, so Rosie did the same, riding over to her grandparents' house via the trails at the bottom of Ilkley Moor. It was too hot to ride for very long. She was meeting Gus later, but wanted to speak to her nanna first.

'I don't like the idea of you out riding those hills all alone,' Nanna Felicity said as Rosie placed her helmet and gloves on the garden bench and drank a large glass of fridge-cold water.

'I'm fine, Nanna. I'm pretty good on a bike.'

'Oh, I don't doubt that. It's the other idiots out in the world I worry about. Don't you have a friend you can ride with?'

'Nan, we live in a spa town. I'm perfectly safe.'

'Hmmm.' Her nan was clearly not convinced. Rosie watched her neaten the gloves and helmet on the seat next to her.

'Can I ask your advice?'

'Any time, sweetheart.'

'It's about Dad. He's been acting really strange the last few days. I know he's sad about Mandy but he's also obsessing about something. He's kind of distracted and always buried in his laptop or his phone.'

'Well, he does have a busy job and that can be stressful.'

'I s'pose. It's just . . . we went to visit Uncle Greg this morning, and Dad asked him all these inappropriate questions. It wasn't like him at all.'

'Oh, how is Greg?'

'I met his new girlfriend.'

Nanna tutted and shook her head.

'But . . . he was OK, I think.'

'And what was your dad asking?'

'Have you heard of Audrey Raye?'

'Oh yes. There's another poor girl. She was hit by a car, they say.'

'I know, and Dad was asking Greg about her. Don't you think that's off? Like, insensitive, considering Mandy?'

Felicity watched her husband pass by with a watering can, on his way to see to his tomatoes in the greenhouse. 'Sometimes, when something bad happens, it reminds people of other bad things. I'm sure your dad didn't mean any harm. Was Audrey a friend of his too?'

'No. Dad doesn't seem to have known her at all. He was asking Greg about her accident like he was trying to find out what happened to her. He said he'd listened to a podcast and was just interested, but Dad never listens to true crime stuff. Camille loves it but he always says it's too depressing.'

'You're a good girl, Rosie, worrying about your dad, but he's a grown man. He's grieving and that can make people act out of character. In my experience, when you're going through a bad time having people close to you looking out for you makes a big difference. If you want to help, make him an extra few cups of tea, ask him if he's OK, that kind of thing.'

Rosie and her nan sat for a while in peaceful silence. She didn't know if saying the next thing would make her sound dramatic, but she really needed someone else's take on what she'd heard.

'Isobel said someone was targeting her and Dad, and that this person may have caused Mandy to step into the road on purpose.'

'Oh, Rosie, I'm not sure people should be saying such things about poor Mandy.'

'I know, but what if it's true?'

Her nanna looked at her for a long moment. 'Do you want me to have a word with your dad? We always got on well, so I could try. If something's upsetting him he might not want to tell you.'

'I don't know. He might be mad at me for telling you.'

'True. Look, whatever goes on between your mum and dad, I have a lot of time for your father and I know he wouldn't want you worrying about him. So, let me speak to him for you. I promise I'll be subtle.'

39

PAUL

Tuesday, 10.30 a.m.
3 days, 5 hours left

'Do it,' Vanessa had said when he'd told her about the ultimatum.

Her reasoning was that Ryan's secret would only affect Ryan, whereas if Paul's came out it would undermine justice. There were a fair few people he had successfully put away for rape, murder and organized crime who would have justifiable cause to request an appeal if his past came to light. Then there were others, guilty people who he'd defended unsuccessfully, who could argue he had not represented them fairly. They could all be released or have their sentences reduced. To Vanessa, this was an unthinkable consequence for the victims, their families and society as a whole. She made a compelling case.

But he had no evidence Ryan had cheated, and he believed in the innocent until proven guilty principle. So, after a restless night's sleep, he had sent a text.

I need proof. What evidence is there that Ryan Fallon cheated?

It's your job to find out, Paul.
But remember, the clock is ticking. 3 days to go.

'Oh, I have had enough of this,' Paul said to his empty office. He would get the proof he needed, but he also needed to find out who this bastard was while he was at it. He wasn't being pushed around by some lowlife who took pleasure in judging others. He'd read back through the posts on @BeAshamed and found them stomach-churningly petty and vindictive. Pictures had been posted of people who'd apparently affronted this guy with nothing worse than poor service or incompetent parking. *I don't see a disabled badge, Mrs Land Rover Discovery* was one such post, from what looked to be a supermarket car park. Such badges were only technically intended for on-street parking, but that wasn't what riled Paul the most. It was the stream of inane drivel that followed from idiots who failed to engage their brains and consider if there might be a reason for this action. That they didn't know this woman, or her life, or her health or the stresses she may be under.

Paul was by no means a bleeding-heart liberal. He knew there were bad people doing bad things in the world and he believed they should be justly punished. But you had to have the facts – all the facts – before you had the right to tell someone else they should be ashamed.

He took a stack of Post-it notes from the desk drawer and moved the large print of David Hockney's *Salts Mill* down to clear space on the wall. Then he got to work. On the green Post-its he started to write everything he knew about Ryan's cycling career, including people he might be able to contact for any insights on potential doping, and on the yellow ones he noted what he already knew about @BeAshamed. Then he stuck them all on the wall in two neat columns, and stepped back.

The yellow notes included the fact this person had also targeted Isobel and most likely Mandy and Ryan as well. If Paul had been given Ryan to expose, and Isobel was tasked with exposing Paul, it made sense that Ryan was in this too. So, @BeAshamed must be someone they all had in common. And if what Paul was guilty of was any indication, it was someone who'd been in their lives for a long time. He figured this because he had been in his twenties when he had been a regular at the Royal Oak, so unless someone was really very proficient at research, it made sense that they had known him back then and seen or heard something. He paused and thought about that. They had all grown up in the same town and now lived within half an hour of it. That provided a vast suspect list, from schoolmates to families to any resident of Ilkley who for one reason or another had taken against him and his friends.

He had to consider the why. That was where the answer would be. Was it jealousy, because they had all done pretty well? He had worked on some high-profile cases, both Mandy and Ryan had experienced some fame and notoriety, and Isobel must be fairly well known locally as a senior doctor. Or was it more than that? Had they done something together which had pissed someone off?

40

ISOBEL

Tuesday, 12.30 p.m.
3 days, 3 hours left

The house was quiet when she arrived home. Annie had taken Joshua over to her parents' in York for the day and Isobel was relieved. She was finding it hard to look her wife in the eye, knowing what the truth might do to their family.

She opened the fridge, removed the half bottle of white wine Annie had placed there the night before, and poured herself a generous glass. This had become so much bigger than she'd feared. Whoever was doing this was some anonymous blackmailer who was after her friends too. How do you fight that? What can you do to stop someone from telling true stories about you? Where was the crime? She took a long drink, hoping for escape.

Ryan had called earlier to say Greg had advised him to get the keys for Mandy's house from her brother. He'd sounded shaken, and she wondered if being so close to Greg's grief had upset him more than he'd expected. Sometimes she took for granted the fact she was used to being around grieving people. Like anything in life, the more you're exposed to something, the less impact it has. It becomes normal. By comparison, Ryan had led a charmed life.

He'd ridden bikes well enough to win medals and now helped children to embrace sport. It was like he lived in Disneyland while her world was a misery memoir. Not that she was bitter. She wouldn't want anyone to find grief normal or easy to deal with.

Paul had also tried to call her earlier, but not left a message, so once Isobel had finished her wine, she called him back.

'I wondered if you'd had any success with your cryptic question?' he said on answering.

Isobel filled him in on the fact that Ryan had received a fake BBC news broadcast and that he was heading over to Mandy's house to see if there was any evidence on her computer that she had been targeted too.

Paul was quiet for a moment before speaking again, and when he did his voice sounded thick with emotion. 'So does Ryan have a cryptic question?'

She told him about Audrey Raye and the enquiries Ryan had already made. 'I mean, it's a mystery that no one has solved for years so I'm not sure he's got much chance of answering it. I think the questions are impossible to answer – this person is taunting us and has no intention of giving us a way out.'

'Did Ryan have any thoughts on who might be behind it?'

'No. He wanted to sound out Greg but I said it was too risky.'

'God no. He doesn't want to do that. Weren't you told no police?'

'Yes, I stressed that. It's OK, he agreed not to say anything.'

'Good. I don't think you should do anything rash with this and I think you might be right about your questions. I wouldn't spend too much time on trying to work them out. It would make more sense to think about who might be doing this and why. Could you start making a list maybe?'

Isobel's work pager began to bleep. It appeared her afternoon off was about to be cancelled. She shouldn't have had that wine.

'Sorry, Paul. I've got to go.'

Isobel hung up and dialled the number for work. She had misjudged Paul yesterday and she felt bad about that. Paul understood the criminal mind as well as any police officer, perhaps even better. Having him in their corner was a huge asset. It made her feel like there was a chance she might get through this after all.

41

RYAN

Tuesday, 12.45 p.m.
3 days, 2¾ hours left

On arriving home after visiting Greg, Ryan had taken his bike out for a spin. He'd made many a life decision out on the hills while feeling the burn, so it felt natural to consider what he'd learned about Mandy and Audrey Raye this way.

He had checked the date of Audrey's accident. It had been on 28 November 2006, near the end of his first term at university. He couldn't recall exactly when Mandy had dropped out of her course. Had it been in her first year or later? He knew it was after her mum's stroke and that she'd come home to help her dad, but he had no idea when that had happened. Her mum had lived a few years longer, but had been wheelchair-bound and unable to speak.

He rode over the huge cow painted on to a steep section of road near the Cow and Calf rocks. It had been done when Yorkshire had hosted the Grand Départ for the 2014 Tour de France. He lost himself in a few minutes' reminiscence of that day. People often asked him about his stage win, but to him, racing a Grand Tour on roads he'd grown up riding had been the most memorable day of his career. Despite fellow Brit Chris Froome being the reigning champion and pre-race favourite, Ryan had been as big an attraction that day. By then, just a couple of years after his stage win, he knew he wasn't going to be in the mix for the big titles. In some ways, that day was the pinnacle. Not for the first time, the thought made him sad, and he turned his thoughts back to the matter in hand. He tried to imagine what it must have been like for Mandy's dad when his wife had her stroke. His life had changed for ever in the blink of an eye.

Something he'd forgotten came back to him. As with many a farmer's child, Mandy had been the first of their group to pass her test, and then to have her own car. Her dad had done up one of the farm workers' old Vauxhall Novas for her and in the summer before they all left for uni they had piled into it for trips out to Bolton Abbey and Whitby. What had happened to that Nova? And why could he not remember Mandy ever driving it again after that summer?

A scenario played out in his mind, one where Mandy was driving home on the night Audrey Raye was walking along the dark lane near to the Rogers' family farm. Perhaps she'd been driving a little too fast, or not paying attention? None of them had been particularly skilled drivers at that point. And then it would have been so easy to make it back to the farm unseen . . . Could that have contributed to Mandy dropping out of uni and dumping Paul? Ryan had been so wrapped up in his training, he'd paid little attention to Mandy's woes. He recalled hearing about her mum being sick and being told she had dropped out. He also recalled the many long, ranting phone calls from Paul in the weeks and months after Mandy dumped him, but he couldn't recall if these things all happened at the same time.

If she had been the driver who hit Audrey, she would have been in shock and traumatized by the guilt, but why hadn't she gone to the police? She was a good person, not someone who would cover up a crime. Plus, she'd gone on to marry a policeman. He had to be wrong.

But he knew there was one other factor that supported his theory. If Mandy had been hiding such an awful secret all her adult life, and then someone had sent her one of those articles saying everyone now knew all about it, that might very well cause her to step into a busy road.

Ryan pulled into a small layby and took a few deep breaths. The road ahead snaked away from him; a smooth tarmac racetrack slicing its way through the green fields. For a few moments he held his phone in his hand, wanting to delay the whole thing and live with the reassuring comfort of not knowing for sure. Then he opened his messages and selected Shame@pm.me. He knew this was the quickest way of finding out if he was right. Which he really hoped he wasn't.

Did Mandy Coulters hurt Audrey Raye?

'Hi Dad, I was making us a sandwich. Do you want one?' Rosie was buttering bread. On the table in front of her she had cheese, ham and a jar of pickle. At her side stood Gus Phillips, wearing a North Face T-shirt and board shorts.

'Is Camille here?'

'No. She's taken Ethan to soft play.'

Ryan didn't like the idea of Rosie being alone here with her boyfriend, but he would speak to her about that later. He didn't want to embarrass her.

'Is your dad all right?' Ryan said to Gus. The lad didn't look much like his father. He was slimmer and blonder and lacked the Toby Phillips swagger.

'He's good, thanks. He told me to ask you why you chose to road cycle over doing the real thing? His words, not mine!'

'Did he now? Has he got himself a motor on his mountain

bike yet?' Ryan did his best to smile even though the banter felt forced.

Rosie spoke to Gus. 'Oh yeah, I found out yesterday that Dad actually started out mountain biking with your dad.'

'Yeah, I know.'

'Do you? Why didn't you say?'

Gus shrugged and smiled at Rosie but avoided looking Ryan's way.

'Rosie tells me your dad knew my friend Mandy, too? She was Rosie's godmother.' If he was right about Mandy and Audrey Raye, the fact Mandy's brother had cheated on Toby's little sister might be significant. Did he hold a grudge against her too? Rosie had said something about Jimmy cheating with one of Mandy's friends. Ryan considered the idea that this could have been Isobel. He knew she'd had a few heterosexual encounters before coming out. Could Jimmy have been one? Was that a shameful little secret Izzy and Mandy had kept between themselves?

'Yeah, sorry to hear about her. Rosie said she was lovely.'

'Did you want a sandwich?' said Rosie, clearly keen to change the subject. 'Or a cup of tea?'

Ryan shook his head. Truth be told, he hadn't been able to face food since Friday. He ate because his body needed fuel, not because he wanted to. 'We loved her very much and we'll miss her.' Ryan swallowed the lump in his throat. Rosie came around the table to hug him as a text arrived.

You are correct.

But do you know how?

Ryan tilted his head up to the ceiling and closed his eyes. How had Mandy lived with it? She had always been the most fun-loving and light-hearted member of their group, and yet she hid

153

this dark secret. After a moment or two, he typed a reply that broke his heart.

She was driving the car.

Ryan wondered how he would have reacted if Mandy had ever confided in him. No doubt he'd have advised her to confess, if only for her own mental health. He knew from personal experience that carrying guilt was a heavy burden, and he'd not left someone with life-changing injuries.

Who the hell had uncovered this? Toby Phillips? Greg and his new woman? He could see how the latter might be more likely; Greg might have even known of Mandy's involvement all along. Would he have kept something like that to himself? The man was conservative with a small c. There were no grey areas in Greg's world view. Doing wrong was doing wrong. Or so Ryan had thought. But maybe that was only in a legal sense; perhaps he was more sanguine about moral wrongdoings, hence his affair. And if he had kept her secret and then she'd done everything she could to ruin his new life, would he have used it against her?

A message pinged on his phone.

If you want your secret to stay hidden, Ryan, you need to tell the world what Mandy did.

You need to ruin her memory.

Welcome to the Shame Game.

Ryan swore, causing Rosie to exclaim, 'Dad!'
'Sorry, Ro.'
He stared at the message.
Welcome to the Shame Game. It made him feel sick that someone thought this was a game, as if there was fun to be had.

42

PAUL

Tuesday, 2.30 p.m.
3 days, 1 hour left

Paul had printed off the statistics page for Ryan from procycling-stats.com. It displayed a bar chart of points earned each year from 2000 to the present day, along with the number of wins and race days. Ryan's first points in senior races came in 2009, and showed a clear and distinct peak in performance in 2012, when Ryan had earned double the points he'd gained in both the year post and the year prior. He had also ridden in sixteen more races that year. Looking at the detail below, Paul saw that the bulk of the points in 2012 had come from Ryan's Tour de France stage win, an achievement that appeared even more stark considering he had dropped out of his only previous Grand Tour, the 2011 Giro d'Italia, due to a bad crash.

It was looking highly likely that some performance enhancement might have gone on, but it was by no means proof. To get that, he'd need to speak to someone who'd been there. He knew Lance Armstrong's sports masseuse had been critical in outing him, so perhaps there was someone like that he could find. Someone who'd travelled with the team and witnessed all that occurred.

A medic would be ideal, because they would have been monitoring bloods.

And if he got that evidence. What was he going to do?

Paul paced across the office. This was how he prepared for all his court battles, and this might just be the fight of his life.

If he was to expose Ryan, how would he do it? Posting something on social media didn't feel significant enough. He didn't have a huge number of followers, so chances were it would do nothing more than raise eyebrows among his friends and colleagues. He could tag in @BeAshamed and immediately prove to the blackmailer that he had seen this through. They might well then retweet it to all their thousands of followers, effectively destroying his friendship with Ryan once and for all. But that felt weak and petty. If he was going to retain any personal integrity, he would have to do it in such a way that it looked well-meaning. He could go to the press with his concerns over Ryan working with children, given his history with drugs. As a well-regarded barrister, his account would surely attract some press attention. Could he justify that? Ryan and Camille would be furious, as would Ryan's parents. They were such a huge part of his life and this would undoubtedly destroy all those relationships. He had a slim chance of winning Isobel round. She was all about kids since fostering Joshua, so he could plead his case for wanting to protect them. Maybe he could use Annie? If he went to her with the story and convinced her to help him to expose Ryan, that would tie her and Isobel into the whole thing.

Rosie was the real kicker. She'd hate him for sure and that would hurt. But maybe, in time, he could win back her trust. Make her see that his heart was in the right place, argue that he was simply doing the right thing. Could he live with that?

He thought about Vanessa's ultimatum. If his past came out, she'd walk out. The divorce lawyer would be on speed dial. Losing his friends might be the price he had to pay for saving his marriage. After losing Mandy, he wasn't sure he could cope with losing Ness too. He wasn't good on his own.

And what if he couldn't find the evidence to prove Ryan's guilt? Would he be willing to accuse Ryan anyway to save his own skin? He knew the answer. True or not, if the idea that Ryan had doped came out, his career would be terminally damaged. His TV work as a cycling pundit would be done and his charity – which relied on his reputational brand – would either fold or oust him. It would be financially and personally devastating for the Fallon family. But that was as far as the wreckage would go. One family.

If Paul's past came out there would be two dire consequences. The immediate impact would be similar to what he would be inflicting on Ryan. Loss of reputation, loss of job, chance of being disbarred, but then, as Vanessa had said, the ripples would go wider. Serious criminals he had put away, or some he'd unsuccessfully defended, would be instructing their legal teams to appeal on the basis of his potentially flawed or prejudicial representation. Some might win and have their sentences lessened or, God forbid, they'd walk free. What impact might that have on the victims and their families? It was huge. And that's before he even started to think about Kyle Renton and the people who might be pissed off if Renton's claims of an unfair trial were finally substantiated.

And so exposing Ryan was a given. He'd have to do it, proof or not.

He did need to consider the chance Isobel might uncover his secret and choose to expose him. That might need some management. He knew she was, so far, totally off track with her interpretation of the question she'd been given. He just had to make sure she continued down that wrong route.

On the wall to the left, Ryan, Mandy and Isobel's names were written on separate sticky notes. Under each, on more sticky notes, Paul had listed the relationships they'd had, jobs they'd done, places they'd lived; everything he could think of that might give him some insight into what they might have done or who they might have upset. He had already added a note under Isobel's name saying, 'Indiscretion at work years ago', and now he added 'Doped @ TDF', under Ryan's. Then he pressed his fingers against the question Ryan had been set: Who hurt Audrey Raye? The answer to this was something he was struggling to think about. He hadn't written his own list up because he didn't want Vanessa thinking too hard about the whole thing. She was too intelligent and curious for him to risk her delving too deeply into his past.

Paul began pacing again. He did have one other option, of course. Find the bastard who was doing this and stop it at its source.

43

ISOBEL

Tuesday, 3.30 p.m.
3 days left

The neonatal unit was busy. It cared for some of the sickest, smallest and most vulnerable babies in the region. On the unit today there were a set of premature twins born that morning who were both experiencing breathing difficulties due to their lungs being unprepared for life outside the womb. Isobel had been working closely with the registrar to manage their care, as well as assisting with the planned delivery of a baby with a congenital heart condition. The job was stressful, but she viewed the stress as her penance for the mistake she had made. After that day, she had dedicated her life to making amends. It was a choice that became all the more challenging when she discovered that she could not bear children herself. But she would do anything to stay. The idea that she could be banished from this world, and that her ability to help these babies and their families would be taken away, was a whole new kind of hell. She couldn't let herself think too long about it.

In twenty minutes, she was due to meet the CMO to discuss

their impending review of the cardiac unit. She grabbed a can of Coke from the vending machine knowing she needed energy to get through the day. In the consultants' lounge, she took out her phone and dialled a number she had not used for over five years. Paul was right. They needed to work out who was doing this to them.

'Hello?' His voice was just as she remembered, and Isobel immediately felt the anger bubble within her.

'It's Isobel. I need to ask you a question about what happened at Harrogate.'

The man said nothing for a long time. 'I don't know what you're talking about.'

'Yes you do, Jed. I just need to know if you ever told anyone, because someone is threatening to destroy my career.'

'I'm sorry. I can't help you, Isobel.'

She stared at her phone not quite believing he had hung up, but then what had she expected, really? He had never been man enough to own up to what they had done. What made her think he would start now? He had told her it was not their fault, that these things happen, that even if she'd responded to that first bleep the outcome would have been the same. She'd revered him so much, as her more experienced registrar, that she believed him.

He was some big-shot plastic surgeon now, having given up on paediatrics not long after it all happened. She felt embarrassed about having admired a man who turned out to be such a big arse of a disappointment.

The memories from that day intruded into her thoughts again, but this time his smug face was there too. She should have ignored him and done the right thing. She should have seen him for what he was. She shouldn't have put herself first.

She picked up the can of Coke but then quickly placed it down because her right hand was shaking. She rubbed the palm with the fingers of her left hand, pushing deep into the muscle in an effort to stave off the tremors, but they wouldn't stop. It was beyond her control. This was her comeuppance. Her karma. And she knew she deserved every painful, humiliating thing that was coming.

44

RYAN

Tuesday, 4 p.m.
2 days, 23½ hours left

Mandy's ground-floor apartment was in a converted psychiatric hospital a few miles away from Ilkley, in the neighbouring village of Menston. Ryan had never visited Mandy here. She and Greg used to live in a large detached property a few miles away and he wondered if she'd felt embarrassed about downsizing to a ground-floor flat. He hoped not. He and Camille would never have judged her.

Ryan turned on to a long straight road that led up to the imposing main building with its central clocktower. Matching manicured gardens spread out either side of a wide gravel pathway. He passed two female runners who were moving at quite a pace but still managing to have an animated conversation which involved lots of hand gesturing. He envied the women for the normality of their days. They were not reeling from the shock of losing a life-long friend or scared that some sadistic arse was about to expose their most shameful secret.

Parking in the bay next to Mandy's, Ryan took a moment to steel himself. It felt odd to come here without her. He had collected the key from her brother, Jimmy, on the way, explaining again that he and Isobel wanted to retrieve some photos. He could tell Jimmy was not really listening. The guy looked like he'd not slept since receiving the news.

There was a faint smell of oriental spices when he opened the front door. The lounge was bright and warm thanks to two large windows, and Mandy had a couple of grey sofas, scattered with orange cushions, facing each other in front of a woodburning stove. Around the corner to the right was a small but neat kitchen. A mug and plate were still on the draining board and a cafetière was in the sink, filled with water. Ryan emptied it out and placed it next to the plate and mug. She had left it here to soak, thinking she would be back. The thought brought a lump to his throat.

Ryan opened the fridge. As always it was well stocked, as Mandy only ever cooked food from scratch. He searched the kitchen drawers until he found a stash of plastic bags, taking one and placing the meat and vegetables into it. He would hand it all over to Jimmy on his way back as he wasn't sure anyone else would be coming in here soon and he didn't want it going off and starting to smell. Maybe he could ask about Toby Phillips's sister and their break-up too. Or was that really damn insensitive?

On the notice board next to the fridge, he saw a photo of him, Mandy, Paul and Isobel in fancy dress. He took it off the board to look more closely. He had no recollection of the event. He was wearing a bushy blonde wig and swirly orange shirt, Paul was in an open neck white satin shirt and gold medallion, and the girls had flowered garlands around their heads and fake eyelashes. They looked young and they were laughing. Ryan popped the photo in his pocket. He wanted Izzy and Paul to see it.

Moving back into the hall, he found the bathroom and then Mandy's bedroom before coming to the office she had set up in the box room at the far end of the corridor. It didn't pass him by that the photo on her bedside table was from her and Greg's wedding day. He remembered that the black and white shot had taken pride of place on their mantelpiece when they were together. Once more, Ryan felt grief grip his chest. She had struggled with losing Greg more than he'd realized. She always said she was fine. She always kept laughing. But he could see now that this was all for their benefit.

He found her laptop in her desk drawer. It was a MacBook, which was good. Hopefully this meant her phone messages were backed up on it. He typed 'Julia0611' – her mum's name and birthday – in as her password. Jimmy had told him what it was.

Mandy's home page couldn't be more different from his own, which was organized into folders with everything arranged neatly on the right side of his screen. In contrast, Mandy had what looked like hundreds of documents packed on to her home screen. How did she make any sense of it? He noticed a folder called 'wedding photos' and wondered how often she had been tempted to open that in recent months.

He clicked on the speech bubble icon. A list of messages popped up and he selected the most recent. It was from Jimmy, and had a link to a funny meme about animals dressed up as chefs. He scanned the ones below, which looked like they were mainly phishing.

He turned his attention to her photos. He had set up an album called 'Mandy' on his phone and for the next twenty minutes he AirDropped any pictures he thought people would like to see. She was clearly a fan of the selfie hug. In pretty much every photograph, friends and family were laughing and hugging Mandy. Ryan paused on a few showing her with him and Camille at last year's Ilkley Food Festival. They had eaten jerk chicken burritos on the lawn near to the rugby club as they watched Ethan play.

Then they had run up to the closest coffee shop when the heavens opened; the four of them laughing as they went. He remembered that Greg hadn't been able to join them because he was working. Had that been the truth, or had he really been with his new girlfriend? Ryan had no doubt that these were the kinds of questions that would have tormented Mandy.

In a few of the most recent pictures he noted that Mandy's face was less rounded and he could see her collar bones protruding through her top. Steph had said something about Mandy suffering more than any of them knew, that they had all been too busy to notice, and he had put it down to his ex's typically dramatic nonsense. But she was right. He had certainly missed it.

He sat back in the chair and looked at the quote framed on the wall above the desk. *I don't trust anyone who doesn't laugh.*

Although he desperately wanted to tell Mandy to not do what she did, that the bad times would pass, on some level it was a relief to know that she wasn't in pain any more.

As he was closing the laptop, he noticed that Mandy's messages had refreshed and three new ones had appeared. The first was from Shame@pm.me, and had a link that led to the same 'website unavailable' page he had found when trying to go back and find his article. Isobel was right. Mandy had been targeted too. He tried not to think about the panic Mandy must have felt seeing the truth about her and Audrey Raye writ large. In a matter of minutes, she had decided she could not face it. The second text was from Jimmy, asking her to call him ASAP, which was received not long after her accident, and the last was received at midnight that same day. This one began with words Ryan recognized only too well. He opened the message and read down to the question Mandy never knew she'd been set.

WHO BROKE THEIR VOW IN THE WOODLANDS?

It made no sense to Ryan, so he photographed it to run by Isobel later.

The decision he needed to make churned his guts. Me or Mandy. That was his choice. There was no getting out of it. One of them would be shamed and he just had to decide who.

45

THE SHAME GAME:
A TRUE CRIME DOCUMENTARY

Episode 2 of 3 – The Play

EXT – COMMON HOLME LANE, ILKLEY –
DAYTIME

The camera zooms in on a blue sign attached
to a gap in the wooden fence, which reads
'Ilkley Golf Club, First Tee'. Then it moves
to a section of perfectly straight road
bordered on the left-hand side by a row of
densely packed conifer trees.

AUDIO plays of an historical news report
about a young woman who was found injured on
a country lane in Ilkley.

The camera drops down into the valley and
homes in on a farmhouse that sits next to
the River Wharf.

TEXT on the screen: MANDY COULTERS'S CHILDHOOD
HOME.

INT - ROGERS FAMILY FARM, ILKLEY - DAYTIME

Two men sit side by side on a grey sofa.
The older man is wearing a flat cap and
a checked shirt. The younger man wears a
similar shirt and has thick black hair with
wide sideburns.

> VOICE (O.S.)
>
> Can I ask what you were charged
> with, Alan?

> ALAN ROGERS
>
> Accessory after the fact.

The older man sits forward a little as he
speaks.

TEXT on the screen: ALAN AND JIMMY ROGERS.
FATHER AND BROTHER OF MANDY COULTERS.

> JIMMY ROGERS
>
> Dad did what he thought was best
> at the time.

> ALAN
>
> She was in such a state. I'd called
> her home because her mum had

had a stroke, she was upset and
distracted. I should have told her
to come the next day or sent Jimmy
to fetch 'er. It wasn't her fault
that young lass was dressed head
to foot in black, or that the road
'ad no street lamps.

VOICE (O.S.)

I think many people would
understand that it was an
accident, but why not report it?

ALAN

Well, she didn't know she'd hit a
person. I called my lad, Bob, to
come over. Said I needed him to
watch the farm while I went to sit
with Julia. I didn't say Mandy had
hit sommat but I knew he'd pass
by the spot and I was 'oping he'd
say it was a sheep or the likes,
but he never arrived. He called
from the hospital saying he'd
found a girl.

VOICE (O.S.)

How did Mandy react to that?

Jimmy looks at his dad as the old man
speaks.

ALAN

Well, I didn't tell her. She had
enough to worry about. We didn't
think her mum was going to pull
through at that point. I sent her
and Jimmy to the hospital and I
took her car to the scrapyard.

VOICE (O.S.)

So you got rid of the evidence?

Jimmy looks at the camera.

JIMMY

That's what accessory after the
fact means. Covering up a crime.

VOICE (O.S.)

When did Mandy find out?

ALAN

It was on the news the next day.
She was a bright lass, she worked
it out. She wanted to go to the
police, I want people to know
that. She was a good girl but
I told her I'd take care of it.
She wasn't to say or do anything.
Not yet.

JIMMY

Dad told me Mandy said that what
Dad had done stopped her from
coming forward. She knew he would
be in trouble and she couldn't
bear the idea of him being taken
away from Mum when Mum needed him
so much.

VOICE (O.S.)

Did you know about the accident,
Jimmy?

JIMMY

No. I would have told them both
they were idiots if I had, and
I'd have marched the pair of them
straight down to the station.

VOICE (O.S.)

Did Greg Coulters know that his
wife was involved in the accident?

Jimmy looks at his dad, who is staring
straight ahead.

ALAN

How would we know?

FADE TO BLACK

INT - WALTERS FAMILY HOME - DAYTIME

The back of a woman's body is briefly
seen in front of the petite blonde woman
in the chair. The blonde's wispy hair and
smattering of freckles give her an elfin
look but her eyes are sharp and intelligent.
Once the microphone is put right the
standing woman moves out of shot.

TEXT on the screen: ANNIE WALTERS, WIFE OF
ISOBEL WALTERS

Annie takes a sip of water and places the
glass down on the coffee table in front
of her.

                    VOICE (O.S.)

     You were friends with the group
     for many years.

                    ANNIE

     I loved them all. We had some
     cracking parties and they fed my
     people-watching tendencies well.
     They were vibrant and successful,
     flawed and fabulous. But I had
     no idea any of them had secrets
     and it's my job to know these
     things.

VOICE (O.S.)

Greg Coulters is reported to have
said it shows how little we really
know about our friends.

ANNIE

Is he? Well, I suppose he
would know.

VOICE (O.S.)

How do you mean?

ANNIE

I think I've probably said enough.

VOICE (O.S.)

Are you referencing his
extramarital affair?

ANNIE

Like I said. I've said enough.

There is a beat of silence before the
interviewer speaks again.

VOICE (O.S.)

Did you suspect he knew about
Mandy's involvement in Audrey
Raye's accident?

                    ANNIE

He said he didn't.

There is another long silence.

                 VOICE (O.S.)

Some people may find that hard to
believe.

                    ANNIE

Some people *did* find that hard
to believe. I mean, the first
thought I had when I found out
someone had dug up dirt on Isobel
and her friends was, *who has the*
wherewithal to do that? Who has
the skills to investigate people's
lives?

                 VOICE (O.S.)

You do.

Annie laughs.

                    ANNIE

Yes, but I was still friends with
everybody. I was trying to think
of people who had a reason to hate
them enough to hurt them.

46

I wish I could have seen your face when you realized the truth, Ryan. Were you appalled by Mandy's actions? Disappointed in her? Sad? How I would have loved to have seen the look in your eyes when it dawned on you.

I can still recall the moment I first suspected the truth. It was within weeks, maybe even days, of the incident. I remember it was Christmas, because the tree was up at the end of the Grove and the whole of Ilkley centre was decked in golden lights. The town really does do a classy festive season. I had been talking to a friend on the street, I don't recall who now, but they must have been boring me because I was more interested in the conversation Mandy and her dad were having with a man outside the butchers. It was about the girl that had been found by the golf club and this man was saying how awful it was, but I couldn't take my eyes off Mandy. Her whole body screamed 'Get me away from here!' Her pupils were like pin dots that kept jumping from one position to another and she was biting her thumbnail so hard I expected it to bleed at any second. The man was saying how he thought it was most likely the boyfriend who'd done it, as someone had heard them arguing, and I watched Mandy's dad take her hand as he said, 'Let's hope they put the whole thing to bed soon, aye,' and then he looked at Mandy and do you know what he said?

He said, 'It could have been much worse. At least she survived.' He was speaking only to Mandy, not to the man.

It was a fortuitous moment. If I hadn't been in Ilkley that day, I would have been in the dark about Mandy's crime like the rest of you. I like to think it was the universe handing me a gift. You see, it planted a seed in this fertile mind of mine. A seed that waited for the seasons to pass and the time to be right.

47

RYAN

Wednesday, 9.30 a.m.
2 days, 6 hours left

There were more people in the conference room than he had anticipated. Ryan took a deep breath. This was going to be rough.

A few hours earlier, he had woken Camille and said he needed to tell her something. He explained that someone was threatening to release an article accusing him of having doped when he won his stage of the Tour de France. This achievement was a great source of pride for Camille and her French family, so he quickly reassured her.

'I promise, when I won the stage I did it clean. But—'

'Oh no, Ryan?' Camille's hands went to her mouth.

'A year earlier, when I was training for the Giro d'Italia, I had a friend who was riding with another team and he introduced me to his doctor. The guy had a bit of a reputation for working with some of the best riders, so I was in awe. He told me I couldn't win without the drugs because everyone who wins takes them. He said I was holding myself back, that I had so much potential, and it would be a shame, blah, blah blah.'

'You didn't.'

'I was young and stupid and I figured trying it wouldn't be so bad. Who would ever know? But then, a few stages in, about a hundred k into the day's racing, I knew I'd messed up. I didn't feel right.'

'It made you sick?'

'Ha, no, quite the opposite. I felt good. Too good. My legs felt like they were someone else's and I had all this energy. I was moving up the field and I realized if I carried on like that, I was going to raise suspicion. I became paranoid that everyone knew. I was terrified they would do a blood test at the end and then it would all be over, so I rode into a high kerb on purpose. It threw me off my bike, damaged my shoulder and my elbow and I was out of the race.

'After that I never touched the stuff again. I swear. But I did chase that feeling. I wanted to feel that strong naturally, which was no easy task. I trained and trained. The team coach had to have a word at one point as I wasn't resting enough, or fuelling myself properly. But it worked. I did it and I won clean.'

'But the world won't believe that.'

'Sophie says my one chance of coming out of this with any of my reputation intact is to head it off. Tell my story first.'

'OK. But. What if this threat is just that? They don't have their facts correct so they can't have done any research. What if they want money because . . . we can give them money.'

'They don't want money.'

'How do you know? If you jump the knife you may ruin your chance of keeping all of this private.'

'It's jump the gun, babe, but it's not only me they've threatened. It's Isobel and Mandy too. Whoever is doing this wants to shame us for some reason.' He told her about the articles and subsequent messages they had all received. Now he knew that Isobel and Mandy had also been targeted, and that he had been given

Mandy's secret to uncover, it was obvious that whoever was doing this had a personal vendetta.

Camille swore in French. 'Did you say your threat came just before my party, the day that Mandy . . .'

Ryan nodded and watched a single tear roll from his wife's eye.

'And what about Paul?' she said.

'What about him?'

'Has he not been threatened?'

'No. Isobel has been talking to him about her situation and he hasn't had anything.'

'That's odd, don't you think? The three of you are threatened immediately before my party and then given an ultimatum at the end of it. A party Paul and Vanessa refused to come to.'

'They didn't refuse. Paul was working late on a case. Don't let your suspicions that they don't like you influence you on this. They love you, by the way.'

'Vanessa thinks I'm an airhead and Paul hates the fact that I am your person rather than him. These are the facts. You said to me when we got together that if I marry you, I marry your friends, because you are a gang. So why is Paul not targeted too? That's all I'm saying.'

'That's not all you're saying. You're implying he might be behind it. He's my best friend, Camille. He wouldn't do something like this because we're his friends and he has no reason to.'

'I thought I was your best friend.'

'Now you're being childish. I need to speak to Rosie.' Ryan stood up.

'Is there not another way to stop this?'

He looked at his wife. She had taken the news better than he'd expected. There had been no suggestion that she was so appalled by his confession, or the ramifications of it coming out, that she might not want to be with him any more.

'I don't think so. I need to own this, Camille. I'm determined to try and make the best of the situation. It's not the first mountain I've had to climb. It will be hard and painful and I'm really sorry for all of that, but I've never failed to reach the top before. There's no reason this should be any different.'

He had decided this was his only real course of action when looking through Mandy's photographs. She was universally loved by her friends and family. He couldn't taint their opinions of her by allowing the truth about Audrey Raye's accident to come out. Who would it benefit other than him? Audrey wouldn't understand well enough to feel any sense of justice and her mother had passed away. It would only act to smear Mandy's name and change how people thought of her. Ryan loved his friend too much to let that happen and so he had to take the hit.

He took a deep breath and knocked on Rosie's bedroom door.

'Ryan?' Camille met him in the hall as he was about to leave the house and straightened his tie. 'Good luck. We love you.'

'Thanks, babe.'

'And . . . I know you think I'm a crazy conspiracy theorist but if you speak to Isobel just ask her to be careful . . . with Paul.'

'That's enough, Camille. This is bad enough without you stirring up trouble.'

48

ROSIE

Wednesday, 10 a.m.

The first notification sounded about halfway through her dad's press conference. It was followed by another and then another. She didn't dare look. She was scared to see what her friends had to say.

Her dad had woken her up before he left and sat on the end of her bed.

'When I was cycling,' he said as she rubbed her eyes and yawned, 'I did something very stupid, something I shouldn't have done because I should have known better and it's something I've regretted ever since. And now I need to come clean because it's important to own up to things, especially if keeping it secret might hurt others.'

'What did you do?'

'I took a substance called EPO. It's medicine they developed for cancer patients which increases your red blood cells, making your body better at moving oxygen around.'

'So you doped?'

He looked surprised that she knew the terminology. 'I did. I'm sorry.'

She shrugged and then curled back under her duvet cover.

He told her about the press conference and what he was going to say. She didn't comment or look up at him again. He kissed the top of her head before leaving her room. 'Love you, Ro. I'm sorry.'

She refocused on her phone screen. The banner across the bottom of the BBC News report said, 'British cyclist and sports presenter, Ryan Fallon, confesses to doping in the 2011 Giro d'Italia'.

Rosie hugged her knees tighter to her chest as more notifications pinged on her phone.

Why had he done this?

49

PAUL

Wednesday, 10 a.m.
2 days, 5½ hours left

'*The Fallon Foundation are pleased to announce a new initiative focused on using sport to help young people who may be personally struggling with drugs or who have parents struggling with them. This is a cause close to my heart. As a professional cyclist in an era when doping was an inescapable reality of the sport, I saw how easy it was for people to be attracted to using them and how hard it then was to stop.*'

Paul turned up the volume on the news. Was Ryan about to do what he thought he was? He studied his friend's face. Ryan looked weird, like his facial muscles were out of place. His jaw was tense and his cheeks oddly puffed out, and then there was his top lip – it had become nothing more than a straight line above his teeth.

Ryan swallowed and his eyes flicked briefly away from the camera.

'*Indeed, I'm sorry to say I once participated in their use. I was encouraged to take erythropoietin, or EPO, prior to the 2011 Giro d'Italia and I stupidly agreed. I immediately regretted the decision and found it hard to focus. This inevitably contributed to the crash which caused me to drop out of the race.'*

Paul stared at the screen, not quite believing what he was hearing.

'I want to reassure my teammates from the time, the cycling fans who have supported me over the years, and my own friends and family that this was a one-off. I never touched EPO again nor did I take any other performance-enhancing substances at any point in my cycling career. I decided if I wanted to ride better I needed to work harder, and that's what I did.'

'Fuck! You total bastard,' Paul said realizing there was no way he could stop his past from coming out now.

50

NO! NO! NO!

This was not part of the deal. You don't get to opt out of this thing, Ryan, and you certainly can't use it to try and benefit your profile and enhance your charity work.

What was with these people? How dare they refuse to take their punishment. Did they give others the same opportunity? No, they did not.

Did you think you could beat the game, like Mandy did? If you think this will save you both, then you are more of a fool than I thought. Because this is not really a game. Perhaps you hadn't realized. I am not playing. I am serious. And if you try to avoid my punishment, I will find another way to make you suffer.

Mark my words, Ryan Fallon, you are going to regret this.

51

ISOBEL

Wednesday, 10 a.m.
2 days, 5½ hours left

'Babe, you need to hear this!'

Annie's voice called up from the kitchen. It sounded urgent so Isobel quickly finished changing Josh's nappy and hurried down.

'Did you know about this?' Annie said, pointing at the iPad and the image of Ryan dressed in a blue suit and pink tie sitting behind a table with a serious looking blonde woman sporting a sharply cut fringe. 'Ryan doped when he was cycling. What is he thinking? This could tank his career. He should have spoken to me before he decided to do this.'

Isobel hugged Josh closer to her chest and leaned against the fridge.

Annie looked at her. 'You don't tell the press this stuff, even if you are trying to help kids addicted to drugs. They call us "the press pack" for a reason. We're wolves who will come for you if we smell blood. Jesus.'

Isobel stared at her friend's face on the screen. On Monday, he wouldn't tell her what shameful secret someone had threatened to expose about him, and now he was admitting it to the world. What had changed? And why hadn't he told her what he was going to do? Her shock was mixed with rage. This affected her too, and Annie and Josh. It wasn't only happening to Ryan. How could he be so thoughtless and selfish?

Or had he found something at Mandy's yesterday? Surely he would have told her if he had. They were in this together. Or at least she'd thought they were.

'Iz?'

Isobel looked at her wife.

'Are you going to tell me why you look terrified all the time. Has it got anything to do with this? Did you know about Ryan?' Annie's eyes widened so much that Isobel could see the whole circle of each bright blue iris. 'Oh God, you didn't help him back then, did you?'

'No! This is the first I've heard.'

'So, what then?'

Isobel closed her eyes, she had no choice but to tell Annie something now. 'On the afternoon of Camille's party, Ryan, Mandy and I were all sent press articles about something in our past and threatened with exposure. We think that was the cause of Mandy's accident, either she was distracted or . . .'

'Why the hell didn't you tell me? That was five days ago. I could have been helping you to stop this or finding out who's behind it. You need to tell me everything. What is it that some-one's got on you?'

'It doesn't matter.'

'Well, clearly it does if someone thinks they can threaten you with it. Tell me, Izzy. I can help you. If someone attacks you, they attack us.' Annie had both hands on her hips in her 'don't mess with me' stance. 'Is it something you did with Ryan and Mandy?'

Isobel shook her head and hugged Josh closer to her side. 'It's no one else's business.'

'You mean it's not *my* business.'

'I don't want to talk about it.' Isobel walked out of the room. Today was her admin day and she had a stack of paperwork to get through.

'Don't walk away from me. What are you hiding, Isobel? I know it's bad because you've not been sleeping and you're doing a lot of school-night drinking. I thought we said we'd always tell each other the truth.'

That stopped Isobel in her tracks. She felt Josh wriggle in her arms as he reached back towards Annie. She had never lied to Annie. When they met, she knew she had finally found a person she could completely be herself with and it was liberating. She had given Isobel the courage to be who she really was. But this was different. Isobel hadn't been afraid to tell people she was gay because she was ashamed of it – rather, it was something other people in her life felt uncomfortable with, so she hid it to save their feelings. But this thing – the thing she had done – was not at all the same.

'I can't, honey. I don't want to say it out loud. I don't want to see your face . . .' The next few words caught in her throat and she took in a long breath that quivered in her chest.

Josh began to wriggle more and cry in her arms.

Annie walked around her so they were face to face. Josh reached across and Annie took him. The boy didn't want to be near Isobel's emotions.

'What the hell, Iz? Nothing you tell me will ever change anything. Do you hear me?' Annie moved her head to catch Isobel's eye. 'Nothing.'

'This would.' The tears came now. Isobel couldn't stop them. 'Believe me. This would.'

Isobel shut herself in the office, knowing her wife would not leave it there. How was she going to stop herself from letting it all spill out? The thought of Annie knowing the truth felt like a physical pain; as if someone had taken hold of her insides and twisted them out of place.

Her phone began to ring. It was Ryan. She let it go to voicemail.

52

STEPHANIE

Wednesday, 10.30 a.m.

'Ryan, answer your phone! Why do you always ignore my calls and messages? I have been trying to reach Rosie since yesterday and she will not reply. You need to tell her to respond to me. She can't treat me like this. I know you're making her do it. Filling her head with lies about me. But I'm her mother. I'm on my way to your house and if you're not there you need to tell that frog of a wife to let me see my daughter OR ELSE!'

Stephanie hung up the phone and hit the brakes too late for the lights. Her tyres screeched against the tarmac and the car crossed the lines, leaving her bonnet sticking out into the junction. She swore and looked in her rear view. The 4x4 behind was right up her backside so she couldn't reverse.

Her hatred for Ryan burned hot in her veins. How dare he keep Rosie from her? She was the mother. Rosie was hers. He was nothing more than a walking, talking sperm donor, and a mediocre one at that. She was never, ever leaving Rosie with him again. This was the end of it. She couldn't risk him dripping his lies into the girl's head. Rosie wasn't bright enough to know what was the truth.

Her phone rang and she hit the answer button without reading the name.

'Ryan, why do you never answer my calls. It's really rude.'

'Mum it's me.'

'Rosie? Are you crying? What's happened? I've been trying to get hold of you since yesterday.'

'Have you seen Dad on the news?'

The lights changed and Stephanie pulled away from the junction.

'What are you talking about?'

'It's awful, Mum. Can you come and get me?'

'Of course, sweetheart. I'm on my way over anyhow. I've been worried about you. What on earth has he done?'

Steph listened as Rosie filled her in on Ryan's press conference.

'Everyone is laughing at me.'

'What is he thinking? Your dad always puts himself first. Always has. Always will. But they are not laughing at you. They are laughing at *him*. And if any of your so-called friends have a go, they'll have me to deal with. I'll be there in five.'

53

PAUL

Since Ryan had blown a large gaping hole in Paul's planned defence, the only option now was to go on the attack. Logic told him someone from their shared history was running this Shame Game, so chances were they lived in and around Ilkley, or used to. His only real leads were the email address and Twitter handle, but neither provided anything useful to a lay person. He'd discovered that the @pm.me address was from an encrypted email service called Proton Mail which, if used with the Tor network, masked a sender's IP address, making them anonymous and untraceable. He needed expert help.

Greg could possibly access it, but going to him was too risky. The next best thing was a decent IT geek. A quick search of 'IT specialists near me' saw one name jump out. Stuart Fraser. Paul looked at the guy's website followed by his Facebook and Instagram pages. It was the same Stuart Fraser who had been in Paul's year at school, the kind of boy who didn't ever look you in the eye and preferred to hang out with the girls. It seemed he was now running his own computer repairs service, but that wasn't what attracted Paul's attention. Fraser had shared all manner of articles and comments online about the use of AI to produce deep fakes, and how to spot a phishing scam. Given that the articles Paul and the others had been sent had looked so impressively real, it seemed Fraser was a person he needed to talk to.

He typed Fraser's name and the town of Ilkley into 192.com and two records came up. He registered for an account and a few seconds later – boom – there was Stuart Fraser's home address.

It didn't take Paul long to find the place. The white bungalow had two large windows either side of the front door and a large sloping roof topped with a brick chimney. Attached to the side was a flat-roof extension, most likely a converted garage. The garden was overgrown and full of dandelions and as he walked to the door he noted that the windows were dirty.

An older woman in sweatpants and crocs answered, telling him there was a sign on the window saying no cold callers.

Did cold callers still exist in the digital world? Paul thought.

'I'm here to see Stuart.'

The woman's eyes narrowed and she half closed the door.

'We went to school together and I need some computer advice. Is he here?' In the background Paul could see the décor was highly floral, with picture frames covering every spare space on the walls. Did Stuart still live with his mum? Is that what the garage conversion was about – the thirty-seven-year-old son who had never left home?

'What does he want?' called a voice from down the hall.

'Stuart? It's Paul Reece-Johnson. We went to school together. I was just Paul Johnson back then? I need your help, mate, have you got five minutes?'

Stuart stepped into view. He wore baggy grey jogging bottoms with flip-flops and a *Star Wars* T-shirt. The thick head of hair he'd had at school had thinned down to almost nothing and his skin looked pale and spotty, like he didn't get enough sun. Paul felt overdressed in his Ralph Lauren T-shirt and smart shorts.

'Why didn't you email or call?' said Stuart.

'It's a bit of a sensitive matter. I wanted to discuss it with you in person.' What he meant was he didn't want any record of him having contacted Stuart hanging around. He didn't want to leave a trail.

'You'll have to speak in your room. I'm watching *Homes Under the Hammer*,' said the woman Paul assumed to be Stuart's mother.

Paul followed Stuart into the converted garage. The guy did not look happy about having a visitor, and Paul could see why when he clocked the discarded plates, mugs and food wrappers which covered most of the available floor space. The room had a ripe, musty smell that made Paul want to throw open the windows. There was a crumpled bed in the far corner next to a door which Paul presumed led to a bathroom, but the majority of the space was taken up by a large desk covered in laptops, monitors and wires alongside Stuart's own computer. In comparison to the mess in the rest of the room, this section was neatly organized and clear of clutter.

'So, how've you been?' Paul wanted to get this over and done with as quickly as possible but he knew a bit of polite interest always went a long way.

'Fine. You?'

'Looks like you're pretty savvy with technology.' He nodded towards the desk behind where Stuart stood. 'Do you know much about copycat websites and scam notifications?'

'No,' Stuart said.

Paul wasn't sure what to say. It was not the answer he'd expected. Given all that Stuart had posted online about deep fakes and phishing tactics, he expected the guy to launch into a whole load of technical jargon about how these things were done.

He'd met enough expert witnesses in his years at the Bar to know how a passionate specialist communicates.

'Nothing?'

'No.'

'But you posted all that stuff online about phishing and spotting scams. How can you not know?'

Something in the air changed. Stuart was no poker player. His forehead had started to look a little sweaty and he was swallowing far too much. Another skill Paul had learned from the Bar was spotting signs of guilt.

'OK. Let's try something more specific. How would someone create a copycat news website containing a fake article?'

The range of emotions that ran across Stuart's face were almost too fast for Paul to keep up with, but he caught the gist of them: surprise, fear, pride.

'I don't know.'

Paul stared him down. 'You don't know?'

Was Stuart involved in all of this somehow? It didn't seem possible. He was a creepy little nerd, but why was he being so shifty?

'It's my job to spot a bullshitter, Stuart, and you are smelling particularly bad right now.'

'I can't help you. You need to leave. I only do repairs.'

A memory came back to Paul, as if it had been waiting for an opportune moment to reappear. Mandy had once said Stuart tried to lift up her skirt in the dinner queue, causing Paul to have a quiet word with him near the boys' toilets. Stuart had run away almost in tears, tripping over his shoelaces as he went and making some passing kids laugh. Is that why Stuart looked so nervous when he saw Paul at his front door or was there some other reason?

Paul placed his hands in his shorts pockets to hide his balled-up fists.

'What are you hiding, Stuart?'

'You need to go. Get out. Go away.' Stuart moved to push Paul then thought better of it. He wasn't making any eye contact and his pasty skin had become blotchy and red.

Paul felt the rage he had been suppressing towards the black-mailer and Ryan's confession and Mandy's death all fighting its way to the surface. He'd become adept at keeping a lid on it over the years, but that hadn't always been the case. His dad had been a boxer who had taught him how to fight. He had also been a bully who had shown Paul how to beat people down in more than one way. Paul had been on the receiving end of daily verbal attacks. It was where he learned to spar.

'If I find out you had anything to do with Mandy's death, I swear to God I will come here and—'

'Mum! MUM!'

'What are you calling her for? How is she going to help you?'

'LEAVE ME ALONE.' Stuart tried to barge past Paul to get to the hallway, but Paul sidestepped and blocked him again. The guy was really sweating now.

'Why are you running away? Hey, look at me. Look at me, Stuart. Just tell me what you know about those articles? Was it you? Did someone put you up to it?'

'I don't know anything. I don't know what you're talking about.'

'You're lying.'

'Leave me alone. MUM!'

Paul couldn't keep a lid on it any more, his temper erupted and he grabbed the neck of Stuart's T-shirt. 'You know something and you are going to tell me what that is or I will hurt you, do you hear me? I've already lost too much this week and I'm not losing anything else because some weirdo feels like playing games with my life.'

Stuart grabbed Paul's hands and tried to wrestle them free,

and when this didn't work, he made a big mistake. He threw a punch.

By the time Paul heard the sirens, Stuart was doubled up on the floor, crying, with blood dripping from his nose, and his mother was screaming in the hallway.

54

ROSIE

Wednesday, 10.45 a.m.

Her mum hugged her on her dad's driveway as Camille watched from the doorway.

'Take care, darling,' Camille said as Rosie climbed into her mum's car.

Rosie spotted her mum throwing Camille a dirty look. The antagonism between the two of them was irritating but Rosie was used to it. She used to wish they'd get along because she loved them both, but she had long ago come to terms with the fact that was never going to happen.

'Let's go to Nanna's and get some lunch. Your real family will look after you.'

Rosie felt relieved to be out of Dad's house. Camille had been on the phone most of the morning talking in French and laughing. How could she laugh when all this was going on?

'Leaving school and working for your dad might be out of the question now. I told you he was not a good role model.'

Rosie stared out of the window. So, this was what she had to deal with. A stepmother being weird and her mother revelling in her father's failings. She desperately wanted to call Gus but couldn't face what he might say.

'He's ruined your life. I can't believe he's done this. What is wrong with him?'

Rosie looked at her phone as a new message arrived.

'Just put that thing away and don't look at any of it,' her mum said, pointing to Rosie's phone. 'You are going to lose a lot of friends.'

'Wow, thanks, Mum. Way to cheer me up.'

'I'm serious, Rosie. Put that thing away.' Her mum grabbed her phone and threw it on the back seat.

'Hey!'

'People will vent their hateful opinions and you won't be able to stop it or challenge it. Your only option is to ignore it.' Her mum's voice was shrill and her movements jerky, the way they always were when she was losing it.

Rosie stared forward and bit her lip, willing herself not to cry.

55

PAUL

Paul needed to get out of this place fast. He felt the tension in his jaw and tried to concentrate on relaxing. Every step he took now risked some nosey copper taking too close a look at him. *Be calm, think straight*, he repeated in his head, but the sight of Detective Chief Superintendent Greg Coulters walking through the interview room door brought back the rage. Paul squeezed both of his thighs hard.

Greg sat opposite Paul and held his gaze. 'What on earth got into you?'

'It's a personal matter. No one else's business.'

Greg's eyebrows rose. 'You turn up at the home of a guy you went to school with, scare the living daylights out of his mother, and risk a charge of affray or grievous harm. That makes it our business too.'

'Your wife died a few days ago. What are you doing at work? Surely you're not fit to work at the moment.'

'I'm not at work. They asked me to come in to see you.'

It was Paul's turn to raise his eyebrows. 'You're no friend of mine any more. I don't require your help or support.'

'That wasn't why they called.'

Greg sat forward and lowered his volume as if he was sharing a secret. His eyes looked red and the bags underneath were charcoal grey. 'They told me that when you had Stuart Fraser up against the wall you were screaming in his face about blackmail and the fact he'd murdered Mandy.'

'I never said that,' Paul said, though he couldn't be sure.

'It's an odd thing for Fraser's mum to make up. Why would you think Stuart had anything to do with Mandy's accident? He wasn't the driver of the van. He wasn't in the city centre that day. Indeed, according to him, he hasn't seen Mandy since school.'

'I told you I never mentioned Mandy.'

Greg sat back and eyed him closely for a moment. He wasn't buying Paul's story but no doubt knew there was not much he could do. It was Stuart's mother's word against Paul's. All Paul had to do was keep denying he'd ever mentioned Mandy.

'You were out of control today and I'm wondering why someone in your position would do something so risky. What has you so angry, Paul?'

'What are you talking about? I'm as cool as a cucumber. Nothing to see here.'

'You and I both know when someone does wrong they need to be held to account.' Paul could have been mistaken, but he thought he saw a brief smile on Greg's face.

'They do indeed.' Paul stared unblinking at Greg.

'Was something going on between you and Mandy?'

'Oh, you have a fucking cheek asking me that. She was too good for you.'

Greg dropped his gaze to the table and sucked in his cheeks until his face looked sunken and angular. 'Tell me about Audrey Raye.'

Paul prided himself on keeping calm under pressure, but this took some effort. 'Who?'

Greg looked him in the eye. 'Don't tell me it's a coincidence that Ryan turned up at my house yesterday bent on quizzing me about the woman, and then the very next day you beat up her cousin.'

Paul let the intel sink in and then he leaned forward. 'You said I'd *risked* a charge of affray, so I'm assuming Stuart's not pressing charges, so I'm going to go.'

56

STEPHANIE

Wednesday, 2 p.m.

Rosie looked younger and more delicate than she had in years. It reminded Stephanie of what it was like to be a teenager. While Ryan was busy every lunchtime, playing sports with his never-ending roster of friends, she had sat alone. She would never admit it, but she'd always felt grateful that their daughter had inherited her father's easy popularity. And now he'd gone and done this.

'Don't worry, Rosie, worse things happen at sea,' Felicity said, one arm around Rosie as she spoke. Stephanie's mum had never been a hugger. Even during her years as a local MP, she had avoided physical contact with other humans as much as possible, choosing to wear gloves whenever she did a meet and greet. *You never know where they've been*, she'd once told Stephanie. 'Are you feeling any better about that last exam? It must be nice to be all done and dusted, if nothing else.'

'Oh no!' Stephanie's hands flew to her mouth. She'd totally forgotten Monday's exam. 'Why didn't you remind me? I was so busy at work and then with all the stress around Mandy. Someone should have told me. Mum, why didn't you remind me?'

'It's OK, Mum. Don't get worked up.'

'I'm not getting worked up. I'm just saying someone could have reminded me. I can't be expected to remember everything and I'm having an awful week.'

'I think Rosie is having a tough week too, Stephanie.'

'I know. I know. You don't have to tell me that. That's why I've collected her so I can take care of her.'

'Yoo-hoo, anyone home?' Stephanie's friend Fleur was wearing her usual blue T-shirt and black sweatpants. She was a larger lady who was forever on a diet. The kind of diet where she insisted on having Diet Coke with her fish and chips or McDonald's. 'I've just been to yours, Stephy. I've been meaning to call in all week after Mandy but then this thing today with Ryan. My God. Are you OK?'

Felicity guided Rosie towards the kitchen. 'Grandad made his famous rhubarb and custard cake this morning. How about the two of us steal a slice while these two catch up?'

'Ooh, I'll take a piece if some's going spare, Felicity.'

'I'll see what I can do, Fleur. Stephanie?'

'I'm fine.'

'Right, tell me everything,' said Fleur, sinking into the sofa. 'I mean it couldn't be happening to a nicer person, right? Did you have any idea about him taking drugs?'

'God no! Rosie is devastated.'

'Finally seeing her dad for the first time. That sucks. Poor kid. Have you spoken to him?'

Stephanie shook her head. She knew she was the last person Ryan would ever speak to when facing tough times, but she wasn't about to share this with Fleur. She liked people to think she and Ryan were still close. Fleur was one of the few friends that had stuck by her over the years, even if she was the type of friend who thrived off drama. When things were going well for Steph, Fleur was nowhere to be seen, but as soon as the shit hit the fan,

Fleur was there with a box of tissues and a good dose of indignant anger to throw in the pot.

'Do you think the frog model will scarper now?'

'Sshh, Rosie might hear and she likes Camille.'

'Sorry.' Fleur dropped her volume. 'She'll be packing her bags as we speak though, yeah?'

'Here's hoping. It would make my life a lot easier if she wasn't around.'

'And any goss on what happened to Mandy?'

'They were all gathered at Ryan's afterwards. Isobel, Paul and the others. Nobody even bothered to tell me, Fleur. That's not on, right? I mean I'd been so good to Mandy, really looked after her when they were too busy to care.'

'Your problem is you're too nice. I'd have steered well clear. The woman made her own bed.'

Stephanie smiled at Fleur. It was nice to have at least one person on her side.

57

PAUL

Wednesday, 4 p.m.
1 day, 23½ hours left

'What the hell were you thinking?' Vanessa was standing in the doorway of his office when he walked through the door. She was not impressed that he'd spent the last few hours at the police station. 'You're acting like an idiot. You have got to start using your brain.'

'I was using my brain. Whoever has cooked up this campaign has to have been there in the background, snooping into our lives and gathering their dirt for years.' He moved past his wife and over to the wall of sticky notes. 'Stuart Fraser is an obvious culprit. The weird little fella lives in his mum's converted garage, probably playing computer games and raging inside about how unfair his pathetic existence is. He fits the profile.'

'And what does he have against you and the others?'

'Huh?' Paul was looking at his notes.

'What does he have against you? What did you do to him?'

'I've no idea,' Paul said, knowing it wasn't wise to bring up how he'd defended Mandy's honour at school. Vanessa didn't react well to tales of his and Mandy's time together. 'But I bet there's something.' *Something to do with Audrey Raye?*

'You didn't find out?'

'He wasn't exactly talkative.'

'Does he have the IT skills to pull off those fake news sites?'

'I expect so.' Paul riffled through his drawer.

'But you don't know? You didn't find out?'

Paul found a pen and began to write a thought on a new Post-it.

'Did you at least find out why he's doing this now?'

'I just told you. He's a weirdo.'

'But why now, Paul? Why wait over ten years to expose Ryan, and even longer with you? Why *now?*'

'I just said. He wasn't talking.'

'Why not? You can make anyone talk.'

Paul stuck the new Post-it to the wall.

'Paul?'

'What?'

'Why couldn't you get him talking?'

'I lost my temper, OK? The guy was standing there, denying everything to my face. He was taking the piss.'

Vanessa physically recoiled from his words. 'You attacked him? For God's sake, Paul, this is what I mean. Use your brain. You're a lawyer. You know how to beat him with intelligence, you don't have to use your fists.'

'No, Ness, I don't know how to beat him. I don't know how to stop him. Isobel told me someone had contacted the Fallon Foundation about a mystery cyclist who'd fucked up, then she said the local MP had told her bosses at the hospital about a tip-off that one of their neonatal consultants was hiding a wrongdoing from their past. This sicko, Stuart, is serious. He's not playing, Ness, and I can't go to the police, can I? I have to find a way of stopping this myself.'

Vanessa looked at his latest Post-it note, which read, '*Stuart Fraser – blackmailer?*'

'What if it's not Stuart?' Paul stared at his wife. 'So he's a weirdo who lives with his mummy, but that doesn't mean he could pull this off. What if it's not him?'

'He's Audrey Raye's cousin. His mother's sister is Audrey's mum.' Vanessa looked confused and Paul pointed to the Post-it with Ryan's question written on it.

'That could be nothing more than a coincidence. This is a small town.'

'Yeah, like the fact Mandy was standing in the middle of a busy road at exactly the same time we all received those articles is a coincidence.'

'All right, point taken. So, who is Audrey?'

'A girl from our school who was hit by a car years ago and left . . . well, she lived but not in any state you'd want to.'

'And how is that relevant to all of you?'

Paul bit his lip then spoke more to himself than his wife. 'Maybe he thinks we all know something, or covered something up . . .'

'Why would he think that? Paul?'

Paul was not listening. He was looking at Ryan's question and thinking about his own and Isobel's. He took another Post-it, wrote on it and stuck it to the wall.

'"Daisy Chain". What does that mean?' said Vanessa, reading it. 'Paul! Seriously, what are you thinking?'

Paul blinked at his wife as the options ran through his head. He'd messed up by attacking Stuart. He couldn't negotiate with the guy now. Chances were, Stuart would be even more determined to drag Paul's reputation through the dirt. The guy clearly wanted them all to pay for something, and he wanted them to punish each other. *What does he think we are guilty of?* Paul looked at the wall and the names of his friends. Was he caught up in a mess of their making? He'd been studying in Sheffield when Audrey's accident had happened. He remembered it was around the time he and Mandy had split up, because his dad had sensitively pointed out that Paul should be grateful he'd only been dumped as he could have had his head squashed into the road instead.

'I don't know what to do,' he said to his wife. 'This is going to come out now Ryan has done what he's done, and it is going to be so bad and I don't know how to stop it.'

Vanessa scanned the wall.

'Cut a deal,' she said after a few moments pointing at the orange sticky which said, '*Indiscretion @ work*'. 'Find out what Isobel did, then cut a deal to expose her instead of Ryan.'

58

ISOBEL

Wednesday, 4.30 p.m.
1 day, 23 hours left

'Oh my life, Isobel. What happened? Are you OK? What are you doing? Isobel? ISOBEL?'

Annie's words made their way into her mind but couldn't quite find a place to land. Isobel tried to sit up straighter but the arm bracing her against the floor gave way and she slumped back into her half sitting, half lying position.

'Leave me 'lone,' she managed to say.

'Good grief. Wait there. How much of this have you drunk?'

'Go 'way.'

'I'll put Josh in his play pen. One minute.'

'NO! GO 'WAY.'

Isobel heard Annie telling Josh to be a good boy.

'I've given him a breadstick, that should keep him busy. Now let's get you off the floor.'

Isobel grabbed Annie's arm and shook her head. 'Leave me.'

'You're not staying on the floor. Come on, put your hands around my neck.'

'Leave me. Please.'

'Iz, honey I don't know what's happened but I'm not leaving you on—'

'You have to leave me. Take Josh. Start again. You can't stay with me. I'm damaged. I'll hurt you.'

Annie sat back on her haunches. 'Now you're talking nonsense.'

'I. Am. Not.' Isobel concentrated on forming the words. The white wine coated all her neurons, making them drowsy and unresponsive. 'I'm bad for him. I'm bad for you. You need to go now before . . . before it's out, so it doesn't faint . . . taint . . . you.'

'I'm not going anywhere. Stop being silly.'

'Not silly. Listen. LISTEN. I want him . . . him to have the best life and the best mummy . . . and that's not me, it's you. Just take him away so he won't have to have this on him.'

'That's your solution, is it? Josh and I scarper tonight and get a free run at life without you. Not only is that the stupidest thing I've ever heard because – newsflash, wife of mine – we love you, but we also can't wipe you out of our lives by walking out of the door. You'll always be my wife and Josh's mummy even if we're living somewhere else.'

Isobel shook her head and the room spun like she was riding the waltzer. 'Don't say that. You have to get him away and make him free of it, of me, because I'm a bad person and I don't want him to know that. Can't you see. I can't let him know that . . . or . . . or . . . you.' The sobs took over and Isobel collapsed on to the kitchen tiles, hoping the world would stop spinning and let her get off.

59

RYAN

Wednesday, 7.30 p.m.
1 day, 20 hours left

Camille flicked on the light switch, illuminating the windowless snug where Ryan sat without his phone, without any TV or music playing, without a book or magazine. Just him, alone. He waved his hand for her to switch it off again but she ignored him and perched on the end of the corner sofa where they had spent many a night snuggled up in front of a movie.

'I have put your phone on silent. It wouldn't stop.'

Ryan nodded. He had seen that his agent for the TV work had called numerous times, as had Sophie at the office. The fallout was bigger than any of them could have imagined. Either they had picked a slow news day or people really did revel in the idea of someone falling from grace.

'There are reporters outside. I asked them to stop ringing the bell as Ethan was getting upset. They were nice about it.'

'Do you want me to speak to them?' It was the last thing he wanted to do, as he was sure Camille could tell from his lifeless words.

'Non. Sophie said to stay quiet. Let it die down.'

Sophie must have called Camille when she realized Ryan wasn't answering his calls.

Let it die down.

'Are the kids OK?' he asked.

'Ethan is asleep.'

'And Rosie? How's she taking it?'

'She went back to her mum's.'

Of course she did.

Rats from a sinking ship. The image of scrambling, desperate animals falling over each other to get away had never felt so apt. Even his own daughter. How many more would he watch racing out of his life? How many after that would wait to slink away once the dust had settled?

He reached out and took hold of Camille's hand. At least she was still here. He wouldn't have blamed her for wanting to take a long visit to her parents and it meant the world to him that she had stayed.

He had only dared to take the briefest of looks at social media after the press conference. Part of him hoped for a glimmer of support, admiration even, for the fact he'd owned up to his crime, but that was not what he saw in the seconds he spent looking. Disdain and derision were writ large in the words of the public.

But none of that stung as much as the expressions on the faces of the reporters in the room for the press conference. One by one they had looked up from their notepads, some continuing to scribble his words blindly, others holding their pen aloft, but all of them staring at him with the same mixture of delight and disbelief. He was voluntarily handing them a stick to beat him with. In their eyes, he was nothing but an idiot.

Annie had sent him a one-word text immediately afterwards that summed up the media's position perfectly: *WHY?*

Of course he would never be able to tell anyone why. He had

done this to protect Mandy and now he had to see it through. He couldn't complain about the person who'd goaded him in to doing this, he couldn't blame the media for making a big deal of it, or his friends and family for changing their opinion of him. Because he had chosen it all. He just had to suck it up.

60

THE SHAME GAME:
A TRUE CRIME DOCUMENTARY

Episode 2 of 3 - The Play

AUDIO from Ryan Fallon's press conference
plays over clips of his cycling career.
In the final video he sits upright in his
seat and raises both arms as he crosses the
line. Behind him a dozen other men race to
finish with their heads down and their bikes
rocking from side to side.

INT - FALLON FAMILY HOME - DAYTIME

Camille Fallon folds her hands together and
places them delicately on her lap.

> VOICE (O.S.)

What happened after the press
conference?

CAMILLE

The whole thing blew up in the
media. It was on the six o'clock
news and the ten o'clock news.
They played footage of Ryan
alongside Lance Armstrong. Then
they showed him commentating on
races and talking about doping
and they made it look like he
was so . . . what is the word . . .
ingenuine?

VOICE (O.S.)

Disingenuous?

CAMILLE

Oui. The coach from British
Cycling said they were all shocked
and disappointed, that Ryan had
tainted the reputation of his
more talented colleagues and I
know that broke Ryan's heart. He
was so proud to be part of that
generation of athletes. I think
they should have backed him up
and not hung him out to dry.
People from that world dropped
him overnight. The sponsorship
deal he was about to sign with a
big American cycling brand fell
through, leaving the Foundation
in an impossible position. The

governors had no choice but to ask
Ryan to step down as MD.

> VOICE (O.S.)

Clearly this significantly damaged
his career, but did it do more
harm than that in your view?

Camille nods and bites her bottom lip.

> CAMILLE

He was so ashamed, like he was
in physical pain, and after his
father came to see him I really
worried that Ryan would do
something stupid.

FADE TO BLACK

INT - WALTERS FAMILY HOME - DAYTIME

Annie Walters runs a hand through her
blonde hair.

> ANNIE

I was gutted he didn't speak to
me before he did it. I don't know
what that PR woman was thinking.
You can't go around saying, *Hey, I
took drugs and I cheated but let
me look after your damaged kids.*
I mean, it's preposterous. It was

always going to end in disaster.
He torpedoed his career. And I
simply could not understand why
on God's earth he would choose to
do that.

                    VOICE (O.S.)

Until Isobel told you about the
threats.

                    ANNIE

But she didn't know the whole
story. If he had come to her and
told her what was going on and
what he was thinking, maybe . . .

Annie blinks a few times before turning away
from the camera.

                    VOICE (O.S.)

Would you like a minute?

61

Isobel, what is going on with you? The boys have been really quite proactive and are fully informed about the choices they need to make, but you have been strangely silent. Should I be worried? Have you worked it out? You are the smartest of them all I expect, so it's possible. You were always my weakest link. Little Goody Two-Shoes. I didn't even realize you were gay until it was all out in the open. You protect your privacy well and I respect that. But don't confuse that for a willingness to let you off the hook. You are in this thing for good reason and I will make damn sure you wriggle and writhe on the end of my line like the other stinking fish you swim with.

62

ISOBEL

Thursday, 9 a.m.
1 day, 6½ hours left

For the first few seconds she struggled to remember where she was. Perhaps the on-call room at work? Her back certainly ached enough for her to have slept on its thin, hard mattress. She blinked at the unfamiliar ceiling, her head pulsing with a dull ache and her mouth feeling like it was coated with cotton wool. She rolled a little and then had to brace herself to prevent a fall on to the floor.

How had she ended up on the sofa in the dining room? She slowly sat to ensure her head remained as stable as possible and noticed someone had brought down the pillow from her bed and the spare blankets from the cupboard on the landing. She was still wearing the jeans and T-shirt she'd had on yesterday.

Isobel checked her watch but was unsure if she was late for work – she couldn't remember what day it was. In the kitchen next door, someone was singing nursery rhymes. It wasn't Annie, as the voice sounded younger and higher pitched. Wrapping one of the blankets around her shoulders, she stood and made her way to the kitchen, stopping twice on the way to stem the nausea threatening to engulf her.

Josh was giggling in his highchair. His face was covered in butter and jam and he had a scrunched-up piece of toast gripped in one podgy fist. Rosie was singing, 'The Grand Old Duke of York', as she broke off chunks of banana and placed them on Josh's plastic plate. She turned when Isobel coughed.

'Sorry, did we wake you? Annie said to let you sleep.'

'It's fine. Where is Annie?' Isobel made her way to the kettle and flicked it on. She needed a strong coffee ASAP.

'She said she had to go somewhere for work. How are you feeling? She said you were poorly.'

'When did she ask you to come over?'

'Last night. She called after dinner.'

Isobel nodded. Parts of yesterday were coming back to her like pieces of a jumbled-up jigsaw. She recalled standing in this very spot and downing her first two glasses of wine. When the cold liquid drenched her throat and the alcohol raced into her brain she had felt the elation of imminent escape. She also recalled sitting on the floor. There was an image of Annie trying to lift her up. Also, she remembered the cold tiles against her cheeks. Had she thrown up in the downstairs toilet?

There was a note on the table in Annie's handwriting. Isobel picked it up.

I called work and told them you had food poisoning. Rest up and drink lots of water. I'll be back by lunchtime. Love you, A xxx

She finished making the coffee then sat at the kitchen table with the mug untouched in front of her.

'Thank you,' she said to Rosie, who was helping Josh to take a drink from his sippy cup.

'S'OK. I like helping with Josh. I used to do it for Ethan.'

Isobel smiled. Rosie was a lovely girl. She hoped Josh grew up to be so kind and helpful.

'You don't look very well, Aunty Isobel. You can go back to bed. I'm OK here. I'll play with him until Annie gets back.'

Isobel was seriously considering it when her phone began to ring. She looked around and found Annie had placed it on charge next to the Ninja blender. It was Paul.

'Hi, are you in work today?' he said when she answered. 'Because I've found something out about your Royal Oak question.'

'What?' she said, feeling a little more alert.

'It's hard to explain over the phone. Can you come over? I'm here all day.'

63

PAUL

Sweat stung his eyes as he ran full pace across the moor path towards the Cow and Calf rocks, jumping over craggy outcrops and deep ditches. He couldn't believe he'd put himself in that bastard Greg's domain yesterday. He used to tolerate the man for Mandy's benefit, but God knows why she had been attracted to such a strait-laced, superior arsehole.

He was only running down so he could turn and punish his legs on the run back up. The pain and the effort would help him to focus.

Paul had texted Isobel five times last night without response and by this morning he'd been restless and impatient. He needed to talk to her soon; time was running out. Vanessa had been certain that his best move now was to find out what Isobel had done and offer to shame her to save himself. There was a logic to it, he knew.

He had been given Ryan to out and Isobel had been given him, which meant Ryan had either Isobel or Mandy, and Ryan had presumably outed himself to save whichever one of the girls he had. That left Isobel home and dry, as neither Ryan nor Mandy would be outing her. When she'd failed to respond last night, he thought she must have figured this out, but clearly not, as when he'd called her this morning she'd sounded grateful for his help and agreed to head over to his later, leaving him just enough time for this run so he could think it through and get it straight.

The only obstacle was getting Isobel to confess, but he didn't see any real problem with this. He would ask non-threatening questions until he found a chink, a way in, and then he would circle and pick, and circle and pick, until the chink was wide enough to make an educated guess. *Did this thing happen at work? How long ago did it happen? Was it just you or were others involved? Does anyone else know about it? Was anyone upset by it? Was anyone hurt by it? Why do you feel so ashamed? Was this something you did because of particular circumstances? Was this something you did on purpose?*

Eventually, she would give something away.

It must be something to do with a child she had treated in the past. When they'd been discussing who might be sending them this shame game in his kitchen, Isobel had commented that some parents of deceased children could be driven to take revenge. People don't make observations like that unless they have some personal experience of it.

Once he knew the gist of what she'd done, he could probably find any further details he needed in public records, and after that make an offer to Stuart.

He'd checked the dates and it all fit. Paul and Mandy had been happy and planning their future until the night she'd called to say she was rushing home because her mum had had a stroke. He remembered calling and calling the next day, but she never picked up and then finally when he'd headed back to his dad's house from uni to see her, she dropped the bombshell. They were finished. Her family were more important than him. Her mum needed her. She didn't have time for a relationship. And the thing that had hurt him most was the look in her eyes. She had looked at him as if he was nothing and he couldn't understand how she'd gone from, *I love you* to *I don't care* so quickly, even with a sick mum. How could she just turn off her love? But she hadn't turned off her feelings for him, she'd turned off her feelings full stop. She had been in shock. It was a realization that made him feel oddly better.

If Paul had interrogated Stuart instead of losing his temper he could have gained an advantage. He should have quizzed him on his computer skills, put pressure on him by using Mandy's death to force him to admit something. But that was the problem. He had needed someone to take it all out on. Mandy dying had brought everything back; all the anger he'd worked so hard to compress and pack away had burst free and filled him up entirely. He needed it to go somewhere so he could feel the release of pressure and Stuart had been a prime target.

He was going to need someone else to question the scrawny bunglefuck if he stood any chance of finding some evidence to end this thing. He had no problem going to the police if he was certain the person he was pointing the finger at really was the blackmailer. Paul couldn't send Vanessa; he needed someone that wasn't related to him.

And then it struck him. The perfect person was Annie.

She was not only skilled but motivated. Stuart was threatening her family too. Would Stuart speak to her? Would he know who she was? Probably. If he'd been involved in stalking them, he'd know exactly who Annie was, but if she played it smart, bumped into him when he was out and about, showed sympathy for him over Paul's unreasonable attack, he might talk to her for just long enough . . .

But could he ask Annie for a favour like that while he was also looking to betray Isobel?

If it stopped this bunglefuck in his tracks and saved them all from exposure, absolutely.

64

ISOBEL

Thursday, 11.30 a.m.
1 day, 4 hours left

Despite the coffee, the paracetamols, and the pints of water, Isobel's head continued to throb. The pain came from somewhere deep in her brain and she knew she had no choice but to accept its presence for the rest of the day. Only a good night's sleep would tame it now. She glanced at Josh, who was spark out in his cot. If only she could join him.

'Are you sure you're OK to stay with him?' she said to Rosie. 'I won't be long.'

Rosie said it was fine. She had her phone. If Josh woke up grumpy, she'd call.

Isobel parked on the drive outside Paul and Vanessa's five-bedroom house. What on earth they used all those extra bedrooms for she had no idea. She and Annie had stayed over a few years back after a New Year's Eve party and she remembered the peacock-themed bedroom and accompanying en suite with its black fixtures and lime-green tiles. The whole house looked like a photo shoot from *Country Living* or *House Beautiful*.

Isobel rang the doorbell and waited. Paul opened the door

while talking on his phone and beckoned her in. He went back into his office, which was halfway down the hall towards the huge kitchen. Isobel heard him say, 'I told you, I have something important on this week so you'll have to rely on Stephen and Manreet.'

Isobel stooped to untie her pumps as she wondered if grieving for Mandy was the important thing he had on. Paul's call did not sound like it was coming to an end, so she padded towards the kitchen on bare feet. Paul had half closed his office door so she pushed it open a little, intending to gesture to him that she would make a cuppa.

The entire side wall of his office was covered in brightly coloured Post-it notes. Isobel stepped forward to get a better look. Was this how he prepared for a trial? Annie did something similar when working on a story but her notes were always scattered randomly across whatever wall space she could find when inspiration hit. This couldn't be more different. Each column of squares reached from above head height almost to the floor and was perfectly lined up against its neighbour, with gaps in between that looked equally spaced. She was struck by the patience this must entail, and totally fascinated.

When she saw her name written in capital letters above the two orange columns, the first thing she thought was that it must refer to a defendant or victim. But then she saw that Ryan's name topped the green columns and Mandy's the pink ones. Isobel's eyes moved down the orange squares one by one, finding that they recorded her own life history; where she'd studied at university, where she'd done her residency, the part-time jobs she'd had as a student, the medical jobs she'd had, her relationship with Annie – when it began, when they married, when they'd fostered Josh – it was all there. Paul had tracked and traced her every movement and it looked like he had done the same to Mandy and Ryan. The final note at the bottom of the orange columns read, '*Indiscretion @ work*'.

Isobel looked at the back of Paul's head as her heart rate increased.

Hold out on talking to Paul until we speak. I'll explain later. This was what Ryan had said at the end of the voicemail he'd left her yesterday.

Why had Ryan warned her not to talk to Paul? What had he found out? Something so bad he couldn't leave it in a phone message?

She looked back at the Post-it notes. She knew Paul had said he would help but who goes to this much effort to help others? Plus, she had only told him that Ryan was also being threatened on Tuesday afternoon. How had he gathered this much detail on all of their lives so quickly? Unless . . .

I have something important to do this week.

Isobel looked at the single column of yellow sticky notes that were closest to her on the wall. The moniker at the top of this section was @BeAshamed. Underneath that, Isobel's week from hell was listed in chronological order: 'Article sent as a warning', it said on the first sticky, then 'Someone is hiding something from you. You have until Friday 3.30 p.m. to uncover their secret.' After that it went on to, 'Offer of a clue sent', 'Example Twitter feed sent', and finally, 'Shame your friend to save yourself.'

What on earth did that last one mean? And how did Paul have all this detail on what she and Ryan had received?

A few moments later, Paul ended his call and turned to face her. She had not managed to move from her spot inside the doorway. Her eyes met his, and the realization hit her.

Paul was the one who had threatened her and Ryan. He was the one who had driven Mandy to take her own life.

Move, Isobel, move! a voice screamed in her head.

65

PAUL

Thursday, 11.45 a.m.
1 day, 3¾ hours left

He didn't understand the look in her eyes or why she ran, but he chased her anyway. He couldn't let her leave no matter what was going on, he had to find out her secret, and so he beat her to the front door and blocked the exit.

'What are you doing?' he said.

'Get out of my way.' Isobel tried to move his arm from across the door.

'What's going on?'

'You know exactly what's going on. Let me out now or I'm calling the police.'

Paul strengthened his stance. That was not happening.

'Fine, have it your way. Do you know what you've done to us? To Mandy?' Isobel took her phone from her jeans pocket and began fumbling with the screen. 'Why? Why would you do it? There's something wrong with you. You're sick.'

'Put your phone away, Isobel. I don't know what you think I've done but I will not let you call the police.'

She took a few steps away. 'You will not tell me what to do,' she said, putting the phone to her ear.

Paul made a grab for her arm. Isobel snatched it away but lost her grip on the phone, sending it sliding across the polished wood and into the skirting board with a crack as a voice on the other end said, 'Emergency. Which service?'

'Oh no you don't.' Paul ran to the phone and kicked it away as Isobel tried to pick it up.

She scrambled after it and he followed. As they both reached the handset Paul stamped on it with all the force he could muster.

Isobel looked up from the floor next to her smashed-up phone. 'Why would you do that?'

'No police,' he said.

'You can't keep me here,' she said as she stood.

'Well, I could if I wanted to.' He meant it as a joke to lighten the mood and get them back on track, but she missed the humour in his eyes and the lightness in his tone.

Her eyes flicked to the front door and then the kitchen.

Don't do it, Isobel, he thought.

She chose the front door, making another dash for freedom. Paul didn't even have to move – he simply grabbed her right arm as she passed him and pulled her back. She was no match for his strength. But good God did she try everything she could to wrench herself free. She hit out at him, tried to prise his fingers off her forearm and then attempted to twist and turn it in every direction. Neither of them spoke during their weird dance. He was aware of their heavy breaths and the odd grunt from him or frustrated cry from her. And then she started hitting him in the chest with her free hand, flat slaps at first but then punches with the side of her fist. He pushed her whole body away from him but kept a tight grip on her right forearm as she stumbled backwards.

'Calm down, Isobel.'

His words had some kind of incendiary effect. His friend, who was always so delicate and neat, looked half crazed. Her hair fell over her face and her eyes blazed.

What the fuck? he thought as she ran at him, hurling her whole body at his.

He didn't mean to throw her, but the rage inside him had been patiently waiting for an excuse to take a run-out again, and she gave it one.

66

ROSIE

Thursday, 11.45 a.m.

Little Josh was snoring lightly in his cot next to her as she read her book. She couldn't face scrolling through her phone for fear of what people were saying about her dad today. Aunt Isobel and Annie had never trusted her to look after him alone before, and the responsibility felt significant. Like the time her dad first gave her a key to his house and told her she could come whenever she wanted. She and Mum had been having one of their arguments. Dad knew how difficult Mum could be when she was in one of her moods. Not for the first time, Rosie wondered how much of her character came from her parents. Whenever Dad took the mickey out of her being stroppy or Nanna chastised her for being cheeky, it made her worry. Josh shuffled and one of his legs jerked out straight, stayed there for a moment and then relaxed back down. When she was sure Josh wasn't waking up, she went back to her story.

She hoped Josh would stay asleep – she liked being alone with him and she wanted Aunt Isobel to think she'd done a good job taking care of him. Ever since Rosie was young, Isobel had always looked her in the eye and spoken to her like she was an adult. She wanted to live up to that.

She read for a little longer, until Josh woke up and began to cry.

She carried him down to the kitchen, singing 'The Grand Old Duke of York' as he had liked that earlier, but he was grouchy and kept shaking his head and rubbing his face against her shoulder. It was kind of cute, although she was a bit freaked out that his nose was running and she was probably getting snot smeared all over her new T-shirt. Mum would not be happy about that.

Josh began to cry even louder and call out, 'Mama. Want mama.' Maybe there were some snacks she could give him. She found a bag of dinky breadsticks in the cupboard which stopped him from crying, but he was smelling a bit pongy. She hoped Isobel would come home soon.

When Josh had finished his snack and grew bored with Rosie's nursery rhymes, he began to really cry. Rosie called Isobel but it went straight to voicemail. She left a message to say Josh had woken up and wanted her. Then she took Josh into the playroom to try and distract him with his stacking cups, but the little boy was not interested. He started screaming and pushing her away. His face was bright red and snot was pouring out of both nostrils. Rosie was out of her depth. She tried Isobel again but once more it went to voicemail, so she called her dad.

'Hey, Ro.' Her dad sounded tired and a bit sad. 'Who's that crying?'

'It's Josh, Dad. Aunty Isobel asked me to watch him while she went to Paul's but he's woken up and I can't calm him down. Isobel's not answering her phone. I gave him snacks but there aren't any more and he smells bad.'

'Rosie, slow down. What are you saying? Where are you?'

67

PAUL

Thursday, 12 noon
1 day, 3½ hours left

Isobel had hit her head hard on the door frame of the office. The thud was enough to make Paul wince. He hadn't meant to hurt her. He only wanted her to calm the fuck down. She had landed in an awkward position on the floor. She wasn't out cold, but she was stunned enough to not respond to him when he asked if she was OK. Her eyes looked glazed and there was a stream of blood coming from her mouth where she had presumably bitten her tongue or her cheek.

He had to make a choice. Either he called an ambulance and faced the questions that would follow, or kept her here with him.

'Isobel, can you hear me? You've banged your head really hard. Should I lie you down or will that make things worse?' She didn't respond and he knew better than to google it. He might need to deny all knowledge of this thing. The thought caused him to pause. Was he really considering how to cover his tracks in case she died? He hadn't hurt her that badly, had he? But the truth was, he didn't know.

In the end, he decided to gamble on the fact she had a bit

of concussion and would come round. He hooked his arms under hers and half lifted, half dragged her to his office. He thought she might need to stay upright, he didn't know why, but he figured if the idea had occurred to him it had done so for a reason. He perched her on the chair and leaned her gently against the wall. She made a few muffled sounds but nothing he could discern as communication. When he was sure she wasn't going to topple off, he stood back and looked around for something helpful. Then he remembered that there were two robes he and Vanessa used to walk to and from the hot tub on the back of the utility room door. He fetched the belts off them and wrapped one around Isobel's waist and the back of the chair and the other across her upper torso, knotting them tightly. Hopefully this would stop her from sliding onto the floor or rolling to the side.

He needed to explain to her that they should work together to find out who was blackmailing them. She wouldn't want to listen after he'd hurt her, so he'd need to make her listen.

Was he really going to keep his friend tied up and pump her for information like a kidnapper? He knew Isobel had been given his secret to uncover and he had no idea how much progress she might have made. Was that why she had looked scared of him and run? Could be. Or, more likely, it was the wall of research she had seen in his office. He imagined that might look a touch suspicious, especially as he hadn't put his own name and details up there.

Even if he could convince Isobel to tell him her secret so he could use it against her, could he be sure she wouldn't then out him? She was an intelligent woman. It wouldn't take her that much longer to figure out that they had all been pitted against each other. It was a race against time. He had to expose Isobel before she suspected him. That way she'd be too busy dealing with the mess of her own life to pay him much attention. But all that relied on their blackmailer accepting the trade, and he had no idea whether they would.

Taking out his phone, he decided to play his hand and see what he got. After a few moments of thought he typed out a message and hit send.

Ryan's confession presents a problem for me.

I need another trade to ensure you will keep my past in the past. So how about I out Isobel instead?

That is unless I can find out who you are and stop you that way.

68

RYAN

Thursday, 12.30 p.m.
1 day, 3 hours left

Ryan felt bad about Isobel. When he'd told her he'd been threatened too, she'd said she hadn't been sleeping, that she'd been waking in the early hours in a panic, unable to get back to sleep. She had been feeling isolated and alone.

'It's awful to say this, but at least it's happening to you too, so I have you in my corner,' she'd said.

They were words that had come back to him during the night when he had awoken to face his own bout of insomnia. He should have clued her in to what he was doing. He hadn't wanted to tell her what was making him do it. He didn't want her to know about Mandy. He didn't want anyone to know.

And so he hadn't called until it was done. She would understandably be hurt and, knowing Isobel, angry.

He pulled into her drive and tried not to feel a little jealous that Isobel had turned to Paul. He knew he couldn't blame her.

'He's really smelly,' were the first words out of Rosie's mouth as she opened the door and handed over Josh.

Ryan couldn't help but laugh at the look on Rosie's face. She'd always flat out refused to handle anything in the nappy department with Ethan.

'Give him here, you big princess. Everyone poos, you know. Oh crikey, bud,' he said as he took the boy. 'What have they been feeding you?'

'See!'

'I'll go and change him.' Ryan carried Josh up to his nursery where Isobel and Annie had a changing table.

'Aunt Isobel is still not answering,' said Rosie. She stood as far away as she could on the landing.

'Have you tried Annie?'

Rosie nodded. 'Same. No answer, but she's at work. Oh, that's gross.'

'Rosie, little Josh is uncomfortable and I can make him feel better, so stop your moaning and see if you can find me a nappy bag in one of these drawers.'

Rosie came into the nursery making it obvious she was holding her breath. Josh stopped crying as soon as the dirty nappy was off his body.

'Right. You take Josh downstairs. I'll tidy up here and then we'll call Paul.' His phone buzzed. 'I bet this is Izzy now.'

That confession took balls, Ryan.

Tough days to come, no doubt.

Hope Rosie is doing ok.

Ryan concentrated on relaxing his jaw. The message was from Toby Phillips.

69

ISOBEL

Thursday, 1 p.m.
1 day, 2½ hours left

'Where am I?' Isobel's head felt heavy, as did the rest of her body. She tried to force herself conscious but every cell of her resisted. It felt like her very essence was pulling her back into the dark depths of slumber.

'Izzy? Hi, it's Paul. How are you feeling? How's your head?'

'Huh? Where am I?' Her words sounded muffled as she forced them out of her dry mouth.

'Izzy? Hi, it's Paul. Can you hear me?'

The fog lifted a little, just enough for her to fully open her eyes. Paul was kneeling at her feet, looking at her. She was sitting in his office. Her mouth tasted of metal and the left side of her tongue felt swollen and sore. Her dull headache had risen a good few notches and taken on a spikier pain which she put down to some kind of injury to her skull. She looked down. He had tied her to the chair. *What the hell?*

Isobel strained her arms against the ties but there was no real give.

Paul placed his hands over her wrists. 'It's OK, Izzy. I just need to talk to you.'

His warm smile threw her for a moment. He was a good man. A rational man. He wouldn't have wanted to hurt her. She began to smile back, but then she recalled the scuffle and the rage in his eyes as he'd pushed her, after which she couldn't remember anything until she'd woken up here. What had made him hate her so much? Hate all of them? Even Mandy. He loved Mandy.

Isobel looked at the wall covered with Post-it notes again.

You need to get out of here and tell someone.

She began to twist and turn her body in ever more frantic movements to loosen the restraints.

'Hey, hey. Careful.'

'You attacked me.'

'I really didn't mean to hurt you but you were acting so crazy. I thought you were having some kind of episode.'

'You tied me to a chair.'

'I didn't want to lie you down in case that wasn't the best thing to do with a head injury. I tried to ask you what I should do but you were not with it at all. I thought sitting you upright was the best thing to do.'

'But you tied me to a chair?' She couldn't get her head around this part.

'I think I know what freaked you out. It's this wall, isn't it?' He nodded towards the Post-it notes. 'I can see how that might have looked to you, but honestly this is how I work and I'm really frickin good at what I do. I'm getting close to working out who's behind it all, but I need your help.'

Isobel blinked a few times. To be honest, she was only half listening due to a strong wave of dizziness that made the room spin as if she was a teenager on her first bar crawl.

'Untie me, Paul. Now, please.' She spoke softly but firmly. She didn't want to make this situation any worse.

Mandy had once told her that Paul had worked really hard to control his anger issues following the treatment he'd received at the hands of his father when he was a boy. Isobel had only seen him lose his temper once before – way back after Mandy ended things, he had punched his fist through a stud wall outside the pub toilets. Ryan had asked Isobel to take a look at it. She was only a first-year medical student at the time, but still her friends had already started to consult her on their various ailments and illnesses as if she had access to some secret stash of solutions. She had cleaned Paul's hand as he'd ranted to Ryan about Mandy and the audacity of her finishing with him. Since then she had all but forgotten about the incident, until she'd seen the same anger in his eyes as he threw her across his hallway.

'If I do, will you promise not to freak out at me again?'

Isobel held his gaze until he looked away.

'I'm sorry I pushed you. There is no excuse for a man to strike a woman, even in self-defence.'

Self-defence? Is that how you're justifying it? thought Isobel, but decided this was not the time to debate things.

'Can I show you my thinking so far?' he said, standing up.

Isobel was not at all interested in his theories or questions any more. She just wanted him to untie her and let her go.

70

PAUL

Thursday, 1.30 p.m.
1 day, 2 hours left

'So, I'm thinking whoever is behind this has been snooping around you for a good few years. I mean, Ryan doped back in 2011 if we are to believe his account.'

Paul took the note from under Isobel's name that read, '*Indiscretion @ work*'.

'That's what you told me in the kitchen on Monday.' For a moment he held his breath, thinking she might simply confess everything off her own bat, but no such luck.

'How long ago did your thing occur?'

Isobel frowned. 'Untie me, Paul.'

He hesitated. Would she run? Fight him again? He could tell by her expression she was not answering any questions while she was tied up, so he had to risk it. He removed her restraints and stepped back, ready for her to bolt. She started to push herself up from the chair but then sank back down again and closed her eyes. This was his chance.

'So, how long ago did it occur?' he said again.

'Why?'

'Under ten years? Over?'

Isobel opened her eyes to look at him. 'Does it matter?'

'Maybe. Someone has been lurking in the background and stalking your lives. If we can get a clear timeline of when that might have started it would give us a clue to either who is behind this or why they're doing it.'

Isobel frowned and he could tell she was still weighing up the idea he might be responsible for all of it.

'Isobel, if I was behind all of this, I would already know your secret. Why would I be asking you about it? I promise, I'm trying to help.' Isobel seemed to soften. 'Was it at the hospital?'

'I'd rather not . . .'

'It's OK. You don't have to tell me the details, but the context might help. Where has your stalker had to gain access to? How might they have uncovered your secrets?'

Paul waited. When Isobel offered nothing, he knew he had to try a different tack. He needed to know her secret so that if she found out his he had some collateral to use. He moved to stand alongside Mandy's notes.

'Do you have any idea what Mandy might have done?'

'No. You?' she said.

'I wish I did. What could have been so bad?' He smoothed down the Post-it note under Mandy's name that read, '*Died Friday, 3.34 p.m.*'. 'Why do you think they're doing it, whoever it is? Is it jealousy, revenge?' He looked at Isobel and used the most powerful tactic he had for making people talk: silence.

71

ISOBEL

Thursday, 1.30 p.m.
1 day, 2 hours left

After a long while, she finally spoke.

'I want to know why you care so much. You say you're not behind all of this, so why have you put so much effort into it? Why that wall and all the obvious research? Why are you so desperate to know what Mandy, Ryan and I have done?'

'Oh for pity's sake, Izzy—'

'No. Why do you care what I did in my past?'

'So I can find out who's doing this to you. I told you that!'

'Bullshit. Why would knowing what I did make a difference?'

'Well, if you think about it rationally, if I know what happened, and where and when it happened, I could look at who might have found out.' He pronounced every word carefully, as if she was slow on the uptake.

'How?'

'How would I find out? That depends on what happened and when.'

Isobel held the base of her palm against her forehead as a spike of pain seared through her brain. She stared at him for a long moment as her aching mind worked hard to put things together. 'You think if I tell you my secret now, it will stop me from telling them that you hurt me. That's why you tied me to the chair?'

There was a look in Paul's eyes that sent a small chill through Isobel and the next few moments passed in slow motion. He moved towards where she sat, and she tried to stand, but the dizziness had her slumping back into the seat once more. She raised her hands in front of her face.

'I'm not going to hit you!'

He grabbed the arms of the chair as she tried to spin it away from him, using her feet to walk it across the floor on its wheels, but the carpet was too thick and her efforts did nothing more than jolt her already painful brain against her skull.

'What on earth is going on?' Vanessa stood in the doorway with her hands on her hips. 'Isobel? What happened?' She looked at Paul. 'What happened to her? She looks awful.'

'She fell and hit her head.'

'You mean you pushed me and smashed up my phone.'

'What are you both, twelve?' Vanessa came over and placed her hand on Isobel's forehead. 'Paul, go and make some camomile tea. The bags are in the yellow box in the cupboard.'

'I don't want tea.'

'No, but you look like you need it. You're as pale as a sheet.'

When Paul was out of earshot, Isobel grabbed Vanessa's arm. 'Your husband knocked me out and tied me up because I discovered he's been tormenting us all. Have you seen all his creepy little notes about every aspect of our lives?'

'You really did bump your head, didn't you?'

'I'm serious, Vanessa. Not only did he attack me, but if I'm right, he made Ryan torpedo his career, and don't get me started on Mandy.'

'Isobel, I don't know why you would blame Paul for all this

245

nonsense. Those notes are him trying to figure out who's behind this whole thing. He told me all about it. He's trying to help you.'

'You would say that.'

'Why? Why would I say that? Do I strike you as the kind of woman who would sit back and let her husband stalk his friends and his ex-girlfriend? Do you think if he was doing such a thing he would stick Post-it notes all over the walls of the house where I live and where visitors such as yourself might easily see? My husband and I are by no means perfect, Isobel, but please do not insult us.'

'One camomile tea,' said Paul, returning with a tall china mug.

'Did you put sugar in it?' When Paul shook his head, Vanessa tutted. 'She's in shock. Give that to me.'

Paul avoided Isobel's eyes as they waited.

'Here you go.' Vanessa said a couple of minutes later, handing the mug to Isobel.

'I just want to go home. I don't need a drink.'

'I know. I'll take you now. I'm meeting a client for a boozy lunch in town. I was going to call a taxi but I'll drive your car down and drop you home. I can walk from yours. Just take a few sips for me. Do you have your keys?'

'Ness?'

'I don't want to hear it, Paul. You've done enough. This has gone too far, do you hear me?'

Isobel took a few sips of the hot tea as she watched Vanessa stare Paul down. She had always imagined Vanessa wore the trousers. In fact, she and Annie had joked about it, but it was still interesting to see.

'Right, let's get you home,' Vanessa said when the tea was all but drunk.

Vanessa helped Isobel up and walked with her to the car. Isobel stumbled a couple of times but Vanessa was on hand to steady her.

'Do you need a doctor?'

'I just need to get home. I left Josh with Rosie.' Isobel sat in the passenger side of her car. She was struggling to keep her eyes open. Should she be worried? Had that bang on the head done more damage than she knew? If someone told her they were feeling exhausted and lightheaded after a head injury she would without doubt tell them to get to hospital.

Vanessa opened the driver's door.

'I think I need to go to A and E,' Isobel said, closing her eyes and leaning back against the headrest.

72

PAUL

Thursday, 2 p.m.
1 day, 1½ hours left

'Vanessa?' he said under his breath as she opened the driver's side door of Isobel's car.

She closed it and walked back to where he stood in the doorway. She looked more furious than he had ever seen her.

'What are you doing? As soon as she gets home she'll call the police. She already tried it and that was before she fell.'

'You pushed her.'

'What?'

'She said you pushed her.'

'She attacked me! I was defending myself. She was half crazed.'

'And was Stuart Fraser half crazed too?'

'That's not fair.'

'I tell you what's not fair, Paul, my having to clean up your mess because you can't stop yourself from having a temper tantrum. What did you think was going to happen when you tied her to a chair?'

'I was scared she'd slip off it. She was unconscious.'

Vanessa's eyebrows rose and her expression said, *WOW*.

'She overreacted. Lost her shit and I had to stop her from call-ing the police because we all know what happens then. You can't take her home. I'm telling you it will be the end of us. Everything will come out.'

'How stupid do you think I am?'

'I don't think you're stupid at all, I'm just saying—'

'Get my car keys. They're in the kitchen.'

'What for?'

'So you can drive my car out of the garage and I can drive Iso-bel's in. I have no intention of taking her home.'

'How will that help? She'll just raise merry hell. We have to talk to her, convince her.'

'And that was going well, was it? The talking? I heard you and it was crystal clear she was telling you nothing at all. She thinks you're doing all of this to her. She's paranoid and scared.'

'So what are you suggesting we do?'

'Let her sleep.' Vanessa looked back at the car and Paul fol-lowed her gaze. 'I figured two of your pills would do it.'

'Oh, God.' His sleeping pills were prescription strength. He had been advised to only rely on them two or three times a week at most, and only to take one tablet at a time.

People at work often said he could be ruthless and he would always smile to himself and think, *If you want to know what ruthless looks like, you should meet my wife.* He had sometimes wondered if she was wired up differently. She could destroy some-one's business and crush their career without breaking sweat or losing a wink of sleep.

'Don't "Oh, God" me. You're the one who's put us in this awful situation. Now we need to buy ourselves time. Once you've betrayed Isobel, she'll have a bigger issue with you than you push-ing her over. But we can deal with that at the time because we'll be in the clear.'

'But she wouldn't tell me anything. I have nothing to trade.'

'Of course you do. Just guess. She's a baby doctor with a shameful secret. I wonder what that could be? I reckon your blackmailer's guessing anyway. They looked at Ryan and thought professional cyclist, probably doped, which is why they said he did it at the Tour de France. But he said that's wrong, he doped but not at that race.'

'Well he would say that, the Tour stage was his biggest win.'

'Or they guessed. Which means they look at Isobel and think *paediatrician*, so she probably messed up and a patient died. You do the same when you send them your trade – you make it vague enough that they think you know. You can do that. "I think Isobel broke her vow to do no harm", yada yada.'

'And then I go to the press with what?'

'Oh for pity's sake, Paul, the print media are not the people who ruin lives these days. You need to be thinking TikTok, Insta, Twitter. Those people couldn't care less about facts. They only want a fire to burn someone with.'

Paul thought about what Vanessa had said as he fetched her keys and opened the garage door with the electric fob. He pulled her convertible out on to the drive and watched her reverse Isobel's car in. Isobel's head was tilted back and her mouth was open wide.

'I think we should see this as an opportunity,' said Vanessa as she watched the garage door close. 'I was getting pretty sick of spending all our time with your friends anyway. Remember how we used to talk about earning enough money so we could work for six months then travel for six? We do earn enough now, so why don't we do that and live the lives we want instead of living in the pockets of your childhood buddies?'

Paul looked at his wife. He wasn't sure why she was helping him with all of this but he was glad of it, and it was the least he could do to give her the life she wanted afterwards.

'No one could have guessed my past,' he said. 'Or Mandy's.'

That was the problem with her theory.

'What, the fact a farmer's daughter isn't thrown by a bit of road-kill?' Vanessa smirked at Paul's shocked expression. 'You were given Ryan to shame, Isobel was given you, that means Ryan's Audrey Raye question must be about Isobel or Mandy, and given the accident happened yards from Mandy's house, it's not rocket science. But you are right. Your past is different.'

'Which means what? I'm the only real target? The rest of them are noise?'

'The rest of them are your punishment, darling. Anyone look-ing at your life would see you can't get through a week without seeing or speaking to one of them.'

73

RYAN

Thursday, 1.30 p.m.
1 day, 2 hours left

Ryan had called Paul but there was no answer. Next he tried Isobel but, like Rosie said, the phone immediately went to voice-mail. Finally, he called Annie.

'Have you heard from Izzy in the last hour or so?'

'No. Why?'

Ryan explained how Isobel had left Rosie and Josh to go to Paul's house and now they couldn't get hold of her. Annie said she was on her way home.

As soon as Annie came through the door, Josh called out 'Mama', and reached for her out of Ryan's arms then gripped her tightly around the neck and buried his head in her shoulder.

'I'm sorry, Ryan. I found her pretty much passed out on the kitchen floor last night – she'd downed nearly three bottles of wine on her own. Drunk herself into oblivion. And that's not all, she's been restless and stressed out for days. She told me someone was threatening her and it's all to do with something that happened years ago at work. I've been out trying to find out what that could be because she won't tell me. She just said I needed to take Josh and leave her because . . .' Annie swallowed, 'because she doesn't deserve us.'

Ryan assured Annie that Isobel would be fine. 'I'll drive over to Paul's and see what's going on.'

'Who is doing this to you all?'

'I've no idea.' He wondered if he should mention Toby Phillips but thought better of it. If Izzy really had been involved in splitting up Toby's sister and Mandy's brother, and that had in some way incurred Toby's wrath, that was a box of mess he didn't want to be responsible for opening with Izzy's wife. Better to speak to Izzy herself.

'And why on earth did you do that press conference? It was career suicide. You should have come and talked to me.'

Ryan forced back his irritation. This was not the time. Annie was worried about Izzy. 'I had no choice.'

'What do you mean you had no choice? There's always a choice.'

'OK then. I had my reasons. Can we leave it at that?'

'No. No, actually, we can't. Isobel is not OK and she says this idiot is planning to go public with something in her past, tomorrow. I trawled through all the press reports I could find this morning, from when she was at uni and the time she was at Harrogate, but I couldn't find anything troubling related to paediatrics or Isobel. Nothing jumped out. Do you know what it is? Has she told you?'

Ryan shook his head.

'Jesus, Ry, we've got to do something. She's not coping. Whatever this is she seems to think everyone will hate her so it must be bad. Have you told the police?'

'No, and you mustn't, Annie. Whoever is doing this made it quite clear – we go to the police, they go to the press.'

'They're going to go to the press anyway, aren't they? So why not try to stop them before they can?'

'Because it's not only Isobel they're threatening. It's bigger than that. Did she tell you what she's been asked to find out?'

'What do you mean?'

'We were given a question and told if we could find out the answer before tomorrow then whoever is doing this will keep our secret, but the problem is, these questions relate to someone else we know, someone else's shameful secret, and so then you get a choice – you or them?'

Annie was quiet for a moment as Ryan's words sank in.

'Right, so what is Isobel's question? What has she been told to find out and about who?'

'All I know is it was something to do with someone betraying her at the Royal Oak.'

'She asked me about that the day we found out about Mandy, she asked me how I could find out something that happened at the Royal Oak. Which Royal Oak?'

'I have no idea. Look, the question said something about it not being the first time. And then she got a clue that related to the Red Cross but I couldn't make any sense of it.'

'Ryan, tell me exactly what it said.'

'OK.' Ryan thought for a moment. 'It was kind of weirdly phrased, something along the lines of, "Who betrayed you in England first at the Royal Oak?"'

'In England? That's ridiculous. How many bloody Royal Oak pubs must there be in England? This person is having a laugh. They're setting you challenges you can't possibly solve.'

Ryan looked at his feet as he thought about Mandy. 'I was able to answer mine.'

Annie stared at him for a long moment. 'You chose to shame yourself instead of your friend. Well, I hope they are bloody grateful.'

'Dad, can we go soon? I'm hungry,' Rosie called from the front door.

'Why don't I go and check on Isobel? And I'll get this madam some lunch while I'm at it. Then you, me and Iz can sit down and talk this out, decide what to do.'

'If I had it my way we'd be calling the police now, but I'll give you this afternoon.'

Ryan nodded. That was fair enough. It wasn't his decision to make now. He'd made his choice and done his deal. Now it was about Isobel and Annie's life. It was their decision.

As they drove away, Ryan turned his attention to Rosie. She must be wondering what the hell was going on and why everyone was so stressed. 'Come on then, we can grab a sandwich from the Co-op on our way back.'

'I'm fine. I'm not really hungry.'

'What? You just interrupted Annie and me to say . . .' Ryan stopped talking as they reached the lights and he looked at his daughter. He could see the tracks of tears running down her cheek. 'Ro, honey?' He placed his hand on her leg.

'They won't stop, Dad. It's everywhere. I can't go on Snapchat or TikTok. They've made memes of you cycling with needles poking out of your arms.'

The car behind beeped its horn and Ryan turned back to the road. 'I'm so sorry, love.' His words were so quiet he wasn't sure she'd heard them.

'It's so embarrassing. People at school used to ask me all about you, especially the boys. They thought you were cool and I . . .'

'You liked that. I know.'

'Why did you do it?'

Ryan blew out a long, slow breath. He should have known this question was coming. He should have been ready for it. 'I was young, and stupid, and I suppose—'

'No! Why did you tell everyone about it? Nobody needed to know. Everything was fine. You've ruined my life.'

The lump in his throat felt large and heavy. He swallowed over and over to try and force it away but it sat there, stable and stubborn. When he'd thought about the consequences of coming clean they'd all been about him; his reputation, his relationships, his work. He'd not stopped to think about how it would harm everyone else. How his daughter might be harassed and how she'd have to carry his shame with her throughout life: 'Oh, you're Ryan Fallon's daughter, the drug cheat.' The same would be true for Ethan. He'd never be proud of his dad like Rosie had been. He'd grow up with a different father, one he most likely wouldn't talk about. Then there were his parents; they would be treated differently too, possibly even blamed for raising a cheat. His father was such a proud man. How would he cope with that? They should be enjoying their retirement and he'd landed a whole dump truck of crap on their lives.

'Have you spoken to Gus?'

Rosie shook her head.

The message from Toby was bugging Ryan. The guy was bragging, he felt sure. *Tough days to come.* And how dare he express concern over Rosie?

'That's probably . . .' he was going to say for the best but then realized that was a bit too pointed. 'You know, honey, in tough times you often find out who your real friends are. The people who care about you will stick with you. They'll call and they'll be there on the other side.'

'Like Uncle Paul and Aunt Izzy with you?'

Ryan nodded as he realized neither of them had actually called following his press conference.

'Isobel's car's not here.'

Rosie's words broke Ryan from his woes. She was right; only Vanessa's Mercedes was parked in front of the double garage. Its roof was down.

'OK, wait here, honey.' He half climbed out of the car then turned back. 'I'm sorry I've let you down, Rosie.'

'It's OK.'

'No, no it's not. I'm going to do my best to make everything OK and I love you.'

Rosie's eyes filled with tears again and she nodded.

Ryan knocked on the door and waited. There was no answer. He looked through the small window into the hall but it was empty, as was the kitchen at the far end.

'No one in?'

Rosie made Ryan jump and he put a hand on her shoulder. 'Seems not. I'll try one more time. He knocked again and rang Paul's phone at the same time. 'I think I can hear it ringing inside.' He looked through the window again but there was no sign of Paul.

'Rosie. Come away from there, that's rude.' Rosie was standing on a flower bed and peering in through Paul's office window.

'Look at this.' She beckoned her dad over.

There was no answer from Paul, so he searched for Vanessa's number as he carefully stepped across the shrubs to reach Rosie.

'Look at all those notes, and your name is at the top with Isobel and Mandy's.'

Ryan couldn't quite believe his eyes. Isobel had said Paul was helping her, but this was something else.

'Er, what's going on?' Vanessa exited the house holding her ringing phone. She was carrying a bag over one arm and her car keys.

'Sorry. I thought I could hear Paul's phone ringing.' Ryan ended the call to Vanessa. 'Is Isobel still here? We can't get hold of her.' He carefully stepped off the garden and back on to the drive, encouraging Rosie to follow.

'She left not long ago.'

'Did she say if she was going home? Her phone is going straight to voicemail, which is odd for Izzy.'

'No, she didn't say. Anyway, I have to go, I'm meeting a friend for coffee.'

'Where's Paul?'

'He was called into court.' She climbed into the convertible. 'Sorry, can we? I'm running late.' She gestured to his car, which was blocking her exit.

Ryan climbed back into the driver's seat. He was a little irritated with how dismissive Vanessa was about Isobel not answering her phone, but then she and Paul had the advantage of not being directly involved in any of this mess.

'I'm going to go back to Isobel and Annie's. What do you want to do?'

'Can you drop me at Nanna Felicity's?'

Ryan always felt a little gutted when Rosie wanted to be somewhere else other than with him, but he couldn't blame her, and it wasn't right for her to be listening to all of this anyway.

74

Oh you think you are so very clever, don't you, Ryan? You actually think you've won.

But you don't get to choose how this ends.

I do.

I have been patient and diligent in my preparation. I have watched your smug, smarmy self breeze through life, and it has sickened me to my very core. The idea of you being happy, achieving your dreams, and having friends by your side fills me with a disgust that I can't abide.

You are forever in my sights because you put yourself there. You and your friends did not need to step into my crosshairs, but you chose to do so anyway. And a fundamental truth of life is that you never really know the people you cross and what they are capable of. Who they really are. Whether they are going to operate by the same rules and laws of life that you expect.

Because some of us run our own race and dispense our own justice. And we believe you reap what you sow.

You may think you've played a good game. That you delivered checkmate. But it was only check, because I have one more move to make that will remove your crown for ever. One final, deadly move.

75

RYAN

Thursday, 2.30 p.m.
1 day, 1 hour left

Stephanie's father, Graham, was in the garden pruning his roses when Ryan and Rosie pulled into the drive.

'Hello, sunshine,' Graham called to Rosie as he saw her climb out of Ryan's car. 'Nanna's inside, unless you've come to help me out here?'

Graham nodded to Ryan. They had maintained a civil enough relationship over the years, although Ryan suspected Graham and his wife had fuelled some of the conflicts with Stephanie.

'Is it OK if Rosie hangs out here for a few hours?' She had already let herself in.

'Always. Sorry to hear of all your troubles, young man. A bit of a silly thing to do taking drugs, though, only yourself to blame there.'

Ryan always hated it when Graham called him young man, as if he was still Stephanie's teenage boyfriend, but he couldn't really argue with anything else the man had said.

'Ryan? Wait a sec.' Felicity appeared at his car window as he was about to drive off. 'Rosie came to see me the other day saying she was worried about you. I know you wouldn't want to stress her out so I said I'd check in to see if everything's OK . . . I mean, clearly things are not, given that press conference.'

Ryan sighed. 'Thanks, Felicity. There's a lot going on at the moment, so you could say I'm stressed, yeah, but I didn't mean to worry Rosie. Thanks for letting me know. I'll speak to her.'

Felicity looked at him for a moment as if she was expecting more detail. 'Is everything OK with Isobel? I saw her in town yesterday and she was terribly fidgety. She kept looking around as if someone was following her.'

'She's having a tough time with Mandy's death, I think.'

'Ah, yes, of course. Very sad news. Stephanie is terribly cut up about it. But Isobel looked ill. Maybe she needs to see the GP.'

'Right. Thanks for letting me know. We're trying to find her, actually. She's gone AWOL.'

Felicity sucked air in through her teeth. 'What is going on, Ryan? Rosie overheard Isobel saying someone was targeting you both, and maybe Mandy too.'

Shit. When had she overheard that?

'If that's true, I hope you've informed the police. I know Inspector Holland at Ilkley station if you need a friendly ear.'

'No. No. Honestly, Felicity, it's nothing, just a bit of internet trolling Isobel experienced. No need for the police.' He couldn't afford for Felicity to call her inspector friend on their behalf. He needed to close it down.

'And now you can't find her?'

'It's only been a few hours. She'll have gone for a swim or to see a friend. She'll turn up soon I've no doubt. But look, thank you for tipping me off about Rosie. I appreciate that and I will take care of it.'

As Ryan drove away he saw Felicity watching him from the driveway. He wasn't sure she had accepted his brush off that all was OK. He wasn't in the best frame of mind to bat off the questions today. He imagined her hand hovering over the inspector's number. As much as he believed Felicity's concern for Rosie was genuine, he also knew Felicity and Graham didn't rate him very highly as a father.

He just hoped he'd said enough to convince Felicity to not make that call.

76

PAUL

Thursday, 2.30 p.m.
1 day, 1 hour left

A message pinged on his phone at the same time as it began to ring. He had ignored a couple of calls from Ryan but this number was unfamiliar and so he answered it, just in case it was the blackmailer calling with a response.

'Paul, it's Mira Hussain from the *Guardian*. We spoke last Friday.'

The knot in Paul's stomach tightened a few notches. 'What can I do for you, Mira?'

'That reporter you called about, Carl Baker, he just emailed and offered me a story about a King's Counsel with a dodgy past.'

The knot of nerves unfurled like a snake and rose up Paul's throat in a flash of rage. *Motherfucker.*

'Did you take it?'

'I didn't say no. I've asked him to send me a draft but he wants payment first. I've never heard of this Baker fella so I wanted to check him out. Is this about you? If you want to give me an exclusive I'm sure I can sort out a story that will treat you more favourably, or would you prefer that I pay the man?'

'He's a shyster, Mira, that's why I called on Friday to tip you off. I've had dealings with him professionally and let's just say he may not be the most satisfied customer.'

'You got him convicted?'

'I'd prefer not to go into details, but you know as well as I that sometimes people hold a grudge, and when they have time on their hands they can come up with many a hare-brained scheme. I wouldn't want you to fall foul of his fraud.'

The line was worryingly quiet. He needed Mira to buy this and back off.

'Mira? You still there?'

'I'm going to need more than that, Paul. He made the story sound meaty. If you can send me details of your history with him, something I can corroborate to prove this is a revenge pitch, I'll send him packing.'

'How long have I got?'

'Shall we say twenty-four hours?'

Fuck, fuck, fuck.

Paul hung up and opened the message that had arrived. It was from Shame@pm.me. Hopefully this would give him the go-ahead to shame Isobel and end this hell.

I will make a trade but not using Isobel.

Ryan's actions present a problem for us both.

He is a fraud who thinks he can cheat his way out of this game too. He cannot.

And you are going to teach him that for me.

Only then will I keep your secret.

Paul read the message a couple of times and then sent a reply.

What is it you expect me to do?

He paced back and forth in the summer house at the bottom of his garden. He was livid with this whole situation but, more than that, he was scared.

The shot was already lined up with Mira Hussain and if Paul didn't do whatever was asked of him, he had no doubt the trigger would be pulled, and the fact he had hurt Isobel would not work in his favour. In fact, it would act as the final nail in his coffin. He couldn't out himself like Ryan. It simply wasn't an option. Not only would it wreck his career, it would endanger his life. Kyle Renton's boys wouldn't hesitate to use it as an excuse to exact their own particular brand of revenge.

Take him out of the game. Permanently.

And make it look like an accident.

Do we have a deal?

THE SHAME GAME:
A TRUE CRIME DOCUMENTARY

Episode 3 of 3 – The Price

EXT - REECE-JOHNSON FAMILY
HOME - DAYTIME

The screen shows a large Yorkshire stone
house with three curved steps leading up
to the front door. To the right there is a
picture window and then a double garage with
a grey-green door.

Annie Walters stands in the driveway. Her
curly hair is blowing in the breeze and she
brushes it back with her left hand and holds
it in place.

The camera zooms in on ANNIE'S face.

                    VOICE (O.S.)

        So this is where Isobel was kept?

                        ANNIE

        That's right.

Annie Walters shakes her head.

                        ANNIE

        I don't like to think about it.
        Was she unconscious the whole
        time or was she coming round
        and calling for help? If so,
        did they ignore her? They were
        our friends. How could they do
        something like that?

                    VOICE (O.S.)

        And you had no suspicions about
        them at the time?

                        ANNIE

        We didn't even know they were
        involved in all of this. Ryan
        and I thought Paul was trying to
        help Izzy.

Annie's laugh is bitter.

ANNIE

I always liked Paul a lot. He was
quick-witted. He could be a little
brutal at times, but I always
believed he was a good man. A man
who was trying to make the world
a better place. I knew Vanessa was
less principled but I couldn't
argue with her work ethic, you
know. She put more hours in than
any of us so she deserved her fancy
life and house. But I don't think
any of us would have believed what
they were capable of.

78

PAUL

Thursday, 3.30 p.m.
1 day left

How long had he been sitting, reasoning it out?

As if it was possible to reason out murder.

That's what was being asked of him. Premeditated murder to save his own skin. He had been more than prepared to betray Ryan and wreck his life. But taking it away altogether? That was something else.

He knew he had two simple questions to answer in order to decide. Could he justify it to himself? And if he could, could he get away with it?

He started with the second. It was easier. He had spent his career reviewing and rewriting the stories that took people from a calm life to one of chaos and catastrophe. He knew there was always a journey: a dot-to-dot trail that led from one incident to another, one seemingly insignificant decision followed by an unintended consequence. Then add to that the matter of human emotion, which in most cases defied all logic. So if Ryan was going to die, there needed to be a dot-to-dot trail that explained things independently of Paul.

He pondered on the events of the week. Mandy's death, the blackmail, Ryan deciding to come clean and having it blow up in his face spectacularly. In the space of twenty-four hours, his TV contracts were gone, he'd been sacked from his charity and he must be having a hard time walking down the street. All of which made despair a good emotional option.

Is that what Mandy had felt?

He pushed the thought away. He couldn't afford to get sentimental.

So how might despair affect Ryan's judgements? What might it drive him to do?

Mandy stepped in front of a van.

Paul closed his eyes and tried not to picture Mandy crumpled on the road.

He could invite Ryan out for a run. Take him up across the moors to where it was isolated and desolate. And then what? Make it look like he'd jumped off something? Or like he'd succumbed to an error of judgement. Runners sometimes fall foul of a bad fall or dehydration. Could he make it seem like Ryan had been so distracted by the week's trauma that he'd run too far and drunk too little? It was particularly hot this summer. But Ryan was an ex-professional sportsman. Would it follow that he made an error in hydration, and how would Paul ensure it all happened? Tie him up like he had Isobel? Hit him over the head? Push him down a ravine? The truth of the matter was, not only could he not risk leaving some physical evidence of himself at the scene, he didn't want to be there. Ryan was his closest friend. He didn't want to see him hurt and suffering.

Which brought him to the next question. If something bad did happen to Ryan, could Paul justify it?

And the answer to that was Kyle Renton.

Renton was Paul's greatest achievement as a barrister. Paul was revered far and wide for being the man who put Renton behind bars. The case had made his career. He'd fought for it too. Charmed the clerk at the chambers to make sure when the request came in, Paul was the next in line to prosecute it. He wasn't the most experienced barrister in the area but he had good numbers and, as it would transpire, a special something that set him apart from most of his privileged peers. He knew what it meant to be part of a gang. He knew the kinds of brutal bastard it attracts. And he knew how to push their buttons.

The case against Renton was based on a long-standing rivalry with Mitch Bleacher's gang that had led to an attack on Bleacher's twenty-year-old son, Sean. Sean claimed three men jumped him outside his gym and then Kyle Renton chased him through the streets of Bradford city to the home of Sean's girlfriend. When she opened the door with her two-year-old son at her side, Renton took a shot at the fleeing Sean, missing him and killing the child. A week later, Sean Bleacher's girlfriend miscarried their second child. It caused a public outcry. The image of the little boy's mum sobbing on her knees made the front page of every paper. Everyone expected Mitch Bleacher to administer his own revenge, but instead he tipped off the police as to Renton's whereabouts and let justice take its course.

'I want him rotting in a cell for the rest of his days,' Mitch had told Paul when they first met.

For a good few weeks it looked like Renton might get away with it. He was sticking to his denial and the only evidence from a CCTV camera on the street outside Sean Bleacher's girlfriend's house revealed nothing more than a figure in a black hoody. No weapon had been found. No DNA linked Kyle Renton to the scene. It was Sean's word against Kyle's and Kyle was smart. He came across as charming, said he was appalled at the loss of a child, how he had kids of his own and couldn't imagine the pain Sean and his girlfriend were experiencing. He was sorry for their loss but he didn't do it, he didn't order it and he didn't condone it. End of.

Paul had begun by stroking Renton's ego. He was a powerful man who had made a success of his life, albeit through crime, but his house was big and his reputation bigger still. Everyone in Bradford and Leeds knew who Kyle Renton was. It was a tactic that did the trick. Paul could see Renton becoming all puffed-up and proud, which is when Paul turned to goading him. His empire was crumbling, he'd lost ground to Mitch Bleacher, his gang members were defecting and he himself was looking old at forty-three. He must be frustrated, angry and bitter about how things were going. Wasn't he smart enough to stop the decline? Wasn't he tough enough to drive away the competition? Wasn't he brave enough to be the man? Eventually, after hours of picking and picking at Renton, the man lost his temper and the mask slid. Which is when Paul took his chance. That final interaction was etched in his memory as if it happened yesterday.

'Mitch Bleacher and his rat, Sean, are nothing,' Kyle had shouted in a rage.

'Still more impressive than you, though.'

'No. Not even a little bit. They're nothing but a pair of nobodies meddling in a world they don't have the balls to be in.'

'Did that justify an attack on Sean?'

'Look at the way he ran away like the rat he is. He wasn't man enough to stand up for himself so he ran to his missus and she was dumb enough to bring their brat to the door.'

'Was the boy in her arms or by her side?'

'By her side.'

The silence in the courtroom took on its own energy; a sizzle in the air as every person realized what Kyle Renton had said. This detail had not been released to the press. Only someone who had been there would know. Renton was a little behind the groove. It wasn't until Paul asked his final question that the realization dawned in his eyes.

'So you saw the little boy and fired anyway?'

Since his conviction, Renton had launched appeal after appeal and vocally challenged his conviction on the grounds of poor representation at trial, misconduct by the judge, jury bias, everything he could think of. None of it had been upheld but still the man cried foul. If Paul's past came out, particularly the truth about what he had done to ensure the conviction of Leonard Phelps in 2013, that could be a game changer because, like Phelps, Kyle Renton was black.

He thought of Vanessa's hypothesis. She thought that this was all about him and his friends were being used as collateral damage, a way to attack his whole life.

But what if Vanessa was wrong? What if Kyle Renton had no idea about any of this? What if it was a weak-minded weasel like Stuart Fraser exacting some petty revenge in the name of his cousin because he thought they'd all been complicit in what Mandy had done?

If that was the case, and Paul failed to do what they asked, his past would come out and Kyle Renton wouldn't hesitate to take advantage. And if Renton walked free, that would not only be bad news for the local area, it would bring personal danger to Paul and Vanessa.

The reality of the situation was clear. Either Renton was behind this whole thing and Paul was fucked already, or he wasn't, and Paul had one chance to stop him from finding out.

Could Paul justify things if Ryan was to experience an accident? There was a high chance he could. He also knew exactly who he could call on to help him; someone who wanted to keep Kyle Renton locked away even more badly than he did.

Paul walked back through the house and into the garage. Isobel was still in her car, spark out. He watched her chest rise and fall a few times to reassure himself she was only sleeping and then he climbed into his own car and drove to a supermarket, where he bought a pay-as-you-go phone. He then walked across town to ensure he was nowhere near his own car and phone in order to make the call.

'Yup?'

'Mitch, it's Paul Reece-Johnson. You said if I ever needed a favour I should call . . .'

79

RYAN

Thursday, 4.30 p.m.
23 hours left

'Izzy's phone is still off. I called the hospital and her mum's but she's not at either.' Annie sat at the table chewing her nail and bouncing Josh on her knee.

'What about friends?' said Ryan.

'Just Mandy, you and Paul locally.'

'No one from work?'

'Since starting at Leeds she's avoided building friendships. She says it makes it harder to manage the team.'

'Might she have gone for a drive or a walk? Felicity said she didn't seem well when she saw her in town yesterday, that it seemed Izzy thought someone was following her.'

'Why would she think that?'

'I don't know. Maybe all of this is making her paranoid. You said she hadn't been sleeping.'

'Or someone *was* following her. This person persecuting you all knows a lot so it's not beyond imagination they might be a stalker. Where is she and why is her phone off?'

Ryan thought about that moment at Camille's party when

Isobel had looked off into the trees, said that she had an odd feeling. He'd felt similar, like someone was out there watching him. 'Let me call Camille and get her over here to look after Josh. Ethan will love it and you and I can go looking for Izzy. Make a list of any places you think she might go.'

By the time Camille arrived, Annie had called all the local hospitals to check if Isobel had been admitted but there was no sign of her. Ryan and Annie agreed to take separate cars and drive around the local area. Annie had made a list, but it was a short one.

'Keep in touch,' Ryan said.

'Wait, I forgot to mention,' Annie said, walking to his car, 'Isobel had it all wrong with that question she was sent. I'm pretty sure it's not a medical thing. After you left I kept replaying it in my head and that phrase – "betrayed you in England first" – just struck me as odd. Look at this.' She opened the internet browser on her phone and showed Ryan a Wikipedia page.

Ryan looked at the gold circle with 'England First Party' written around the circumference.

'And look at their emblem in the middle.'

'A red cross.'

'A St George's cross, from the English flag. They were a far-right nationalist group from the Blackburn area.'

'And someone Isobel knows is a member?'

'Was a member. They've disbanded, but yeah.'

Isobel had a Syrian mother. In the eyes of these people, she would be seen as an aberration. Who the hell in Isobel's life would think that and, if she found out, why on earth would she choose to protect them?

Ryan's phone buzzed to alert him to a message. It was a voice recording from Felicity.

'Hello Ryan. I hope you managed to track Isobel down. I wanted to let you know I spoke to Inspector Holland and asked if he had

any experience with internet trolling, is that what you called it? I didn't mention you specifically I just said I was asking for a friend. Anyway, he said he hadn't dealt with anything like that himself but he has colleagues in Leeds and Bradford who specialize in something he called . . . digital crime. I wrote that down to make sure I got it right. Anyway, I hope that helps. I'll text you his number.'

Ryan closed his eyes and blew out a slow breath. This was the last thing he needed. Stephanie's mum loved nothing more than to use her local contacts to find help for others. She had spent two terms as the Conservative MP for Ilkley. He knew she was trying to help, but this sailed dangerously close to informing the police of what was going on. Thank God she'd not mentioned him or Isobel by name. He quickly texted back in the hope it would stop her from taking it any further.

Thanks, Felicity. Please do send his number.

I'll pass it on to Isobel so she can make contact if she wants to.

80

PAUL

Thursday, 6.30 p.m.
21 hours left

When Paul returned from buying the phone to call Mitch Bleacher, Vanessa's car was not in the driveway, so he parked his car next to Isobel's in the garage. She never reacted to his arrival. Her head had lolled to one side and her mouth was still open. How long would two of those sleeping pills knock her out for? He cautiously moved to the car window beside her and watched her chest to check she was still breathing.

By this time tomorrow it would all be over, one way or another. He couldn't bring himself to think about Ryan and the things he had set in motion.

His brief to Mitch had been clear: I'm being blackmailed. To make it go away, Ryan Fallon needs to die. It needs to look like an accident. Nothing can be linked back to me and it needs to happen tonight.

Mitch had been reluctant at first. He couldn't organize things so quickly. He wasn't running an on-demand service, but when Paul stressed the consequences of this not happening – that

Renton, among others, might have a valid reason to appellate their convictions – Mitch had changed his tune.

'Bloody hell, what did you do? No, don't tell me. The less I know the better,' Mitch had said, and Paul knew the man understood. If you help me, Kyle Renton stays where he belongs.

Paul had given Ryan's address to Mitch, who had assured him that he would see to it straight away. Just before Mitch hung up, Paul had an idea. For the purpose of insurance, he told Mitch he suspected the blackmailer might be Stuart Fraser. Mitch took his address, too.

Afterwards, Paul walked back to his car in a daze. Had he really just done that? It took all his willpower not to call Mitch back and cancel the whole thing. Memories of Ryan rushed through his mind in a slideshow of their lives. The banter, their competitive games of Scrabble, Battleships or Monopoly (which usually resulted in one of them jumping up, arms aloft and dancing around the other). The times Ryan had built Paul up, backed him in chasing his dreams. Straightening his tie on his wedding day and reminding him to go back into the house to collect the personally written vows Vanessa had entrusted him to bring.

Maybe if he'd handled this differently he could have avoided this awful ultimatum: his friend's life or his own. If he'd not been so distracted by Mandy's death, perhaps he would have found Stuart Fraser earlier, spoken to him more calmly and found something on him he could have taken to the police, or perhaps he would have sounded out Mitch Bleacher about Renton to see if he'd heard anything about a revenge attack on Paul.

Hindsight is 20/20, as Vanessa liked to say. Too late now.

They were where they were, and he'd done what he'd done.

81

ROSIE

Thursday, 6.30 p.m.

The town centre was busy. People strolled in pairs or groups, chatting and laughing as they headed out to the many bars and restaurants. A few of them smiled at Rosie as they passed. She kept moving and weaving.

Her mum had turned up to Nanna's house furious about something that had happened at work and ready for a fight. Rosie hated it when she was in that mood. Why couldn't her mum be like her friends' mums? The ones who told their daughters they were brilliant and beautiful, helped them with their homework and gave them lifts to and from their friends' houses? Rosie's mum had nothing but criticism to throw Rosie's way.

Why didn't you tell me when Isobel left you alone with the baby? Why did you call your dad for help? What's wrong with me? Why is he so brilliant all of a sudden? You know he's a druggie, that he'll have no money soon and then neither will we. The job you wanted at his company is gone now too, so you'll have to knuckle down and do some schoolwork.

She should never have told her about babysitting Josh and not being able to reach Isobel. It had given her mum something to latch on to. When Rosie had said she was going back to her dad's because she'd had enough, her mum had shouted after her.

'Go on then, why don't you stay there and never come back!'

As Rosie closed the door behind her, she'd heard Grandad tell her mum off for saying mean things.

Rosie moved past the last of the people walking along the Grove and turned left into the quiet streets towards her dad's house. She took out her key and let herself in. The house was quiet.

Dad had said they were having lasagne for tea and it was nearly Ethan's bedtime so they would all be home soon, but she was relieved to have a bit of time on her own. She made herself a drink before sinking down on the sofa in the snug and turning on the TV.

82

RYAN

Thursday, 6.45 p.m.
20¾ hours left

When his phone rang, Ryan had been driving around for over an hour. He'd been to Mandy's flat in Menston, driven past Mandy's dad's farm and circled around the car park of the Ilkley Lido where Isobel liked to swim. Isobel's car was nowhere to be seen. His eyes felt gritty and sore from straining to check out every vehicle he passed. He hadn't realized how many silver Audis were around. Each one he saw brought a glimmer of hope that was then dashed when he focused on the driver or the registration plate and found it wasn't Isobel.

'What is your problem, Ryan?'

The sound of Stephanie's voice made his heart sink. He couldn't deal with this right now. 'Good evening to you too, Steph.'

'You and your friends are putting stupid ideas in her head and making her run around after you. It's not on, Ryan. You're the parent here. She's the child. Stop putting all this stuff on her. What was she doing at Isobel's house all alone with the baby?'

'I believe it was you who agreed to her babysitting Josh, not me.'

'I didn't know Isobel would go out. Annie said Isobel was sick.'

'Rosie was fine. She's a sensible girl and she's looked after Ethan many times.'

'Oh you have an answer for everything, don't you?'

'Was there something you wanted, Steph?' *Or are you just calling to have a go?*

'Rosie has stormed out on me and headed from Mum's to yours. Are you not at home?'

'Not at the moment. What happened?'

'What do you mean what happened?'

I mean what did you say to cause our easy-going daughter to get so upset she stormed out? He decided he didn't want to ask again. He'd get a more truthful version from Rosie anyway.

'What is it you are asking, Steph?'

'I'm not asking anything. I'm calling to tell you to try and be a proper dad for once and take care of your child instead of treating her like she's one of your mates. She needs discipline. Everyone says so.'

'Who exactly is everyone?' He knew he shouldn't bite but sometimes it was impossible not to.

'My mum and dad. Fleur.'

'Not everyone, then. Just three people.' Ryan ended the call as quickly as he could. He had little time for the opinions of Stephanie and her friends.

Ryan called Rosie. Her phone rang half a dozen times and then went to voicemail. He'd never reached her voicemail before. That girl was glued to her phone. This is what he'd done to her. She was hiding from all the abuse people could send her way through her mobile. Life was never going to be the same for any of them, he knew that now.

THE SHAME GAME:
A TRUE CRIME DOCUMENTARY

Episode 3 of 3 - The Price

INT - HOTEL LOUNGE, ILKLEY - EVENING

A heavy-set gentleman with wisps of white
hair at the sides of his head sits on a
white sofa. He's wearing a pale pink, fine-
knit jumper with beige slacks.

TEXT on the screen: GRAHAM GRANGER,
GRANDFATHER OF ROSIE FALLON.

                GRAHAM GRANGER

    There was an argument that
    evening before Rosie left our
    house. Between Rosie and her mum,
    Stephanie. That's my daughter. It
    was the usual teenage thing. Rosie

was starting to exert her opinion
more forcefully and I think that
was tough for her mum.

                VOICE (O.S.)

And Rosie went to her father,
Ryan's, house, is that correct?

                GRAHAM

Yes. Ryan and his wife were not at
home so she was there all alone
when those men arrived. I'll never
forgive Ryan for that. I know
this wasn't all his fault but
still, those men came for him,
not my granddaughter. She should
never . . .

Graham shakes his head.

                VOICE (O.S.)

She must have been terrified.

                GRAHAM

I don't like to think about that.
This was nothing to do with her.

84

ROSIE

Thursday, 7.30 p.m.

When the doorbell rang, she was snoozing on the sofa to the sounds of a wildlife documentary she had found on the animals of Antarctica. She loved anything to do with penguins. The way they walked made her smile.

She left her phone on the arm rest only noting how late it was when she reached the clock in the hallway. Where were her dad and Camille?

The two people standing on the doorstep wore baseball caps with neck warmers pulled up over their noses. Rosie's first thought was how odd it was to be dressed this way on such a warm summer's evening. Her second was that this must be Gus and his mates fooling around. She had been avoiding his calls so expected he might simply show up at some point.

'Who are you?' the man in the blue neck warmer said.

'Who were you expecting?' she replied with an almost-smile.

'We're here for Ryan Fallon.'

Rosie took a very small step backwards. It was the way the guy said they were here *for* her dad and not to see him. She looked from one set of eyes to the other. There was no humour in them. This wasn't a joke.

'He's not here.'

'Are you alone?'

Rosie swallowed.

'I said are you alone?'

Rosie considered lying. She could say Camille was here, or Gus, or she could try to close the door. She placed her hand flat on the wood. She would need to be quick. They were standing really close. *It's not going to work*, a voice said in her head but she didn't know what else to do. She just wanted this to be over. She didn't like how the one in the blue neck warmer was looking at her.

'She's scared. Look at her face,' the man said and then he laughed.

Rosie knew it was now or never. She pushed the door as hard as she could, hoping it would catch before they could react.

The man in the black neck warmer jammed his foot into the space and pushed the door towards Rosie so hard that she stumbled backwards into the hall. Out of nowhere, a third man appeared wearing a black balaclava. He pushed past the other two to reach her. Rosie began to scream but the man wrapped his arm around her head and clamped his hand over her mouth. He pulled her close to him so she could feel the heat from his body.

'Is Ryan here?' Balaclava Man demanded.

Rosie shook her head.

'Go and check,' he said to Black Neck Scarf, who went inside the house. 'Are you his daughter?'

She hesitated.

The man squeezed the hand he had over her mouth a little tighter until it hurt.

Rosie nodded. She didn't know what else to do.

When Black Neck Scarf came back and confirmed the house was empty he had Rosie's phone. He handed it to Balaclava Man.

'Scream and I'll hurt you, do you hear me?' He briefly took his hand away from her mouth so that the phone recognized her face then he clamped the hand back in place. 'Good girl. You might survive this after all.' He handed Rosie's phone to Black Neck Scarf and said, 'Text Daddy and get him back here,' and then he said to the other one, 'Open the boot.'

Rosie wriggled and tried to bite the man's hand as he put his free arm around her waist and lifted her off the floor, but it did nothing to slow him down. He carried her across the driveway to a BMW with blacked-out rear windows.

Blue Neck Scarf moved away from the open boot to make room for his colleague and Rosie.

'What are you doing? The boss said nothing about taking a kid,' said Black Neck Scarf, walking their way.

'Fallon isn't here, is he? The plan has to change, and this is our insurance.'

Rosie kicked out her legs as the man began to lift her. She was trying to make herself too big for the space, or to brace herself against the outside of the vehicle, but the man was too strong.

'Leave me alone!' she had chance to shout before the lid was shut, locking her in the small dark space. She could hear their muffled voices outside.

'Take her to White Wells and wait for me there. I'll deal with Daddy.'

'I told you. I ain't doing nothin' with a kid. That wasn't the job.'

'The boss said Fallon had to be dealt with tonight, and I'm in charge, so do what the fuck I'm telling you and stop whining like a pussy. The girl's a fucking witness now.'

Rosie was determined not to cry even though her whole body was shaking uncontrollably. The boot smelled bad, like old socks mixed with wet dog. Her ankle hurt where the man had shoved it into the boot. She tried to reach down to check if she was bleeding but the car went over a bump that jarred her whole body. Rosie curled up in the dark space to make herself as small as possible and tried not think about what might happen next.

85

RYAN

Thursday, 7.45 p.m.
19¾ hours left

He was on the phone to Camille when a message from Rosie came in. It flashed up on the screen.

Dad, can you come home quick.

'Hon, I'll call you back in a mo,' he said, ending his call.

As he drove towards the house he dialled and redialled Rosie's phone, but there was no answer. He tried to tell himself his daughter simply needed to see him after the row with her mum, but the fact she'd sent that message and then wasn't answering his calls scared him.

It only took a matter of minutes to get there but it felt like an age. When he saw that his front door was ajar, Ryan left the car and ran inside, shouting Rosie's name. The house was quiet apart from the distant sound of the TV.

'Rosie, are you in here?'

He ran to the snug, ignoring whatever person was talking on the screen.

'Rosie?'

There was no sign of her or her phone. He ran back to the hall and up the stairs to her room but that was also empty, as was the bathroom and the en suite to his and Camille's bedroom. He raced back downstairs, calling his daughter's name but knowing somewhere deep in his gut that she wasn't going to answer.

Why did she tell him to come quick? Why would she leave the door open?

He didn't immediately see the figure sitting in a corner of his kitchen. It was only when he called Rosie's phone again and it rang behind him that he turned to face the man in the balaclava. Ryan's body stiffened.

'I expect you'd like to know where your daughter is?' The man twisted Rosie's ringing phone between his gloved fingers.

Ryan didn't recognize his voice. It was deep and gravelly, and sounded too old for any of Rosie's friends. The man was dressed in black from head to foot and when he stood up, he towered above Ryan.

'I suggest you put down the phone and come with me.'

Ryan looked at his phone. *Why didn't I call Camille back and tell her something was wrong with Rosie?*

'Where is my daughter? What have you done with her?'

Ryan glanced at the front door. It was directly in his line of sight from here. The masked man was a big fella who could probably hurt Ryan quite significantly, but could he run fast? Ryan could knock on one of his neighbours' doors. Neil at number twelve was probably home. He and his wife didn't go out much.

In the time it took for Ryan to think about running, the man in the balaclava had moved a step towards him.

'Put. It. Down. And come with me.'

86

ROSIE

Thursday, 8 p.m.

Rosie was the type of girl who didn't let anyone get the better of her, but when the two men with neck warmers opened the boot, she felt small and vulnerable and the terror made her limbs heavy and her mouth dry.

'We are going for a little walk and if you try to run or scream or attract any attention, we will hurt your dad very badly. Do you understand?'

Rosie could do nothing more than nod as the three of them began walking from the car park up towards White Wells Bath House. Black Neck Scarf held on to her right biceps, his grip tight enough to be painful. The message was clear. Don't try anything stupid.

On the hill above, she saw the flicker of mountain bike headlights weaving across the moor. She had done those rides; focusing on the trail ahead as if your life depended on it and feeling totally and completely free. The memory brought tears to her eyes and Rosie bit her lip.

'Please let me go,' she mumbled, but the men didn't respond.

The white cottage with its small café high up on Ilkley Moor was a favourite place of Rosie's to stop when she was out riding or walking with friends. It was a place of peace and beauty, but tonight it felt isolated and eerie. She could see that the café door was closed and that there was no one around. Darkness was falling and all the ramblers had headed home, or back to their B&Bs, for a well-earned meal.

Next to the café door was a small porch that extended outwards and she watched Blue Neck Scarf pick the lock to this door with a growing sense of dread. The White Wells plunge pool had been there since Victorian times, but it was only open to the public when the flag was flying, or on New Year's Day, when streams of people from the town trekked up the hill with their swimsuits to take a freezing dip.

Rosie remembered the breathtaking feeling of sinking under what felt like ice-cold water then rushing out as fast as possible. She and her dad had laughed at the sensations. It was a tradition he always participated in, and she had joined him until she was thirteen, at which point she found it embarrassing.

Do not go in that room, said a voice in her head. It was a small space with no windows and thick walls. No one would know she was in there or hear her scream.

Rosie began to struggle against Black Neck Scarf's grip. 'No! Get off me. Let me go!' Her eyes skittered around the cobble-stoned area looking for something to help her. She spotted the stone steps attached to the building wall. Originally designed for dismounting a horse, the flat-topped triangle was a place she and her friends had photographed each other jumping off over the years. She struggled towards it now, hoping that gaining a bit of height might enable her to twist herself free or use her weight to unbalance the man. Then she would run as fast as she could. Not back down the path, but over the moorland where it would be hard for them to follow. She was good on a downhill, her dad had said.

But her attempts proved futile. The men worked together to restrain her before she made it to the bottom step. Then they marched her into the Bath House.

'Get her in the water,' said Blue Neck Scarf as soon as they were inside.

The deep, round pool was surrounded by waist-high metal railings and the gate to the stone steps down to the water was padlocked shut. Gus had told her just a few weeks ago that he and his younger brother always plunged at New Year, so she had considered jumping in again. But not like this.

'Why?' said Black Neck Scarf. He had protested about bringing her here in the first place. Rosie stared at him, hoping he would be her saviour.

'You really are a pussy, aren't you?' said Blue Neck Scarf as he used the small screwdriver he had picked the door lock with to release the padlock. 'Trust me, when people go in here, they get real compliant.'

'You been 'ere before with others?'

Blue Neck Scarf shrugged. 'It's a favourite of ours. Best torture chamber for miles around.'

To Rosie's horror, this convinced Black Neck Scarf to do as his friend suggested and the two of them began to manhandle her towards the water.

'Please, no, please. I don't want to—'

'Shut up, princess,' said Blue Neck Scarf as they walked her to the gate and used her upper arms to direct her down the first of the steps.

Rosie looked at the water. It was clear and undisturbed, unlike on New Year's Day, when the amount of people jumping in stirred up the silt, making it impossible to see the bottom. Today she could see the many coins that people had thrown in for luck carpeting the floor.

She used to jump from where she stood now, holding her nose

and her breath and knowing that it would be over as soon as it had begun.

But not today.

Without warning, one of the men, Blue Neck Scarf she guessed, shoved her hard from behind. Rosie slipped down the next step, stubbing her toes on the hard stone before landing face first in the water with a loud splat. She was only wearing a hoody and shorts with her Vans but the clothes seemed to pull her downwards, deep under the surface, where it felt like hundreds of freezing needles were piercing her skin. The pool was shallow enough for her to stand in, but her feet hit the sides and then slid across the many coins on the floor, making her panic. She scrambled to swim as her lungs demanded a breath. Rosie couldn't stop it. It was as if her body was in control of her rather than the other way around. Her mouth popped open and she took in a gulp of water that burned her chest before she managed to force her head upwards and above the surface.

As she grabbed the railings, coughing and retching the dank, icy water out of her shivering body, the two men laughed.

87

RYAN

Thursday, 8.30 p.m.
19 hours left

The ride in the boot was hard. His left elbow was crushed underneath him and his knees whacked into the walls. Who were these people? Was this the work of his blackmailer or something else? Had his confession caused some crazy anti-dopers to take it upon themselves to punish him? And had Rosie endured this? The idea made him more angry than he had ever been. She was a child. A sweet-natured, loving child. How would this affect her? What scars would it leave, being bundled into a car by a masked man? Ryan couldn't even bring himself to think of her alone somewhere with one of these men.

When the car stopped and the boot opened, Ryan was ready for a fight. He had suffered pain that this tough guy couldn't tolerate. He had pushed himself physically and psychologically to the edge on so many rides, in so many races. He was stronger than any of them could imagine.

'Where is my daughter?' Ryan jumped out of the boot and saw they were parked in one of the small number of spaces in the car park at the base of the moors. 'White Wells?' he said. He looked up the hill. In the moonlight, the long white cottage shone brightly against the dark moor.

'I'd hurry if I were you. She'll be getting cold.'

Ryan began to run. They were in the middle of a summer heatwave and it was still warm enough to go outside in a T-shirt, so there was only one reason Rosie would be cold up there. The plunge pool was at a constant temperature because the water came directly out of the ground, and he knew from experience that was below ten degrees Celsius.

It was only about a quarter of a mile from the car park to the Bath House but it was uphill all the way. The path was gravelly and uneven but once he'd crossed the stream it widened and smoothed a touch so he was able to stride out and make better progress. His mind raced as quickly as his feet. He needed to figure out what these people wanted if he stood any chance of getting them away from Rosie.

As he neared the cottage, he noticed there was light coming from the door into the plunge pool room. He heard a few mumbled words of a conversation and a quick laugh before whoever was in there heard him coming and fell silent. Ryan burst in to find two men with neck scarves covering their noses standing on either side of the pool. They were leaning on the top of the railings as if they were neighbours having a Sunday afternoon chat over the garden fence. In between them, in the water, Rosie clung to the bottom of the railings. Her face was pale and her lips were blue, she was shaking and he could see the tracks of many tears on her face.

'Da—' she tried to say.

'Rosie, honey, it's OK. I'm here now.' Ryan focused on her and didn't even glance at the two men, who by now had stood up straight. He didn't want to give them the satisfaction of his attention. Behind him, the balaclava-clad man entered, panting deeply.

Ryan removed his T-shirt and threw it into the corner of the small stone room, then he waded into the pool, taking deep breaths to steel himself against the cold and reach his daughter.

'He's putting himself in there.'

'Making our life easier, cheers mate.'

Ryan continued to ignore the men. He unhooked Rosie's arms from the bars and placed them around his neck. She was not capable of helping, which scared him. He could feel her whole body shivering as he took her weight and walked her back across the small pool and up the steps.

'Whoa, what do you think you're doin'?'

'It's OK. Let him take her out.' The man in the balaclava was clearly the boss. He coughed and took in a few deep breaths. Running up that hill had hurt him, Ryan was pleased to see, but still the man filled up the entire doorway. There would be no barging past him.

Ryan led Rosie to the side and sat her down. She tried to talk but her lips struggled to form the shapes.

'It's OK, sweetheart. You're OK now. I'm here. Let's take this off.' He unzipped her hoody and peeled it off her. Underneath she wore a T-shirt and shorts. He sat beside her and wrapped his arms around her torso, trying his best to share his body heat. He needed to get her out of these wet clothes and into his dry T-shirt but first he needed her to gain some muscle strength back. He rubbed her arms vigorously, hoping it would speed up the blood flow as he held her close to him.

The men silently watched. Ryan waited until he managed to get a small but significant smile from Rosie, at which point he turned his attention their way.

'Who are you and what do you want?'

88

ROSIE

Thursday, 8.45 p.m.

The warmth of her dad's body felt so good that Rosie began to cry again. She had fought to contain the tears as she'd stood in the water, feeling weaker and more numb by the minute. The men had been discussing someone who'd been brought here to confess his role in a stabbing. The men had laughed when the one in the blue neck scarf said their victim had pissed himself.

Her dad was demanding to know who the men were and what they wanted, and the man in the balaclava said all they wanted was to get the job done. Knowing the reason wouldn't help them at this point. Rosie squeezed herself closer to her dad when that was said.

'Rosie, take my dry T-shirt and go up to the changing rooms.'

'I don't think so,' said Balaclava Man.

Her dad stared at the man with an expression Rosie recognized from the videos of him riding up a mountainside. 'Your problem is with me. Not her. She needs to get dry and warm and she is not changing here in front of you.'

The steel in Dad's voice had the desired effect. Balaclava Man sent Blue Neck Scarf up the small, wooden staircase that led to the changing room, to check there was no way out. When he came back down, the man nodded to indicate that she was OK to go up. She didn't want to leave her dad's arms. Maybe they wouldn't hurt him if she was with him.

'You need to get warm, Ro. Go,' he said, and he was serious.

Rosie did as she was told, taking his dry T-shirt and using it to replace her top and shorts.

When she walked back down the stairs to the main room, Black Neck Scarf suggested to Balaclava Man that he take her outside to wait. Both Dad and Balaclava Man protested at this idea.

'Hey, I'm not trying to be alone with your girl or anything, honest.' Black Neck Scarf held both hands up. 'But the boss said nothing about involving a kid, so I don't think she needs to be here, know what I mean?' He briefly looked at Balaclava Man and then back to Dad.

Her dad reached for Rosie's hand and pulled her into a hug.

'I don't want to leave you. I'm not leaving you,' she said.

'It's OK. This will be over soon, promise.' He looked into her eyes. 'I love you, Rosie, and I love Camille and Ethan.'

Rosie began to shake her head.

'Go, babe, and remember how strong you are.'

Rosie wanted to stay and argue but she knew her dad would never listen.

'Please don't hurt my dad. Please,' she said as Black Neck Scarf tugged her reluctantly towards the door. Balaclava Man blocked the way and as they neared him, he leaned in close enough for Rosie to smell a mixture of cigarette smoke and sweat.

'Your dad's a cheat, and he's brought this on himself. Brought this on both of you.'

89

RYAN

Thursday, 9 p.m.
18½ hours left

Ryan stood still in the middle of the pool with his arms folded. The water rose halfway up his bare chest but he'd taken his fair share of ice baths and knew how to ignore the discomfort. They had ordered him back in after Rosie left. When Ryan had protested, the man in the blue neck scarf had produced the longest knife Ryan had seen outside of a kitchen from within his jacket. Ryan realized the man must have had this on him when he had abducted Rosie, and the idea that she might have been threatened with it horrified Ryan. His poor girl.

The one in charge instructed Ryan to hold his arms out so they could handcuff his wrists to the bars.

'Just tell me what you want. You don't need to handcuff me,' said Ryan.

'If you don't do what I say, I'll let my friend here cut you, and then I'll let him cut your girl,' said the man in the balaclava.

Ryan let the man attach steel handcuffs to both his outstretched wrists. The rings were closed so tightly that when he tried to move, the metal cut into his skin. The man with the knife thrust his boot between the bars behind Ryan's back and struck him hard in the middle of his shoulder blades. Ryan's body jerked forwards, causing his arms to take his weight and his wrists to jar against the cuffs. He cried out in pain.

Outside, Rosie screamed.

'Shut her up or I will,' shouted the man in the balaclava without taking his eyes off Ryan. 'Now then, chief,' he said, 'my friend here is going to prepare something special for you. We understand you enjoy a little trip, so we're happy to oblige. A little send-off present for you to enjoy.'

'Tell me who's behind this.'

'Don't you worry about that.'

Out of the corner of his eye, Ryan saw the other man produce a syringe from a bag.

'What difference will it make if you tell me now?'

'It won't make any difference – you're still clocking out.'

'Do you have my friend Isobel too?'

The man frowned.

'She went missing this afternoon. Was that you lot?'

'Never heard of her.'

'But your boss has heard of her. Might he have arranged for someone else to—?'

'Have you got the hots for this woman or something? You been cheating on more than a bike, Mr Fallon?'

The guy with the knife wolf-whistled.

'She's my friend and she's a good person and she just adopted a baby boy.'

Ryan saw something shift in the eyes of the man in the balaclava. 'Like I say, I've never heard of her. The boss only mentioned you.'

'So, you will let my daughter go? You have to. Your boss only mentioned me. Please don't hurt her.'

'I'm not sure you're in any position to bargain,' said the man

302

with the syringe. 'And she's a witness, kid or not. Maybe you decided to take her out with you. Fellas do that I hear.'

The man in the balaclava came to the top of the pool steps and stooped down on his haunches, resting his arms on his knees and clasping his hands together. 'And why should I listen to you?'

Ryan thought about that shift in the man's eyes.

'Because you're a decent person. You have a daughter yourself, or a younger sister, a niece maybe, and if anyone dared to harm a hair on their head, I expect you'd—'

'Kill them,' the man finished.

'Well, yes. So you get my point. She's innocent of whatever it is you think I've done.'

'You only *think* you've done something. Funny that. I meet a lot of folks who don't know what I'm talking about when they come to face their comeuppance. Maybe I'm just a poor communicator, hey?'

'I'm not trying to piss you off. I'm just asking you to let her go, and then you can do whatever you want.'

The man took out a cigarette, lit it and took a long, deep drag before blowing the smoke in Ryan's direction.

'I can do that anyway. You're the one fastened to the railings.'

90

ROSIE

Thursday, 9.15 p.m.

The air outside the cottage was warm and she finally had some sensation back in her toes. Her feet still squelched inside her soaking wet Vans when she moved, but she tried to ignore it. The view down to the town was pitch black and there were no stars above. The sky was overcast with clouds and only the odd dash of moonlight was breaking through.

'Are you all right?' Black Neck Scarf had let go of her arm as soon as they stepped outside. She wondered if he had kids, and was about to ask when her dad shouted out in pain.

Rosie darted back towards the cottage. She didn't realize she was screaming until Black Neck Scarf grabbed her.

'Shut her up or I will,' called the voice of Balaclava Man from inside.

'Ssshhhhh,' Black Neck Scarf hissed in her ear. 'Just keep calm, OK?'

Rosie shrugged him off her and folded her arms.

'What are they doing to my dad?'

'Just asking him some questions.'

'Will he be OK?'

The man didn't answer.

Rosie had a horrible feeling she might not see her dad alive again.

Why had she been so mean when he'd confessed to doping? She should have told him it didn't matter. Now, she thought that people could laugh at her all they liked. Her dad was brave for telling the truth. He had always told her not to lie and now he'd had the courage to show her how important the truth was.

A break in the clouds lit up the moors above. Rosie looked up. She could just make out the crag behind them and the outline of the trees. And then she saw something else: a flash of light weaving and bobbing before it disappeared again.

'Do you do this often?' she said.

The man made a huffing sound and waved his head from side to side. She took that as a yes.

'Why?'

'What?'

'How does someone end up doing this kind of thing?' She wanted him to like her enough to grant her a small favour, and her dad had always told her if you want someone to like you, show an interest in them. 'Is it a tough guy thing?'

'You're a nosey one, aren't you?'

The man perched on the end of a picnic table and lit a cigarette. Rosie moved to stand alongside him. Uncle Paul had once told her that people open up more when you're side by side rather than face to face.

'Sorry. I babble when I'm nervous,' she said.

He was quiet for a while and then he said, 'Maybe, when I was young.' He looked at the plunge pool door and Rosie guessed he was referring to Blue Neck Scarf and all his swagger. 'Now . . . it's all I know.'

Rosie visualized the small muddy strip, just beyond the cottage to her right, that wriggled its way upwards towards a patch of trees. Behind where she stood, she knew that a similar muddy strip continued downhill, cutting through the ferns and the bracken.

'Thanks for being nice to me.'

The man nodded and Rosie knew it was now or never. She might miss her chance if she waited too long.

'I need to wee. Is it OK if I go over there where those ferns are? I won't be out of your sight.'

'Can't you hold it?'

'Please, I really need to go. I'll be quick. I promise.'

The man looked around. The dark moor was quiet and deserted.

'Be quick,' he said.

Rosie rushed to where the tall ferns started and stooped low behind the first few. For a second she thought he was going to watch but then he turned to angle himself away and give her some privacy. *Go, now*, said a voice in her head and she knew it was her one chance. Staying low, she began to scramble through the ferns behind her as quietly as she could using her hands and her feet to forge a pathway up and away.

'Hey! Hey!' The man was moving too now. She could hear his boots trampling across the ferns to get to her. They had grown lush and tall in the summer sun and she heard him swear a few times as he most likely became tangled.

It was hard going but Rosie was well practised. She and her best friend, Katie, used to chase each other through the summer ferns all the time as kids. She knew you had to lift your knees high, land your feet firmly and push the big green branches away with both hands. It was more like swimming than running and she deftly moved in a diagonal direction towards the trail. The moonlight was dimming again and it was getting harder to see but she knew the path well. She'd cycled it many times. She just needed to get to it through the ferns.

'Get back here!' she heard Black Neck Scarf shout and was pleased he sounded farther away than she had expected.

When she reached the trail the moonlight was all but gone, but her eyes were adjusting to the dark and her squidgy feet felt the change in the ground. The trail was compacted from bike after bike which had come weaving, skidding and flying down the moor. She had seen the lights earlier. It was Thursday night. She knew the local mountain biking club met here on Thursdays. She had joined them a couple of times since dating Gus because his dad organized the rides. She only hoped some of them were still here, flying down then racing back up to go again.

Her heart pounded in her chest and her throat burned from the effort, but she kept running and running, up and up and up towards that small group of trees, hoping to find somebody, anybody there.

91

RYAN

Thursday, 9.30 p.m.
18 hours left

This was it then. This was how it was all going to end. *Murdered.*
There was an epitaph no one ever expected to have.

He imagined the headlines: DISGRACED CYCLIST RYAN FALLON
DIES AFTER DOPING SCANDAL

Don't worry about the future. Concentrate and take control.

Somehow, the mantra didn't fit any more. What else was there
to do in your final moments other than think about what you
would be missing? How life would go on without you. Babies
would be born, wars would be fought, tsunamis and eruptions
and forest fires would wreak their havoc and the world would
recover and keep spinning. Days would continue to come and go.
He just wouldn't be in them.

How had it come to this?

What would happen to Rosie? Would they let her go? Would
they bring her in here and let her see how he'd died, half-dressed
and pumped full of drugs? Would they hurt her? His mind raced
away from the thoughts of what she might go through, how
scared she'd be and how he'd be helpless to stop any of it.

And if by some miracle they let her go, he would not be there to celebrate her GCSE results. He knew he'd already messed up her plan to come and work with him at the charity, but he'd liked the idea of them doing something together, someday, maybe after she'd been to university. And now none of that would happen. She would be left with Steph as her only parent, a woman who seemed to revel in undermining Rosie and chipping away at her confidence. How would his beautiful girl cope without him there to shield her, to provide respite and all the unconditional love she deserved? Would Camille stay in touch with her? God, he hoped so. They had become so close but he also knew Steph would do anything in her power to untangle that bond.

And then there was Ethan, his little man. Thinking of him growing up without his dad was too much to bear and Ryan had to stop his train of thought. It would do no use to sink into the grief anyhow. It wouldn't change anything. All he could do was hope that all of them – Rosie, Ethan, Camille, his parents, Izzy and Paul – knew how much he loved them and how thankful he was for every moment they had given him.

'She's gone, I can't find her, she's gone.' The man in the black neck warmer ran in looking flustered and sweaty. 'She said she needed a pee and then she bolted.'

'What the fuck, man?' said the guy with the syringe.

The one in the balaclava hung his head. 'Go after her before she reaches the town.'

'That's the weird thing. She didn't run to town, she went uphill.'

'Why didn't you chase her down?'

Ryan curled his hands into fists. Rosie was away, running across the moors; moors she had walked, run and cycled since she was a kid.

'I tried but it's all bracken and brambles and shit up there.'

'Get back out there and keep a lookout. This won't take me long.' The man in the balaclava smiled at Ryan.

Please, please keep going, Ro. Get as far away from here as you can, Ryan willed in his head. If she was away and free that's all he needed to know for now. If it was the only peace he would be getting, it was enough.

92

ROSIE

Thursday, 9.45 p.m.

The fall was stupid. She knew she should be watching the ground ahead. Rocks and boulders were embedded all over the place, it was what made mountain biking down these trails so much fun – they were gnarly, you had to really concentrate to complete them clean. But she had been looking up, trying to spot lights or hear voices. She hit the ground hard, skidding along the side of her left knee and landing with her face buried in the ferns. She knew she had grazed her palms as they broke her fall and her left knee protested as she rolled on to it and pushed herself up. A fresh set of tears bubbled inside her eyes and she swallowed a few times to rein them in. This was useless. It was dark, she was tired and she was running in the wrong direction, away from her dad.

And then she heard it. A sound that filled her with so much joy she laughed out loud.

'YYYEEEEEEWWWWWWW!'

As mountain biker calls go, it was one of the best.

Rosie began moving again seconds before she saw them. A handful of lights bobbed towards her, moving erratically from side to side as the riders jumped and dabbed across the terrain.

Only at the last moment did she realize they wouldn't see her. She yelled for them to stop as she leaped sideways into the ferns.

'Holy crap!' she heard the rider at the front shout as he swerved to avoid her. 'WALKER!' he yelled.

'STOP! PLEASE STOP!' Rosie stepped back on to the path and held both hands up high, hoping the bikes that followed would see her in their lights in time. And of course they did. These riders were at one with their bikes, fully in control and able to skid stop with a moment's notice.

'Whoa. What's going on?' said a voice from the back.

Rosie counted four of them.

'I need help. It's my dad. I need—' The combination of the run up here and the relief at finding people caused her to lose control of the tears. She coughed out two loud sobs in quick succession then covered her mouth with both hands. 'Sorry.'

'Are you OK?'

'What are you doing up here?'

'Are you hurt? You're bleeding.' The front guy pointed to her knee.

Rosie looked down and in the glow of the bike lights she could see the large graze across her knee and upper thigh.

'STOP! STOP!' shouted one of the guys as another set of riders raced towards them.

The rider at the front put his bike down and came to her side. 'What's that about your dad? Is he hurt?'

'Hey, do I know you?' said another rider before one of the new riders pushed forward through the group to reach her.

'Rosie?'

She looked up and was blinded by his bike lights for a moment. The man moved so she could see his face. It was Toby, Gus's dad. The sobs really did escape then and Toby climbed off his bike and grabbed her in a tight hug.

'What the hell has happened?' He turned to the group. 'Tell Gus it's Rosie. His girlfriend.'

Rosie took a deep breath and focused on Toby. 'They've got my dad in the Bath House. You need to go and help him. They're going to hurt him.'

93

RYAN

Thursday, 9.45 p.m.
17¾ hours left

The two men were discussing who should administer the injection that would end his life. The man in the blue neck scarf waved the syringe around as he talked about how he was 'Ripe for it', and 'Had been waitin' too long for a chance to take one out.'

Ryan tried to go to that place in his mind where he always went in the final kilometres of a race, when your muscles were wrecked and your lungs were protesting at the pace. A place where you can rise above the pain, acknowledge it but not truly feel it, a dissociation that allowed you to pedal on.

'What the hell? GUYS! WHAT THE HELL?' came the shout from outside. 'What is that? Come out here, you need to see this. I don't know what it is but it's all kindsa wrong.'

The two men and their syringe went outside, leaving Ryan alone.

'What are they? They're everywhere!'

'Lights.'

'I know they're lights, Hinchy. I can see they're fucking lights, but on what?'

'Shit, they're coming fast!'

Ryan guessed what the lights were. It was Thursday night, the mountain bike club would be out in force. *Rosie ran uphill.*

'What the hell?'

All Ryan heard for the next few moments were shouts and thumps amidst the clickety clack of whirring bike chains and the thunder of bike wheels across the cobbles. He twisted his hands inside the handcuffs but there was no give, so he shouted.

'IN HERE! HELP! IN HERE!'

The sound of chaos continued from outside and Ryan strained to hear what was going on.

'IN HERE!' he shouted again, and louder, 'IN HERE. HELP!'

A high-pitched wail of pain from the outside silenced Ryan for a moment. He pictured the large knife and hoped it wasn't the cause of that wail. There was more shouting but Ryan struggled to separate the voices.

He was about to call out again when he heard someone coming his way. He braced himself for the return of the man in the balaclava or his knife-wielding friend, so the sight of a mountain biker in his helmet, padded zip top, knee pads, elbow pads and black gloves was quite something.

Ryan laughed in relief but then he heard an all too familiar voice.

'All right, Ry? Just taking a cold bath, naked, with your buddies 'ere, were you?' Toby wore a smirk that was all kinds of smug.

94

RYAN

Thursday, 9.45 p.m.
17¾ hours left

'Is this you . . . God . . . I never thought . . . I mean I suspected, but what the fuck man, how could you? To Rosie? What makes you hate me so much?'

'I don't hate you, Ryan.'

'I kept telling myself it couldn't be you. I didn't want to believe it but here you are. You just happen to be riding by the Bath House. Did you want to see the fruits of your labour?'

'The fruits of my what?'

Ryan tried to ignore the numbness of his freezing body as he met Toby's gaze. 'You've had a chip on your shoulder ever since I switched to the road. You just hated that I was so successful. And I imagine you were elated when someone told you about the EPO. But that doesn't give you the right to mess with my life and my family. Who was it? Another rider? The doctor?'

Toby let the silence hang as he looked from one shackled wrist to another. 'Have you finished?'

'Are you're going to deny it's you, behind the articles and

the blackmail and this?' Ryan raised his arms as far as he could against the shackles.

'I'm going to assume you've got brain freeze, cos you're making no sense, man. I have no idea what you're on about.' Toby whistled and a skinny mountain biker came in. 'See if either of those two have the handcuff keys, will you?'

Ryan tried to work out if Toby was playing with him or being genuine. The cold had slowed his mind and he was struggling to make sense of things.

When the skinny biker came back with the keys he also carried the knife. 'They had this, too.' He handed it over to Toby who raised his eyebrows and whistled.

'Those lads weren't messing about. There's a carrier bag in my rucksack. Take it out and put that thing in it. Nobody touches it without gloves, OK? It might be evidence,' Toby said to the skinny rider before freeing Ryan from the cuffs.

Ryan rubbed his wrists as he climbed out of the water. The temperature was taking its toll and he was shivering.

Toby pulled a raincoat out of his rucksack. 'Put this on.'

Ryan took it as Toby told the skinny lad to wait outside and make sure the two men didn't leave.

'There were three of them,' Ryan said.

'Aye, I know. One of them jokers scarpered like a bunny from a fox. Now, I think you better tell me what's going on.' When Ryan said nothing, Toby sighed. 'All right. If you won't talk, let me. You say I hate you, that I'm so jealous of your achievements that I've taken me bat and ball 'ome, and, yeah, I was jealous that you got to go live your dream even though you had a kid, like me, but I was also really goddamn proud. It was you that changed. You were the one who wouldn't look me in the eye when you came back. You thought you were sommat special and you made that very clear.'

Ryan shook his head. 'That's not true.'

317

'Well, it's the way I see it. I 'ave no idea what's going on 'ere, and I know nothing about any blackmail.'

'Look. If I'm wrong, I'm sorry, but—'

'*If* you're wrong? *IF*?' Toby stepped up close to Ryan.

'OK, OK. I'm sorry.' Ryan held his hands up. 'Is Rosie OK?'

Toby locked eyes with him. 'She's fine. My Gus is a good lad. He'll take care of her.'

Ryan sank down to the floor and put his head in his hands. They'd survived. The realization brought tears that he couldn't hold back.

'Shit, man. What is going on? Talk to me.'

The kindness in Toby's tone brought Ryan to his senses. The man had just saved Ryan's skin and in return Ryan had accused him of being a vindictive lowlife.

'Someone threatened to break the story about the EPO, they forced me to come clean but then these guys took Rosie and . . .'

'And you thought this was all my doing?'

'I thought . . .' Ryan looked at Toby. 'I figured you'd judge me for doping and expect me to fess up.'

'Jeez, man, I don't judge you for that. I'd have probably done the same in your shoes given how rife it was back then. In fact, I'd probably not have had your good sense to stop after trying it once, know what I mean?'

'Right.'

'Look, like I said in my text, what you did took balls, but it was the right thing to do. It's not about us any more, is it? It's about the young 'uns, and you've raised a cracking girl there who just saved your bacon. That's what you should be focusing on. Anything you did on a bike – win, lose, cheat – is nonsense compared to that. Yeah?'

Ryan nodded and swallowed back the lump in his throat. 'Thanks.'

'Now, are we calling the police?'

'I need to buy some time before involving the police. This is not only about me.'

'You're not suggesting we let them go?'

'No, but . . .' Ryan wrapped himself in the raincoat as he thought about it. 'These fellas weren't messing about. That one who scarpered might be coming back with others. I'd say we all need to get out of here sharpish.' He looked at Toby's hands. 'What do you think? As soon as we're away we can call it in anonymously.'

Toby followed Ryan's gaze to the handcuffs. 'Might do 'em good to feel the chill for a bit. Why don't you get yourself home and get dry. You can take my bike. I've sent Gus to my camper with Rosie. He'll drop her back at yours. Me and the lads will sort things 'ere.'

Outside, the two neck-scarf wearers were sitting against the wall. Neither had their faces covered any more. Around them, the togged-up bikers still wearing their helmets made for an intimidating set of guards. At least one bike was crumpled to the side of them, but by the looks of the two men on the ground, the bikes had won.

'Now then, Hinchy,' Ryan said to the younger man. The young man looked up at him in surprise. 'Are you going to tell me who your boss is, or do we have to get the police?'

The man spat in Ryan's direction, which resulted in whistles and jeers from the bikers.

Ryan looked at the other guy. He was older, in his forties maybe. 'Who sent you? Who is this boss who wanted me dead?'

The older guy shrugged. 'I don't know nothin'.' He had a scar across his chin and a tattoo on his neck. Ryan guessed he was not easily intimidated.

'Right, well, thanks for letting my girl go. I owe you one.'

'Want us to see what me and the lads can find out?' Toby had wheeled his bike over.

'Just get away from here as quick as you can, especially if the other guy comes back with reinforcements. I don't want your lads getting caught up in this. Then make the call.'

Toby smirked. 'I'll have to see if I can remember where I put my phone.' He passed his bike to Ryan.

Ryan took it. 'Thanks. I owe you. And . . . I'm sorry about . . .'

'I'll put it down to you 'aving a bad day.' Toby nodded to the bike. 'You take care of her now. You can ride a real bike, can't you?'

Ryan smiled as he put Toby's helmet on and set off.

'Remember: that bike's more precious than my kids. I'm not joking,' Toby shouted after him.

'They all are. I'll treat her as if she were mine,' he called back.

95

ISOBEL

Thursday, 9.45 p.m.

17¾ hours left

How did I get here?

Isobel remembered being outside with Vanessa. Then what? The memories floated away from her. She was pretty sure she was now in Paul's garage. She wasn't sure she'd ever been in here before but the small amount of light coming in from under the door meant she could make out the shape of a Porsche parked next to her.

She opened the car door and tried to move but the searing pain in her head took her breath away. A wave of nausea rose up from her centre. She clamped her hand to her mouth and half stepped, half fell out of the car before throwing up on the floor.

Why would Paul and Vanessa keep her here? Unless Paul had done something to Vanessa to stop her taking her home. Isobel felt a fresh bout of nausea and took a few deep breaths. *Why is he doing this? What has happened to him?*

Across the room, she could make out the door that led into Paul and Vanessa's utility room. Should she go that way or try to open the garage door? She was pretty sure the latter was electronic, so there must be a release button in here somewhere.

Using the car to help her, she carefully stood. Her vision blurred and she tried to blink it away but apparently it was here to stay. She moved slowly towards the utility room, checking for a garage door release on the walls as she went. Her fear was all-consuming now. She had lost movement in her left arm. She kept trying to wriggle her fingers and twist her wrist but they felt more and more like dead weights with each attempt.

That was not good. She was fairly certain she had an intra-cranial haematoma. Such a bleed would be slowly increasing the pressure on her brain and, if she was right, her symptoms would only get worse. She needed to get to help before she passed out again or had a seizure.

96

RYAN

Thursday, 10 p.m.
17½ hours left

By the time he reached the house, Toby's camper was already parked in the drive.

'Rosie?' he called as he walked into the hall.

His daughter ran down the stairs and flung herself at him, almost knocking him over, then they clung to each other in a tight hug.

'Are you OK, Ro?'

She nodded. She felt warm and dry and was wearing one of his hoodies over some sports leggings.

'You were so brave, honey.' He lifted her head with both of his hands and looked into her wonderful blue eyes. 'You saved us both. You and Gus's dad. You saved us.' He hugged her back into his body as Gus walked slowly out of the kitchen, looking unsure of whether it was OK for him to intrude on this family moment.

Ryan held his hand out to the young man. 'Thank you for taking care of my girl, Gus.' He shook the boy's hand and was pleased to find the lad's grip was strong. 'Thank you.'

'You're welcome,' said Gus, looking at the floor, 'Why wouldn't I?'

'Why wouldn't you indeed,' Ryan said, hugging Rosie a little tighter. 'Your dad told me you were a good lad.'

A phone began to ring in the kitchen.

'It's Camille,' said Rosie, lifting her head and drying her eyes. 'She keeps calling but I didn't know what to say, I didn't know if you were OK.'

Ryan kissed her head before moving through to the kitchen.

'Sorry, Camille,' he said on answering.

'Oh my goodness, Ryan, where have you been? Why haven't you answered your phone? I've called a million times. What is going on? Annie and I have been frantic here, first Izzy and then you.'

'Cam, it was bad. Rosie was kidnapped and they made me leave my phone to go to where she was, they took us both to the Bath House on the moor, Rosie was freezing in there, then they forced me in and Rosie ran, she managed to get away, God knows how, but she did and she was amazing, she managed to find Gus and his dad, they were out biking and there were loads of them, bikers I mean, like a good dozen and they just came en masse and took these guys down. Well two of them, one got away and he was the boss one so that's not good. Anyway, I'll tell you more about that when I see you. But Rosie was amazing. Oh my God, Cam, I'm so bloody proud of her.'

'What are you saying, Ryan? Someone kidnapped Rosie?'

'It's OK. We're OK. We're home now and I'm heading over to you. Just let me put some dry clothes on. Any sign of Izzy? Did Annie find her?'

'No. She called the police but they said Izzy is a grown woman who's only been missing a few hours. They said to call back tomorrow if she wasn't home. Have these people taken her? The ones who kidnapped Rosie?'

'I don't think so. I think this was about me coming clean. I'll explain when I get there.' Ryan wanted to ask how much Annie had told the police but figured that could wait.

He quickly changed into a dry set of shorts with a T-shirt and hoody like Rosie. When he came back downstairs, Gus had made steaming hot tea for them all.

'Are you OK to take Rosie back to yours, Gus? I need to help find Izzy and I don't want you guys here alone in case those blokes come back.'

'Do you think the same people might have her?' said Gus.

'I'm coming with you,' said Rosie.

'No, honey. Stay with Gus until this is sorted. It's safer.'

'No! I want to be with you. I need to be with you.' She left her tea and came to hug him again. Ryan could understand it. She might be sixteen but she was still a child, and when you're a scared child, you only want your parents.

'OK, OK. You can come along.' He kissed her head. 'Gus, can you text your dad and tell him I'll need to speak to him later? Are you OK taking his bike home?'

'Sure.'

'Come on then, superstar,' Ryan said to Rosie. 'Let's go.'

'What happened to those men?' Rosie asked as they drove. 'You told Camille one had run away, but what happened to the others? Did you call the police?'

Ryan turned right on to Cowpasture Road at the mini round-about. 'Not right away. Toby's going to call the police once they're safely away from there.'

'What, why? What if their friend comes back and then they come after us again?'

'It's complicated, Rosie. I need to find Isobel first, OK? I will speak to the police . . . later.' He wished he could tell her everything and explain that there was more at stake here, but he had to agree with Steph on this – not everything should be shared; she was his daughter, not his friend.

'What if those men have Aunt Isobel like Gus said?'

Ryan didn't have an answer for that. If they did, him not calling the police immediately might be something he came to regret.

'Why did they want to hurt you?' she said quietly.

Ryan reached out for her hand. 'I don't know, honey.'

Rosie sat silently for the remainder of the journey. Ryan wanted to ask what she was thinking, but he didn't want her to push him for information again.

97

ISOBEL

Thursday, 10 p.m.
17½ hours left

Very carefully, she tried the handle of Paul and Vanessa's utility room door. Having failed to find anything resembling a garage door release, this was her only option. The mechanism disengaged and she slowly pushed the door open. The smell of Indian spices filled the air and she could hear crockery chinking, as if someone was loading or unloading a dishwasher. Isobel moved slowly into the room. The light in here was off but the door to the hallway was ajar and light streamed in, as did the sound of a TV or radio playing.

She paused at the doorway, listening for Paul or Vanessa, and also to be sure she wasn't going to be sick or pass out again.

The ringing phone made her jump. It sounded closer than the chinking and she felt her pulse rate quicken, which did nothing for her aching head.

'It's Ryan.'

Paul's voice was close. Isobel could picture him sitting on the same bar stool he'd sat on when she'd confessed to him about receiving the article blackmailing her. She wished she could go back and change that now, but how could she have known back then? She would never have thought he could betray her, never mind attack her.

'He probably wants to know if you've heard from Isobel.'

The sound of Vanessa's voice made Isobel's heart sink. Why would Vanessa help Paul do this to her? She needed medical attention. Something very wrong was happening in her head.

'Yeah . . . but . . .' Paul said.

'Yeah, but what?'

'Nothing. Shall I answer?'

'I imagine he'll only keep ringing if you don't. I told him you'd been called into court.'

'Hi, mate. Everything OK?'

Isobel strained to hear. Ryan was looking for her. Annie would be too. Isobel checked her watch. She had left home over nine hours ago. Her wife would be going spare with worry by now.

'Shit. You're joking. When? Where?'

The chinking sound stopped and the radio or TV went off. Everything was quiet. Isobel could hear her own breathing.

'Bloody hell. Are you OK? Is Rosie?'

What had happened to Ryan and Rosie? Isobel shuffled forward a bit.

'How the hell did you get away?'

Isobel froze. Something in the tone of Paul's voice sounded off; as if he was making an accusation rather than an enquiry.

'Right. Blimey. I don't know what to say. Is there anything we can do?'

'What's happened?' Vanessa's words were spoken quietly.

'Yeah, sure, thanks for letting us know. Like Ness said, Izzy left here mid-afternoon. I was called into court . . . OK . . . yeah . . . I'll let you know if I hear anything. Take care, mate. And Ryan, send my love to Rosie.'

Isobel couldn't believe he had lied so easily. She thought she knew these people. They must know she was going to dispute their version of events when she got out of here.

Unless . . .

She couldn't let herself finish that thought. This was no time to panic.

'Go on . . .' said Vanessa.

Paul said something about Rosie having been kidnapped and held at the Bath House.

Isobel clamped her hand over her mouth to stop herself from making any noise. Coming in here was the wrong move. She needed to find another way out. *How the hell did you get away?* Had Paul sounded annoyed when he'd said that?

Moving back as quietly as she could, Isobel used the light from the open door to look again at the garage walls, searching for a release switch. She spotted it to the right of where she stood, above a shelf. An orange button with a label stuck below that said 'Garage Door' in Paul's handwriting.

Isobel closed the utility room door as carefully as she had opened it then breathed a sigh of relief. No one had spotted her, no one had heard her. With any luck they thought she was still passed out in her car and wouldn't check for a while. The room spun and she steadied herself against the wall, waiting for it to pass.

She was running out of time.

Isobel breathed in the fresh air as the door began to lift, making only a low hum. It provided a pleasing relief from the smell of vomit. So far, so good. She was going to crawl out and get help from a neighbour.

As she moved towards the door she caught the shelf with the side of her hand, unbalancing a large spanner that rested at the edge. She watched as the metal tool spun out towards her, teetered for a moment and then tumbled towards the floor. It clanked hard against a tin of paint, the sound bouncing off the walls, and then it landed with a loud thud on the concrete.

98

PAUL

Thursday, 10.15 p.m.
17¼ hours left

How had this all gone to shit so badly? Why had Mitch's men taken Rosie, for fuck's sake? And how the hell had Ryan got away? The blackmailer wanted Ryan out of the picture and clearly Mitch's men had messed up big style, which had sent Paul back to the drawing board. He still had until 3.30 p.m. tomorrow to work something out. He needed to go back to his original idea of taking Ryan somewhere and engineering an accident.

A loud clattering came from inside the garage. Vanessa's eyes met his and they moved together.

The garage door was almost up and Isobel was on her feet, moving towards it. Without discussion, Paul went one way around the car to reach her while Vanessa went the other. The classic pincer movement.

'Get away from me.' Isobel held one of his large spanners in her hand and waved it towards Vanessa, who had to jump back to avoid a direct hit. 'I said, GET AWAY!'

'OK, Isobel. OK.' Paul held his hands up.

'I need to go to A and E now. One of you needs to take me or call an ambulance,' she said.

'No. No hospital.'

Isobel swung the spanner towards him and he stepped back. Although she was not as strong as him it was a decent slab of metal, so it would hurt if she hit him right.

'The hospital might call the police and you can't afford the police.'

'You mean *you* can't.'

'Isobel. You told me yourself this person threatened to go straight to the press if you speak to the police. Is that what you want? Your darkest secret splashed across every lowlife rag in the land?'

'Paul, I'm not well. I need to go to A and E. I'll tell them I fell. There will be no need for the police.'

Paul looked at Vanessa, who raised her eyebrows. She was waiting to see what he was going to do, but before he had chance to decide, Isobel swayed, reaching out to grab some non-existent item to steady herself as she headed for the concrete floor. Paul just managed to step in and break her fall in time.

'Now what?' Paul whispered to Vanessa. 'Was that the pills or the knock on the head? Because she was going down hard.'

'Does it matter? Find out what she did, back then.' Vanessa pushed the button to close the garage door again and crossed her arms.

'I thought you said to make it up?'

'You're not finding out for the blackmailer, you're finding out for us, to stop her from telling the police what you did to her. Once you find out what we need to know, we can take her to A and E. But you know as well as I do that without knowing—'

'I know, I know.' Paul waved a hand at his wife. This was a nightmare with no end. He propped Isobel against a shelving unit and crouched in front of her. He placed his hands on her knees. She flinched away from him and he pulled back.

'Right, we need to cut to the chase, Isobel. You need to tell me what you did. The indiscretion at work. And you need to tell me now. Then I will take you wherever you want to go.'

Isobel lifted her head. There was a deep frown across her brow and her eyes blazed with anger. 'And what if I tell you to fuck right off out of my business?'

99

RYAN

Thursday, 10.15 p.m.
17¼ hours left

Annie met them at the door, speaking at a million miles an hour as they made their way inside.

'How long has it been since anyone has seen her? Paul and Vanessa are not answering their bloody phones and I'm going frantic here. I swear, Ry, if anything has happened to her I will never forgive you for telling me to hold off on calling the police. I'm surprised they haven't got you down at the station doing statements.'

Ryan felt Rosie's gaze on him as he gave Camille a long hug. His wife squeezed him tightly and then beckoned for Rosie to join them.

'Let's all just take a breath. We need to think this through,' said Ryan, breaking away from his family.

'How can you say that after what's just happened to you? What if Isobel's out there suffering and scared, waiting for someone to help her?'

'I asked the men who took us if they had Isobel too and they said they didn't.'

'And you consider them a good source of intel, do you?'

Ryan chose his words carefully. 'I don't see why they would lie. They didn't expect me to be walking out of there, plus they seemed like the kind of guys who might enjoy twisting the knife if the opportunity presented itself. If they had her too, I think they'd have bragged about it.'

'You can't be sure of that.'

'No, but . . . if they don't have Izzy, we don't want to do anything to make her life blow up in her face when we're not there to support her. Not given how you say she's been.'

'But if they do have her, she could be dead by now.'

'In which case, we're too late.'

'All right, she could be dying or about to die. We can't find her. I've been everywhere and tried everyone, we need the police but they won't bloody do anything until tomorrow.'

'I told her to ring Greg, but . . .' Camille shook her head.

'It wouldn't be right, after Mandy.' Annie picked up a tea towel, half folded it then threw it on the side.

Rosie left the room and Ryan remembered Steph's words: 'She's not your mate, she's your daughter.' She shouldn't be listening to all of this.

'I agree. When I visited Greg on Tuesday he said something pointed about everyone having secrets. It's probably nothing, but I think we should be careful.' Ryan was mindful of the mistake he'd made accusing Toby.

'What are you saying?' said Camille.

'He'd have a better chance of digging up dirt on you all than most,' said Annie.

'Non. He wouldn't,' protested Camille. 'He is a principled man.'

'Someone is doing it though, aren't they?' said Ryan. 'So until we know who, let's be careful about who we're talking to.'

'So what are you suggesting we do?' Annie crossed her arms and stared at him.

'Those men had been sent by someone they referred to as "the boss", and they were not novices at this kind of thing. Rosie overheard them talking about torturing someone for information about a stabbing. They mean business. It must be part of the Shame Game – punishment for me cheating it, or something. I think the whole thing was partly a message for Isobel, letting her know she had to play by the rules. By coming clean, I messed up the blackmailer's plan – that's why they came for me.'

'So, we need to find Isobel, and then what?'

'Answer her bloody question and shame whatever lowlife was a paid-up member of a far-right group. I don't know about you, but that seems like a fair trade for keeping quiet whatever it is that's traumatizing Izzy.'

'I just think all of it – "no police or I go to the press", "you've only got a week", "you need to betray your mate" – is foreplay for the main event. What if all your secrets come out at three thirty tomorrow no matter what you do?'

'If that's the case, then it doesn't matter what we do. But if it isn't the case, if this boss really will let Izzy off the hook . . .'

Annie sighed. 'Then it's worth a shot.'

'It's worth a shot.'

'But where the hell is she?'

100

ROSIE

Thursday, 10.30 p.m.

Rosie went upstairs to the bathroom and locked the door. She couldn't believe her dad and Toby hadn't called the police and had those men arrested, and the scariest one, Balaclava Man, had escaped. What if he came back for her dad and what if they had Isobel somewhere? Her dad had nearly died because of this Shame Game thing. Someone had to sort it out before those men decided to finish the job.

When they'd been at Paul's house earlier looking for Isobel, she had photographed the wall of coloured Post-it notes she'd seen through the window of his office while her dad was talking to Vanessa. She opened the picture now and zoomed in to take a closer look. It was split into four sections. The first section was a single column of yellow notes. Next to that, there were three columns of green notes under her dad's name, followed by three columns of orange notes under Isobel's name, and finally four pink columns under Mandy's name. As Rosie scanned the information she noticed something on one of the yellow notes that made her stop and zoom in even closer. It triggered a memory of something else and she closed the picture, not wanting to think about what that might mean.

Scrolling down the list of names in her phone contacts, Rosie found the number she wanted and dialled.

'Hiya, it's Rosie,' she said when the call was answered on the second ring. 'I need your help.'

101

ISOBEL

Thursday, 11 p.m.
16½ hours left

Just tell them and get out of here.

Isobel knew this was her best option but the anger and disgust she felt towards Paul and Vanessa wouldn't let her. They were supposed to be her friends and they were more interested in digging into her past than protecting her future. She should never have confided in Paul, should never have let him in on what was happening to her and Ryan.

A wave of nausea rose up from her centre. She clamped her hand to her mouth and ran back into the house, heading for the downstairs toilet. Unsurprisingly, the house-proud Reece-Johnsons did not try to stop her.

Kneeling on the floor with a tissue to her mouth and her head resting against the cool tiles, Isobel began to cry. She was getting worse. She had no option. If Paul wanted her secret she'd have to give it to him, but she wanted something in return.

Paul called to her from the kitchen when she stepped into the hall, and she made her way there. He and Vanessa stood at the kitchen island. They both had a half-drunk glass of wine in front of them. They had not offered her any.

Isobel sat on the nearest bar stool and rested her now totally numb arm on the countertop. 'I'm pretty sure I have a brain bleed and need to go to hospital, so I'll tell you, but I have a condition, two conditions.'

'Right?' Paul sipped his wine as he kept his eyes on her.

'I want to speak to Annie.' She didn't say that this was because she thought there was an outside chance it might be her last opportunity to tell her wife she loved her.

'And?' said Paul. 'The other condition?'

'If you're willing to withhold medical attention, I want to know why that is.' She was proud of herself for articulating things so well. Her blurred vision and constant waves of nausea were distracting and it was taking all her effort to force out the point. 'But first. Annie.' She held her hand out for one of their phones.

Vanessa looked at Paul and gave a small shake of the head.

102

RYAN

Thursday, 11 p.m.
16½ hours left

The knock on the door brought the conversation to an end. Ryan looked at Camille and Annie as he placed a finger on his lips. He then walked slowly and quietly into the hall, holding a hand up to Rosie, who was halfway down the stairs. He reached the door and took a couple of deep breaths. If this was Balaclava Man, could Ryan and the three women overpower him? He knew it was unlikely if the man was armed.

The sight of Greg was a relief.

'Evening, Ryan. Some of my colleagues just found two men in the Bath House pool, handcuffed to railings. Care to explain?' Greg walked past him and into the kitchen.

Ryan met Annie's gaze and nodded an unspoken agreement: *Be careful.*

Greg focused on Rosie, who had followed her dad into the room.

'Hi, sweetheart. Are you OK?'

Rosie nodded then turned to her dad. 'I'm worried about Aunt Isobel, so I called Uncle Greg.'

Ryan's heart sank. He should have explained to Rosie that he wasn't calling the police in order to protect Isobel. And perhaps he should have also mentioned his worry that Greg knew more than he was letting on.

'Thank you for coming, Greg. I didn't want to call because of Mandy. Can I get you something?' Annie said.

'Rosie tells me this involves Mandy, so I think I'm exactly who you should have called.' Greg's expression was stern and his gaze lingered on Ryan for longer than was polite. This was Detective Chief Superintendent Greg Coulters, not his old friend and drinking buddy. And he looked angry. 'I think you better tell me what on earth's been going on. Rosie said someone is blackmailing you all, and it involved Mandy too.'

Rosie, Rosie, Rosie. He hoped the fact that Greg was dressed in jeans and a T-shirt meant he maybe was here as a friend rather than a copper.

'Fine. Someone unknown has threatened to expose us all for things we did in the past, like my doping.' He watched Greg closely as he spoke, looking for any tells in his reaction.

'And what does this person or persons unknown want?'

'They've been given the option of exposing a friend in order to save themselves,' said Annie.

Greg's eyebrows rose and he looked genuinely intrigued. 'And how exactly does this involve Mandy?'

Ryan took a breath. If Greg wasn't involved in all of this, the next bit might hurt him. 'I had Mandy, so that's why I came clean, so no one would ever need to find out her secret.'

Greg's jaw twitched. 'Go on.'

Ryan looked at Camille, who gave a little nod. 'You remember I asked you about Audrey Raye?'

'The brain-damaged girl? Yes.'

'And you said Mandy knew her at school and took her birthday cakes every year. Well, we didn't know her at school. She was older.' Ryan tried to think of how best to say this without causing too much upset. 'But one night, years ago, when Mandy's mum had her stroke, Mandy raced home from university and the road was unlit and Audrey was dressed in dark clothes and . . .'

The realization in Greg's eyes stopped Ryan. Clearly, this was the first Mandy's husband had heard of it.

'She never told you?'

Greg shook his head then looked at Annie. 'Who knew about this?'

Annie had a hand over her mouth. 'I had no idea. Does Isobel know?'

'I didn't want anyone else to know. I didn't see the need because . . . I think maybe Mandy couldn't bear the thought of it going out in the world,' said Ryan.

Greg swallowed and looked at his feet for a long, silent moment. Then he placed his hands in his trouser pockets and focused on Ryan.

'Let's discuss these guys at the Bath House, then. How long were you planning on leaving them there, Ryan?'

'Wait, did you not receive a call about them?' Ryan saw Rosie shuffle on her spot and realized it was her who had told Greg about them. That's why Greg knew Ryan was involved. If Toby had called, it would have been an anonymous tip-off. Ryan tried not to be angry with his daughter, but it was tough. She had landed him right in the middle of this when he didn't need to be. He had more urgent things to be doing than talking to the police, like finding Isobel. 'They were planning to kill me, for going public with the doping,' said Ryan.

'They said Dad was a cheat, that he'd brought this on himself,' said Rosie.

Greg raised his eyebrows. 'You're sure of that?'

'Well, unless that syringe was empty, yeah, they seemed serious. I'm pretty sure they intended to make it look like I'd taken drugs and drowned or something. But then only Rosie was home when they came for me, and they had to improvise. I dread to think what would have happened to her.' Ryan knew the men had no intention of letting Rosie go but he didn't want to repeat that in front of her. She was set for bad enough nightmares as it was.

'I see. And who sent them?'

'Whoever is behind the blackmail, I imagine.'

Greg nodded slowly. 'And you haven't seen Isobel since before you and Rosie were taken by these men?'

Annie bit her lip as she shook her head.

'I know it's late, but are you two OK to come with me to see Paul?' Greg looked at Ryan and Annie.

'I can watch the kids. You all go,' Camille said.

'Why do we need to see Paul?' said Annie.

'I think he might have information that could help us to find Isobel.'

'What kind of information?'

'One of the men we found at the Bath House had a tattoo—'

'On his neck, yeah, I saw that,' said Ryan.

'Distinctive, isn't it? Not the cleverest bit of ink to get. Easily recognizable, especially when you're already known to the police. That guy works for Mitchel Bleacher, who is something of a crime boss in the Yorkshire region. Bleacher is a slick operator.'

'Why would this Bleacher character have a grudge against all of us? I've never even heard of him,' said Ryan.

'That is the big question here. What you are talking about is not Bleacher's style. He's a drug dealer and he's all about the cold, hard cash in my experience. This all sounds far too . . . emotional for him.'

'Wait,' said Annie. 'Wasn't it Mitchel Bleacher's son who was shot by that Renton bloke?'

'Kyle Renton, yes, but it was Mitchel's grandson, the two-year-old, who died.'

Ryan saw the connection before Greg spelled it out.

'And Paul prosecuted Renton, which means he worked closely with the Bleacher family.'

Had Paul done something to upset this Bleacher character? Is that why the man was coming after Paul's friends? But why not Paul himself? Camille had flagged this. She thought it was odd that Paul wasn't being shamed too.

'Dad?' Rosie said as they were all moving to leave. 'Can you drop me at Nanna's on the way?'

'No, hon, it's late. Why don't you stay and help Camille with the kids, you're good at that.'

'I don't want to stay.'

'Why not?'

Rosie's eyes flicked to Camille.

Ryan took a few steps away from his wife into the hall and Rosie followed.

'What's going on?' he asked.

'Nothing, it's just ... Camille was acting weird yesterday. Nanna and Grandad will be awake. They never go to bed before midnight. They won't mind.'

'Weird how?'

'She was laughing on the phone with someone after your press conference when everything was going wrong. She was speaking French and laughing. I didn't like it.'

'Honey, she will have been getting some moral support from her family. We're all going to deal with this differently.'

'I know, but still. Can you drop me? There's nowhere for me to sleep here anyway. I'd have to be on the sofa if you all stay and I don't want to go back to yours.'

Ryan nodded. What choice did he have? She was scared to go back to his house and he couldn't blame her. He looked at Camille, who was reading a magazine at the kitchen table. She glanced up and smiled. Ryan blew her a kiss.

'Back soon, babe.'

103

PAUL

Thursday, 11.30 p.m.
16 hours left

Isobel's body shook violently as Paul stared at her from across the room.

Vanessa walked to the dishwasher and turned it on. Should he be worried that his wife didn't seem at all concerned that their friend was having a seizure on their kitchen floor? Then again, he was standing frozen to the spot and doing nothing to help, so what did that say about him? They were terrible people. He should have taken Isobel to A and E when she'd asked. Why didn't he do that? She was a doctor. She knew something was ser-iously wrong and he'd ignored her. Had part of him known he was risking her life? On some level, had he figured that if Isobel succumbed to her injuries he would be home and dry? He actu-ally didn't know, and that scared him. How dark did his soul go?

Isobel had seemed so composed when she'd demanded one of their phones to call Annie. It had felt almost reassuring to Paul, like another escape route had opened, but then Vanessa had shut it off with that simple shake of her head. And she'd been right. Isobel had screamed, pleaded, and the effort must have been too much. It had pushed her over the edge, pushed them all over. Or had he stepped over the brink days ago . . .

All of these thoughts skittered into hiding when there was a loud knock on the door. Everything after that happened in slow motion. The front door opened and Detective Chief Superintendent Greg Coulters filled the space. Vanessa moved quickly to block his view of the kitchen floor where Isobel lay, but she wasn't quick enough to get into the hall and close the door behind her. A howling sound filled the air, like the call of an injured animal, and Annie ran from behind Greg towards her wife, shoving Vanessa aside and dropping to her knees.

'Izzy, babe. Oh my God. Call an ambulance!'

Greg was already on his phone.

'What the hell happened?' said Ryan.

'She fell and hit her head against the door frame in the hall,' Paul said.

He watched Ryan fetch a cushion and place it under Izzy's head then move all the chairs away from her.

'Is she OK? Why's she making that noise?' Annie looked terrified.

'The ambulance is on its way. ETA five minutes,' Greg said.

Ryan touched Annie's arm. 'Give her some space. It will pass . . . I hope.'

The group all silently watched as Isobel's body continued to jerk and arch. Paul avoided everyone's eyes. When the seizure finally stopped, Annie held her hand as she slowly regained consciousness. The ambulance arrived a few minutes later. The paramedics asked Isobel for her name and whether she knew where she was. She didn't answer. Then they asked Ryan about her injury. He looked at Paul.

'She fell and hit her head against the door frame in the hall,' he said again. *Keep it simple. Don't elaborate.*

'How long ago?'

'Huh?'

The paramedic looked at Paul. 'How long before the seizure did she hit her head?'

'Not long.' He made sure to avoid Vanessa's eyes.

'Did she lose consciousness after she fell?'

'Yes.'

'Oh, God. Izzy. Come on babe, look at me,' said Annie. 'You're going to be OK.' She looked at the paramedics. 'She is going to be OK, isn't she?'

They reassured Annie they'd get Isobel to hospital and checked out as soon as possible, but Paul noted that they stopped short of confirming she would be OK.

Paul knew Isobel would tell Annie everything he and Vanessa had done to her as soon as she came to. Annie would undoubtedly report him to the police. It was only a matter of time before he was questioned about it all, so he'd need to make sure his version of events was consistent and capable of convincing the authorities that it was all a terrible accident. He hadn't meant to hurt her, and that was true, he really hadn't.

As his friend fought for her life, he was thinking about how to protect himself.

104

Scrappy Paul Johnson. I expect you added the Reece when you married your posh girl in the hope some of her class would rub off. But it really didn't, did it? How could it? You were already soaked to the bone with fire and fury. Look at you, agreeing to do away with your oldest friend in order to hide your dirty little secret.

It was finding out what you have been hiding that helped me to finalize my plans. The whole thing was losing momentum. Life takes over, I suppose, and I found myself distracted. And then, quite by chance, I met an old friend of yours. When I said I was from Ilkley he said, 'One of ours is from that neck of the woods, do you know him?'

'One of ours.' At first I thought he meant you were family, or even of the same profession, but it was neither of these, was it? Oh, you had been a naughty boy. How would Isobel feel if she knew? It was that question which gave me the idea of how I would use your shame against you: the chance to not only ruin your life, but to tear apart your friendships.

105

RYAN

Friday, midnight
15½ hours left

The atmosphere was tense when he and Greg returned to the kitchen. Annie had gone in the ambulance with Isobel. Paul and Vanessa sat at the island, and Ryan sensed he and Greg were up against a united pair.

'I think you'd better start explaining,' Ryan said. He saw the muscles in Paul's left cheek twitch. It struck Ryan that for the first time in as long as he could remember, Paul looked nervous.

'What happened to you and Rosie?'

'No. You do not get to change the subject. I know how you work. Tell me what the hell has gone on here with Isobel.'

'Come with me.' Paul led the way to his office and stood in front of the wall of notes Rosie had pointed out to Ryan through the window earlier. 'Isobel thought I was behind all of this because I've been trying to find out who's doing it. She went mental. She attacked me.'

'So when you said she fell?'

'I didn't mean to hurt her. I only pushed her away from me. I swear on Rosie's life, I would never hurt Isobel intentionally.'

'Don't do that. Don't use Rosie.' Ryan studied the wall properly. The notes reached high and wide, covering pretty much all of the space. 'This is a lot of work. I can see why it freaked out Isobel.'

'They threatened him, too,' Vanessa said as she joined them. Paul looked furious with her. 'What? I'm sure Ryan has already worked that out. And if he hasn't, Greg certainly has.'

Greg stood silently behind Ryan and didn't react.

Paul swallowed and sucked his cheeks in before speaking. 'I'm pretty sure Stuart Fraser has something to do with it. Do you remember him? He was a proper nerd at school. A bit creepy around the girls.'

'The guy you beat up yesterday?' Greg said.

'You've already confronted him?' said Ryan. He knew Paul used to be quick to use his fists, but he'd grown out of that years ago, or so Ryan thought. And now he was pushing Isobel around and attacking people.

'Not many words were exchanged, no. He was shifty as shit,' said Paul. 'Whoever is doing this has stalked us and uncovered things that are buried deep. Fraser has the means and the motivation. He's been around us all for decades, is undoubtedly a man who spends more time lurking around on the internet than living in the real world and clearly he wants to punish us all for something.'

'You have no proof, though,' said Vanessa. 'It's just a theory.'

Ryan tried to picture the socially awkward Stuart Fraser he remembered from school morphing into someone those three men who'd just tried to kill him would call 'boss'.

'No. Not a chance. Whoever is doing this is violent. Stuart wouldn't be capable.'

'But this Shame Game thing has taken skill and patience. It's someone who has a lot of time on their hands and nothing better to do. Stuart fits.'

'Are you suggesting we ignore the fact that these people attacked my daughter and tried to kill me?'

'You know what I mean.'

'No, actually, I don't.'

'I'm telling you, it's Stuart.' Paul met Ryan's gaze and held it for a second. 'He's Audrey Raye's cousin. Our friendly Detective Super here gave me that little nugget of intel.'

'You knew about Mandy?' Greg's words were clipped and curt.

Paul didn't look Greg's way. 'Not until I worked it out earlier. But you fell on your sword for her, Ryan, so I assume you and Izzy have known all along. That's why Stuart's got it in for us all. Did you help her cover it up or something?'

'No, Paul. I had no idea until this week and as far as I know Isobel has no idea at all. If Stuart thinks we were involved, he's very much mistaken.'

'Well, we still need to stop him. It's the only way now. Time is running out and I can't let this all come out. *We* can't.'

Ryan saw something in Paul's expression that made the hairs on his arms stand up. There was something very off about his friend's behaviour, even considering the extreme situation.

Paul continued, 'It's all very creditable, you covering up what Mandy did to Audrey, but the rest of us can't afford that. Izzy wouldn't even tell us what she'd done. Although we're pretty sure she killed a child.'

'What the hell? Izzy hasn't killed a child.'

'She told Paul her threat was to do with an indiscretion at work,' said Vanessa.

'That doesn't mean she killed a child, for God's sake.'

'People do awful things without intending to,' Paul said. 'She's a paediatrician. Her whole career has been focused on children, mainly babies. What else would make her so desperate? She's been behaving crazily, accusing me of all sorts, attacking me.'

Ryan didn't want to think about that, so he considered the other things Paul had said. Like the fact that if Stuart Fraser was behind it, this whole thing might be about Audrey's accident.

'Let's think about the questions we were all set, then – are they all related to what happened to Audrey? Because Annie has a theory on Izzy's and I think she might be on to something.'

'What theory?' Vanessa said.

'That someone Izzy knows was part of the England First Party – a far right group.'

'Really? I didn't get that from what she told me.' Paul's response was quick and calm but it wasn't enough to mask his reaction. For the briefest moment, he'd looked like he'd been slapped in the face, and Vanessa's whole body had tensed just a touch. They were such small things, and yet for Ryan they screamed the truth aloud.

I was given Mandy to shame, Isobel was given Paul.

Ryan stared at his best friend. How could that be right? Ryan had never detected any racist views in Paul. He'd been close friends with Isobel most of his life. Had she found out? Ryan knew that would have broken her heart. Is that what their fight had really been about? Or had Paul hurt Isobel to silence her?

Ryan scanned the wall of Post-its again, looking for clues. His whole life was recorded up there, from where he'd lived with his parents, their names, his schools, qualifications, teenage jobs in the local newsagents and cycling shop, children's births and marriage to Camille, then one whole column was dedicated to his cycling races. His eyes paused on a note that read, '*Drug use @ TDF July 2012*' and another recording his question: '*Who hurt Audrey Raye?*' He scanned a similar level of detail for Isobel and Mandy. He noted that under Isobel's name, the question read, '*Who betrayed you in England at the Royal Oak?*' The word '*first*' had been omitted.

'How come there's nothing about you on here?' Ryan pointed

at the wall. 'If you were targeted too? Is it because you don't want the fact you are a racist written up there?'

'Shit,' said Vanessa under her breath.

'I always knew you were angry, but white supremacy? Jesus.'

'Says the drug-taking cheat.' Paul's cheeks flushed scarlet.

'Yes, says the drug-taking cheat. I was an idiot. I did a stupid thing and now it's ruined my life, but I owned up. And I didn't try to ruin the lives of others, did I?'

'Yes, but this won't just ruin our lives, will it? If it comes out, people will be able to appellate their convictions. Or say I didn't represent them properly. The court of appeal will not be able to say no to retrials. This is about justice.'

'I was given Mandy to expose. Isobel was given you to expose. So were you given Isobel? Is that why you attacked her, because she wouldn't confess?'

'No. I didn't attack Isobel. She came after me, I've told you. I had *you* to expose. "Who cheated justice on twenty-second July 2012?"'

This was the same claim that he'd been sent in the fake article, but he hadn't cheated then: 22 July 2012 was the date of his Tour de France stage win. He'd taken EPO a year earlier, for the Giro. Ryan realized that whoever was doing this had their facts wrong.

'Mandy must have had Isobel,' Paul said.

Ryan thought about the question Mandy had been sent. The one he'd found on her laptop when he'd visited her flat. *Who broke their vow in the woodlands?* He had wondered if it was about Greg breaking his wedding vows, whether he'd consummated his fling with his detective inspector in some wooded area. But it could be Isobel. He'd never had the chance to show the wording to her, or to anyone else for that matter. He knew she would never cheat on Annie, but another word for 'vow' was 'oath', so could it relate to Isobel's career? Had Isobel broken her oath to do no harm? The nausea he had felt before confessing to his own crime rose up in a fresh wave.

'Why were you so keen to know what Izzy had done then?' he said.

'Because you came clean,' said Vanessa. She sounded irritated. 'You took yourself out of the game and so did Mandy. Paul had no choice.'

Ryan stared at Paul as if he was an alien.

'Your only way out was to expose Isobel.'

How could he be so cold? What right did he have? And then Ryan looked again at the note stuck to Paul's office wall – *Drug use @ TDF July 2012*. If he hadn't come clean, his best mate would have thrown him to the lions.

Ryan eyeballed Paul. 'So what now? What do you propose to do now there's no one left to betray?'

106

PAUL

Friday, 12.30 a.m.
15 hours left

Paul felt sweat beginning to soak the back of his shirt. He was losing control of this. Greg now knew about England First, and soon Annie would too. The police and the press; a marriage made in hell. How long before someone looked into Leonard Phelps and found out what Paul had done, the evidence he'd sat on which pretty much proved Phelps's innocence? He had done it to impress the England First leadership. He wanted them to see he was committed and useful and he hadn't cared about the lives it would ruin. And now it was about to ruin his.

'Tell me again what happened with Isobel,' said Greg.

Paul knew the tactic. Keep asking the same question and listen for variations.

He explained again about her seeing this wall and thinking he was the blackmailer and how she then lost her temper and began screaming and hitting him. He said he had tried to restrain her but she was crazy strong and so as a last resort he'd pushed her off him which is when she fell and hit her head. He kept it factual and simple.

'Mandy told me how you used to scare her. She told me about your temper and how she would want to get away.'

God, Paul hated this arrogant bastard.

'No, she didn't. And don't talk to me like you knew Mandy better. You lost that right when you broke her heart. You know that Mandy did what she did on Friday because she couldn't take any more, because she was so damn depressed about the way you treated her. She would never . . . not Mandy . . . she would never, but what you did to her destroyed her before this all began. You had already destroyed her.'

Greg turned to Paul, his feet planted firmly on the carpet and his voice calm and measured. 'Don't paint me as the villain. This is about what you did to Isobel, not about Mandy and me.'

'You brought it up. Do you know why she married you? To punish herself, that's why. Imagine knowing you'd committed a crime and then hidden it, imagine feeling that guilty and ashamed and then putting yourself in bed with the law every night. She didn't love you. It was penance. You were her penance and you were too stupid to see it.'

Vanessa walked out of the room and back towards the kitchen.

Greg placed both hands together under his nose. 'Here's the thing that's bothering me. Everything I've heard you say about this blackmailer and what they've been doing implies they're trying to embarrass you all. But the attack on Ryan and Rosie feels like a major escalation. Suddenly, we have organized crime involved.'

'That's what I was thinking. I can't make sense of that,' said Ryan.

'Paul?' Greg looked at him.

Paul shrugged. 'I think Fraser hired these thugs.'

'Interesting. I was thinking that Bleacher wouldn't be afraid to take people out for the right price.'

The room fell silent for a long moment before Greg spoke again.

'Did it annoy you, Paul, when Ryan took your get out of jail free card away? Is that why, later the same day, you attacked Mr Fraser in a rage?'

'There is no getting out of jail for free, don't you see that? Either the blackmailer shames you or your friend does. It's a lose-lose. I wouldn't have exposed Ryan. I was trying to find out who was behind it. I still am.'

'A lose-lose. No way out. And if your past comes to light it affects the very justice you've dedicated your life to applying. That is a conundrum.'

Paul couldn't look at the guy. He was such a smug arsehole.

'Enough to make a man desperate . . .'

'How do you mean?' said Ryan, looking first at Greg and then at Paul.

'Well, in my job, you learn not to put too much store in coincidences. Like the fact that the day before all your dirty secrets come out, Isobel ends up in hospital after injuring herself at Paul's house, and someone puts a hit out on Ryan with none other than Mitchel Bleacher.'

Paul tried to find a counter argument, a way to discredit Greg's theory, but his ability to think was inhibited by the hot, raging anger compelling him to knock the smug bastard out.

'You can't possibly be suggesting that Paul orchestrated a hit on his closest friend?' Vanessa stood in the doorway. Her words sounded like they were in support of Paul, but their delivery was flat and monotone. Her heart was not really in it. She was simply expressing surprise to Greg in the hope that her innocence in the matter would be assured.

'Of course he isn't, because that would be a blatant lie. You have no proof of any of this. It is a skewed speculation based on your personal hatred of me,' Paul said.

Ryan's phone rang.

'It's Annie,' he said, before walking out and towards the kitchen.

107

ROSIE

Friday, 12.15 a.m.

Shame is a burden some must bear
It hides within the soul
Its roots are deep
Its tendrils creep
As you try to plug the hole.

Shame tells you every win you've won
Is nothing you are worth
And all the bad things that occur
Are just what you deserve.

If you let shame into your heart
It will make a home for life
Lurking below
Waiting to grow
Feeding on all your worry and woe

So beware of the parasite known as shame.
Do not let it call your name.

Rosie sat back against the side of the bed and read the poem again. She had rooted it out from underneath the linens in her mum's old bedroom at Nanna's house. She'd first found it years earlier, when she'd been using the sheets to build a camp. It was with a stack of framed pictures, including a pencil drawing of a girl carrying a teddy bear and a print of the cover of Roald Dahl's *Matilda*. Nanna had said they used to hang on the walls when Rosie's mum was a girl, and she couldn't bring herself to get rid of them.

Did this mean what she feared it did?

Greg had dropped her off at her grandparents' house on the way to Paul's, and her dad had walked her to the door. He'd offered to come inside and tell them about the events at the Bath House, but she'd asked if he could come over tomorrow and do it then.

As Rosie had watched him walk away, she felt a large weight form in her stomach. The little girl inside her wanted to run after him and beg him to take her with him, but she had to be grown up. She knew she had something important to do and she knew she might be the only person able to do it.

Back at Isobel and Annie's, when she'd looked at the picture of Paul's Post-its on her phone, she'd spotted a name she knew well: Stuart Fraser. He was a lifelong friend of her mum's. Rosie recalled that when she was younger, Stuey would come and babysit. He would let Rosie watch TV on his phone while he hooked up his PlayStation to Mum's TV and played games. It was seeing Stuart's name that had reminded Rosie of the poem from her mum's bedroom. Had Paul discovered that Stuey was involved somehow? Could he even be helping her mum do all this?

It wasn't only that the person doing this to Dad and his friends called it the Shame Game, it was the fact that her mum had still been with her dad in 2011, when he'd doped. Had he confessed to her back then and had Mum kept that to herself until she was ready to use it against him? It was time to find out.

Rosie took out her phone and texted her mum.

I'm at Nanna's. Dad just dropped me off. Can you come?

She knew that saying Dad had dropped her off would fire Mum up to come over. She loved any opportunity to present Dad in a bad light. *How could he drop you off at this time? He's supposed to be looking after you. What kind of father does that?*

108

RYAN

Friday, 12.45 a.m.

14¾ hours left

'How is she?'

'Not great, Ry. She has a brain bleed so they're operating now. I can't believe this is happening. What was going on there? Have you got anything from Paul?'

'God, I'm so sorry, Annie. How long will the surgery take?'

'They're not saying, but everyone is telling me she has the best people working on her.'

Ryan sat on the small sofa in Paul and Vanessa's kitchen. Could Greg be right? Could Paul be behind the attack on him and Rosie? Ryan couldn't wrap his mind around why his friend would do something so extreme. Had he really misjudged him so badly all these years? He knew Paul could be a bit distant and aloof at times, but he was a good person, a kind person.

'Look, Annie, it seems Paul was trying to get Izzy to tell him what she'd done so he could use it to stop her from exposing him. That England First group you found, Paul used to be a member.'

'What the actual . . . ? You *are* kidding? Paul is one of Izzy's best friends. We've stayed over at his house, how can that be possible?'

'I don't know. I can't make sense of it. Anyway, I think there's a good chance all this stuff about us is going to come out, Izzy's secret included, unless you can win her a pass before three thirty tomorrow. Do you have Izzy's phone?'

'No, she told me Paul smashed it up. I managed to get a bit of the story out of her before she went into surgery. She said Paul and Vanessa kept her there, in the garage.'

Shit. Paul really was a thug.

'OK. Can you access her phone messages on a laptop or iPad? They should upload there from the cloud.'

'Yeah, I think so. Izzy's iPad is at the house. I could ask Izzy's dad to fetch it here for me, maybe. Why, what are you thinking?'

'There will be messages from Shame@pm.me and I think you need to reply as if you are Izzy. Say Paul Reece-Johnson is the person who betrayed you in England First. They will respond, telling you to expose him if you want to protect yourself. Do you understand?'

Ryan sensed someone watching him and looked up to meet Paul's furious eyes.

He had no time to ask Annie to keep him posted on Isobel, or even to say goodbye. His phone was thrown out of his hands as Paul launched his attack. He grabbed Ryan's shirt and yanked him to his feet before landing a punch on the side of his face that felt like he had been hit by a brick. Ryan fell face first into the cushioned back of the sofa and before he could push himself up Paul landed more blows on his head and back as he shouted that he was going to kill him. Ryan tried to twist his head to find some air. The weight of Paul's attack was pushing his face into the cushions. His skin felt hot and sweaty and his throat burned in protest at the lack of oxygen.

'That's enough,' Ryan heard Greg say, before the blows paused momentarily.

Ryan twisted on the sofa, relieved to be able to breathe again, then Paul landed another punch that smashed into Ryan's nose.

Greg hooked his arms around both of Paul's from behind and was fighting to get control as he told Paul to calm down. Paul struggled and strained against the restriction, his eyes blazing and his mouth almost foaming. He looked to Ryan like a wild animal.

'You don't know what you've done,' Paul shouted. 'You have no idea what you've done. Get off me!' Paul suddenly twisted in Greg's hands and threw a punch which missed the policeman's face but landed squarely in his chest. Greg winced but then stood taller and grabbed Paul's arm by the wrist and twisted it behind his back.

'Whatever else you may have done, Paul, that was a stupid move. Assaulting a police officer is a serious offence.'

'Fuck you,' spat Paul.

Ryan rolled into a seated position on the floor; his mouth tasted of metal and he could feel blood running down his face.

109

ROSIE

Friday, 12.45 a.m.

'What is he thinking, dropping her off at this time? This is all I need after the day I've had – it's been non-stop and I've got a crashing headache. You know the GP is referring me for tests to check all these headaches aren't a tumour or something.'

Rosie rolled her eyes at the sound of her mother's complaints. She was always having the hardest life. Always feeling the most ill. Always the most downtrodden.

Grandad looked up from his book as Mum came in and launched an attack on Rosie.

'What have you got to say for yourself, swanning out of here and then not bothering to let me know if you're OK? Do you know how frantic I've been? And then you expect me to drop everything and come running when you snap your fingers. You are quite awful, you know.'

'*I* am?' said Rosie.

'All right. Let's calm it down.' Grandad didn't like the arguments. He usually escaped into the garden or to his study if things started to kick off.

'I want to know why you hate Dad so much.' Rosie stood up

so she was eye to eye with her mother. 'I think it's time you told me the truth. You've done nothing but bitch and moan about him since I was little, taking every chance you can to try and turn me against him or stop me from seeing him. Why? What did he ever do that was so bad?'

'He left us.' Her mother spat the words.

Nanna entered with a tray of mugs and exchanged a look with Grandad.

'Lots of dads leave their wives and vice versa. I have loads of friends with divorced parents, but they don't hate each other, they share a beer at summer barbecues, and chip in together for birthday parties. Why can't you be like that?'

'Because he left me with a baby. Left me destitute and unable to take care of myself. You have no idea how hard it was back then. You were a nightmare, always screaming and refusing to sleep and I was all alone.'

'You moved in with Nanna and Grandad and they looked after you. You weren't alone or destitute. You're such a drama queen. Why can't you ever tell the truth?'

'Why are you defending him? He doesn't deserve it,' she shouted.

'But that's not the point, is it, Mother?' It was Rosie's turn to shout now. 'It's not about whether he deserves it, it's that I deserve a father who loves me. You have a great relationship with your dad. You love him to bits, so why would you want to stop me from having the same? What right do you have to try and take that away from me?'

Her mum stormed out in tears. Nanna went after her. Rosie sank on to the sofa. She could hear the blood pumping in her ears and her cheeks felt hot.

'What is wrong with her, Grandad?'

'She's not a bad person, you know. Your mum's just not very good at handling things.'

Rosie huffed. *Whatever.* 'There is something very wrong with her, you must know that.'

After a few moments of silence, where all Rosie could hear was her mother sobbing in the kitchen, her grandad said, 'People are not born broken, you know. It's life that makes them that way.'

Rosie had had enough of all the drama, and the lies, and the cryptic comments. She strode into the kitchen determined to get the answers she needed.

'OK, if you won't tell me why you hate Dad so much, tell me what you have against Isobel and Mandy?'

'Oh, for heaven's sake, Rosie, leave me alone.' Her mum had a large bunch of kitchen roll grasped in her fingers that she was using to dab her tears.

'Just tell me why you hate Dad and his friends so much.'

'Stop being so awful to me! Why are you being so awful? Mum, won't you tell her to stop it. I can't take it, I'm not well.'

'Why don't you go and have a lie down, then?'

Her mum nodded to Nanna and mouthed the words, 'Thank you', before leaving the room without even looking at Rosie.

'Sit down and have your cup of tea, love.' Her nanna pushed a mug of tea towards her.

'I don't want a cup of tea or to sit down.' Rosie was sick of the lot of them.

'I know. You want answers and it's about time you had them. So sit down. I need to tell you a story.'

110

STEPHANIE

Friday, 12.45 a.m.

Sitting on the bed in her old room, Stephanie raged inside at the injustice of it.

How can she say that I tried to turn her against Ryan?

She remembered the laughter and the cheering and the look in their eyes as she had pleaded with them to stop. Stephanie changed her position on the bed and tried to force the memories away but they wouldn't go. She hadn't been much older than Rosie. Afterwards, her mum had said they needed a common enemy to feel good about themselves, but Steph knew differently. They just thought she was less; that she wasn't as clever, or funny, or popular. They had made the voice in her head true. The one that said horrible things about how useless she was, what a failure she was, how nobody liked her because what was likable about her really?

Something is wrong with me. Something so bad that even my own mother can't love me no matter how much I try to make her care.

The thing that hurt the most, that enraged her the most, was that since Rosie had become a teenager, Steph had seen the same judgement and disgust in her daughter's eyes. And she knew for a fact that was down to Ryan and his awful friends.

111

ROSIE

Friday, 1 a.m.

'It was only a few weeks before her A Level exams began. I was working in the big Estate Agents on the Grove. There were three of us mums who worked there part-time at that stage and I was doing an afternoon shift, which meant Steph was taking the bus home and putting on the tea. Your grandad liked a meal on the table when he got home at 5.30. I remember when I got in, your mum was a bit quiet and she had a couple of scratches on her face but that wasn't unusual for Stephanie – she was a clumsy child. Then a day or so later, I was at work again and it was the office manager, John, who alerted me. He had one of these new video phones, you see. I just had a little Nokia thing at the time. I could make calls and send texts but nothing more, but his had the ability to play back recordings and apparently this one had been doing the rounds in the town. Teenagers with these new phones would target some other child and then film themselves pushing them around. It wasn't the best footage but I could see it was our Stephanie on the back seat of the bus with her arms covering her head as they pushed her and slapped her and then grinned back at the camera. They called it "Happy Slapping".

'It wouldn't have been so bad if it had simply been a bit of bullying that was over as quickly as it began, but this video kept it going. Your mum said she would hear people watching it and laughing. I don't know if that's really what was happening but that's what your mum believed and so she became very insular. She revised for her exams but then she walked out of two of them because she said she was sure people were looking at her and laughing.'

'Are you saying my dad was one of the people who made this video?'

'Oh yes, he was doing the filming, you could hear him laughing as he watched the others humiliating your mum.'

'And the others were?'

'Paul, Isobel and Amanda.'

Rosie tried to process this shocking detail about her parents' history. Her dad – her kind, caring dad – had been part of a gang who had physically and psychologically attacked her mum when they were all teenagers. For the first time since Rosie was very young, she felt genuine sympathy for her mum. In fact, the whole thing made her feel sick and furious with her father and his friends.

'Your grandad wanted us to involve the police and complain to the school but I said to him, *What's the point, they're kids; they'll get a slap on the wrist and that'll be that.*

'But this was why your mum never went to university. She didn't get the grades and she refused to retake. It was awful. Stephanie had aways been difficult, she was a high-maintenance child, not like you, Rosie, and we needed a break. We hoped she might meet someone in her university town and put down roots so we'd have the freedom to do the things we'd been unable to do since having her. But she never left. She lived with us until she fell pregnant by your dad, which to me seemed like the stupidest thing in the world. I think she wanted to prove to everyone that all those supposed friends accepted her now, that by going with your dad she became one of them, but we could see it was doomed from the start.

'Your grandad set them up in a rented flat above where Toast café is now. That's where they lived when you were born. We paid for it and furnished it in the hope things would work out, but your dad was always out riding or away racing and your mum wanted someone there helping her all the time, not just occasionally. She's not the most capable, as you know. And then one day he upped and left, said he couldn't cope with it all any more, like you can just hand a baby back if you find it hard.' Felicity tutted loudly. 'So you and your mum moved back here and your dad went gallivanting around Europe with models.'

For a few quiet moments, Rosie sat thinking about everything her nanna had revealed. The secret past that began to explain why her family was so full of bitterness. She looked at her phone on the table and scrolled to her dad's number. She didn't know what to do with the new information she had learned about him. She didn't want her opinion of him to change, but how could it not? He had hurt her mum. Rosie tried to imagine how she would feel if Gus and his mates turned on her. If they started laughing at her. She couldn't picture any of them physically pushing or hitting her but there was enough mental abuse that went on at school for her to know you didn't need bruises to feel under attack. Happy Slapping may have been how they did it in her parents' day, but now it would be via social media; like the memes some of her supposed friends had been circulating about her dad being a druggie.

And if Gus and his friends did turn on her to the extent that it ruined her life, would she want to take her revenge?

'Do you think Mum has held a grudge against them all for ruining her life?'

'Rosie, sweetheart, let's be quite clear about this. Your dad,

371

Isobel, Mandy and Paul did not ruin your mum's life. Your mum did. She refused to retake her A Levels despite our support, then she got that part-time job at the restaurant and never left. Although, in the early days, I'd have Malcolm on the phone pretty much every week telling me they'd have to let her go if she kept calling in sick and letting them down. Your grandad had to agree to do Malcolm's accounts on the cheap to make sure he didn't fire your mum.' Nanna sighed. 'She was always hard work. Even as a baby she'd have your poor grandad walking circles around the garden in the middle of the night as she screamed and refused to sleep.'

Rosie had heard this story all her life, about poor Grandad walking Mum in circles. It struck her that despite what Grandad had said about people not being born broken, Nanna's view had always been that something was wrong with her mum right from the start.

112

RYAN

Friday, 1.30 a.m.
14 hours left

How had it come to this?

In under a week, Mandy had lost her life, Isobel was fighting for hers and Paul had tried to have him killed. It was like something out of a horror movie. He couldn't wrap his head around it.

After Greg had dropped him back at Isobel and Annie's house, having dispatched Paul off to the station with two uniformed officers, Ryan had to sit on the step before going inside because his whole body was shaking. He had nearly died, and worst of all his little girl, Rosie, had been caught up in it all. What if those men had hurt her? He could never have forgiven himself and he didn't like to think about what he might have done to Paul.

'I can't get this little mite to settle,' said Camille, bouncing Josh as he began to make a low, droning sound. 'He wants his mummies and I'm sure he can tell something is wrong.'

'Let me take him for a bit,' Ryan said, taking a long breath in when his nose met the top of the little boy's head.

'I need to see your injuries.' Camille lightly touched Ryan's face and the tenderness of her touch brought a lump to his throat.

As Camille wiped the cut on his face with warm, salty water, Ryan tried to fill her in on all that had happened. She stopped tending his wounds and swore in French when he told her Paul had hired the men who attacked him and Rosie.

'What on earth did Vanessa say about that?'

Ryan shrugged. 'To be honest, she didn't show too much emotion about any of this.'

'Good grief, I would divorce you in the drop of a glove if you tried to kill one of our friends.'

'Drop of a hat, babe,' Ryan said with a smile. 'And I'd bloody well hope so.' Josh started to feel a little heavy against his shoulder, so he kept up the slow bouncing motion that was hopefully sending the boy to sleep. 'Did Izzy's dad come by for the iPad?'

Camille shook her head.

'Can you have a look around for it, hon? There's something I need to do and I don't want to disturb little nibs here.'

'Izzy is out of surgery, by the way,' Camille called from the hallway. 'It went well, Annie said.'

Ryan had to swallow a couple of times to stop himself from crying. 'Thank God,' he said.

His phone vibrated in his pocket as Camille came back in with a black iPad in her hands. Ryan retrieved the phone, having to adjust his position quickly as the motion caused Josh's now heavy head to slip from his shoulder.

'Oh, he's gone. Well done,' said Camille, rubbing Ryan's back.

It was Rosie calling.

'Hi, Ro,' he said, putting the phone on speaker.

Ryan could hear talking in the background.

'Rosie? You there?' he said, putting the phone on the table. He was about to hang up, assuming that she had pocket-dialled, when he heard something that stopped him.

'Might Mum have wanted to take revenge on Dad and his friends?'

Ryan looked at Camille and placed a finger on his lips, then he turned the volume up high on his phone and leaned in closer to listen.

113

ROSIE

Friday, 1.30 a.m.

Her phone was face down on the table with the volume turned low. She played with it a little as she spoke so she could make sure it sat between her and Nanna. She had no idea what was going to be said but she wanted her dad to hear. Despite what he'd done in the past, he was still the person she trusted most in the world.

'Your mother doesn't have it in her to take revenge,' Nanna was saying as she swilled their mugs in the sink. 'She's as flaky as a cream horn.'

'But you said the Happy Slapping thing had ruined her life.'

'No. I said it didn't ruin her life. She gets her washing done, her meals cooked for her and babysitting on tap. I pretty much raised you myself because she found it all so hard.'

'Do you sometimes wish you hadn't had Mum?'

'Rosie! What an awful thing to say. Of course not. I love your mum.'

'Yeah, but you don't like her, do you?'

'Whatever do you mean?'

'You tell her she's lazy and awkward all the time and I can't count the amount of times you've told me she's a terrible mother. I remember the first time you said it, after Mum had been shouting at me for spilling orange juice on the new carpet. You apologized for cursing me with her. I must have been six or seven and I was so upset I told Dad.' Rosie watched her nanna frown and neaten her hair. 'You think there's something wrong with her too, don't you?'

Nanna sat down heavily in a chair.

'That poem about shame that used to hang on Mum's bedroom wall,' Rosie said. 'Where did that come from?'

'Which poem?'

'The one that goes, "Shame is a burden some must bear, it hides within the soul".'

Her nanna shook her head. 'I have no idea. I think it's anonymous.'

'Did you put it up for Mum in the hope she would heal herself?'

114

RYAN

Friday, 1.45 a.m.
13¾ hours left

He wasn't sure how long he'd been holding his breath.

Why was Rosie talking about the Happy Slapping? Who would bring that up? He and Stephanie had discussed it over and over when they were together. Nobody hated her, but she was wrong to have told Mandy that Paul had made a pass at her. It was bound to stir up trouble. Paul and Mandy had wanted to make sure Steph didn't do something like that again. Ryan hadn't liked it, even then, but he didn't want them to think he was a wuss. Plus Isobel thought it would be a laugh. They didn't have to hurt her, she'd said, they could smack their hands together to make it look worse than it was. And so he'd agreed to hold Isobel's fancy new phone as the girls 'pretended' to slap Steph about, but of course once all the clapping and cheering started from around the bus everything changed. Next thing Ryan knew, Paul was in there pulling Steph's hair and telling her he wouldn't make a pass at her if she was the last girl alive.

If he was honest, all that had probably played a part in him and Steph hooking up years later. He'd felt guilty and when he'd been home on a break from training she had seemed so different. She was caring and sweet, because it turned out Steph could do caring and sweet so long as you were doing what she wanted you to do. Plus she had really been into him and, as a twenty-year-old, that had mattered. He wasn't proud of any of it. He didn't regret them falling pregnant and having Rosie, because that baby girl was the best thing that had ever happened to him, but he had always known he couldn't spend his life with Steph. She was too broken and needy.

Was Steph behind this whole thing? He had to admit, he also thought Steph would be too flaky.

Ryan heard Stephanie's voice on the end of the phone.

'Are you talking about me? Are you? What are you saying? TELL ME!'

Ryan stood up. 'Take Josh.'

Camille nodded and carefully moved the sleeping baby from Ryan's shoulder on to hers. 'Go,' she said, knowing he would want to be at his daughter's side.

'I love you,' he called back as he left.

115

THE SHAME GAME:
A TRUE CRIME DOCUMENTARY

Episode 3 of 3 - The Price

INT - FALLON FAMILY HOME - DAYTIME

ROSIE has her feet curled underneath her as she sits on a yellow sofa. She is wearing cropped jeans and a lilac checked shirt.

                    VOICE (O.S.)

    OK, Rosie, are you ready to start?

                    ROSIE

    Sure.

Rosie hooks one arm around her legs.

VOICE (O.S.)

We are fascinated by how you
worked this out and how you feel
about the various members of your
family at this stage, but first I
need to ask about that night at
your grandparents' house. Can you
tell us what happened?

ROSIE

I just wanted everyone to tell the
truth. There were so many secrets
and I was fed up of them. I'd
nearly lost my dad because of what
she'd done. I thought it was the
right thing to do. I didn't intend
for anyone to get hurt.

116

ROSIE

Friday 1.45 a.m.

'What are you saying?' Mum looked from Rosie to Nanna and back again. 'TELL ME!'

Rosie looked at her mum's face. It was contorted in anger, making her look really ugly. Rosie realized this was how she visualized her mum in her head when she thought about her.

'Oh, calm down, Stephanie, we're just having a chat,' said Nanna.

'About me, I know, I heard. You were talking about what's wrong with me. There's nothing wrong with me.'

'Are you sure about that?' said Rosie.

Her mum turned on her. 'And you can shut up. You don't get to judge me, you're nothing special.'

'Wow. Thanks. You know, whenever I was upset at some awful thing you'd said to me, I'd tell Dad and he'd say you were not a bad person, but I could always see the sadness in his eyes and how he wished he could protect me.'

'Your father wouldn't know good parenting if it slapped him in the face. He was about to let you leave education and become cheap labour in his ridiculous charity, leaving me penniless *again*.'

'What on earth is going on?' Rosie's grandad had his reading glasses pushed low on his nose and was holding the latest cosy crime novel he'd been reading.

'OK, explain this then,' Rosie said to her mum. 'You've been telling everyone all week that Mandy was your best friend, but I checked your phone because I don't recall you ever being close. I found lots of messages from you asking for her to call or meet up, or demanding to know why she hadn't replied to you even though you could see she'd been on WhatsApp that day, and all she sent you back were polite one- or two-word answers. She clearly didn't want to talk, but you just kept badgering her, telling her how Uncle Greg was as bad as my dad.'

'How dare you look through my phone. You have no right. You're invading my privacy.'

'Thing is,' Rosie continued, 'someone threatened to tell everyone about something Mandy had done and that's why she stepped in front of that truck. I think all that stuff about you being best friends was you covering your back so people wouldn't know it was you tormenting her.'

'What are you talking about? I don't know anything about what Mandy has done.'

Rosie felt her blood boiling. How could her mum lie like that? 'Nanna literally just told me that when Dad and his friends did that Happy Slapping thing, you said it ruined your life, so I think you decided to punish them.' Rosie saw her mum flinch at the mention of Happy Slapping. 'How did you feel when Mandy killed herself? Did you feel guilty at all? You can't have, because you kept going. And then . . .' Rosie looked at her grandparents. 'I was kidnapped tonight by three men who wanted to kill Dad.' She watched the shock land in their eyes before turning back to her deranged mother. 'You're a psycho. You don't care about anyone but yourself.'

Her mum lunged at her across the table, screaming like a crazy person. Rosie pushed her chair back and stood up so her mum couldn't reach her.

'Right, I think that's enough,' said Grandad, stepping in to try to control his daughter.

Her mum pushed him roughly away and started raging across the kitchen, picking up whatever she could find and throwing it to the ground. First a mug smashed, then the sugar bowl scattered its contents across the floor.

'Stephanie!' Nanna shouted, but it was too late to stop Mum from knocking the draining board with all its plates, knives and forks to the ground. The crockery smashed and the cutlery skittered in every direction.

'Do you believe her?' Mum screamed at Nanna. 'She's awful. She's lying! Nobody tried to kill Ryan. He put her up to saying that.'

'So you think I imagined being bundled into the boot of a car and thrown fully clothed into the Bath House pool earlier tonight, do you?' said Rosie.

'Rosie, leave it,' said Grandad.

Rosie rounded on her grandad. 'Maybe if you'd stepped in more and stopped all this fighting things wouldn't be so bad.' Her grandad recoiled. She'd never raised her voice to him before and she felt instantly guilty.

Mum and Nanna were going at it now, shouting about how Mum was hard work and Nanna never did anything to help. It was the same old argument Rosie had witnessed on a weekly basis. She clenched her fists and dug her nails into the palms of her hands to stave off the frustrated fury. The argument was too familiar. The outcome too predictable. Nothing would change.

'Why can't you ever stick up for me?' Mum was shouting. 'Why do you always take other people's sides? Me and Dad hate you.'

Rosie watched her grandad shake his head. She expected he wanted to walk out, like he usually did when everything kicked off, but he couldn't after what Rosie had said. He started to collect all the cutlery from the floor and kick the shards of broken crockery to one side.

'Stephanie, you say the most disgusting things. I don't know how I ended up so unfortunate as to have you as my daughter. What did I ever do to deserve it?'

'I hate you,' screamed Mum as she lashed out at Nanna, scratching the side of her face.

Grandad moved quickly to stop things from escalating. Rosie watched him step between his wife and daughter and hold his hands up to them. Nanna batted his arm away as she continued to give Mum a piece of her mind, but Mum grabbed his wrist and shook it. Then, to Rosie's horror, her mum focused on the cutlery clutched in Grandad's hand and made a grab for the kitchen knife. Grandad tried to yank his hand away but Mum had already pulled the knife from his grip.

'Don't you dare,' shouted Nanna, as Grandad tried his best to block Mum, who was now waving the sharp knife in Nanna's direction.

Mum lunged to one side of Grandad and then to the other. He mirrored her movements but she continued twisting to try to get past him, all the time jabbing forward with the knife and screaming something unintelligible.

'Get away from me!' shouted Nanna. Her back was up against the side of the counter and Grandad was blocking her exit as he tried desperately to hold Mum back. He made a grab for the knife and the blade slid through his grasp, causing blood to splatter on to the floor, but he didn't seem to notice as he continued to fight against his crazed daughter.

'Stop it!' Rosie shouted. 'You're hurting him.'

Mum looked wild. Her eyes were open far too wide, her mouth was twisted in a lopsided sneer and the sound she was making was more of a growl than any words. She pushed Grandad hard with her empty hand, causing him to stagger and make a kind of 'umph' sound.

'Don't you dare, don't you dare,' shouted Nanna, realizing Mum had a clear run on her now.

'Stop it, PLEASE!' shouted Rosie. 'Stop it!'

Mum lunged again and Nanna managed to jump out of the way.

'Whoa, whoa, whoa! What are you doing?'

Rosie turned to the door on hearing her dad's voice. His face was bruised and there was a cut on his forehead. Rosie looked back at her mum in time to see her spot Ryan. If she had looked crazed going after Nanna, the look in her eyes now became one of pure venom. Her mum drew the knife back, away from Nanna, held it high in the air and ran at Rosie's dad.

117

RYAN

Friday, 2 am
13½ hours left

Steph ran at him so quickly there was no time for Ryan to dodge her. If Graham hadn't stepped in her way, it would be him injured on the floor now.

'Oh my God! Oh my God!' Stephanie was leaning against the fridge with her hands over her mouth.

Ryan kneeled next to Graham, who had sunk on to the floor with the knife sticking out of the left side of his chest.

'Felicity, call an ambulance.'

Felicity nodded and reached for her phone, then she stared at it for a long moment, as if she didn't know why she had picked it up.

'Here, Nanna, I'll do it,' said Rosie, putting her own phone to her ear.

'No police,' said Graham through rasping breaths. His face was glistening and pale.

'I don't think you can avoid that, Graham. Just take it easy,' said Ryan, as Rosie requested an ambulance and told them her grandad had been stabbed by her mum. No chance of avoiding the police now, then. Rosie was taking no prisoners tonight. He could see her point. She no doubt thought all the adults in her life were a huge disappointment.

'Take it out,' Graham said, reaching for the knife. His movements were agitated and Ryan placed a reassuring hand on the man's shoulder.

'No. Leave it,' said Ryan. There was only a small amount of blood at this stage and he had no idea where that blade might have landed. 'Best to leave it there. We might make things worse.'

Graham dropped his hand to the floor and took a few more rasping breaths. Ryan hoped his lung wasn't damaged. The knife was too far left on his torso to have hit the heart, or at least he hoped it was.

'What on earth has been going on?' Ryan looked at Rosie.

'It was Mum. The Shame Game. She did it with Stuey's help.'

Ryan glanced at Stephanie, who still had her hands over her mouth and was now making a low moaning sound.

'Is that true, Steph? Did you dream up this madness?'

Steph met his gaze, her eyes wide and scared.

'What did you do?' said Felicity, quietly and then again more loudly. 'What did you do?'

Stephanie continued to shake her head and moan.

'He's got a knife sticking out of him! What did you do? ANSWER ME!'

'Don't shout at me.'

'Don't shout . . . Don't SHOUT! You stabbed your father!'

The two women started to holler over each other. Ryan watched Stephanie put her hands over her face at one point and stamp her feet. A few moments later, the shouting was interrupted when the second set of paramedics Ryan had met that night rushed in.

They moved Ryan out of the way and went about checking Graham's vital signs. Ryan watched them cut away Graham's shirt and check the wound.

'BP one hundred over seventy-five,' said the older paramedic. 'Resp rate thirty. Oxygen saturation is ninety per cent on air. I'm struggling to get a line in here.'

'Are you finding it hard to get your breath there, Graham?' said the younger paramedic.

'I didn't mean it. I didn't mean it,' said Stephanie.

'I need to go with him,' said Felicity as the paramedics prepared to move Graham into the ambulance. 'I'm his wife.'

The police arrived a few moments later, speaking briefly to the paramedics before telling Felicity one of them would accompany Graham to the hospital as well, presumably to get the story of what had happened from them as soon as possible.

Felicity looked back at Stephanie before she left.

'I will never forgive you for this. Never.'

Ryan looked at Stephanie and thought, *If you really did all of this, I couldn't agree more.*

118

ISOBEL

Friday, 2.30 a.m.
13 hours left

The world came back to her slowly in a haze of confusion and muffled beeps. She knew from the smell that she was in hospital but she couldn't recall how she got here.

'Hey, baby,' she heard Annie say as she opened her eyes.

That was when all the memories flooded back in a mass of images. She remembered lying on the floor with Annie calling her name, she remembered being tied to a chair, almost escaping from the garage and Paul pumping her for information on what she'd done.

And then a whole other set of memories rushed in.

The sound of the crash call with its eerie, disembodied crackle: 'Neonatal crash call. Labour ward. Room Seven.' The sight of the silent baby still being worked on by a desperate midwife, the heart monitor showing his heartrate had dropped below sixty, which should have triggered chest compressions, the demands of, 'Where have you been?' and then the lie. The instinctive, self-serving lie.

Isobel looked at Annie and squeezed her hand. 'I need to tell you something.'

'It's OK, just rest, there's plenty of time to talk later. You had to have surgery but it went well they think.'

Isobel tried to shake her head but the motion hurt so she concentrated on staying still. 'I was young and stupid and in total denial about my sexuality.' Isobel squeezed Annie's hand again when it looked like her wife might interrupt. She needed to get this out. 'I thought he loved me and that I loved him but I was just in awe. That day, when it happened, we were in the on-call room. Together.' She looked Annie in the eye to check her wife understood. She didn't want to say the phrase 'having sex' out loud. 'I don't recall hearing the bleeps, but apparently they did bleep us twice. He was my registrar, I was the Senior House Officer. It had been a quiet night so we didn't expect an emergency. Eventually, the midwife demanded a voice call, but it was too late. He'd been deprived of oxygen for too long, the official line was that this was down to his heart defect and that there was nothing we could have done, but that's not true. If we had been there . . .'

'Hey. Is that it? A patient died because you didn't get there quickly enough? That must be an everyday occurrence in a busy hospital.'

'No. That's not the worst of it. When the midwife asked why we hadn't responded I lied. I said we'd been at another emergency, but we hadn't and then I stood there and watched him, the man I thought I loved, write in the notes that the APGAR score was low from birth. That's how we rate the health of a newborn. A low score means they are floppy, unresponsive, pale and not crying from the off, but I know this wasn't the case from what the midwife later told me. That lovely boy and his poor parents. I don't deserve to get away with that. I don't deserve to have this wonderful life we have, our boy, you. I don't deserve it, don't you see?'

119

ROSIE

Friday, 2.30 a.m.

Rosie couldn't believe what had just happened. The image of her grandad sitting on the floor with a knife sticking out of him brought tears to her eyes.

'Hey. Come on. It's OK. He'll be OK,' her dad said, as if he'd read her thoughts. 'He's a strong man, your grandad.'

Rosie nodded and leaned into the hug. Small tremors that she couldn't control kept running through her body. She looked at the door to the kitchen, where the police were speaking to Mum. She and Dad would be next.

'There's something I need to tell you, about Paul.' Her dad swallowed. His face was swollen and large bruises were forming across his cheek and around his right eye.

Rosie listened as he told her that Paul was probably responsible for hiring the men who'd attacked them, that he was being blackmailed too, and that he'd hurt Isobel so badly she was now in hospital.

'Why would Uncle Paul do all of that?' Rosie's heart felt heavy in her chest. She should feel relieved that her mum wasn't behind those men coming for her and Dad, but she just felt numb.

'I don't know, Ro, but he's in a lot of trouble.'

'What will happen to him?'

Her dad told her about Greg arresting Paul. 'We need to go to the station first thing tomorrow to provide statements on everything that's been happening.'

Rosie wished she could call Aunt Mandy and tell her how great Uncle Greg had been. At least he hadn't let her down.

'What on earth made you accuse your mum? I'm not mad. None of this is your fault. I only want to understand before we speak to the police.'

Rosie sat up and pulled away so she could look him in the eye. She suspected he didn't believe her. 'She had this poem on her wall when she was a teenager about not letting shame infect you. I think that's what gave her the idea.'

'Right?' Her dad looked sceptical.

'She hated that you all left her out though, didn't she? She always hated how close you were to Aunt Isobel and Aunt Mandy, and she just hates Paul.'

'I can see why you might think that, but I'm not sure your mum has it in her, hon. I don't mean she's not . . . angry enough or . . .'

'Mean enough?'

Her dad nodded. It was a rare moment of honesty from him. He usually refused to badmouth Mum.

'I think Stuey helped her. Paul wrote his name on one of those notes on his office wall and he's been close to Mum for years.'

'Stuart Fraser?' Her dad sounded surprised.

'Yeah, he would babysit for me when Mum and Nanna fell out. Or sort out Mum's new phone or broadband for her. You know, the stuff Grandad isn't so good at. He's good with IT and Paul had a note saying the person doing it had strong technical skills.'

She watched her dad mull this over and wondered if she should ask him about the Happy Slapping, but then Dad's phone rang. It was Uncle Greg.

'Hi, mate, thanks for calling me back and sorry about this, I know this is the worst time for you but something else has happened.'

Rosie headed upstairs to use the bathroom. She paused outside her mum's old bedroom. She could see the framed poem still sitting on the top of the chest of drawers where she had left it. Had her mum seen that when she'd come up here? Had she known someone was on to her?

Her family had always been odd. She'd known it from the start. To her, the idea that children take things for granted and assume what they experience is normal didn't ring true. Maybe it was because she'd had Dad and Camille providing an alternative home; one filled with love, respect and laughter. It had been obvious when she went on playdates that other families didn't routinely drag each other down or scream and shout, and she had felt embarrassed when her best friend from school said, 'Jeez, your mum's hard work, isn't she?' after one particularly testy visit. But on the whole, Rosie had kept her head down and got on with things. She didn't like the drama and the conflict. She had coped because no one really knew what her life was like at her mum's, but they were about to find out. Mum was going to be arrested for stabbing Grandad and questioned about the Shame Game and then she might be charged and taken to court. In the space of one week, Rosie's life had taken a nosedive. She was now the daughter of a drug-taking cheat and a vengeful woman who had gone out to destroy lives and ended up taking at least one.

Rosie thought of Aunt Mandy, Aunt Isobel and her grandad, and the tears came again.

THE SHAME GAME:
A TRUE CRIME DOCUMENTARY

Episode 3 of 3 – The Price

INT - FALLON FAMILY HOME - DAYTIME

Rosie still sits with her feet curled beside
her on the yellow sofa.

> VOICE (O.S.)
>
> How is your grandad?

> ROSIE
>
> Good, thanks. He was really lucky.
> If the knife had been just a
> few inches over, we might have
> lost him.

                    VOICE (O.S.)

Your mum was charged with grievous
bodily harm and questioned over
the Shame Game threats. Is that
right?

                    ROSIE

She denied everything. Not the
stabbing, although she did insist
she hadn't meant to do that –
apparently we had all upset her
so much she'd lost her mind so it
wasn't her fault.

Rosie smiles a little.

                    VOICE (O.S.)

But she denied being behind the
Shame Game?

                    ROSIE

Yes.

                    VOICE (O.S.)

And could the police find any
evidence that it was her?

                    ROSIE

They didn't look.

                    VOICE (O.S.)
        Why not?

Rosie stares directly into the lens.

                    ROSIE
        Because I was wrong.

121

RYAN

Friday, 12.30 p.m.
3 hours left

'What happens now?' Ryan and Greg stood outside West York-shire Police District Headquarters in the centre of Bradford. He and Rosie had been there all morning, speaking to officers about Stephanie stabbing Graham and the whole incident up at the Bath House.

It had been tough listening to Rosie's account of things, especially the way she had been manhandled and threatened by Bleacher's men, and when she had mentioned the Happy Slapping incident as a reason her mother might have orchestrated this whole ordeal, Ryan could tell his daughter couldn't look at him. He needed to speak to her about it soon, try to explain how it came about and how sorry he was for the effect it had on her mother.

He watched her from where he stood. She sat, staring straight ahead, in the passenger seat of his car, having asked for the keys as soon as they'd left the building.

'We've seized Stephanie's phone and computer and we'll be interviewing Stuart Fraser as soon as we can track him down. His mother claims someone broke into their home last night while she was at the pub because all of Stuart's IT kit is gone. But she also admitted that she hasn't seen her son since yesterday morning. I suspect the guy was spooked by Paul's attack and scarpered.' Greg's complexion was grey and the bags under his eyes dark. 'We'll do our best to find him before the deadline passes, but if not we have our digital team on alert to try and trace the source.'

'And Paul?'

'He's still being questioned.'

Ryan could just imagine how slippery Paul would be as an interviewee. He wasn't sure what he'd do if Paul walked free.

'Did you listen in to Steph's interview? Do you think she did this?'

'I can't tell you that at this stage.'

'I know, sorry. I shouldn't have asked. If I'm honest, I'm not sure what I'm hoping for. I don't want it to be Steph because I don't want Rosie . . . you know . . . but then again, if it is her, then this is all over.'

'Well, I suppose we'll find out at three thirty, won't we?'

122

ISOBEL

Friday, 3.27 p.m.
0 hours left

Sitting in the hospital bed in the private room she had been given – one of the privileges of being a fellow NHS employee – Isobel watched the minutes tick down on the clock.

3.27.

3.28.

3.29.

Annie sat on the seat beside her with her laptop on her knee. Ryan had called first thing to fill them in on all the drama of the night before. He'd also said the police were questioning Steph about the Shame Game threats. Annie had been furious on hearing this. They both knew of the many struggles Ryan had experienced with Steph over the years. She had been continuously disruptive and obstructive. Rosie had never been allowed to go abroad with her dad before the age of fourteen. Annie had pointed out that Ryan was quite within his right to order her a passport and just take her, but Ryan couldn't stomach the grief it would cause. The amount of times Isobel had wanted to pick up the phone and tell Stephanie to back off or calm down were more than she could count, but she never had because it was none of her business. Now, she was wondering if she should have stepped in and tried to play mediator. Maybe if she had, Mandy would still be alive.

Despite the news about Steph, Annie had sent the text to Shame@pm.me asking if Paul was the person who had betrayed Isobel with England First. She'd done so at 10.45 a.m., when Isobel's parents had visited and brought along her iPad. 'We can't take any chances,' Annie had said, but there had been no reply.

And now it was 3.30 p.m.

Annie had multiple articles ready to fire off to various local and national press outlets and to post on social media, all presenting Isobel's version of events and aimed at reducing the collateral damage. These had all been Annie's idea and Isobel sensed her wife had needed something productive to do as they waited. Isobel, on the other hand, had made her peace with it. She had already spoken to her medical director and given an account of what had happened all those years ago. It was pointless trying to outrun it. It would be so much worse for her if this thing hit the press and her bosses were blindsided. The medical director had made it clear he would have to refer things to the GMC, and warned Isobel of the most extreme consequences, which were being struck off and facing a compensation claim from the family of the deceased boy.

It turned out her head injury had scared her into imagining something so much worse than letting Annie and Josh down. What did it matter if she wasn't a doctor any more? If she had to start over and find an alternative way of living, at least she would be alive.

'It's here,' Annie said, sitting up straight and beginning to type. 'It's started.'

Isobel closed her eyes and thought of how good it was going to be to cuddle Josh when he came to visit.

123

PAUL

Friday, 4.14 p.m.

The house was quiet when he finally returned from his sixteen hours at the police station. He desperately wanted a shower and something to eat. He called out to his wife but there was no answer, which was explained by the note on the kitchen island which read, *Don't wait up. V.*

Paul checked the clock. There had been no call back from Mira Hussain at the *Guardian*. He'd phoned her as soon as he was released to offer his side of the story: he had joined England First because a friend was in it and he was intrigued about the people. He had seen it as useful research. He understands that the optics aren't good, but his intent had been sound. He held no prejudicial opinions about any minority group, now or ever.

It was a version of events he had generated while sitting in his cell awaiting the next round of questioning. It transpired Mitch Bleacher had despatched a set of singing canaries to take out Ryan. They had name-dropped Paul all over the place, claimed Paul had hired them directly and that Bleacher knew nothing about it. Paul hoped the coppers were bright enough to see that load of bull for what it was.

He looked at his phone and willed Mira to call back. She had said she needed to check the story with her team. She wasn't sure it would work now they already had the story exposing him.

It had been sent to them at precisely 3.30.

Paul headed for the shower. He couldn't sit staring at the unringing phone for ever. It would drive him mad.

There was something familiar about the feeling he had. It reminded him of being on a vertical-drop ride. They always began with a long slow pull up a steep climb, each click-click of the tracks telling you to prepare yourself, something big was coming. That's what this week had felt like; a slow movement towards impending doom. Then, once at the top of the ride, the little cart you sat in would trundle to the edge of a drop and tilt just enough for you to see what was coming, which was an impossibly steep fall into a black hole. For a few heart-stopping moments the cart stayed there, teetering, just long enough for you to change your mind – *I don't want to do it. Let me off* – before it dropped you.

That's what this felt like, as if he was sitting in that cart, teetering on the edge and waiting to fall face-first into the darkness.

124

ROSIE

Friday, 5.30 p.m.

She wasn't aware of the drive from the police station to the hospital. Her mind was full of what ifs. What if she hadn't accused her mum? Would Grandad be at home doing his garden now? What if Grandad hadn't stepped in Dad's way? Would her dad have been injured, or worse? What if her mum was the reason Aunt Mandy stepped in front of a truck? What if Paul really had hired the men who'd tried to kill Dad? And what if her mum had caused that too? But mostly she was thinking, what if I was wrong about it all?

What if I accused Mum of all those awful things and she didn't do any of it?

She had learned a lot in the police interviews. She had learned that Mandy was responsible for injuring Audrey Raye and that her Dad had confessed to his doping to protect her and prevent the world from ever finding out. She had learned that Paul was once part of a far-right group called England First and that he was friendly with a crime boss who employed the three men who attacked her and her dad.

She had also learned that the police were struggling to trace the source of the texts because they were created using an anonymous email account called Proton something, and sent using the Tor browser, which hides your IP address.

On arrival at the hospital, Dad said he'd go and see Aunt Isobel while she visited her grandad. Grandad was asleep, so she sat and gently stroked his hand. It was dry and wrinkly with little brown dots covering the skin. The nurses said Nanna had popped home to have a shower and bring in some things for him. He had not needed surgery, which was lucky. The knife had somehow managed to miss anything really important.

'I'm sorry, Grandad,' she said. 'If I hadn't said you were wrong to keep out of it you wouldn't be in here. I know Mum didn't mean to hurt you. She loves you so much. You're the only one of us she doesn't get mad at. I think Nanna was right too, about Mum not being up to creating this Shame Game, because Dad said the same thing, and that got me thinking about how Mum just lashes out then it's all over and she's fine again. She doesn't plot and plan, she reacts.'

Rosie watched her grandad's chest rise and fall. She wanted him to wake up and talk to her about it. He had always been her calm within the storm. When it was obvious he was not waking anytime soon, she took out her phone and looked at the photograph of Paul's wall again. This time she focused on the reasons it might not be her mum. For instance, although it was entirely feasible that her mum knew about Dad's doping, as they had been together back then, how would she have known that it was Mandy who hit Audrey Raye?

Then there was Paul's involvement in a far-right group. The chances of her mum uncovering something like that were very small. Mum was hardly worldly-wise. She rarely left Ilkley town.

Rosie studied Isobel's list to see if there were any clues there about the secret she was being shamed with. All she found was a note saying it was an indiscretion at work years ago. Rosie scanned up the list to look at the various places Isobel had worked. What she saw caused her to take a sharp intake of breath.

'Hello, darling.'

Rosie looked up to see her nanna dressed more like she was heading out for a lunch date than coming to sit with her injured husband. Her hair was perfectly styled, her make-up fully in place and her outfit smart. She carried a bag, from which she began to remove Grandad's pyjamas, slippers and a washbag. A nurse entered to check on Grandad, and Nanna began to tell her about a patient a few doors down whose family were concerned he wasn't receiving the right food because he was gluten intolerant and had been given toast for breakfast. As Rosie watched the nurse trying to make a swift exit from Nanna's pep talk about attention to detail and quality of care, she recalled something Grandad had said a few years back, when Nanna was elected as a local MP.

He'd asked Rosie if she knew what MP stood for, and then he'd winked and said, 'Meddling Person.'

'How long will he need to stay?' she asked Nanna when the nurse had escaped.

'They're not sure. His heart had a little moment in the early hours so they want to observe him. It's playing merry hell with my nerves. They won't give me a straight answer and I was here all night sitting with him, worrying. Anyway, I spoke to the consultant, Mrs Fields, who said it was hopefully down to the shock and things will settle but she wants to be sure.'

'Do you know Mrs Fields?'

'No. I met her this morning. She's Grandad's consultant.'

'I thought you might have come across her when you were volunteering at the hospital.'

'No, sweetheart, I don't do anything at Airedale. I only help out at Leeds Children's Hospital. It's kept me busy since retirement and we all have to be prepared to give something back.' She rubbed a hand on Grandad's arm and he stirred a little.

'Don't you volunteer at Harrogate hospital too?'

'Sometimes, yes. Not as often though.'

Rosie looked out of the window. Little pieces of a puzzle were coming together in her mind. The more she concentrated, the more pieces floated into place. She wondered if she should call her dad and tell him what she suspected. Grandad had given her a clue when he'd said mum had been broken by life, but it wasn't the cruel thing Dad and his friends had done that had broken her. What had Nanna said? *They didn't ruin your mum's life, she did. She's had her washing done, meals cooked and babysitting on tap ever since.*

'So you volunteer at the place Aunt Isobel currently works and the place she used to work?'

'I never knew Isobel worked at Harrogate. What a coincidence. Right, well, it's probably time your grandad woke up. He's slept half the day. I'll see if the nurse can get him a cup of tea.'

'It was you, wasn't it?'

Her nanna paused halfway out of her seat.

'When you said the Happy Slapping thing hadn't ruined Mum's life, because you'd done all her cooking, washing and babysitting ever since . . . It was your life they ruined, wasn't it?'

'Well, I never—'

'It wasn't just Mum who was in Dad's life when he doped, you and Grandad were too. Did you know back then what he'd done? Did he tell you or did you overhear something?'

'Don't be silly. I had no idea until your dad came out with it all this week. If I had, I'd have told him to come clean years ago. No good can come of keeping things like that quiet.'

'But Mandy and Audrey Raye, you knew about that, didn't you?'

'I have no idea what you're talking about, sweetheart.'

'So how come when Mum first spoke to you about the fact Mandy had died, she said your comment was, "Karma is a bitch." Why did you say that?'

407

'I don't think I did. Your mum has a very active imagination, as you know. She doesn't always speak the truth.'

'Was it because you knew Mandy had hit someone with a car? Is that why you said it?'

Her nanna stared her down. 'I told you. I did not say that.'

'And then there's Paul. The England First people he was involved with are a political party, aren't they? So did you uncover something when you were an MP, or did you go snooping into his life like you've been doing with Isobel?'

'That is enough of your cheek, young lady. Don't you be getting all aggressive like your mother.'

Rosie sucked her lips close to her teeth and clamped her jaw together. All her life she had been told, *You're just like your dad* or *Don't be cheeky like your mother*, whenever she had done something to displease her nanna, and Rosie had tried so hard to not be like her parents. She had really believed that this was a legitimate goal in life. But she was starting to wonder if it had been a power tactic all along. If Rosie shouldn't behave like her mum or dad, that meant she should be more like her nanna; the person she spent most of her time with outside of her parents. The underlying message was, *Don't be flaky like your mum or a show off like your dad, be strong and smart like me.* And they were qualities Rosie had long admired, but, if she was honest, she had harboured a concern for a while now, ever since the psychology lesson at school when they'd studied neurodiversity. Miss Potts had said some people were wired up differently, and this made them less caring and more self-absorbed. Everything was about them and they struggled to empathize with anyone else's experience.

All the things her nanna had said about Mum the night before were really about how hard Mum had made things for Nanna: *she was always hard work, she's high maintenance, I pretty much had to raise you myself, she's as flaky as a cream horn*. All things Rosie suspected her mum might have been told about herself her whole life. Rosie knew something of what that was like – her mum had done the same to her – but Rosie had been lucky enough to have her dad telling her she was loved and amazing and capable of being whatever she wanted to be. Rosie thought of her grandad – she had often felt sorry for him when he'd headed out to the garden to avoid Mum and Nanna's fights, but now she realized he was just as much at fault. Why hadn't he stood up for his daughter like her dad had for her? Was he so scared of Nanna that he didn't dare defy her? Rosie realized he probably was, and so was her mum. Well, Nanna was in for a shock, because Rosie wasn't scared of her.

'Was it me saying I was dropping out of school that made you go after them all now? Because if I leave school, Dad will stop paying Mum child support and then you'll have to fund Mum's life again, because she's incapable?'

'Well, that's simply ridiculous,' said Nanna, standing up and taking a look at the clipboard of notes at the end of Grandad's bed.

'You think it's OK to shame my dad and his friends for doing wrong, as if you have the right to judge. How would you feel if I told everyone the truth about you? See how you like it when everyone finds out you caused your own granddaughter to be kidnapped and threatened.'

'Rosie, that is enough. I told you I have no idea what you are talking about. Let that be the end of it. Why would I be interested in these people? It's your mum who has a problem with them, not me.'

'You don't care what happens to anyone, do you? You gave no thought to what people would do when you threatened to shame them. You haven't even shown any remorse for Mandy. She killed herself because of you, Nanna. Because of what *you* did.'

'Is this what you meant when you said you would take care of things?' Grandad's eyes were open and he was looking at Nanna. She looked up from the notes and met his gaze with a frown.

'When I wanted to tell the school and call the police about the attack on Stephanie, you said I should leave it alone, that you would take care of it.'

Rosie held her breath. If anyone could make Nanna confess, it was Grandad. When he had told Rosie she was a Meddling Person, Rosie suspected it hadn't been entirely a joke. He knew his wife liked to gather the dirt on people. She was certainly one to whisper the latest gossip over the dinner table. The only time Nanna and Mum weren't at each other's throats was when they had someone else to have a go at.

It all seemed so clear to Rosie now. Her Nanna was organized, patient and had lived in the same town as Dad, Paul, Isobel and Mandy their whole lives. She was also familiar with Stuart Fraser, and more than capable of convincing such a sweet man to do her dirty work for her if she wanted to.

'You cannot let Rosie believe her mum did this if she did not, Felicity. Unless, of course, you and Stephanie dreamed this idiocy up together?'

'Of course we didn't. Stephanie is, well . . . Stephanie.'

There was a moment of quiet when all Rosie could hear was the beep of Grandad's machine.

'So you did do this, Felicity.'

'All they'd have got was a slap on the wrist, Graham. I needed to wait until they had as much to lose as we had. Wait until I could bring their worlds crashing down. See how they liked it. We had plans and they ruined them because they made Stephanie feel ashamed and she . . . *WE* never recovered. They all deserved it.'

125

Barrister's Membership of a Far-Right Group Threatens the Validity of Multiple Convictions

Mira Hussain – *Guardian* **Law Editor**

King's Counsel Paul Reece-Johnson was a member of the far-right group England First from 2007 to 2013. During this time, he played a key role in prosecuting individuals from various minority groups. In particular, his first conviction as lead counsel saw a black man accused of smuggling migrants in the back of his van imprisoned for five years and ten months. Such convictions have now been called into question due to Reece-Johnson's extreme politics.

Reece-Johnson is best known for securing the conviction of Kyle Renton, a man of Afro-Caribbean heritage who shot and killed a two-year-old white British boy when chasing a member of a rival gang. Renton has always protested his innocence and applied to the Court of Appeal many times.

Reece-Johnson told the *Guardian* he had joined the group simply to learn about those with extreme views and that he never shared their politics. The Bar Standards Board said they had suspended Reece-Johnson's practising certificate while investigations are ongoing.

The MP for Leeds Central has demanded an inquiry into a senior doctor at Leeds Children's Hospital. He is acting on information that Senior Neonatologist Dr Isobel Walters, Clinical Director of Children's Services, endangered the lives of children when working in the Woodlands Ward at Harrogate Hospital. WTF!

Ilkley Hit and Run Mystery Solved After Nearly 20 Years

By Jonathan Cook, *Yorkshire Post*

On a dark night in November 2006, 21-year-old Audrey Raye was hit by a vehicle and left injured in the road. She suffered life-changing injuries that resulted in her needing around-the-clock care. No one ever admitted to hitting Audrey, and the police could find no evidence of who the driver might be. That was until the *Yorkshire Post* received an anonymous tip-off that a local woman, Amanda Coulters, was the person responsible. After passing the information on to the police, it transpired that Mrs Coulters had indeed been the driver. Her father admitted to scrapping the car to cover up her crime.

Following the incident, Amanda Coulters worked as a chef, briefly participating in the TV show *Fine Dining at Home* in 2008. She was married to Detective Chief Superintendent Greg Coulters of West Yorkshire Police, who declined to comment. Amanda Coulters recently lost her life in a road traffic collision.

PLEASE SHARE!

My Grandmother, Felicity Granger, ex MP for Ilkley, is responsible for ruining my dad's career, threatening his life, having me kidnapped and causing a family friend to take her own life. She is evil. She thinks she is better than everyone else and that she can take her own revenge, but I am not going to let her. I want the world to know what SHE has done.

I will keep posting here about the whole story. Please spread the word. I want EVERYONE to know who she really is.

THE SHAME GAME:
A TRUE CRIME DOCUMENTARY

Episode 3 of 3 – The Price

EXT - ILKLEY TOWN - SPRINGTIME

Yellow daffodils floating gently in a breeze
fill the screen before the camera moves up
to reveal the town's main street, where
cherry-blossom trees line both sides of the
road and the Yorkshire stone buildings house
gift shops and Betty's tearoom, with its
Victorian glass canopy.

FADE TO AERIAL VIEW. The camera follows a
winding river next to a large park, where
children play and dogs run across the grass.

VOICEOVER announces that Ilkley was crowned
the best place in the UK to live in 2022 by
the *Sunday Times*.

FADE TO HILLSIDE VIEW. The camera views
the town from high above on Ilkley Moor,
showing how it is nestled within a valley;
the hills that surround it abundant with
bright green fields and clusters of darker
green trees.

INT - FALLON FAMILY HOME - DAYTIME

Rosie uncurls her legs and sits up straight
on the sofa as a tall man with tanned skin
sits beside her. He is wearing blue jeans
with a white linen shirt.

TEXT on the screen: RYAN FALLON, EX-
PROFESSIONAL CYCLIST AND VICTIM OF THE
SHAME GAME.

                    VOICE (O.S.)

     So, Ryan, you must feel very proud
     of your daughter for working all
     of this out?

                    RYAN

     Yeah, of course. Although I really
     wish she hadn't had to have any
     involvement in it, Isobel and I
     are very grateful for how she put
     all of it together, and also what
     she has tried to do since. She's
     an impressive young woman.

VOICE (O.S.)

Rosie, how do you feel about your
mother's side of the family after
all of this?

ROSIE

Gosh, it's complicated. I don't
hate them. I wish Mum hadn't hurt
Grandad and obviously I feel awful
that my nanna did these horrible
things to my dad and his friends,
and that they all lost so much as
a result.

Ryan leans forward a little in his seat and
places his forearms on his legs.

RYAN

Look, Paul, Isobel and I can no
longer do the kind of work we were
doing before, and some would say
that's how it should be. We all
did things wrong in our respective
professions, so our punishment
is that we are now excluded from
those environments. But none
of that compares to what Mandy
lost. Her future.

VOICE (O.S.)

Felicity Granger exposed Mandy as
well, even though you had admitted

416

to doping in order to protect her
secret about the accident with
Audrey Raye?

                    RYAN

I believe Felicity probably
thought I had cheated her game.
Paul said at one stage that there
was no way to win. She was going
to expose us or we were going to
expose each other. I don't think
she had any intention of letting
any of us get away without our
shameful secrets coming to light.
She wanted us to pay for what she
thought we'd done to her, and she
was not going to let us off the
hook. That week was just a bit of
sadistic torture. She was making
us wait for the hammer to fall,
but the hammer was always going to
fall. I can see that now.

                 VOICE (O.S.)

We looked into some of the ways
Felicity pulled this off, and
it became clear she'd had a lot
of technical help from an old
schoolmate of yours, Stuart
Fraser.

                         RYAN

      Yes. Stuart was another victim of
      Felicity. It's very sad.

                      VOICE (O.S.)

      His body was found a few days
      after the Shame Game came to an
      end, is that right?

Ryan nods and places a hand on Rosie's arm.

                         RYAN

      He went missing on the day Rosie
      and I were kidnapped and they found
      his body in the river a few days
      later. It's not certain if he fell
      or something else. Paul has denied
      mentioning him to Mitchel Bleacher,
      but all his computers went missing
      along with him, even the ones he
      was repairing for his customers,
      and they have never been found.

                      VOICE (O.S.)

      So you think something darker than
      an accident happened to him?

                         RYAN

      I have no evidence of it, but
      given what happened to Rosie and
      me, I think it's a possibility.

VOICE (O.S.)

How did he become involved in all
of this?

                RYAN

Felicity discovered that Stuart's
mother had lied on a disability
benefits claim and she used this
to blackmail Stuart into helping
her. His mother received a visit
from the benefits fraud team the
day the Shame Game concluded.
They'd received an anonymous
tip-off.

A petite lady with caramel skin and dark
hair comes to sit on the other side of
Rosie. She wears a green floral dress with
orange flats.

TEXT on the screen: ISOBEL WALTERS, EX-
NEONATAL CONSULTANT AND VICTIM OF THE
SHAME GAME.

                VOICE (O.S.)

Isobel, there is one fascinating
element to this whole thing which
relates to your past. Felicity
never really uncovered what you
were ashamed of. Is that right?

ISOBEL

It is, yes. She had tried - I
believe she volunteered at the
hospitals where I had worked with
a view to digging up dirt, but she
failed to do so. The social media
posts she put out about me on that
second Friday were all supposition
and bluster. I do wonder if this
is why she waited so long to take
her revenge on us all.

VOICE (O.S.)

But she somehow made you believe
she knew? What about the first
article you received, did that
not expose your misdemeanour like
Ryan's did?

ISOBEL

We think not. I've talked this
over so many times with Ryan and
my wife. I clearly remember the
headline and the fact my name was
there, but I was in such a state
of shock I couldn't take any of it
in. I think I assumed the article
mentioned a specific event because
it was something that played so
heavily on my mind, but maybe it
didn't. Felicity was smart enough
to know that we all have something

in our past that we're ashamed of.
I think she put enough suggestion
in there to make me think whoever
had written it knew things about
me, like the fact she named the
agency decision-maker who was
signing off on our son's adoption.

                VOICE (O.S.)

So you could have simply
ignored it?

                  ISOBEL

Perhaps.

                VOICE (O.S.)

How does that make you feel now?

                  ISOBEL

The posts she put out suggested
I had endangered the lives of
children when I was working at
Harrogate. I think she figured
I was a young doctor back then,
so probably messed up along the
way. Anyone who spends any time
in a hospital will see how deaths
affect the staff. We all carry
some guilt around about things
we did or didn't do, even if the
outcome was unavoidable. It just

so happened Felicity was right. I had been young and stupid, and I had messed up.

By the end of that week, after everything that happened with Mandy and Ryan and Paul, I was ready to come clean about my mistake and the actions I took to cover it up. That's why I went to my bosses and the General Medical Council. The outcome of that is that I'm not allowed to practise medicine any more, but I can lecture and pass on my lessons to the next generation. Ryan and I work together now, trying to educate people on the importance of owning up to your mistakes and speaking up against bad practices you might see. We hope we can help the next generation avoid the traps we fell into. Make them braver and more honest. More like Rosie, really. She was very courageous in uncovering the truth of things, even when it hurt her and the people closest to her.

                    VOICE (O.S.)

And how do you both feel about Paul now? Do you have any contact with him?

Isobel shakes her head as Ryan answers.

                    RYAN

        I get that Paul was desperate, but
        what he did was unforgivable. There
        is no friendship left there. And I
        don't know where Vanessa is now.

                 VOICE (O.S.)

        Vanessa spoke to us. She is
        divorced from Paul and now lives
        in London.

Ryan and Isobel exchange a look but do not
comment.

                 VOICE (O.S.)

        I have to ask about the Happy
        Slapping incident which kicked all
        of this off.

Ryan glances at Rosie before answering.

                    RYAN

        I think I can speak for all of us,
        Mandy and Paul included, when I
        say we are very sorry for the hurt
        we caused to Stephanie. It was a
        stupid thing, a craze at the time
        that we thought was funny.

He looks at Isobel, who shuffles in her seat.

                    ISOBEL

    I'm ashamed to say I had
    forgotten all about it. I feel
    genuinely awful that it affected
    Stephanie so badly for all those
    years. If I'd have known, I'd
    have tried to put things right
    and I'm sure Mandy would have
    felt the same.

                    VOICE (O.S.)

    Have you spoken to Stephanie about
    it since?

                    ISOBEL

    I've tried. I sent messages to
    apologize and offered the chance
    to talk about it, but so far I've
    had no response, which I also
    understand. I do hope that someday
    I can make some kind of amends.

                    VOICE (O.S.)

    Ryan?

                    RYAN

    It's true to say Steph and I find
    it hard to communicate at the best

of times. I have also told her I'm
sorry, which I hope she believes.
It would be nice if she could have
some peace.

                    VOICE (O.S.)

How about you, Rosie? What's your
take on all of that?

                    ROSIE

When I first heard about it, I was
angry and disappointed in Dad, and
all of them.

                    RYAN

You had every right.

                    ISOBEL

Agreed.

                    ROSIE

But I also think they were young
at the time and young people do
stupid things. Dad has always
told me childhood is where you
need to mess up and fall down so
you can learn how to get back up.
I would hate to think someone
would hold the mistakes I'm making
now against me later, when I'm

grown. They should have been
made to apologize. I think if my
grandad had his way and the school
or police were told, Mum would
have felt better about it. Or if
my grandmother had put as much
effort into helping Mum as she
did into plotting against Dad and
the others, Mum might have had a
happier life and I might have had
an easier childhood.

Ryan takes hold of Rosie's hand and
squeezes it.

                    VOICE (O.S.)

What drove Felicity to go to such
lengths, do you think?

                    RYAN

When the incident happened,
Felicity and Graham were at the
peak of their lives, from what I
know. Graham had set up his own
accountancy business which was
doing well enough for Felicity to
consider giving up working and
becoming a lady who lunches, but
Stephanie became more and more
dependent on them. Felicity had
always bragged about how wonderful
Stephanie was to anyone who would

listen, and I expect she felt
embarrassed that her daughter
dropped out of school, lacked
qualifications and went on to
became a barmaid and a single mum.

                    ROSIE

I think my grandmother, Felicity,
is a destructive person. My
grandad hinted once that my mum
had been broken by life, but I
think what he meant was by her own
mother. Felicity should probably
never have had children, she'd
have been happier that way, doing
whatever she wanted. I mean,
something horrible happened to her
daughter and she decided to make
it all about her.

Ryan cuts in.

                    RYAN

Rosie has been so brave in telling
the world the truth and trying to
redress the balance for all of us.
So I'd like to thank you all at
the production company for reading
her email and taking her request
for this story to get out there
seriously.

VOICE (O.S.)

Felicity has faced no consequences
for her actions so far?

ISOBEL

We believe she directly caused
Mandy's suicide and that she
incited the extreme actions Paul
took, but from the police's point
of view, there's no hard evidence
to prove that Felicity was behind
any of it thanks to Stuart's
expertise and the fact he's sadly
not here to tell us what really
happened.

RYAN

Rosie has been very active on
social media and she has spoken
to the press and a few podcasts
about getting the story out there,
but she felt strongly that a
documentary such as this would
be the most powerful vehicle for
telling our story and finding some
kind of . . .

ISOBEL

Justice.

Felicity put us through hell. She
doesn't deserve to get away with
that unscathed.

Rosie sits up straighter.

                    ROSIE

I also want to say sorry, publicly,
to Mandy's family for what my
grandmother did. I want to say
sorry to Mandy's dad and brother,
and my Uncle Greg. I loved Mandy.
She was more than a pretend aunt
to me. We all miss her.

FADE TO BLACK

Screen shows a picture of a woman wearing
a large straw hat, her head thrown back in
laughter. She is hugging a young Rosie.

TEXT reads: MANDY COULTERS, CELEBRITY CHEF
AND VICTIM OF THE SHAME GAME. 1988-2025.

FADE TO BLACK

Screen shows a photograph of Stuart Fraser
in a *Star Wars* T-shirt, smiling into the
camera.

FADE TO BLACK

SCROLLING WHITE TEXT FOLLOWS

Felicity Granger has faced no charges relating to the death of Mandy Coulters or the actions of Paul Reece-Johnson, which endangered the lives of Ryan and Rosie Fallon. She was invited to participate in this documentary but declined. She also declined to comment.

Paul Reece-Johnson was disbarred and is currently facing charges relating to perverting the course of justice in relation to the conviction of Leonard Phelps in 2012. No charges have been brought against him relating to the actions of Mitchel Bleacher's men, as no evidence was found to prove his involvement.

The Bar Council provided the following statement:

'The involvement of one of our King's Counsels in a far-right movement has brought our profession into disrepute. We can never accept any form of prejudice that might affect the serving of justice. A full inquiry is being made into all of the cases on which this individual acted as counsel for the defence or the prosecution.'

In a separate statement, the Court of Appeal announced that Kyle Renton has been granted the right to appeal his conviction.

Ryan Fallon rejoined his charity, the Fallon Foundation, six months after he was asked to step down as MD. He now works with schools and sports teams to encourage young people to speak up and speak out in the face of pressure, coercion or bullying. He also coaches his daughter, Rosie, as she chases her dream of making it to the Mountain Bike World Championships.

Isobel Walters now lectures on Ethics and Patient Safety for the medical faculty at Leeds University. She and her wife, Annie, have recently adopted their second baby, a little girl called Amanda.

Greg Coulters remains with West Yorkshire Police and has been promoted to Assistant Chief Constable. He gifted the money from Mandy's estate to Rosie's cycling fund.

INT - FALLON FAMILY HOME - DAYTIME

Rosie now sits alone on the sofa

> VOICE (O.S)

Rosie Fallon requested that we
end with the poem that hung on
Stephanie Granger's wall after
the Happy Slapping incident. She
discovered that her grandfather
had put it there in an attempt to
help his daughter.

Rosie reads from a card.

ROSIE

Shame is a burden some must bear
It hides within the soul
Its roots are deep
Its tendrils creep
As you try to plug the hole.

Shame tells you every win you've won
Is nothing you are worth
And all the bad things that occur
Are just what you deserve.

If you let shame into your heart
It will make a home for life
Lurking below
Waiting to grow
Feeding on all your worry and woe

So beware of the parasite known as shame.
Do not let it call your name.

Rosie folds the card in half and looks into
the camera.

The End

Acknowledgements

When I first had the idea for *The Shame Game*, I ran it by my own school friends when they came to stay for the weekend. After a fun night bouncing around ideas for how to make the story work, we all headed to bed. The next morning, one of my friends admitted that they hadn't slept for wondering what secrets they had told me that might have inspired my idea. I reassured them that this book was not about us as a group of friends, but I couldn't help thinking, *Why? What have you done?*

The idea that we all have something in our past that we feel ashamed of is the seed of my story. The things we would rather keep hidden are – hopefully – not as extreme as those of my characters in *The Shame Game*, but still, that question of 'How would it feel if everyone knew what you'd done?' Would it change how they looked at you, what they felt about you? Would you feel the need to hide away with embarrassment, or would you hold your head high and own it? And if you had the chance to stop it coming out . . . how far would you go?

In my job as a psychologist I see shame writ large in people's psyches. The poem I wrote for Stephanie's wall was inspired by how people describe shame impacting on their peace of mind and their enjoyment of life. It is a huge privilege as a psychologist to be let in to people's inner minds and trusted with such truths. To all of those who have taught me so much about how shame affects you, a massive thanks. I hope I have respectfully represented the experience here.

Specific thanks for help with my characters need to go to ex-England cricketer Jeremy Snape, for helping me to understand the mindset of a professional sportsman – and also the specific mental toughness found in road cyclists. Chief Crown Prosecutor Siobhan Blake not only spent hours discussing the mindset of a typical barrister with me but also read all of the Paul chapters to check for authenticity. Your tip to constantly have him arguing the case for and against every decision in his head was brilliant! Finally, my old school friend, and most excellent consultant anaesthesiologist, Tom Hollins helped me to understand the emotional toll deaths at work have on medical staff, and the importance placed on honesty in the face of mistakes. Thank you all. Your insights were critical for making this story work, but more than that, the time and support you were all willing to give to my 'made up characters' was awesome. Any errors I made in a legal, medical and sporting sense are my own!

In researching a number of shamed celebrities on X, I came across the comments targeted at Lance Armstrong after his cheating came to light. This was what gave me the idea that Felicity could send examples of what sort of public shaming might be coming their way to the friends. Those sent to Paul and Isobel are entirely fictional, but I did use the real comments about Armstrong in the version sent to Ryan – apart from the last one: 'Yeah, like fuck off and die already.' I figured Felicity would add this in for extra oomph.

And so to my wonderful publishers. Thank you to the whole Transworld team for always making me feel so valued and supported. Finn Cotton, you are the rock star of editors: someone who makes me laugh as much as you make me think. My stories always feel like 'our' stories because you are always in it with me. Thank you! Also a huge thanks to Thorne Ryan for your advice and friendship. You have built my confidence and helped me to tackle my imposter syndrome. Thanks to Barbara Thompson (editorial) and Fraser Crichton (copy-editor) for checking and perfecting my words so excellently well. To Irene Martinez for the cover design which is so good! And to Emma Fairey for publicity, Sophie McVeigh for marketing and Anna Carvanova for smoothing the way.

To my wonderful agent, Laura Williams, thank you for taking me on as a client and for all your input on *The Shame Game*. Having you in my corner feels like a massive luxury as well as a powerful asset. I can't wait to see where our partnership takes us.

In my teens I changed schools – a lot (thanks, Mum and Dad) – so I became very good at making friends but not so skilled at keeping them. So a huge thank you to those school friends who have stuck with me even when I'm rubbish at keeping in touch. Kathryn Scott, Nicola Eastwood, Tom Hollins, Rachael Watkin, I'm talking to you.

Finally, thank you as always to my family for all the love and laughter. Jamie, Erica, Ella, Henry and Bagel the Beagle, I love you. Thanks to my mum and Mike and my dad and Gigi for always being the best cheerleaders! And to my sisters, brothers-in-law, sisters-in-law, aunt, uncle, cousins, nieces and nephews – sorry for writing yet another book that you HAVE to read.

THE ESCAPE ROOM
L. D. SMITHSON

CAN YOU UNLOCK ITS SECRETS?

Everything is a clue.
Bonnie arrives on a remote sea fort off the coast of England to take part in a mysterious reality TV show. Competing against seven strangers, she must solve a series of puzzles to win the prize money.

No one can leave.
It doesn't take long for the contestants to turn on one another. Who will sacrifice the most for wealth and fame? And why can't Bonnie shake the creeping sense that they are not alone?

The only way out is to win.
When the first contestant is found dead, the others begin to panic. Because there's a killer with them inside the fort, and anyone could be next. If Bonnie wants to escape, she needs to win . . .

PERFECT FOR FANS OF *THE TRAITORS*

'*I'm a Celebrity* meets *Lord of the Flies*' **Emma Curtis**

'The pace never slackens' **Faith Martin**

'Dark, disturbing and addictive' **L. C. North**

dead good

Looking for more gripping must-reads?

Head over to Dead Good —
the home of killer crime books,
TV and film.

Whether you're on the hunt for an intriguing
mystery, an action-packed thriller
or a creepy psychological drama,
we're here to keep you in the loop.

Get recommendations and reviews from
crime fans, grab discounted books at bargain
prices and enter exclusive giveaways
for the chance to read brand-new releases
before they hit the shelves.

Sign up for the free newsletter:
www.deadgoodbooks.co.uk/newsletter